The Lodger at Sunset

By

E. H. Goodfellow

Published by

LANTERN TOWER

An Imprint of Melrose Press Limited
St Thomas Place, Ely
Cambridgeshire
CB7 4GG, UK
www.melrosebooks.com

FIRST EDITION

ISBN 978 1 906561 82 6

Printed and bound in Great Britain by:
CPI Antony Rowe, Chippenham, Wiltshire

Chapter 1

He was wearing black plimsolls, a yellow shirt and blue dungarees of the type that were becoming known as "jeans". Carrying an apple and perspiring freely, he stepped out on to the after deck of the *Empire Garvie*. Almost immediately he was aware of someone standing back in the shadow of the deckhouse. "Roger, my son," came a voice. Thank God it was only Maguire.

"Hullo, didn't see you there. Too hot below isn't it?"

"Call this hot? Wait till we get past Suez, then you'll see what hot is."

Maguire was a fifty-year old from the far west of Ireland whose warm, peat-soft accent was very easy on the ear. Still in shadow, it came again. "You're on your first trip at sea. Green as grass. Now there's some people on here that're right bastards. Also there's about thirty queer fellers, as I'm sure you know by now. Watch how you deal with them, especially with a name like Roger Wren." The door closed. Roger moved over to the sea – the clean, uncomplicated and welcoming sea. Even now, in late evening, the Mediterranean retained that pristine blueness that so amazed him.

A cool breeze danced along the deck and caressed him like an angel's wing, humming in his ears and fluttering his shirt against his body. He wondered if tomorrow he might find the courage to start sun-bathing. In truth, the idea bored him. He preferred to sit in the shade with a good book, an eccentricity that set him apart. Among the crew, rampant masculinity was the order of the day – except for that special group Pat Maguire had mentioned. But to be considered a man required a number of attributes. Firstly: to be healthy and robust. This was why the sun-tan, with its illusion of fitness, was so sought after by everyone. Secondly: an ability to consume large quantities of alcohol without falling over. And thirdly: sexual experience. Most of the crew were more or less qualified.

Roger of course was the exception. To put it kindly, he was slim.

Nearly twenty and just out of the RAF, he looked much younger. As for drink, one pint and his legs felt strange. Two and he forgot his name. A third rendered him immobile. And the only female he'd shared a bed with was his mother. Although this was not for want of trying. His friend Gordon Watts usually arranged the foursomes that cycled the country lanes of Hampshire or queued up at one of Southampton's sixteen cinemas. There were girls. Among others, there was Isobel. Roger had pursued her with the ardour of a bull-frog in spring but to no avail. Apparently he was too bookish. Not adventurous enough. They'd parted only a week ago after a row at a fairground. He'd declined to take her on the Big Wheel, convinced he'd be sick after one revolution. When he'd telephoned later she'd refused to speak to him.

Gordon said, "Give it up. She's not your type. Try your luck elsewhere. But you'll have to do it solo now. I got my call-up papers. You're OK. You've done your National Service." Watching the sunset, he began to eat the apple, wondering what they might be doing in England. Gordon in a hut somewhere, cleaning his boots. At home his father and elder bother Phil listening to the wireless. Their mother had died three years ago and Roger had taken longer than Phil to get over the loss. Phil had "got on", learned a trade in the RAF and continued it as a civilian. Except for mathematics, Roger was reasonably intelligent, with a rather excessive love of history, travel books and poetry. Phil would throw up his hands in despair.

"Poetry! Very useful."

In his teens Roger's less than impressive physique had attracted the sort of jibes that are a speciality of the young.

"Pay no heed," said his father. "You're a late developer. Fill out later you will." For four years he'd worked in a local battery repair company, a soulless job full of lead and acid fumes. Conscription into the RAF had been a welcome relief. Phil had been a radar technician, but the maths and circuitry were too much for his brother. Roger, it seemed, didn't "apply himself". An assessment made by Phil on many occasions.

"Roger's a dreamer, needs to buck his ideas up." The end of his training saw him at a maintenance unit in Oxfordshire, making simple alterations to radar sets under the guidance of an expert. He learned a little of the mysteries of Gee, H2S, and other oddly named apparatus. In eighteen months he was a civilian again, unskilled and jobless. Throughout his whole term in the Air Force he'd never been near an aeroplane.

When he'd first thought of going to sea he could not now remember. His father many years ago had made some trips as a steward. There was a risk though. If he was queasy on the Big Wheel what would happen on the ocean? His father was reassuring.

"Try it. Good money to be made at sea." So it was that Mr Wren's younger son, one day in June 1950, became a seafarer.

It took all day. He was fingerprinted, photographed and medically examined. They gave him a number of documents. One was his discharge book, a record of his voyages. Another was his seaman's identity card, containing a picture of a surly individual holding a board with his name on it. This "mug-shot" he recognised incredulously as himself. He hurried home in his new role of "Merchant Seaman. British. Aged 19. Church of England. No distinguishing marks". Phil was unimpressed, not viewing life as a seaborne waiter a proper trade as he saw it, but out of deference to their father he feigned an interest."You should join the Royal Mail Line Dad was in. They go to Brazil. Is that travel enough for you?"

"Quite right," said his father. "I was with them a long while."

But Roger's wanderlust had become global. "Brazil's only one country, I don't want to just shuttle between there and here." Mr Wren's patience also seemed about to leave home.

"They don't only go there," he snapped. "They go to Uruguay and Argentina."

"Next door to each other," said Roger who knew his geography. "Uruguay's right on the doorstep of Buenos Aires."

His father stood up. "Oh well, you do as you want then. Get yourself on some old tramp-steamer and stay away for a couple of years. Come back with a dose and no money." He quietly left the room.

"Well done," said Phil coldly.

"I didn't mean to upset him. I'll see him in the morning."

"Yes. I think you should." Later, Roger sat alone sorting through his documents. He wondered how to placate his father, how one got on the Royal Mail and what a "dose" might be.

Next day he announced, "I'm off to Royal Mail."

"That's my boy," beamed his father. Near the docks he stepped off the bus, walked along Queen's Terrace, turned a corner and entered the imposing headquarters of the Royal Mail Line. Here he met a young man in a grey suit with a Woodbine in his mouth.

"You come here for a job?"

"Yes. As a steward. My father was —"

"No good unless you're established. You got to be established. Are you established? Do you know what established means?" Roger, despite hearing it four times, did not. The grey suit began to move away.

"I'm off to lunch. Pool you want to go to. The Shipping Federation over the road."

"Thanks, I will."

Unexpectedly the man removed the Woodbine and said, "Good luck."

The Federation was crowded with men facing a high counter that ran the width of the room. Over one half hung a sign – "Unestablished", while the other half, logically enough, was posted – "Established". This part was shielded from the other by a frosted glass partition, as if to avoid contamination. A man stopped on his way out.

"First time here? Not established and you wish you were, right? Join this one and ask them." He indicated the "Established" line. "They might like your face better than mine."

The queue took a quick forward shuffle and the high counter loomed. The clerk behind it took on the aspect of a Dickensian beadle. Another shuffle and he was there.

"Papers!" the man barked. Not a beadle, thought Roger, more a German border guard. The clerk perused his documents. "You're in the wrong queue. Go next door." Roger took back his papers.

"How do I get established?"

"You can't. Not today." The man looked past him at the person behind.

Roger stood his ground. "I wanted to get on a Royal Mail ship. My father was —" The bored eyes flicked back to him.

"Royal Mail? There's nothing doing there today. In any case you've no experience at all have you?"

"Come on," called a voice at the back. "There's others waiting you know."

"Go next door. We're not signing any more people on the established list till further notice." Roger turned to go and looked back.

"How about Cunard?" The clerk had a smile like the brass plate on a coffin.

"Come back in ten years." The queue guffawed.

On the other side of the frosted glass he joined another queue. Twenty minutes later he again offered up his papers. This time the clerk was an older man who studied them slowly.

"First trip? What are you after? What job?"

"I'd like to get on Royal Mail. My father —" At this point he'd always been interrupted and the man's silence threw him slightly. "That is, as a steward, I thought maybe —"

"Can't help you there I'm afraid. Nowadays they prefer their people —"

"I know, established." It would be very easy to get tired of that word. The man riffled through some papers at his side.

"I can get you on the *Empire Garvie* as a mess attendant. It's not a bad old vessel and Captain Baskerville's alright. The job'll give you some inkling what it's all about – the catering game. Get your sea-legs as the saying goes. Of course it's not exactly the *Queen Mary*, you realise that." Here it was then, decision time. Take this job and he'd be off or wait and go through this whole rigmarole again, maybe for days.

"Where's it going?"

The man at the high counter had spent years matching men to ships. Every kind of seafarer had stood before him. Some had spent their lives at sea. Some were first-timers, young hopefuls who'd read everything and been nowhere. The ones who wanted to see it all now. He looked into Roger's eyes and saw the world there.

"Hong Kong." Roger seemed to see his atlas before him, pages rapidly turning. "And of course," said the man, "a lot of places in between."

Roger decided. "I'll take it."

"Right." A pen skated over the paper, and a thudding rubber stamp made it final. A slip of paper was handed down. "Empress Docks – know it?"

"In the old docks?"

"Correct. Sailing Friday. Sign on aboard now and you got two days to get your gear,"

Outside, he stood remembering all the questions he should have asked. What's the pay? What exactly would he be doing? And most important of all, how long would he be away? A glance at his pink paper told him to "report to HMT *Empire Garvie*". HMT? Sounded like Royal Navy. They used civilians on certain vessels. Royal Fleet Auxiliaries. All grey paint and hammocks and away for years. His first misgivings began. At the corner of Queen's Terrace he collided with someone in a great hurry. It was the grey suit man.

"Hullo again," said he, "did you get to the Pool?"

"Yes. Tell me something. What's the *Empire Garvie*?"

"Troopship. One time German liner." A troopship? What had he let himself in for? "I've got to go," said the man. Roger tried to sound jaunty.

"Aren't you going to wish me luck again?"

The man gave him an odd look. "If you're going on the *Garvie* your luck just ran out."

Roger walked on. Now what did that mean? He turned left into tree lined Latimer Street and the dock gate was before him. A policeman glanced at his paper and he entered the docks. In those first golden years of the fifties, the port of Southampton was filled with ships. Cunard, Royal Mail and Union-Castle dominated the area with their ocean greyhounds. Sleek steel giants born in the hammering din of Belfast, Newcastle or the Clyde. Long ago, the glittering *Titanic* had briefly rested here, before making her short voyage to eternity, and falling two miles deep in a sea of tears and legends. And here Roger Wren walked, in his grey trousers, sensible jacket and crisp white shirt. What was there to worry about? The crew were civilians after all. It would be the soldiers who had it rough. The *Empire Garvie* was not grey. She was white – very white. The whole ship dazzled. Elegant lines hinted at her former role as a German passenger ship. Two biscuit coloured funnels set at a slight rake gave her a confident, Teutonic air and along her hull ran a bold blue stripe. Although at seventeen thousand tons she was of average size for her type, to him she looked enormous. The gangway led him up to a large open doorway in the side where he was immediately aware of the distinctive smell of ship in port, a rich cocktail of paint, oil and hot metal. Before him was a kind of square with a similar (closed) door in the opposite side. To his left was an impressive stairway and to his right a small table with a telephone. Sitting here was a burly man in uniform with a white topped cap. He was regarding Roger as if he were something found stuck under his shoe.

Tentatively, Roger held out his pink paper. The man made no move, but continued to stare. He wants something else, thought Roger and showed his discharge book. Please do not feed the animals, he thought madly. Still no reaction. Why doesn't he speak? shouted Roger silently to himself Of course – identity card! The right offering gave the gift of speech to the granite face.

"Second Steward's office – C Deck."

"Where is that exactly? You see I've never…"

"Where are we now?"

Knowing what was coming and the silly game that had to be played out, Roger glanced around. There was the sign. "D Deck," he said patiently.

"So, where can we expect to find C Deck?" Praying they ran from the top down, he pointed upward. "Clever boy, off you go then."

Mounting the stairs, he looked back. The man had been joined by another. They were both chuckling and shaking their heads. Over the years he'd more or less got used to people making an instant link between youth and low intelligence. His slight build and bookish demeanour generally made him the butt of any would-be humourist holding court with his cronies. Yet he'd acquired some defensive skills. The ability to take a joke was something he'd learned early. But he hated the physical jibes. Smart answers were of little use after the observation that his body was "like a matchstick with the wood scraped off". It so clearly was.

Fifteen minutes later, the Master-at-Arms behind his little table saw the pale youth returning, so obviously on his first ship. Perhaps he'd been a bit hard on him.

"Hullo young man. All fixed up?"

"Yes, signed on. Getting my gear now."

"Good. Well, we sail Friday. Nine in the morning. Don't miss the boat." On the quayside, he looked back at the *Empire Garvie*. She seemed different. His ship. The trip, he'd been told, would take eight weeks, calling at five ports each way and for most of that time would be extremely hot. The vessel was run for the government by the Orient Line, who would pay him £28 a month as a washer-up and general dogs-body in the crew mess-room. When off duty he could go ashore anywhere and he wouldn't need a passport.

Roger was content. True, he wouldn't be a steward, balancing a silver tray and gliding among well-dressed passengers, but it was a beginning. He'd been told to report next day at six a.m. to prepare the mess-room for the voyage so he had this afternoon and tomorrow to get what he required. Out of the docks again, into Oxford Street and there was the Merchant Navy shop, Baker and Sons. When he emerged he had two carrier bags containing various dungarees, shirts and shoes.

As a rule, Mr Wren senior never used strong language unless there was a good reason. This was one, he thought. "You did *what*? Signed on board a bloody *troopship*? What about the Royal Mail?"

"Nothing doing, this is all they had."

His father thought it over. "Do you realise what a rough crowd you could be in, drunks and fights and God knows what? Where's it going?"

"The Far East, China."

"Well if nothing else you'll see the world. What about Isobel? Are you really washed up with her?"

"I fear so."

Thursday came and the Master-at-Arms waved him past with a nod. He reported to Mr Candy the Second Steward and set off to find the crew mess, lower down in the ship. Asking the way twice, he walked aft down a long passage and found two doors with "Crew Mess" painted on one. Inside was a fair sized room with long tables and seats firmly fixed to a white tiled deck. At one end was a stainless steel counter with a set of shutters hiding the pantry beyond. The place seemed empty. Daylight streamed in from a row of portholes along one side. The scene was quiet here on the port side away from the quay. Suddenly there was a loud crash. One of the shutters was down and the rest soon followed. Behind the counter a man was folding them up. Then he saw Roger.

"Breakfast is not till half six." The voice was broad Scots, the statement made with that unarguable certainty of fact the accent seemed to convey. Worlds may collide, nations collapse. But breakfast would take place not one second before the appointed time. About forty, stocky and tanned, he appeared how Roger imagined Fletcher Christian may have looked.

"I'm not here for breakfast. I'm here to work. Mess assistant."

"Ah, you'll be Mario's replacement. Had a feeling he wouldn't be back. What do they call you then?" Here we go, he thought. Roger often caused amusement when he introduced himself. His somewhat roguish first name was so at odds with his personality while his surname – that of a timid bird, seemed just right.

"Roger Wren."

The man didn't even blink. "My name's Jack. Not Jock – Jack. OK? Well now, we got a meal to see to. You can go down the galley and fetch the eggs up." A face looked in the door.

"Too early," said Roger. "Come back at six thirty."

"You catch on fast," said Jack and give him an Orient Line cloth. "Away now and get the eggs, and don't drop them."

The galley was a bedlam of clattering pots and pans, hissing steam and shouting voices. Eggs, he thought. I'm fetching the eggs. A question to one of the many cooks sent him to a large stove where a man in a tall chef's hat was working. To the right was a box of eggs, to the left a bucket while on the stove was a huge circular iron pan. With amazing dexterity, the man was taking an egg in each hand, cracking them and dropping the contents into the pan, the shells going into the bucket. The action was repeated again and again, the eggs going pish – pish – pish in the spitting fat and filling the pan with white blobs, like a stick of bombs.

Roger called out but the cook either didn't hear or ignored him. Waiting till the current brace of eggs had landed, he tapped a shoulder. The cook jarred to a stop with hands in mid-clutch over the box.

"Crew mess," said Roger bravely. "I've come for the eggs."

"Oh and who might you be? Where's Mario? He always fetches them."

"I think he's left the ship, the mess anyway." The cook frowned.

"So now you've grabbed his job I suppose." It was an accusation.

"Yes," said Roger, feeling strangely guilty. "I mean, they offered me the vacancy. I didn't know him, never met him."

"Yeah? Well, I liked Mario, we all did. He was alright was Mario."

The cook resumed his task, shelling and discarding with peevish venom that suggested the loss of Mario was a personal affront never to be forgiven. Then he pointed.

"That's your stuff." On the stove was a large, oblong tray. He lifted the lid. There were his eggs, around fifty of them in long neat rows. A regiment of sizzling yellow eyes staring up at the man who was not Mario. Using the cloth, he picked them up and went carefully along the alleyway. The tray was so incredibly hot he had to refold the cloth more than once. During one of these fumbles he allowed the tray to see-saw a few times. Resting one end on a handrail, he raised the lid. To his horror, several of the bolder eggs had broken ranks and slid to one end, clearly intent on escape. Roger at this point asked himself if he still wanted to see the world. Shaking and poking the errant eggs back into ragged parade order he plodded gamely on. Again the hot metal made itself felt and he almost broke into a run.

Approaching the mess, he faced a new hazard. Bunched around the doors and seething with impatience, a tight knot of men waited for them to open.

"Mind your backs!" he bawled. Hurtling in, he dropped the tray safely into its recess in the hotplate and stood wringing his fingers.

"I nearly lost them." Three faces watched his breathless touchdown. Jack had been joined by two others.

"Look OK to me," said Jack. "Pat now, last trip, he did lose them. Dropped the lot didn't you Pat?" The man addressed was a middle aged Irishman with a face like a smiling apple.

"Ah, what of it?" said he with a cackling laugh. The third man spoke, and this time it was a Hampshire accent.

"Where's Mario?"

"He's gone," said Roger.

"And you're —?"

"Yes. Taking his place." The man snorted and turned away. Roger was obviously a poor substitute for the beloved Mario. Two more assistants arrived with trays of food. The door was opened and a hungry horde surged in. A queue formed, the men taking plates from a pile on the counter. They seemed to have their own "irons" and mugs. He was given a serving slice and told to dole out his eggs.

It all reminded him of his RAF days and he took comfort in the homely fare, the heedless chatter and the coarse repartee between the feeders and the fed.

"How about an extra egg?" asked a deckhand.

"Now why should you get more?" said Pat.

"Because I need it, I been working like two men."

"Yeah, Laurel and Hardy." The laughter rippled down the line. By seven thirty it was all over. A pile of greasy plates waited to be washed. In all they'd served forty-odd men with breakfast. He learned the rest of the crew ate elsewhere. This relatively small room was for deckhands, barmen and others. Jack Cutler was the pantry man, assisted by Pat Maguire and the oddly named Todman (Toddy)

White, the Hampshire man. The general work was done by Roger and the two younger men whose names he'd yet to learn. The senior men seemed amiable enough. Roger felt at home with them. With older men he usually did. Older men remembered the pains of youth. As they selected their own meals and settled at one of the tables, he felt that barring sea sickness the coming voyage would be a walkover.

Only when the meal finished did the first discordant note come, the first cloud in Roger's sky. The two younger assistants were about his age, maybe a little older. During the busy time just past he'd exchanged a few words but not really got acquainted. One was blond-haired, rather cold-eyed. The other was shorter, with a mop of dark hair he kept tossing back from his face. Their heads came together, they whispered and the blond one spoke.

"I'm Bill Vincent and he's Martin. Martin Clifford." He wondered if he would ever shake off the "new boy" feeling.

"Glad to know you."

"So what's your name?" He knew what was coming. Get it over with.

"Roger Wren." A look at each other, then at him.

"Roger Wren?" gasped Bill. "What kind of fuggin' daft name is that?"

With what he hoped was a blissful unconcern, Roger said, "Funny sort of label isn't it? But there you are, could be worse." Not the reaction they expected. He saw Bill's mind searching for a new angle. Jenny Wren perhaps? Or more likely the Lodger. Yes, here it comes.

"Roger the Lodger," said Bill. "We'll call him Roger the Lodger. How does it go now?" We're going to get the rhyme, he thought wearily. How many times had he heard it? The two men said what had to be said.

"Mrs O'Grady, a virtuous lady, said prayers every night to God. But it wasn't the Almighty who lifted her nightie, it was Roger the Lodger the sod." They both hooted and spluttered with laughter. It always amazed him that every person who hung that tag on him thought he was the first to do it. And anyway his name was no funnier than "Toddy".

His earlier optimism had waned somewhat. They were trying him out, seeing if he could take a joke. God, he thought. Nearly twenty and I'm still having to go through this playground ritual. A quick smile and an old reply.

"Well, you can call me that if you wish, but it takes longer to say than just Roger. Could tire you out."

The laughter stopped dead. Their faces froze. Martin said, "You've never been to sea before have you? First trip right?"

"What did you do before?" asked Bill. This was the preliminary probing Roger knew of old. He was somehow different, so every way he was different must be laid out and relished.

"I was at Hampshire Batteries for a few years before I got called up." They would have to know sometime that he was also a non-smoking, non-drinking virgin. One thing at a time.

"Now I wonder what service you were in?" said Bill.

"Oh, they stuck me in the RAF. Wasn't too bad."

Bill's voice rose in disbelief. "The bloody Raff? So we got a Brylcreem boy now then. First that wet drip Mario, now a fuggin' Brylcreem boy!" There was no smile, no disarming "only kidding" lightness to the words. The whole tone of it, the curled lip and hard eyes of the man were saying, here was a feeble creature just out of a poncey outfit, who would think he was special and dodge his share of the work. Not a good start. And they hadn't seen him stripped yet. Another rich field would open up then. One surprise was the insult to the hitherto saintly Mario.

Jack banged his mug down so sharply they all jumped.

"Come on – plates!" A huge metal sink was filled and heated with a steam-pipe. The plates, after scraping into a bin, were plunged into it. Liquid soap was added and the toil began. Bill did the washing, passing the plates to Roger and Martin who stood them on edge in wooden racks. These were then slid into a galvanised cabinet and rinsed with scalding water. Pat stacked them up. Jack and Toddy cleared the pantry and returned the galley articles. The rest of the morning was spent cleaning everything in sight. They washed the walls (bulkhead), the floor (deck), the tables, chairs and doors. Roger was assigned to the six portholes.

Now Roger knew all about brass. Hadn't he once spent eight weeks cleaning it along with other recruits? Equipped with polish, wire-wool and cloth, he made a start. Untouched for weeks, the metal was green from exposure. Busy on the floor-wash, Bill and Martin watched him. Would the new man know anything about hard graft? It took him just thirty minutes to do all six. Pat touched the bright yellow rims.

"Very good. We ought to put something on them to preserve the shine, grease or some such." Roger glanced at Bill. "Maybe I could spare some Brylcreem." Martin permitted himself a disloyal chuckle. Bill frowned. It was a feeble point scored and he guessed he would pay later. After lunch he was taken by Toddy to see where he would sleep. They went down another deck to a place of grubby doors and narrow alleyways. There were washrooms and toilets with cracked tiled decks awash with discoloured liquid. From a door marked "showers" came a naked man drying himself with a ragged towel as he passed from sight round a corner. Undressing in public had always been a trial for Roger but he knew he would have to steel himself for it in the coming weeks.

"This part," said Toddy. "Called the glory hole. Every ship, always called that. Why? Don't know." Toddy's odd economy of speech made everything sound like a telegram. Their cabin, No 17, proved to be directly opposite a toilet/washroom. Convenient, but the odour issuing from the latter suggested a mixed blessing.

"Here we are," said Toddy. "Take Mario's bunk." The man vanished, leaving Roger alone in his new home.

The bunks were three up and three down fixed along one wall. Each had a small shelf and a reading light. Opposite these were six battered lockers, five of them padlocked. Overhead, iron pipes ran fore and aft. There was a porthole, and two wooden chairs with splintered backs repaired using electrician's tape. On a rusting metal table under the porthole a number of empty beer bottles stood in a half dried pool of spilt beer. A squadron of flies competed noisily for the sticky traces. There were fag ends everywhere.

He sat on the nearest bunk and surveyed the scene. Life in the RAF had been spartan. It had never been squalid. Perhaps at sea they had a cleaning rota but nobody bothered in port. Looking out of the porthole he found he was on the starboard side facing the quay. Army trucks were disgorging young recruits. A straight backed Sergeant Major drew a deep breath.

"Stand at EASE!"

The long rows relaxed. They stared around them, at each other, down at their boots and up at the ship, pale faces filled with teenaged wonder and apprehension. But for the Grace of God, he thought, I might have been down there with them. Sent to prop up an empire which was on borrowed time even before the war.

The NCO called, "Right now, pay attention you men. When you get on board…" The pep talk ploughed on through a list of "dos" and "don'ts". Watching their faces, Roger felt a touch of guilt. They had no choice about this voyage, while he was doing it for money and to see the sights. A cut rate tourist, he was ashamed of his own misgivings. This was 1950 and he wasn't on the *Bounty*. You didn't get flogged anymore. Turning away from the porthole, he blew a raspberry at the empty cabin and his demons.

"Stop worrying," he said aloud. Where was the spare bunk? The only one with just the bare mattress was an upper one near the door. This could be an advantage. Going to or from the washroom in a state of undress, say underpants only, he wouldn't have to walk the length of the cabin to a chorus of jeers. Thinking like this was another one of his habits, along with self-analysis and daydreaming. His life had to change. Maybe this global journey – what was the phrase? – would make or break him.

His next foray was to the bedding store on G Deck. Somewhere near the waterline, or below it, he found a heavy wooden door with a sliding panel in the upper part. From this he was watched by the store man, a cadaverous figure in a wrinkled singlet and dungarees.

"Bedding?" said he.

"Yes. I'm not sure what I want."

The door opened fully. "I don't care what you want. What you'll get is what you're entitled to and no more. You're not on your daddy's yacht." He was given two blankets, two sheets and a pillow. "Bring 'em back once a week for a clean set." In the still deserted cabin he stood carefully on one of the rickety chairs and made up the bunk. I've made my bed, he thought. Tomorrow, I'll have to lie on it. The symbolism did not escape him. Back at the mess they'd all gone ashore except Jack who suggested he did the same.

"Tea's at half five. You got a bit of time. Oh, and don't forget your posting dates if you want anyone to write to you. Tells 'em when to write to each port. Ask on D Deck Square."

"Thanks Jack, I will."

In town he bought a few last minute things, among them a small padlock and several rolls of film. His camera, a cheap affair called an Ensign Ful-Vue, was at home waiting to be packed. The evening meal passed with no more open hostility, although it was obvious he was falling between two groups. The three older men accepted him, but clearly his youth and inexperience set him apart. Martin and Bill, nearer his age, had a quite different outlook. Conversation, when they deigned to include him in it, was almost entirely about sex, alcohol, what ships they'd known and the fights they'd been in. Bill was the dominant partner, who supplied most of the sarcasm and obscenities, while Martin's function was to help him out and laugh in the right places.

That evening he stowed his things in Mario's locker, snapped the padlock shut and went home.

"I thought you wanted to be a steward," said his father. "You won't learn anything about first class food washing plates for the crew. And it'll be blazing hot on that run. Wear a sun hat if you go round taking your snapshots or you'll get sunstroke. That's if you get any breaks."

Phil said, "He won't have time for anything like that. They'll work him to a standstill." But they were wrong. Food, pictures and even hats would feature largely in the coming weeks.

Roger packed his bags, two suitcases, large and small. Again it was reminiscent of service life, but without a kit-bag. He also squeezed in a pair of binoculars. There would be a lot of scenery. Most of that night he lay awake, thinking of tomorrow. The taxi arrived at five thirty.

"Good luck. Send us a postcard," said Phil, never one to get emotional.

"I'll come down when you go and see you off," said his father. "Nine o'clock you said?"

"Yes Dad. Thanks." It was worse than his call up had been. Then the summons in the buff envelope had been impersonal, unavoidable. This time the wrench from home was self-imposed, yet like conscription there could be no release once he sailed.

Back aboard, he reported to Candy and struggled with his cases down the now familiar alleyways and stairs. Somewhere he could hear music. A male voice, singing a sentimental ballad, which seemed out of place in the grim confines of the glory hole. It issued from the open door of No 21, a cabin some distance from his own. Out of curiosity he looked in. The room was the same size but with more furniture. Three bentwood chairs and one of wickerwork. On a green baize table stood the wind-up gramophone from which the song came.

"Who goes there?" drawled a voice. "Advance and be recognised." In the uncertain light a figure lay stretched out on a lower bunk. A paunchy, middle aged man, he wore round, pebble-lensed spectacles and had a cigarette in his mouth.

"I heard the music," said Roger. "It's a good tune, whatever it's called."

"Who are you – actually?"

"Name's Roger. Roger Wren."

The cigarette was delicately removed and tapped in an ashtray. "How very unfortunate for you. Still, if you appreciate music I suppose you can't be a total idiot."

"Thank you very much," said Roger with a touch of annoyance. "And what's your name?"

"Don't get mad. It's just my way. I'm Henry Batten and I've done two trips on this thing and I'm still sane which I'd say is some sort of achievement." The music stopped and the needle began a mournful to-and-fro in the centre of the record.

"I was on the *Mary* once. Then I fell out with the Chief Steward and that was me finished with Cunard. Next thing I know I'm shanghaied on to this relic of the Third Reich, running around for the kind of people who wouldn't know a *soufflé* from a *Crêpe Suzette*." Roger didn't know either but it seemed unwise to say so.

"I'd better go," he said, picking up his cases.

"The Old Master Painter," said Batten. "That's what it's called – the record. We've only got seven so you'll soon tire of hearing them. Look in anytime Roger."

"Thank you Henry." Batten winced.

"Not Henry please. Not on the ship. Batten. Just Batten."

A refuge, thought Roger, humping his cases to No 17, a place of music and wit, somewhere to go if Bill and Martin got him down too much. The cabin was again empty although only recently vacated. Suitcases, some opened, were scattered around on or under the bunks, some of which had been slept in. Up at the mess he got cordial responses from Jack and Pat, and a nod from Toddy. Bill and his shadow Martin went into their routine of looking at each other, then him.

"Roger the Lodger made it then," said Bill, stone faced.

Roger picked up the board with the breakfast menu chalked on it.

"Couldn't stay away from grub like this, better than we got in the fuggin' Raff." He would use the all purpose adjective sparingly and only on those who favoured it themselves. Two hours later they were in the cabin sorting out their belongings, fumbling and stumbling in the restricted space. In common with most ships of the period, the crew quarters little more than small steel boxes stuck anywhere out of sight according to the designer's whim and in whatever space was left after all the important things were in place. Thankfully, it turned out that Bill had a low bunk near the porthole with Martin above him. Jack had the next upper bunk over Toddy, leaving Pat in the last one under Roger. The arrangement suited him, as he did not relish being in jeering range of Bill. The table talks had taken the form of an inquisition. Try as he might, it was impossible to hide his ignorance of "life" as these men saw and practised it.

Gradually the cabin got into some kind of order. Lockers filled, cases shoved anywhere out of the way. The five others then formed a loose group round the table and the two end beds. Conversation centred around the coming voyage. They'd all served on other ships. He alone was a beginner.

"Who's got the drink?" said Martin. Bottles of beer were produced from somewhere and he heard the fizz and tinkle of discarded tops. Sitting on the Irishman's bunk he pretended to be still unpacking. What could he talk about with them? Nothing, his interest was not theirs and never could be. If he walked over now they would think him an upstart, pushing into a private circle. So brooded Roger, on the first of his fifty-six days, screwing himself into a hole and ready for someone to fill it in. Then came the Irishman's voice, as keen and fresh as a Connemara breeze.

"Hey there Roger boy – will ye not be taking a drink with us?" Gratitude filled him. The beer had no appeal; it was the offer, the gesture itself that cheered him. The tangy liquid went down a trifle fast but he didn't splutter.

"Do you drink much?" asked Jack.

"I like a drop now and again," he lied.

"Mario wouldn't touch it," said Bill. "Proper jerk he was. Never went ashore. No bag-offs, nothing. Always seasick."

Toddy opened another bottle. "So what? Did his job. No trouble."

Before he could stop himself, Roger asked, "Why did he leave?"

Jack pointed to Bill and Martin. "Them two gave the poor laddie a dog's life." Bill fidgeted.

"Well, he asked for it."

"Not only that," drawled Pat with a sly glance at Roger, "but he wasn't even *English*, was he?"

Roger said, "Oh, where was he from?"

"Cyprus," muttered Bill. Roger saw it all, someone different, like him.

"And now you've got me – how about that?"

Bill opened his mouth to speak then Toddy at the porthole said, "Gangplank's going."

There was a leisurely exodus from the cabin and they all made their way upward through the ship, becoming separated in the growing throng. The quayside was packed. On the ship, soldiers and crew jostled together at the rail. Noise lapped back and forth: shouting, whistling and jocular comments.

"You'll be sor-ry!"

"Aren't you glad you joined?"

A military band began to play. As always, it was "Colonel Bogey" and as always the ribald version of the words roared out from the throats of the men in black berets crushed against the rail.

Scanning the crowd he saw his father at last and was seen by him at almost the same time. They exchanged waves and the distance seemed huge. So they stood like everyone else, filling the final half hour with sign language. A departure by ship is a drama unique. All the actors in it are on stage far too early. Time does not merely stand still. It is cast in bronze. The distance between those staying and those going is small enough to see expressions but too great to be heard. Thoughts and questions must remain unsaid, making the break even more agonizing. One by one the rituals are carried out. The crowd is pushed back, the gangways removed, the Tannoys mouth their crackling gibberish. There was a long blast on the funnel. The *Empire Garvie* was a living beast, bellowing to be freed, to slip the lines and sever at last the clinging bonds of the shore. And now her liberation came. Great loops of rope splashing into the water to be drawn aboard dripping and spinning. On the port side, seen by only a few, tugs began to ease her away. Up to now, she had been simply a wall of steel, as solid and immovable as the quay itself. Now a gap showed, ugly and disturbed, widening by the second. Roger watched it all. In the middle of a march the band stopped and began something else, something plaintive, and crushingly apt. On ship and shore the words of the song rose – "I'd love to get you on a slow boat to China." The water stretched twenty yards, thirty, his father became an unrecognised dot among many. A final wave and the parting was complete. Accompanied by a horde of seagulls, they passed the long foreshore at Netley. The tugs departed, and the troopship set off down the Solent. Next came a boat with PILOTS in bold letters on her side. A man shinned down a rope ladder and jumped aboard. The self important little craft gave a snappy toot on her whistle, made an abrupt about-turn and sped back to Southampton. The seagulls left them. Quite alone at last, the ship turned south-west by south, into the Channel and the teeth of the wind. The *Empire Garvie* (and Roger Wren) were on course for the Orient.

There were women on deck, he noticed, children too. Service families going out to somewhere east of Suez. Where the best is like the worst, he thought, remembering his Kipling. Perhaps he might find time to put his own impressions into verse. Something about the allure of the sea, the voice of the wind and so forth. He found everyone back in the cabin which was now wreathed in cigarette smoke.

"So then what?" asked Jack.

"I got a DR," said Martin. "So did the tiger. They said we were both to blame. I reckon the blood caused it. Treated me like dirt."

Bill spoke. "Fancy the tiger getting a DR."

"Yeah well, I had this show where I had to share with the tiger. She got on my wick all the time and it was her bloods what caused the upset, just had to thump one of them. That's the last trip I ever did on the *Empire Ken*."

"Serves you right," said Bill. "For taking a poncey job like steward."

To Roger it made no sense whatever. Somehow he must learn the jargon. The ship gave a sudden lurch and he staggered. Bill saw it.

"Oh dear, the Lodger's still finding his feet." The ship rolled again and his stomach rolled with it. Dear God, don't let him be seasick. Not when they're all watching.

"Get off your feet," said Toddy. "On your bunk. Better, you'll see." It was his first attempt. Taking off his shoes, he began to climb, putting his feet where he could and reaching up to grasp the overhead pipe work. During this, the ship pitched the wrong way and he dangled from the pipes like a monkey while his feet groped for a hold. The cabin erupted with laughter. Finally he got a leg up and flopped on the bunk. From where he lay he could see down the length of the cabin to the porthole and the sullen water rushing past.

Jack said, "Better close the port." Toddy reached up to release it from its hook. As he did so, the Channel spat in his face. A tablespoonful of water snatched up by the wind. Again a burst of merriment and Roger felt better. The sea could make a fool of any one of them. Toddy lowered the heavy brass port with its inch-thick glass and screwed down the clamps while the salt water ran off his chin.

Half an hour later, they were all on deck again, this time for fire and boat drill. Someone showed him how to don a lifejacket and he stood in a line with others watching the boats swung out by deckhands. This seemed to be the extent of the drill, seeing everything worked up to the point of actually manning the boats. Swaying in the wind with his chin resting on the top of the lifejacket, he realised he was indeed getting his "sea legs". As many had before him, he found it better on deck, where the eyes could warn the organs of balance what was coming. A funnel blast signalled the end of the exercise, the jackets were returned and he was in the cabin again, on his back and thinking of Isobel. Perhaps he should have written before leaving. No, he'd tried to speak to her and she'd refused to see him. Leave it at that. Maybe when he got back? His eyes closed and as quickly opened again. Bill was standing there, soon to be joined by Martin.

Chapter 2

Bill said, "What did you do in the Raff?" The bunk was at a height to put him at their eye level. An uneasy feeling, as if he were laid out on a shelf.

"Nothing much. They had me doing up old radar sets, bits of soldering and testing circuits."

"Where was this?"

"Oxford."

"Oxford, wow!" Bill acted amazed. "Up with all the clever boys. Up with the nobs."

"No, not the university. Outside at an MU. An RAF camp."

"Bit of a change for you then," sneered Martin. "Coming on this tub and having to work with common scum like us."

Not at all. I've often worked with common scum like you. The beautiful riposte leapt into his mind but caution stilled his tongue and it remained unsaid.

"I wonder why you came on here," said Bill, "if you can do bloody radar and stuff like that. I reckon you'll turn out to be a jerk like Mario."

"What makes you think that?"

"Saw you when you first come aboard. One look at you was enough." He remembered himself in tweed jacket and flannels, wandering the deck like a lost choirboy. How he must have stood out. The grilling went on.

"You don't really drink do you?" pressed Bill. "Or smoke even. Bet you never had korey either."

His mind reeled "Korey?"

"Fuggin' 'ell!" muttered Martin in disbelief.

"Nookie!" barked Bill. "Bag off, leg over – you've never had it have you?" It was time to lie. There was no way he could be a virgin of nearly twenty and survive eight weeks among these people.

"Course I've had it."

"Got a girl, have you?" leered Bill. Outwardly offhand, his brain was working overtime.

"Yes. Her name's Isobel, if it's any of your business. I was at her place only last night. Anything else?"

Bill pointed a finger in Roger's face. "Don't you get smart pal, or you'll wish you'd never come on this ship."

"I expect he's already wishing that," said Pat from the lower bunk.

"Look Bill," said Roger, "I don't know what you've got against me. I'm here to do a job the same as you. Why are you picking on me?" It was a mistake. The pleading tone was what they wanted to hear.

Bill grinned at Martin and put his face close to Roger's. "Cos you're a jerk, knew that soon as I seen you." He turned to Martin. "Come on." They left the cabin.

Sick at heart, he lay looking up at the deck-head. The hostility seemed without reason. He'd done his full share of the work, hadn't put on airs or talked too much about himself. An ordinary working man, no different from them. But he was of course. He didn't smoke, drink, or fornicate. In Bill's mind, no one could be like him and still be a man. One of us. One of the lads. So what was the answer? Be himself and keep his head down, or try to conform to their rules of acceptance? The maddening thing was, there was no lofty reason for his way of life. Tobacco simply had no appeal. He'd often accepted a cigarette but never much liked it. Drink did nothing for him. As for sex, he was still trying, still hopeful. It was 11.30, time to start work again. Jack and Toddy passed him on their way out. If they'd heard anything of the recent exchange they gave no sign. He sat up and peered down between his legs at Pat.

"Did you hear all that?"

"I did, yes. Don't let them worry you. See you up at the mess."

Roger was alone again with his jumbled emotions. The porthole drew him like a magnet. This near the waterline the Channel surged past at what seemed an incredible speed. The iron grey seascape was far from empty. Through the wet glass he saw about seven ships. In the middle distance, being rapidly overtaken, a small and scruffy vessel dipped and wallowed its way over the choppy surface.

"Butting through the Channel in the mad March days," he said aloud. But this was June and he had no time to stand there quoting his favourite poets. Reluctantly he turned away from Masefield's coaster and set off for the mess. During the work Bill was taciturn, but not unduly hostile. It seemed he needed an attentive audience to bring out his mean streak. They were all too busy, the rolling causing a few spills that had to be cleared up. Roger, serving potatoes, stood between Toddy and Jack and was able to converse freely with the older men. In their company he felt no need to hide his ignorance. Some of the jargon was explained. "Tiger" was the name given on every ship to the Captain's steward. "Bloods" were passengers, while a "show" was any group of them served by one steward.

"And what's a DR?"

"Decline to report," said Toddy. "In your book, what they put where it says 'Conduct'." Later, the work done, he went exploring, feeding his senses on this great thing that was carrying him. To some the world of a ship is utterly beguiling. The solid oak decks, bleached white by salt and sunlight. The wind in the wires and the soft hum of ventilators.

And the sea. Above all, the sea. Finding himself below the bridge, he went forward (for'ard, he murmured to himself) and stood at the very tip of the bow, resting folded arms on the steel coaming. From here the bow-wave was out of sight so that he seemed to be gliding without support over the water. This sense of detachment got him thinking about his future in a more rational way. Given that he would be living cheek-by-jowl with Bill and his odious partner for weeks to come, he had to deal with that. Clearly there must be no more protests, no more "why me?" If necessary, he would acquire a few new vices.

Thus resolved, he returned to the cabin. The place had been thoroughly cleaned. All the debris from the stay in port was gone, the deck no longer strewn with fag ends but bare and damp from washing.

"Glory hole steward," explained Pat. "She does all the toilets too. We pay her something at the end of the voyage for doing the cabin." There it was again. The feminine pronoun. The word that had made Martin's tiger a tigress. The one piece of jargon no one thought *needed* explaining. He had an idea of course. A niggling notion pushing itself forward as his conventional mind strove to reject it. Even in his National Service, that great melting pot of British youth, the "love that dare not speak its name" had not in fact ever done so. So it was hard to believe what he was thinking. So far, judging by the crew he'd met, any kind of "Nancy-boy" could expect short shrift.

And then the door opened and a man entered. About thirty, he was dressed in immaculate dungarees and a pink shirt. One hand rested languidly on the doorframe and the other held a mop out at an angle like a staff of office. Deep set eyes panned round the cabin and settled on Roger. The voice, devoid of any accent, was slow and deliberate.

"Well now, lookee here. A new face I see."

Martin sniggered. "That's Roger the Lodger."

"Ooh vada *him* then." More slang. Would he ever learn it all?

"Roger Wren," he said. To save time, he added, "Mario's gone. I've taken his place."

"Have you now? And what do you think of this bunch?" The dark eyes roamed over the others as a housewife might inspect second rate vegetables.

"Piss off Linda," growled Bill. "Go and clean your toilets."

"Ooh get you! So *manly*. Been eating red meat again have we?" Bill took an aggressive step forward. The glory hole steward quickly couched the mop head under one arm and thrust the handle out before him like a Bengal Lancer.

"Go on then. Try it. You'll get this up your Khyber."

Bill stopped. "Yeah? I'll punch you up in the air." But he stayed where he was and the man called Linda turned back to Roger.

"How old are you then? Sixteen?"

"No, nineteen."

"Surely not. First trip?" How could they always tell?

"Yes, but learning fast."

"H'm. You have to know who your friends are Roger. Can I be your friend?"

What could he say – no? "Of course, and I reckon you did a good job on this room."

The man gazed happily round the cabin. "There, hear that? Somebody appreciates my efforts. See you later Roger." The door slammed.

"See you later *Roger,*" mimicked Martin. "She'll have you on the turn before we reach Gib. That's if you're not already queer. Are you?"

"Piss off," said Roger crisply. He was indeed learning fast.

That night there were two more hurdles to face. It was not strictly necessary to take a shower so soon but he'd resolved not to put it off for fear of giving Bill something to remark on. The second thing was going to the crew bar with the others. It had to be done he knew. The spit-and-sawdust code does not accept that one of a small party remains aloof. It smacks of weakness, disloyalty to the group. Even disapproval of drink! But first, the shower, how to go about it? Go fully dressed to the washroom, strip, wash and dress again? No, too obvious. Casually he spoke to the cabin in general.

"What are the showers like on here?"

"OK," said Jack. "Sometimes take a while to warm up."

Quickly he stripped to his underpants and draped his towel over his shoulders. Grabbing soap and flannel he stepped back in his shoes and slipped out. Nobody had seen him go. As he'd feared, the showers were open cubicles, streaked with rust and flaky paint and without frontal screening. There was no other person there. The water was cold and stayed cold for several minutes. Naked, he stood clear of the jet, desperately twiddling the control. When he did get under, the shower was quite pleasant, but he didn't want to stay long. A brisk rub with the towel, pants back on, and he was ready for the next ordeal – the return to the cabin! This time he was out of luck. There happened to be a lull in the talk as he entered, so all heads turned to see him.

"Fuggin' 'ell!" exclaimed Bill. "I knew he was thin but I thought he'd have *some* meat on him." Roger pinned a smile on his face and tried to keep it there while he dressed.

"Hey!" shouted Martin, inspired. "When did you escape from Belsen?" This brought a general wave of laughter.

"I bet he had to run about in the shower to get wet," said Bill. "Don't ever go ashore in shorts Roger. You'll be picked up as a vagrant, no visible means of support."

Most of it he'd heard before yet every crack, however old, cut with a pain forever fresh.

It went on. "I can count his bones," said Martin. "His rib cage."

"Looks more like a bird cage," scoffed Bill. There had to be some reply, some counter joke.

"At least I'll never worry about getting fat."

"No," said Bill grimly. "You won't live long enough if you ask me. I got a cousin of thirteen looks more of a man than you do." The older men had stopped chuckling. They'd noticed the change, the drift from mild leg pull to crude insult.

Now it was Martin again. "If I had a body like his I'd bloody shoot myself." Roger stood outwardly cool, inwardly cringing.

It was Toddy who ended it. "Going down the Pig. Open now, should be. Anyone?"

"Yes, said Jack. "Let's go. You too Roger." As they all went down another deck Pat put a hand on his shoulder. "Cheer up son. Come and get a few bevvies down you."

But Roger didn't want a few bevvies down him. Roger wanted to be tossed overboard with a lifebelt, somehow drift back to Southampton, crawl up Netley Shore and run home. The Pig turned out to be similar to the mess but with tubular tables and chairs scattered loosely about the place. The room was thronged with men drinking and chattering under a thick mantle of cigarette smoke. Drink was served from a hatchway in the end bulkhead where a bald barman with a Hitler moustache reigned supreme.

"I'll get 'em," said Jack and the others sat down. Obviously they would all be buying a round. Roger now faced the classic dilemma of every unwilling drinker wishing to be sociable. How to pay his share without having to match their rate of consumption. Jack returned with the beers on a tray and his heart sank. The foaming pints looked enormous. If he stayed for each round he'd have to swallow six of these things. The others drank thirstily, banging the glass on the table with the breathy "Ah-h-h!" that signifies pure bliss. Roger made a start. His hand actually felt small as he grasped the glass, so huge did the pint seem.

Soon he noticed that four of the other glasses were empty. Hurriedly he poured half his beer down his protesting throat and saw he'd overtaken Martin who was strangely lagging behind them all. Here was an opening, a small gap inviting a rapier thrust, sweet revenge for the torment in the cabin, and to hell with the consequences. He drained his glass and stood up.

"Come on Martin, you're slow. What's up with you? Is it too *strong* for you?"

Their faces told him he'd scored. Even Bill was amused. Martin had to both finish his drink in a hurry and make some response. So he did both at once.

"You cheeky (gulp) bastard. You want to (gulp) watch your lip or I'll (gulp) punch you up in the air (gulp) see if I don't." Eyes watering, he put down his glass and gave it an angry shove, sending it sliding along the table as in a Western film. Roger put it on the tray with the others and went to the bar. It was the second time he'd heard the curious threat to "punch up in the air". There seemed no end to the stream of mysterious and colourful slang. Every hour he heard something new. Plates were "strapped up", never washed up. "Gash" meant surplus, not wanted. Terms for sex abounded. Korey, hole, nookie, bag-off and bunk-up as well as the older ones he'd known before. Why didn't they just say sex?

Roger, as was his way, pondered these matters as he waited at the hatch. The barman put the refilled glasses on the tray and as he paid for them he realised he'd forgotten which was which. Perhaps it didn't matter. If he couldn't tell them apart neither could they. From what he'd seen so far, the *Garvie* crew were not unduly obsessed with hygiene and he sensed there were greater hazards to come. Martin took his beer with an ill grace, and there was a ghost of a smile from Bill. Slowly the hours passed. Conversation was not easy in the general din. Roger's contribution was mainly nodding and saying "Really? I never knew that." Sometimes an argument would erupt near at hand. Voices were raised and glasses banged down.

Around him were all the accents he'd heard in the service but Bill and Martin had him baffled, Derbyshire maybe. They were talking loudly together now, voyages and excesses, past and to come; a lurid catalogue of alcohol and flesh that left him both revolted and a little envious. The walls of sound that encased him advanced and receded in his tired ears and the smoky cloud base seemed to be pressing the top of his head down. Halfway into his third pint he banged his shin violently on the table leg and felt no pain whatsoever. Three quarters into it and his hands felt unreal, as if he were wearing thick woollen gloves. There was no clock in the room and he'd left his watch in the cabin. In any case what did it matter? There was nowhere to go, no bus to catch, just a bunk to fall into. If one could fall into something at shoulder level. Still, he had to get away before he collapsed. The long day, the drink and the sleepless night at home were taking effect. Yes, three pints were enough. Finish this one and go. But where was it? His glass had gone.

"There you go my son," said Pat happily. "Get your laughing gear round that. Do you a world of good." A fourth pint stood before him, white froth spilling down the side like an evil, silent volcano and looking to his shocked eyes big enough to drown in.

"Thanks Pat," he mumbled, trying to sound delighted. "I think after this I'll call it a day." But Pat was talking to someone else. Only Martin was facing his way and his expression would have curdled milk. Roger stared him out, took a few reckless swigs and began conversing with Toddy. He was reaching the point where pretence was hard to sustain. It was not the first time in his life he'd sat like this, clutching at the last shreds of lucid thought. Once before, when he'd finished his RAF training, Roger had briefly been "one of the lads". But that was a special occasion shared with other callow youths, not the possible start of a run of such nights in the company of hardened drinkers.

Taking his next mouthful, he raised the glass too quickly and banged the rim on his teeth with an audible click. Now his elbow slipped off the table. And his eyes were playing him up. When he looked at Toddy his gaze overshot and had to be dragged back on target. Next his brain seemed to rotate in his skull. Then it stopped, only for the room to turn instead. God, this must be his last drink. But then – well – he *was* drunk – face it – miles from home – may as well – sheep as a lamb – be hung. Paid my share – can't say I didn't. Very, very carefully he picked up the glass. Taking two huge gulps, he surveyed his shipmates. Shipmates, he thought. Good sound to that. He was a seaman! Hoist yer top gallants! Belay yer – yer mizzen thing! Another heroic dive into the glass. Sod them all! The thing was simply to say "I'm off. Goodnight to you all." He braced himself, tried to stand and found his shoes had become large wellingtons made of lead.

Suddenly there was a commotion nearby. Fired by alcohol, a row between two men had become violent. A blow was struck and one of them crashed back into Roger's table. Some of the others grabbed their drinks in time but Toddy and Roger lost theirs as the table went over. They all got to their feet, Roger finding himself upright without knowing how he got there. Other people separated the battling pair, the table was righted and they began to settle again. Not Toddy. "Had enough, me," he announced in his cryptic way. "Off below."

Salvation, thought Roger. "Yeah me too. Tired out." The barman, cursing freely, came over and began picking up the broken glass.

"Sorry, not our fault," said Roger, visibly swaying.

"No," snapped the barman, moustache twitching. "Never is, is it?"

As the cooler air hit him Roger felt giddy and sick. Toddy leading, they made careful progress along the alleyway, Roger making much use of the handrails and uneasily aware that Martin was following them. Back on their own deck, he heard a door open as they passed it and saw Martin slip into another cabin. In his haze of alcohol and fatigue he couldn't divine what that might signify. Now the nausea increased and he reached the toilets just in time as his evening meal made a lively exit.

Toddy watched him. "Too much booze," he remarked. "You're not used to it. Spew your ring up every time." An observation, thought Roger that was neatly put and entirely correct. Five minutes with his head inverted over the pan sent the blood back to his brain and the giddiness abated. Later on when he'd freshened up and was finally ready for bed, the others had still not returned. Toddy was already turned in. At the porthole he took one last look out.

"What's the weather doing?" asked Toddy. Over a pitch black Channel the sky was the colour of granite in which a few stars winked like fool's gold.

"Looks alright, what I can see of it."

"Got the Bay yet. Don't worry, maybe OK." The Bay of Biscay, thought Roger, another test. His head swam as he left the porthole and he held on to the bunk supports as he undressed. No pyjamas of course. He felt certain they didn't wear such things here. It would be underpants only in this uninhibited company. After a couple of attempts he reached the bunk and lay wondering what would happen next. He'd brought two or three books with him but something told him not to unpack them yet. It was eleven o'clock as he put his watch on the shelf and crawled under the covers. This would be his first night away from home since he left the service.

The door crashed noisily open. Bill and Martin fell into the room and made straight for him.

"Ah, there's poor little Roger," cooed Bill. "Fast asleep and dreaming he's giving Isobel one."

"Him?" said Martin. "He don't know what it's for yet, do you Roger?" The question was driven home by a vicious dig in the ribs. He raised himself on one elbow. Martin must have rejoined Bill in the Pig. They were both drunk. With their bright eyes and half opened mouths they resembled excited spaniels.

"No, I don't. So are you going to show me at one of the ports?" Martin frowned, trying to think of an answer. Bill patted Roger's cheek.

"No need to wait till then. You're going to find out what *everything's* for, much sooner than you think." Martin tittered mischievously, and they went to the other end of the cabin, chuckling at some secret knowledge. As he wondered what this could mean, the remaining two inmates returned, talking quietly and only moderately tipsy. While the four seamen got ready for bed, their voices blended with the sounds of the ship, the hiss of the passing sea, and it was all part of the new life that was so alien to him. The single overhead light went off and he relaxed at last. His first night at sea had begun and he was thankful the long day was finally over. But he was wrong of course. The day was not over. Not for him. Before dawn came, there would be a further shock.

His mind still plunged about, reviewing the day and the jumbled scenes that filled it. There had been a stirring departure from England to see and remember. He'd bruised his leg, and seen a man felled by a savage blow in the face. He'd met a man called – Linda. And the day had been tastefully rounded off by telling a few lies and a little swearing. For an encore, as out of character as the rest, he'd got drunk on four pints and been spectacularly sick in a toilet, and it was only his first day at sea! Peering about, he saw that the cabin was not completely dark. A faint light entered by a slatted air vent in the door, by which he could make out the line of lockers and the clothing hung about on makeshift hooks. Gradually his brain slowed down, and at last, at long last, he slept.

Sometime later he came uneasily awake. Something was in the bed, moving over his legs under the covers. The ship was fairly old – did it have rats? Fighting a rising sense of horror, he put a hand down to investigate. He found not a rat but another hand, which on being touched deserted his legs and grabbed his fingers in eager amity. He jerked free and sat up, switching on the bunk light. Linda the glory hole man stood there, wearing only a towel and gazing at him in puzzlement.

"What's the matter Roger?" His breath reeked of whisky. "They said you wanted me to call. Come back tonight you said." Still under the covers, the hand resumed its travel. Roger rebelled, yanking the covers back and dashing the hand away.

"Look, you got it wrong. I'm not interested, really." For some reason, he added, "Thank you all the same."

Linda was annoyed. "You said I could be your friend – you *did*!" Roger felt sick again and his head hurt. Would this ghastly day never end?

"I know I did, but I didn't know you meant that way."

"Martin told me quite distinctly. You said in the Pig you liked me and wouldn't mind if I came back here later." He recalled that crafty visit on the way back from the Pig. Obviously to Linda's cabin.

"Then Martin is a fuggin' liar!" The word was slipping out more often but he was beginning not to care.

Linda glared down the cabin. "You rotten lousy bitch, Martin. I'll never speak to you again!" Then he flounced out, slamming the door so hard two of the slats fell out of the air vent.

The rest of the cabin had of course heard it all. On the instant the door shut all the other bunk lights came on and the heads leaned out to see him sitting up trying to gather his wits. Audience appreciation was total. They hooted and roared. And they relived the parts they liked best.

"Not tonight Linda," cried Bill in a quavering voice. "Come back tomorrow when I'm not having a wet dream about Isobel."

"Thank you all the same," added Martin and fell back convulsed on his bed. Martin had that way of laughing that grates on the listener, where the sound is made on the intake of breath as well as exhalation, sounding like a person choking. The taunts continued.

It was Bill's turn again, still with the plaintive whine. "I thought you wanted me Roger. How about if I changed my name to Isobel?" Roger's face ached with the good humoured, "take-a-joke" grin he'd stitched in place as soon as the lights went on. As before, during the post-shower onslaught, he felt he couldn't just sit there in dumb acquiescence. An old trick he'd seen in a film came back to him and he quickly adapted it for the occasion.

"Hey Bill," he called down. "Do you know how you can always tell if a bloke's queer?"

"How?"

Roger mumbled indistinctly and Bill said, "What?" Now Roger raised his voice.

"I said if he's hard of hearing!"

For a few seconds there was a stunned silence. Then the laughs rolled forth again from all except Bill. "You shut your mouth Roger. Try to be funny with me – just you shut your fuggin' mouth or I'll – or I'll –" groping, he fell back on the old standby "I'll punch you up in the air."

Roger pictured this man in a fight, his opponents plummeting to earth all around. The exchange had spoiled the flow somewhat. As the lights went out again the word-stream dried up. One amusing bonus for Roger was that if Bill asked him a leading question, he had only to mumble his reply to kill the intended jibe. Bill could not say "Eh?" or "What?" without reprising the hard of hearing joke.

He lay in the gloom hearing the structure of the old liner moving and flexing around him. Having his legs stroked by a man had shaken him. Now as he lay longing for the oblivion of sleep, five decks down and getting ever further from home, he felt a gnawing dread at what might be in store. There would be heavy drinking. There would be tensions and lost tempers. To some, this wonderful voyage was only a job. Tropical heat and grinding boredom would drive them to seek relief, any kind of relief. He thought of that God-like figure, Captain Baskerville and his officers up on the Olympian heights of A Deck. How much control, how much discipline did they actually wield down here in the depths where drink was king and violence settled everything? But when Roger's first day came to an end it was on a high note. As he sank towards sleep he heard Toddy speak. And Jack replied, just loud enough for all to hear.

"Well, I'll say this for Roger. The laddie can take a joke. That's more than you can say for some people in this cabin."

One thing he'd forgotten was an alarm clock, but in the event it wasn't needed, nor ever would be. At 5.30 he awoke. The first thing he saw was the porthole's bright circle, with the silhouetted heads of Jack and Martin. He sat up too quickly and his head fell off. Or so it felt. It took a major effort to focus his thoughts and his mouth resembled Bonneville Salt Flats on a very hot day. As hangovers went it wasn't too bad he supposed, apart from a headache. But it did show.

"God, look at the Lodger," said Bill. "The state of him. Eyes like piss-holes in the snow."

"Are we –?" Why did his voice sound shrill? He cleared his throat. "Are we in the Bay yet?" Martin stopped on his way out.

"In the Bay? We got in the Bay last night."

"That's right," said Bill. "Round about the time your new girlfriend called. Or new boyfriend, depending on who's doing what."

As they left giggling for the washroom, Roger slithered down to the deck and began to dress. Now the change in the weather was obvious. It was a struggle to balance while getting his trousers on. The washroom was crowded, about twenty men using the two rows of sinks. When one became free he put his things on the ledge under the mirror, aware that he was being watched.

"Don't tell me you've started shaving," drawled Martin. "I suppose you got to look nice for the boyfriend."

"I don't know about that. It was you he called a bitch." Filling the sink, he saw Martin in the mirror. The man's face was a picture. All very well, but he wished there was some way of ending this tit-for-tat game. Other than complete submission, Mario style.

Back in the cabin, they all finished dressing and made their way in a straggling line to the mess. The routine was set, one that would order their lives all the way to China and back: the mess-room to keep clean; three meals a day to fetch and serve to the same assortment of men, parading past the counter. And what an assortment it was. The homosexuals, each sporting a feminine name, and many having a boyfriend or "husband". Derisively dubbed "queers", they minced and pouted through the day, hurling waspish insults at any who challenged them. There were the young lions, aggressively masculine and set on proving themselves at every opportunity. Often tattooed, they strutted like roosters and talked endlessly of manly things. And the old men, bodies salted and dried by years of sea winds who droned on about their former ships (The old *Majestic,* the dear old *Aquitania*) as if they were discarded mistresses.

After breakfast, he took his camera and went on deck. Perhaps because it was summer, the Bay had laid its fearsome reputation aside. The roll was lively but smooth. It was gratifying to think he could be one of those fortunates who never got seasick. One thing fewer to worry about and a plus point for someone who needed all he could get. A ship came into view on the port side, and swiftly drew near. A grey-black freighter of around 6000 tons with a red band round her funnel. The Ful-Vue's shutter clicked and the unknown traveller passed and vanished astern, unaware that long after she was scrapped her soul would live on in a small black and white image.

That afternoon he was called to Candy's office and went from there to the ship's doctor. "Mr Wren? Come in, sit down," said the man behind the desk and continued writing notes. Presently he looked up. "This is your first trip Mr Wren."

"Yes." I ought to wear a yellow star, he thought.

"To the Far East I mean."

"To anywhere." The doctor rustled his notes, humming tunelessly.

"Ever had a dose?" he inquired breezily.

"A dose of what?"

The man stared. "Syphilis. Gonorrhea. You know, VD." So that's what it meant. He recalled the RAF lectures with their hideous colour slides and the wave of sniggering that died out as the full details became clear.

"No never."

"I see." The doctor seemed almost disappointed. "Well you must have heard of these things, surely."

"Oh yes. In the RAF. They told us all about it."

The stern face brightened. There would be no need for the lecture. "Good, good. Fine. Just remember the golden rule. A wise soldier always keeps his weapon clean, before and after going into action. Roll up your sleeve." As he always did, he had to look away as the needle went in. The doctor signed a paper and handed it to him. "Any worries, you know where to come. Oh and try to stay off the drink." Out in the corridor, clutching his arm, Roger read the paper. Whatever he might die of in the ensuing weeks, it wouldn't be smallpox.

On this, his second day at sea, he spent some of his free time wandering about the crew deck and adding to his knowledge of the ship. She was twenty-one years old, he learned. Formerly the *Krugersdorp* of the German African Line and one of the spoils of war converted for trooping. Like the *Empire Ken* on which Martin had earned his DR. And the *Fowey*, the *Windrush* and the *Halladale*, all with the *Empire* prefix.

Up on D deck square he found, pinned up behind glass, a chart showing the ship's daily run with a small flag to mark their present position. They were nearing the north west corner of Spain. He hurried out to the port side. Yes, there it was. France had crept past unseen in the night but there was Spain. The faint smudge of green on the far rim of the sea was unmistakably foreign. He had begun to see the world.

From that moment the milestones passed rapidly. Early on Monday he saw the great mass of Gibraltar slipping by. They now entered a sea of truly startling blueness, enclosed by the coastlines of a host of nations. A tideless, sweltering bathtub of a sea, laced with the blood of a thousand battles. To Roger, history and geography were one. He thought of the mariners of old sailing these waters, the Phoenicians, the Romans and so many others. He saw the great galleys, long banks of oars gleaming wet and kissed by the sun, with the big painted eye on the prow seeking out the enemy. And he thought of the recent war, when this now quiet place had seen carnage on a scale unimagined by the men of those long gone vessels.

As the ship throbbed her way towards Port Said the temperature on board commenced a steady climb. More and more people came on deck. Shirts came off and the sunbathers began their homage to the god overhead. Some already found the heat below intolerable, taking bedding on deck to sleep. Roger had by now settled into an uneasy but bearable relationship with his younger colleagues. Bill was still hostile, but wary. Roger's infrequent but telling little victories like the deafness joke had been a new experience for Bill. Mario had never answered back, except to plead for mercy. Jack, who was surely the oldest, treated everyone alike. As brown and steady as a Dundee cake, he dispensed advice in an accent you could grow heather on. It was he, a day or so after Gibraltar, who brought some interesting tidings.

"We're going to Korea. Japan too. It's up on the notice board.

There's a war starting or something."

"Where's Korea?" muttered Bill from his bunk. Roger knew but kept quiet.

"Up by China," said Toddy. "Bit sticking out." There was an animated discussion over the new ports of call, which would add several days or weeks to the voyage. Roger tried to balance the opposing feelings he'd begun to have regarding the whole enterprise, but Japan would be the ultimate in foreign visits. There was no longer any doubt. This voyage was going to be the experience of a lifetime.

CHAPTER 3

THE SUNSET WAS FINISHED AND SO was the apple. He dropped the core into the Mediterranean and considered returning to the cabin. There was still that flutter of unease each time he joined the little circle. The jibes were wearisome and the heat made them worse. However the drinking was less of a problem. They still went to the Pig but he was able to escape before he got too ill. And there had been no more amorous overtures from Linda. During the course of his work he'd got to know a few other people and realised his first idea of the crew as a band of hardened reprobates had been premature. The "queers" in particular were mostly intelligent men who used genuine wit to make a point rather than crude aggression. But he was aware of the pitfalls. His midnight encounter had seen to that. With regret he re-entered the deckhouse. A wave of heat came up the stairwell, becoming more clammy with each downward step. More men were sleeping on deck now, an idea that held great appeal for him, but he didn't want to be the first in his group to do it.

The atmosphere in the cabin was scarcely breathable. An appalling cocktail of sweat, cigarette smoke, spilt liquor and freely expelled body gases. The port was open and the scuttle in place. This was a metal device which slotted into the aperture and supposedly scooped outside air into the cabin. It also tended to collect any debris tossed out of portholes ahead of them. What tiny breezes did enter hit the unyielding foulness and died on the spot. Uneasily he checked the room. Jack and Bill were playing cards under the porthole. Martin watched from his bunk and Pat lay dozing on his. Toddy was absent, believed to be trying to learn more about the new ports of call.

"Where you been?" demanded Bill. "Up on deck again I suppose, creeping around to pick up some rough trade." They were still getting mileage out of the Linda incident.

"Brown-hatter," pronounced Martin firmly. "That's what he is. Him and Linda. Saw the look between 'em that time. What would your Isobel say if she knew you were queer Roger?" He was too tired to retaliate, too tired with the endless stream of body and sex jokes. Maybe he could change the subject.

"Anyone here been to Korea before?"

"No," said Jack. "What's it all about anyway, this war?"

Roger, for all his youth, took an interest in world affairs and read the papers at home.

"It's about the north being communist and the south not wanting to be. The UN is trying to sort it out." Careful, he thought. Don't come across as a know-all.

"Yes," said Pat, waking up. "But why are we going there?" To his alarm, they were all looking at him.

"Why are we going there?" he echoed stupidly.

"Yeah, why?" asked Bill with a gleam in his eye and a quick look at Martin.

"Well, I don't really know. I mean, we're in the UN so we have to send some troops. Maybe transfer some from Hong Kong by way of Japan."

"Tell you what boys," said Jack. "You'll be alright for korey in Japan. If it's Yokohama we go to. I went there before the war. And it's cheaper too." It was the first time he'd heard Jack offer any kind of salacious comment and was a measure of how they all seemed to be gearing up for the coming debauchery. Even the staid Mr Cutler. Who next? Pat?

Sure enough Pat now spoke. "Well now, I wouldn't want to spend too much on a woman in Hong Kong if it's cheaper in Yokohama."

"How much is it in Hong Kong?" asked Roger. His voice, which he'd meant to sound casual, suggested instead a non-swimmer inching along a high diving board.

Bill seized his chance. "What do you want to know for? A good woman would kill you. She'd suck you in and blow you out in bubbles." This sent Martin into his terrible hee-hawing laugh and even the patient Jack winced.

"What the laddie needs," he said heavily, "is someone like you Martin, a man of the world, who can teach him real sophistication."

"Yeah OK," nodded Martin reasonably. "I'll do that if he wants." The sarcasm had passed over his head high enough to leave vapour trails. Jack looked across at Roger and it was a pleasing mischief they shared.

"Why wait for Hong Kong?" said Bill. "Get him fixed up in one of the other ports. If he can't manage it he can have a head job. Ever had a head job Roger?" What use was it to pretend? The erotic slang had him baffled.

"Not that I know of." The guileless reply set Martin braying again. The conversation made Roger uneasy. But it was gratifying to find himself apparently counted back among the heterosexuals. Would he really do it? Sex it seemed would be on tap everywhere they went. Would he actually do it? Pay for it? Such a step was against all his instincts. It was like the drinking all over again. Don't be the odd man out. Roger was discovering what it is that makes soldiers leave their fox holes. Why paratroopers leap into the sky's gaping mouth. And his own frustrations had much to do with it, driving him to the point where he had to do something "manly", but what of the risks?

Again he saw the pictures on the screen at RAF Wilmslow. There had been talk of precautions, "French letters" and all those signs you were supposed to watch out for. No, it wasn't worth all that. Then he thought of the long lusty weeks ahead, the raw masculinity jostling around him and the relentless obsession with sex that seemed to be the sole purpose of the voyage. One thing was sure. If he did venture down that road it would not be with Martin giving instruction. Green he might be, but he felt the Neanderthal method would not be his style.

It was shower time. Bill stared across the cabin as his trousers came off.

"Roger, you're so white and skinny you put me in mind of a parsnip on two sticks of celery."

Martin hastened to contribute. "What he ought to do, with a body like this, what he ought to do is go and jump into the first heap of shit he can find."

"OK," said Roger. "Open your mouth and I'll take a short cut." Jack and Pat greeted this with wicked cackling laughter, while the others eyed each other with what appeared to be consternation. Toddy returned. "Kure," he intoned mysteriously and lay on his bunk with eyes closed. He'd pronounced the word like "jury". If it was a place, no one had heard of it. Not even atlas loving Roger. They all waited.

Finally Jack asked, "Kure? You mean Korea?"

"No. Kure. Place in Japan." A long silence. It was like watching a teleprinter. "We get men at Hong Kong – take 'em to Kure." A longer pause. "Then to Korea, offload 'em, back to Kure. Near the bomb place, Hiroshima." It was quite a speech for Toddy. They left him to his nap and discussed the news.

For Roger the idea that a visit to Hiroshima might be feasible was something to think about. Five years had passed since a B-29 dropped the world's first atomic weapon onto the heart of that luckless city. What did it look like now? Perhaps they didn't let anyone in. The thought of walking with a camera down those tortured streets was suddenly distasteful. Who could he possibly go with? Stick to Kure. Maybe he could take a shot of one of those curious arches they had in Japan. The ones with the top piece turned up at each end. Bill's voice snatched him back to the sweltering present.

"The Lodger's wondering if he ought to get his korey in Japan." The card-game was over. Other diversions were needed. "Look at him. Between Isobel and Linda he don't know which way to turn."

Martin sat up, taking his cue. "Pity Isobel's not here. They could make a daisy chain, the three of them."

"Yeah and bring some tart from on shore. Roger and Linda and the tart in a bunch all at it." The laughter filled the tiny space, mixing with the sticky air and wrapping around him. His rapid education in these matters already included hearing what a "daisy chain" was, but Bill's graphic description brought it to life.

The shower visits began. Pat went first, then Jack and Toddy. He would go next. Finish before Bill and Martin arrived, then nip back and be on his bunk when they returned. Somehow he looked less thin lying down. The shower room was jammed when he got there. In the eight cubicles and the room itself a close pack of naked and semi-naked men pushed and jostled to get under the water spluttering from the jets. His towel was an extra long one he'd made a point of packing. Hung around his neck it more or less hid his torso, only his white legs showing to the world. Around him came the shouts and banter of men thrown together in complete abandon. Free of all restraints, they found release in the wild wetness. He envied them, wished to be among them. He wanted to be tall and tanned and not give a damn about anything. Over the heads of the crowd he saw Bill enter and begin thrusting his way through. At that moment his chance came. Darting under the spray, he nearly died of shock. The water was stone cold.

"Fuggin' 'ell!" he yelped, the word leaping to his lips so naturally now he'd almost forgotten Blimey or Gosh or anything he may have used in his former life. Someone told him the heat had been turned off at source. In the interests of economy and because nobody would want a hot shower this weather. It was fine once he stopped gasping. The room was slowly emptying. With luck he could be gone while Bill and (by extension) Martin were busy showering.

It was not to be. When he reached for his pants and towel they were not there. Naked and wet, he spun around in quiet panic. Could someone have taken them in error? There were about ten men left now, some in adjacent cubicles where they were partly hidden by the short side panels. It was on such a panel he'd hung his things. He grasped the top edge, stretched up and peered over like Mr Chad – and looked straight into the face of Linda.

"Roger, come and join me. I'll scrub your back for you."

"Looking for my stuff," he said hastily and tried the other side.

This time the occupant had his back to him and Roger beheld an astonishing sight. The man was tattooed from the neck down with a vivid rendering of a hunt in full cry; the whole picture writhing in response to his movements as he washed. Hounds and horsemen galloped down his glistening back in pursuit of the fox, which had gone to earth at the only place available, as evidenced by the tail neatly drawn just above the buttocks. Even in his distraught state Roger was fascinated. It was unfortunate that the owner of the back chose this moment to suddenly turn around, so that Roger was now gazing at his genitals. Before he could avert his eyes, a hand grabbed his hair and pulled his head down onto the partition, pressing his Adam's apple against the iron edge.

"What you starin' at?" rasped the man. "I'll knock your fuggin' head off pal so I will." A huge fist drew back and he knew what it was like to die. Then the other hand lost its grip on his wet hair and he fell back into his own cubicle again to sit on the tiles coughing and massaging his throat with trembling fingers. "One of these here perverts," announced the man loudly to observers. Men outside the shower regarded him curiously, then one stepped in to begin his own wash, ignoring the collapsed figure. He climbed miserably to his feet. Where the hell were his things? The prospect of returning nude to the cabin filled him with a dread as cold as the water he splashed around in. He risked a suicidal peek into the lair of the illustrated man, having first waited till his back was safely turned. Not there either.

It dawned on him then, who had taken them. Three cubicles along, Bill was pulling on his shorts while Martin waited for him. Roger approached them with a kind of deadly resignation, holding his head up and trying not to droop his shoulders. His chest looked much the same whether in or out so he left it as it was. But dignity requires clothing. His hair bedraggled, he stood with arms folded, naked as a baby and sopping wet with a red mark across his windpipe. They broke into howls of mirth. And yet there was something else, a tiny flicker of uncertainty. They had taken his things while he was under the shower with eyes closed, expecting him to stay there peeping round the corner in an agony of embarrassment begging to have them back. This was how it had been with Mario. Pleading in his fractured English and trying to cover himself with his hands. They'd made the unhappy Cypriot bend over to be whacked with his own plimsolls and sing *God Save the King* or *I wish I was in Cyprus* to the tune of *Dixie*. Now Mario was gone and they had Roger. But Roger wasn't playing the part. With nothing on, he was walking straight up to them and staring them in the face. It made them feel sort of – well, awkward. Only for a bit, of course. They'd soon get him going.

"What's up Roger?" said Bill. "You're wandering about like a spare prick at a wedding."

Martin said, "He'd be easier to skin than a rabbit."

Roger dredged up the courage to speak. Exasperation was in there too. "Bill, you big asshole, you got my things. Where are they?"

Again, it was unexpected. "Who are you calling – what things?" The disjointed reply sounded uncertain and he dared to believe his boldness might pay off.

"Give me my stuff and quit farting about. I'm tired." For once they were at a loss. His brusque, non-pleading tone was not the thing at all.

"You want it – bloody look for it," said Bill and strode off, Martin scuttling behind him. A kind of victory, but he still didn't have his things. For a moment he thought of going back as he was. Suppose they'd hidden all his other clothes? They could force him to stay nude till it was time to start work. What a scream.

"Roger! What's the matter sweetie?" Linda was close behind him – too close.

"They took my things."

"Who? No don't tell me. Vincent and Clifford right? They were always doing that to Mario." Linda was wearing what appeared to be the lower half of a girl's bathing costume. Pale blue, it had a crinkly texture and the brand name "Jantzen" stitched on the waistband. Not long ago this would have surprised him, now he felt beyond it. Men with girls' names, and men with pictures on their backs. It was an alien world.

Linda now draped a big towel round Roger's shoulders. "Cover your modesty. Standing around like that you'll get yourself raped." Needless to say, the towel was a vivid pink with a floral pattern in the centre. He was led into a cubicle.

Linda pointed. "Is that yours?" His belongings were high overhead. They'd threaded his towel through his underpants then tied it. A disused pipe-end jutted from the bulkhead and here they'd managed to hang it, probably after several throws.

"We can reach it," said Linda, kneeling down. "Come on, get on my shoulders." He saw there was no other choice, despite misgivings about climbing onto *this* man's back. Hastily, he repositioned the gaudy towel, wrapping it round his middle and trying to tuck the free end between his legs.

"Just what an innocent boy like you needs on this ship," said Linda. "A chastity belt. Come on, up you get." He draped a leg either side of the man's head as he came effortlessly to his feet. Reaching up to the pipe he knew with a wretched certainty what would happen next. Linda's towel unwound itself and fell to the floor. And the authors of his woes returned to rejoice at the scene. Naked yet again, he tried desperately to reach the pipe, aware that the tattooed man, who even walked aggressively, was giving them both a wide berth and a look of total disgust as he left the room.

Roger wanted to run after him saying, "You're wrong. I'm not one of them, really." He finally retrieved his things and slid eel-like down

Linda's back to a cheer from the bystanders. The pants were saturated but he was past caring. Thanking Linda he pulled them on. At the door an amazing thing happened. Bill put an arm round his shoulder.

"OK Roger? Only a bit of fun. We used to pull the same trick on Mario, only he never took it so well." There was no mention of his tangle with the tattooed man. Perhaps they hadn't seen it. They were the first amiable words Bill had said to him and he feared some new plot. Yet the cordiality went on as they reached the cabin and it dawned on him that he may have won some degree of acceptance. Well, he'd drunk with them, turned his tongue to a few choice phrases and talked loosely and crudely of the opposite sex. He'd taken all they'd flung at him with outward stoicism while inwardly seething. Was he now qualified to join their company?

Although it was midnight nobody was asleep yet. Roger was ready to turn in but reluctant to do so while he was in favour, so to speak. Worthy of inclusion in the bunk-side chat. They all sat around under the port. Roger found himself next to Bill on the latter's bunk, a position, after all that had gone before, remarkably intimate. Talk was of the war, which gave the older men an advantage in narrative interest. Toddy had been torpedoed in the North Atlantic and he told the story in four concise sentences that made it sound no more than a brief mishap.

"Copped it three days out of Halifax. Then got picked up. Made Liverpool. Train home that night."

Jack had survived an Arctic convoy. "There was this tanker. All on fire she was, and men running and jumping along the deck and the water on fire too with all the oil. Terrible to see." The tales had been told before, maybe grown a little in the telling, yet the horror of it all could not be denied. Roger imagined the shocking explosion, the inrush of water and the blind scramble to escape.

"Saw some Germans once," said Pat. "Off a U-boat they were. We pulled 'em aboard covered in oil. An officer and rating, the only ones still alive. Poor souls, no different to us. One of 'em said he was glad to be out of it. Glad to be a prisoner, safe and out of it. Makes you think, that." It did make you think. Roger, like many of his age, had absorbed his share of war films and tended to think most Germans resembled Conrad Veidt. Listening to the three men telling of war at sea he thought of his own life in the bosom of his family. How close they'd been, how lucky to survive the air attacks on the city and make the post-war adjustment to normal living. He had his health and he had a job. One day he would get married and all the rest of it. But for now he was going to see things. Experience some of those places that had beckoned since he first learned to read. In a couple of days they would be in Egypt; Arabs, palm trees, camels and sand. He would buy postcards and write home. His camera would click busily away.

"Roger!" With a start he came out of his reverie to find Bill standing over him. "Get off my pit. I want to turn in."

"Sorry, I was miles away."

"We're all miles away," said Martin. "Fed up, fugged up and far from home."

It was a phrase that struck a chord with Roger, reminding him of the RAF. "Roll on death – demob's too slow," they'd cried as if eighteen months was a life sentence. The familiar doom-laden humour of the British serviceman appealed to him. There was a quality in it that melted all pretension, reduced everyone to the same degree of comradely misfortune and somehow made it bearable. He swung himself with a now practised ease up into his bunk and lay with his limbs spread as far as the meagre space would permit, so that if a moving piece of air should by chance come his way some part of him might benefit.

What was next? Oh yes. Sunbathing. Tomorrow. More exposure. He wound his watch, shut his eyes and fell asleep almost instantly. Beyond the sweating confines of the ship, North Africa slept too. Inland, the forgotten hulks of burned out tanks still stood in the rustling sand, silent guns drooping like the beaks of dead birds. The *Empire Garvie* passed them unseen, a new generation of untried youngsters off to fight a fresh conflict in another land of strange enemies and unpronounceable place names. On the bridge five decks up, Captain Baskerville reflected that so far the voyage had been relatively quiet, a number of fights, complaints and "drunk and disorderlies" but no deaths or woundings, unlike that other time. That was an ugly affair. Those effeminate types led perilous lives. The victim, who rejoiced in the name Henrietta, had been stabbed after an amorous approach to the wrong man and hovered between life and death for a week in a Hong Kong hospital before recovering and being sent home. His attacker got three years.

It was in the ports of course that most trouble occurred. Seamen would swill freely at the cheap plonk or gut-rotting local spirits till they were broke or comatose. And for some the British Affliction took hold. The main symptom of this was a desperate need to fight someone, anyone. The captain thought too of the soldiers and families, the hundreds of people sleeping down below. It was a large responsibility, one that was all his till they disembarked. He had a word with the quartermaster at the wheel and left the bridge. The *Empire Garvie* ploughed on towards the first stop in the long string of golden days and balmy nights that lay before her.

Roger's new confidence took a knock next day after breakfast. An Army Major had been observed in the galley. The top corner of his chest had carried a small set of medal ribbons, those modest strips of colour which in their British, understated way seem so much more effective that the clanking ironmongery and lurid sunbursts of lesser states. The man had been short and rather thin, prompting a debate on the link between physique and bravery.

"I can't see Roger ever winning a medal," said Martin. "He wouldn't have the strength to wear it, never mind earn it. The weight of it would pull him over." During the ensuing laughter Roger planned his reply. History, he knew, was on his side. He'd read the books, seen the photos. Cheshire, Mannock, Bader and Ball or the men peering through the smoke at Rorke's Drift or Passchendale, heroes all. They were not giants, they were ordinary, scrawny some of them. It was a known fact. There could be no argument. It would be a moment of triumph as he made his point. As the table grew quiet again he spoke slowly and evenly.

"Martin, if you were to look at a history book you would find that physique had nothing to do with it. All those heroes; all those VCs, DSOs and whatnot. It was simply courage, nothing to do with how they looked in the mirror. None of them had a body like Charles Atlas."

"No," drawled Bill. "But they all had a body – that was essential." Again the laughter burst forth. The "moment of triumph" had been short lived. Not to say stillborn.

Later he got ready for his first ever sunbathe. What about his legs? Lacking shorts he would have to roll his trousers up like somebody's father at the seaside. His shirt could stay on until the last minute. Already the qualms were coming. Yet surely, after his prolonged exposure in the shower? Yes. He would get a tan. They didn't call it that of course. On this ship they had another word for almost everything. A "bronzie", that's what the sun gave you. Coming out on deck his resolve faltered again. The sprawled figures lay this way and that with hardly a space anywhere. Wandering on, he found a patch by the rail and sat down. Taking a deep breath he snatched off his shirt. The sun struck his back with the intensity of a swishing cane. Looking round, he saw no one he knew. Feeling easier, he stretched out on the deck.

Lying there, lulled by the warmth, he felt free of the nerves that still bothered him much of the time. What a contrast to the sweltering existence down below! Up here the sun was a beaming friend, the air the cleanest he would ever breathe. Clean air, he would put that in the intended poem. Soft sounds reached his ears but barely registered in the sweet silence. Sometimes the breeze would gather enough energy to raise a sigh before losing itself among the recumbent forms. With only his shirt to lie on he was soon in some discomfort, and sat up, wishing he'd brought a blanket like everyone else. Discreetly, he checked out his neighbours. On one side a man was reading a paperback. On the other, a lean, bearded figure in shorts lay face up, his feet together but arms spread wide. Perhaps to mark his territory, deter anyone from coming too close. A prominent rib cage and jutting beard completed his likeness to a fallen crucifix.

A shadow fell across Roger. The man was about twenty. Clad in black trousers, a white shirt and black leather shoes he looked, in that company, positively overdressed. He wondered what was coming now. Before him, the sparkling sea was framed by the rail uprights. He noticed the paintwork on them was bumpy and uneven. Idly, he pressed one of the bumps with his foot and was startled when a larger blister fell off exposing rust beneath. Perhaps the whole ship was nothing but a thin shell held together with paint.

"I wouldn't worry about it," said the man. "There's plenty of lifeboats." Roger was about to reply when he spoke again. "I think I know you. In fact I'm sure I do."

"Oh?" said Roger. Experience to date made him wary of affable strangers. Although Linda had made no more advances he knew there were many others of that persuasion, around thirty according to Maguire. And they weren't all obvious.

"Yes," the man went on. "You worked at Hampshire Batteries didn't you?"

"That's right."

"Well, I used to be with Baileys, you know, the acid people. Industrial chemists. We supplied all your sulphuric. Remember unloading the lorry with us?" Yes – he did remember those huge glass carboys of acid, the spine-crushing weight of them.

"Yes. Your driver used to pull 'em to the tailboard and you and I lifted 'em down." The man laughed. "And nearly got a rupture doing it!"

Before long they were leaning on the rail and talking easily. The man was also making his first trip. His name was Archie Clayton, but he never used Archie. "Call me Clay, as in 'feet of'. They gave me a bad time in our cabin at first. It was Archibald all the time." So he wasn't the only one.

"Like me, they call me the Lodger." He explained and gave an account of his early ordeals. Clay shook his head ruefully.

"There's some rough diamonds on here. No doubt about that. And how about all these queers?" Roger told him about Linda.

Clay said, "You too?" She had a go at me second night out. I'm settling in OK now, in our cabin, No 21. They're a decent bunch in there, weird but decent. Except one who's a bit mad, a bit bad-tempered. "Clay was a steward in the second class saloon, and about to go on duty. Hence the black and white get-up. Later he would wear a white jacket buttoned up to the neck.

"Hard going in that saloon," he said. "Bloody NCOs' wives and kids. Bring me this, bring me that. And hot as hell. I wanted to be a BRS, bedroom steward, but I could only get this." Roger described his own job which seemed easier in comparison. They turned away from the sea and faced the crowded deck. The bearded man still lay with arms flung wide.

"I see you've got your own crucifix," said Clay in a low voice. The man stirred and yawned.

"Oh, I spoke too soon. Now he's getting up,"

Roger said. "Or perhaps ascending?"

Clay laughed again. "Time I went. Come along to our place tonight. We'll have a drink."

"Thanks, I will." Fate, for the moment, seemed to be smiling on him. "I met one of your people. In No 21. Henry Batten. He's not fond of his name either. Told me to call him Batten."

"That's right. And he's the weirdest one of all. See you later."

Roger was alone again, watching the Mediterranean shimmering past. The business of getting the tan was becoming a chore. Roger, it need hardly be said, had never sunbathed before and thought it was like toasting bread. But by lunchtime the effects of his two hour roast were becoming apparent. It wasn't a tan of course. Not yet. His face and torso had simply been crudely flashed by the sun. But for a person such as Roger, pale all his life, the bright carnation pink glowing back at him was akin to magic. It did not go unnoticed.

"The Lodger's been for a bronzie," observed Martin. "Mixing with the men and pretending he's one." They were at the sink, where Roger was discovering the painful effect of hot water on his scorched arms.

"About time he got a bit of colour," said Bill. "I've seen healthier looking corpses." It was par for the course, a reflex action. For once no-one laughed. Perhaps they really were easing off. Or he was getting used to it, growing a shell.

"Carry on my son," said Pat. "Get yourself a bronzie like all of us." Everyone had a comment.

"Don't see it," said Toddy. As usual they had to wait for his next words. It must have been the oracle-like delivery. "The point. Only to lose it again. When you're home. White again. Don't see it."

Typically, Jack had a note of caution. "You want to watch that sun. Take your skin off it can. Seen a laddie once got so burnt he was laid up for a week. In the sickbay smothered in that calomine stuff."

That afternoon he drew his first "sub", collected an advance from the Purser's Office. The money he'd left home with was gone, mostly in the Pig or on sundry items in the crew shop down in the forward hold. Things like carbolic soap for washing clothes. Drying was done at various hanging places around the after-deck or by festooning the damp articles about the cabin. Now he was drawing on his wages, as many were. The Purser's Office supplied local currency for each port but Jack said it wasn't needed in Port Said. They would only stay a few hours and English money was accepted.

"Save your money for other places," he advised. "Colombo and Hong Kong. Loads of good stuff there."

"Yeah," said Bill. "Loads of korey too. The Lodger'll need his strength for that. You want to get some Spanish Fly in Port Said. Just ask. The bumboats'll sell you some."

"I don't need that," he countered calmly. He'd heard about the alleged aphrodisiac. Bumboats too he'd heard of, native traders that fussed around visiting ships.

That evening he made his way to Cabin 21. As he approached he heard again the wistful song that first drew him there on sailing day. Obviously somebody's favourite. It seemed to be about an unseen artist, the old master painter of the title. A mythical figure employed by nature to put colours in the sky. The lyrics entranced him. They drew a picture, the sort of display to be enjoyed most evenings on deck. At the door he paused. The two stewards, Clay and Batten, had both invited him to call. But – and here again he thought how green he was, what did he know of these people really? Probably he would get drunk again. They would get him into a card game, where his hopeless playing would see his money go in twenty minutes, or suppose they were all like Linda? Even his old/new acquaintance, Clay? Then the door opened and Clay was there in khaki shorts.

"Come on in. Meet everyone." He stepped in and the door was shut rather quickly behind him, followed by a click which he told himself anxiously was not a key being turned.

"Aha!" said a voice. "Just what we need – fresh blood." The room was dim, the main bulb partly obscured by lines of damp undergarments that hung down like off-white stalactites. The usual foetid air was overlaid by something else, something earthy yet perfumed. He imagined eau de cologne dripping onto burning oak logs. A drink was put in his hand and a chair shoved hard up behind him so that he more or less fell into it. In the half light five faces gleamed back at him and he recognised Batten in the centre. The man had a towel round his waist and another over his shoulder which with the round spectacles and balding head suggested an obese version of Mahatma Ghandi. The image was only marred by the cigar in his mouth; a monster of a thing which he now realised was the source of the exotic smell.

"This is Roger," announced Clay. "Roger, meet the inmates. There's Batten, who you know and these gentlemen are Frank Seymour, who could tell you some thrilling some stories about himself – Jim Smith and Mike Nelson."

"Are you married Roger?" asked Smith.

"No, why?"

"Oh, doesn't matter."

Batten chuckled lewdly and removed the cigar, placing it in an ashtray where it smouldered like a shot down Zeppelin.

"Really Jim, and you Clay. The poor lad's barely in our clutches and already you want to snatch away his innocence." His own cabin seemed far away and suddenly attractive. Better the devil you know. He must have been mad to enter this Bohemian den. Surprisingly the glass in his hand held red wine, something he could drink with ease. As they talked he made a discreet study of the men around him. Seymour was the eldest at about fifty, a morose individual sitting on his bunk with a small, battered attaché case on his lap. The raised lid prevented a sight of the contents, which he was sifting through with great care, studying each item before selecting another.

"His secret box," whispered Clay. "Skin books I bet. *Men Only* or *Blighty*. Something like that. Always is when someone's got a private collection they won't let anyone see. I knew one in the army had every copy of *Health and Efficiency*. Give you the creeps they do, people like that." Smith, although only in his thirties, had grey hair cut in an odd sort of all-round fringe. His face was strangely unlined. The fifth man was younger still. A bundle of compressed energy, Nelson twisted and fidgeted as if merely sitting still was an effort.

The record stopped and Clay put on another. This time it was the Inkspots singing the shadow song. Roger finished his wine and put the glass down. Batten promptly refilled it.

"Would you prefer something else? Drop of rum maybe?"

"No this is fine. What actually is it?"

"Beaujolais." The bottle was held out for inspection. "See, I can get all kinds of stuff up in First Class."

"M-e-e-e and my Sha-a-a-a-dow," crooned the record "All alone and feeling blue." The door behind him was suddenly rattled and shaken. So it was locked.

"Who is it?" called Nelson, and there was alarm in his voice.

"Penny," came a voice. A wave of sighs and eye-rolling passed through the group.

"You can't come in now," said Batten. "Mike will see you on deck later."

"Don't say that," croaked Nelson. "I'm trying to end it."

The door was rattled again and the visitor stated calmly, "Let me in or I'll scream the place down."

All faces turned to Batten. He drew on his cigar and regarded the hapless Nelson, who looked ready to exit by way of the porthole.

"Mike, you must be brave. Think of your namesake. England

expects etcetera." Nelson gave a resigned nod.

"Alright, but I'm not saying 'kiss me Hardy'." Roger had known all along there must a sixth person to make up the cabin's complement. Could this be him? Clay turned the key, the new face entered and he saw why Nelson was troubled. It was himself and Linda over again. Penny was a wiry sort of man, a little below average height with close-cropped blond hair.

"Hullo boys. You know I should be very, very cross with you, locking me out like that but I'm not 'cos I know why you did it. You're worried about that awful brute coming back aren't you?" Who, Roger wondered, was the "awful brute"? They all shifted round to make a space and Penny settled into the circle.

"Right Penny," said Batten. "Say hello to your paramour only make it short before he does come back." Roger now became the uncomfortable witness to a strange sight, one man trying earnestly to convince another of his total affection. It was like any romantic comedy he'd ever seen, attempts to embrace, complaints of "not talking like we used to". But for heaven's sake they were both men. He was puzzled, repelled and yet unable to stop watching them. Everyone else conversed, leaving Penny and Nelson to wrangle over their broken affair undisturbed.

"Anybody like this in your cabin Roger?" asked Clay slyly. He pulled his gaze away from the rowing couple.

"Er no. Nothing like that, we're all normal." As he spoke there occurred one of those untimely conversation breaks. A sudden pool of quiet. And his last few words rolled into it, deadly as a primed grenade.

The atmosphere froze. "Oh I see," said Penny with a hiss of venom. "You're normal are you? So we're all loonies – is that what you're saying? Who are you anyway – sitting there passing judgement? Normal he says. Takes a man to be normal, somebody with a bit of flesh on him. Here, see me." Penny stood up and opened his shirt, shaking it down off his shoulders. The man's physique was impressive.

"I may be queer duckie, but I could see a skinny homie like you off anytime!" Roger's head whirled as he tried to cope with all the inverted gender values.

"I'm sorry, I didn't mean..." But there was no placating Penny.

"Coming in here – who is he anyway?"

"First tripper," said Smith as if that pardoned all sins.

"I don't care. I won't put up with it" – The tirade went on.

Batten shouted over it. "Penny!" They all fell silent. "Penny, don't be such a touchy cow. Roger didn't mean anything. He's new to all this. I understand he had a midnight visit from Linda on his very first day aboard. That's enough to confuse anyone."

Mention of Linda switched Penny's anger to an older, more familiar target. "Oh well then. If he thinks we're all like her. Wicked slut. Drop of whisky and she's anybody's, that one." As Penny paused for breath the Inkspots filled the gap. "Not a soul to tell our troubles to – and when it's twelve o'clock –." Clay topped up Roger's glass.

"That'll learn you," he whispered. The crisis was over. The amorous pair bickered on, Batten's column of scented smoke drifted up to the washing line and Seymour began a gentle snoring. The record sang on – "we climb the stair – we never knock –". Smith spoke quietly to Batten, who nodded.

"Penny, you'd better go. The Pig'll shut soon. You don't want him to come back and catch you here." Again the dangerous Mr X. Penny, it seemed, didn't live here. The mystery man did. And they all had a healthy respect for him.

Penny said, "Alright, but I'm fed up with running away from him. I'll report him one day, see if I don't." Roger wondered if he might leave now too. Never mind the unknown man. He'd met enough eccentrics for one day. The Inkspots ground on "– 'cos nobody's there, just me and my –" Penny paid an emotional farewell to Nelson and left, giving Roger a withering glance in passing.

Batten said, "You want to watch yourself with Penny. That one really bears a grudge." Clay opened a pack of Lucky Strikes and offered Roger one. He wanted to decline but after the recent clash he shrank from anything that set him apart. The unfiltered tobacco stung his throat but he managed not to gag.

"Have another," said Clay. "For later."

Roger put it in his top pocket, took a sip of Beaujolais and said,

"Who's this one you're waiting for? Who mustn't meet Penny?"

"His name's Kropp," said Batten. "And he's crazy." For the moment that seemed to be all he would learn, while the others thought about it.

Then Nelson spoke. "He's from Glasgow, despite his name. K, R, O, double P. Kropp."

"Sounds more like a German farmer," said Roger, recklessly witty.

"The thing is," said Batten, "he's unstable. Family background. Something there."

"Unusual name," said Roger. "For a Scot." Batten stubbed out his cigar, which took a while.

"Once when he was sober he told me his great-granddad was a Swiss travelling salesman."

"No wonder he's cuckoo," said Nelson nervously.

"Apparently," Batten went on, "this forebear travelled the length and breadth of Scotland, then settled there. In Glasgow. Well, I did say there was insanity in the family." Roger decided to leave. The visit had been convivial enough, the row with Penny apart. The men of Cabin 21 were a whimsical bunch with a lively sense of humour, the kind that didn't need an immediate victim. A blissful contrast to the personal jabs meted out by Bill or Martin. He finished his wine and took a cautious pull at the cigarette as he considered how to say his goodbyes. Then Nelson said, "What gets me about Kropp is that ridiculous tattoo all over his body."

The effect on Roger was shocking. His sudden intake of breath sucked hot smoke straight through the Lucky Strike. A dragon breathed on his palate. The coughing and hacking went on noisily for a full half minute, waking Seymour who glared and snatched his curtain shut. Roger's back was patted.

"Went down the wrong way," he wheezed. "Wine. Wrong way." Once more his emotional apple cart lay on its side. A minute ago he'd been happy. Now the darker side of his new world loomed again. He recalled the face of the shower man, features twisted with anger at being ogled by a "pervert", and the ham-sized fist heading for his nose. This terrifying figure lived here and was coming home, probably the worse for wear. There was one last hope.

"This tattoo," he asked casually, "is it a fox hunting scene – dogs, horses and that?" They confirmed that it was.

"All over his back and his chest too," said Smith. Roger stood up. The cigarette had vanished in the coughing.

"You know Kropp then?" said Batten.

"Yes I do. And I'd rather not meet him again." It was too late. Some people don't just "come in"; they "Make an Entrance". The door banged open to rebound off the bulkhead. Seymour peeped fearfully round his curtain. Rocking slightly Kropp stepped over the threshold.

A finger jabbed at Roger.

"You. Queer fella – out!"

"Stay here Roger," said Batten. "Kropp, the charge is quite unwarranted. Mr Wren is our invited guest. We have no reason to suspect him of any unnatural tendencies. Indeed, quite early in his career he had occasion to decline offers from a person of that ilk." The formal phrasing struck an unreal note. In that mean place of drooping laundry, fag ash and painted iron walls, delivered deadpan by a reclining shape in a towel and comic glasses, it was almost too much. He saw the others striving to keep their faces straight.

"Seen him," insisted Kropp. "In the showers. Pervert. I'm going to punch his face in. Peeping at other men – skylarking about with that – that whatisname – that Reynolds. Had his legs round his head. Not a stitch on him. Disgusting. Pick-a-back he was. Seen him." They all glanced at Roger with new interest.

"It wasn't how it seemed," he said in a voice he felt compelled to deepen a little. "I was trying to find my belongings. Somebody —."

"Peeping!" barked Kropp. "Peeping at me!" Down in the corner of his sight he saw the man's fingers closing into a ball of hate. "Know what happens to anybody peeps at me?" Kropp's eyes widened and one shoulder began to move back. The blow was coming. Then Roger had one of his rare moments of courage. He turned away and dropped back in his chair as though tired of it all.

"I was looking for my towel. That's all. Then I saw that wonderful tattoo of yours." His back stiffened for the punch he knew must come. But Kropp's gaze had swivelled too quickly as his target shifted. The sudden turn of his head, the zip-panning effect of the moving background, were too much for the fuzzy brain. Kropp had consumed eight pints, by his standards a moderate night's intake. But a number of whisky chasers made for a volatile mixture. They saw his jowls tremble, a resigned look come over the flushed face. A hand came up to his mouth and he stumbled from the room.

"Technicolor yawn," said Batten. "At least this time he didn't do it in here."

"I'm off," said Roger shakily. "Thanks for the drink." The party broke up. Roger took a peek outside.

"Don't worry about him," said Clay. "He'll just stagger back and flop onto his pit. We'll try and explain to him tomorrow about you and the damn tattoo. When he's sober he's quite proud of it. He simply hates queers. Sees 'em everywhere."

"They are everywhere," said Smith. "On this ship."

Back in his own cabin Roger found only Toddy and Pat there. The bunks of the missing men were devoid of bedding.

"Sleeping on deck," explained Pat. "I'll start later in the voyage. Don't call this hot yet. Do you Toddy?"

"All one," said Toddy. "Home or abroad, it's all one to me." Later when he was ready he gathered up his blankets and pillow and started up the steps. The promise of fresh air and solitude was irresistible. Up to now he'd been reluctant to try this. It would have appeared that Bill and Martin had driven him to sleep elsewhere.

The night was crisp and starlit. Features of the deck were washed in a soft-edged black and white that neutralised everything else. All the strident colours of the day were banished, replaced by the night's healing touch, when the bright sea darkened and the blistered steel contacted gratefully in the cool air. The deck was not too crowded. Unlike when "bronzie-ing", men preferred to tuck themselves away in dark corners away from clumsy feet or unwelcome attentions. He went aft to where the deck passed either side of the poop structure and joined up again at the stern. Here on the starboard side he found his spot. The deck was about six feet wide between the deckhouse and the rail, which at this point was atop a solid bulwark. He folded the two blankets lengthwise and laid them close to the deckhouse. Starting to undress, he stopped. Who knew what nocturnal prowling there might be? And his clothes – some joker could take them. Or toss them over the side.

It wasn't all that comfortable after the bunk. Sitting up again he felt something in his breast pocket and fished out the extra cigarette Clay had pressed on him.

"Need a light?" said a voice. A lighter flared and he was smoking again, knowing he was starting to find comfort in it. Perhaps it was the American tobacco.

"How do you find it? The ship?" Without his white cap, and no table or phone the Master-at-Arms was more human.

"Thanks. Oh well, you know –" He tried to think of something positive. "I haven't been seasick." The man leaned on the rail and Roger got up to join him, feeling awkward talking to his back. Nothing, he was starting to learn, was more conducive to chatting than two persons at a rail looking at the sea. But this time the exchange would be as short as it was mystifying.

"I expect you miss home," said the man. "Spend time on your own, thinking."

"Yes – a bit."

The man turned and regarded him, sizing him up. Roger, with studied nonchalance, drew on the Lucky Strike, ready for anything. Not the Master-at-Arms – surely? He turned his attention to the passing sea and a far off light on the Egyptian coast.

"You don't want to do too much of that, my son, staring at the water. Not good for you. Sort of hypnotises you. I've seen it happen to people. More you look at it the more it – draws you. Makes you want to jump in. Take care. Goodnight." The man abruptly turned and walked away. Roger considered whether, in terms of shock, his day might now be over. Was nothing safe? Even admiring the view?

Rather than spend all night in his clothes, he shed everything but his trousers, keeping them on in case of flight. Roger was not a naturally nervous person, but he'd encountered by now a number of disturbing people. That first night in the Pig still came back to him, when he'd seen a man no older than himself struck down to sprawl bleeding in a scattering of beer and broken glass. Now there were the two meetings with Kropp, both ending with a fist heading his way. And he was still adjusting to the topsy-turvy world of the queers, who all seemed to combine effeminacy with a ruggedly manly body. Well, he would cultivate what friends he had, go easy on the drink and try to stay out of trouble while still enjoying this unique trip.

Three thousand miles from home, Roger Wren allowed himself to relax. As yet he hadn't attempted a poem about the sea, but he would – he would. And tomorrow morning he would be in a foreign country. The World would be here. Stubbing out the Lucky Strike in the nearby scupper he closed his eyes and listened to the voice of the sea. The relief from both the claustrophobic heat of the cabin and the tensions he still felt there was a special kind of bliss. He wanted to savour it before tomorrow's treadmill called him back. But he was asleep in minutes. When he awoke it was daybreak and they were there, he could tell. A faint *thrum-thrum* as the ship moved at half speed. Hurrying feet and voices speaking faster than any English tongue could move. The swish of a launch and the creak of pulleys. Excitement gripped him. The solid bulkhead hid it all but he had only to stand to see it. He sat up, knelt up and slowly rose to his feet. *And – Lo! They came unto the*

Land of Egypt, he thought biblically.

Port Said appeared to consist mainly of flat-topped houses with here and there some of four or five storeys. A golden-topped mosque could be seen. There was a exceptionally fine creamy white building with three pale green domes which he learned later was the headquarters of the Suez Canal Company. He saw neat avenues lined with feathery palm trees and shops with un-Egyptian names like SIMON ARTZ in letters big enough to be seen by seaborne customers. At the harbour entrance on a tall plinth stood a statue of Ferdinand de Lesseps, the builder of the canal.

As the ship crept to her assigned place, the long, jostling waterfront unrolled before him. In the distance he made out a thin brown line which he took to be the desert! A let-down, but he hadn't really expected it to be in range of his eager feet. The pyramids and the sphinx, he knew, were at Giza, miles away at Cairo. Yet it was enough to be here at the top corner of Africa, pored over so often in the atlas at home. Now they stopped and were moored to buoys in the centre of the harbour. So it would be a boat ride to get ashore. It amazed him that none of his colleagues were very interested in seeing the place.

"Been here before," said Bill. "Might go for a piss-up this afternoon." There was no mention yet of the much vaunted carnal delights. But there were another six ports after this one. The recently begun war had added two more to the other five.

"How do we get ashore?" he asked Jack. "In one of our own boats?"

"No. We go on the snake." The snake? No, he wouldn't ask. Easier to say nothing and find out later. Sounded like some weirdly shaped, local craft. Later in the morning he received a letter from his father and sent off a reply describing his fortunes so far. Then the great moment came and with it the expected ribaldry.

"Now the Lodger can get his korey," said Martin. "But don't come back with a dose. The quack'll give you the hot wire treatment. Sheer agony that is. So they tell me," he added quickly.

"Go to the Boundary Club in Clermont Avenue," said Bill. "They're all said to be safe there. Tell you what; we're going ashore after lunch. Come with us then. Have a few Stella beers and we'll get you fixed up. Do you a world of good."

"We won't tell Isobel," said Martin. His imagination slipped into top gear. Hopelessly drunk, he is lurching and vomiting down a Port Said street, stricken with some loathsome disease. His bloodshot eyes focus miserably on the departing ship before he falls unconscious into the sand.

"No thanks," he said primly. "I'm just going to take a few snaps." The general amusement this triggered was like old times.

On D Deck square the Master-at-Arms was once more at his table, opposite another one where an Egyptian official drank black coffee from a glass. A chalked signboard informed everyone that the ship would sail at 1800 hours. He was given a knowing smile by the MAA and a landing pass by the Egyptian. The gangway now was lashed to the side of the hull and at the foot of it he saw the snake, a floating string of pontoons forming an undulating path to the shore. With his little cheap camera in its little cheap case slung on his shoulder he joined the throng of wives and children, soldiers and off duty crewmen making an unsteady descent to the pontoons. Stepping on this called for care. Wet in places from the water slopping up between the joins, it earned its name by the serpentine way it moved under their feet. For Roger, another "first" was coming. His habit of dramatizing events had its drawbacks. Sometimes it made him imagine the worst, as in the Kropp incidents and his uneasy relations with various others. Yet on occasion, such as now, his sense of The Moment could enhance the simplest thrill. In short, it was fun.

His foot came down and he was there. Egypt! After showing his pass, he was through and onto the street. The urge to look back could not be ignored, seeing the ship now across the harbour he felt almost affectionate. How could it be otherwise? She was his bed and board as he travelled his long journey across the world. Taking him so far and to such strange places she could never be simply "transport". The *Garvie* was something of home, a piece of England to wrap himself in when that world threatened. Then a voice came. Urgent, pleading and clearly, if inexplicably, directed at him.

"Hey Macgregor!"

Chapter 4

Then the ship was gone from sight, cut off by a horde of jabbering faces. Souvenirs were thrust under his nose then pushed aside by someone with a better offer. Rings, watches, necklaces, things that glittered in eye-aching confusion. Everyone coming off the pontoons was a target. And for some reason every male visitor was addressed as Macgregor.

"Hullo Macgregor – you want necklace? You want nice things for lady friend? For you, special price. You buy now. Two poun' very cheap. No? OK. One poun' ten. I lose money. I starve. You cruel man Macgregor." They stayed with him as he marched in what he hoped was the right direction. He soon learned that the best way of escape was to look straight ahead and not even answer. Such apparent rudeness did not come easily to him, but the alternative was never to get off the waterfront. Any reply, such as "that's too dear" invited the seller to lower his price and continue pitching. One by one they left him.

He found himself in a bright open space. "Ahmed Square" said a sign in English and Arabic. Here were the palm trees that told him he was really overseas, the soft pink or white or turquoise glowing back at him from the buildings, and the hooting tide of traffic rushing past on the "wrong" side of the road. Around him flowed a never-ending stream of humanity. Hawk-faced men of the desert in flowing white robes. Old men in frayed shirts with faces as lined and sand-scoured as the sphinx itself. Men in tight dark suits and red fezzes. Urchins darting in ragged mischief among white-kneed young Britons in pressed khaki trying to look like Desert Rats.

And there were women. In uniform, square-shouldered and slim-waisted, with service badges flashing on arm or cap, sauntering in carefree groups as they window shopped or haggled over jewellery. There were secretary girls, impossibly beautiful with dark eyes and darker hair, glancing at watches on brown arms as they hurried to work. And others, totally swathed in black with only the eyes above the veil showing to the world. The Ful-Vue felt ridiculously small as the shutter clicked. How could all this find its way into a little box? Winding on the film he heard a burst of voices. Coming his way were five members of the *Garvie* crew. Already drunk and looking for trouble, they took up the whole pavement, arguing and squabbling, accosting strangers with the standard "Who are you lookin' at?" challenge. For the first but not the last time he was ashamed of his own countrymen. And if he knew them, they would know him. They'd spot him with that keen vision all drunks seem to acquire when you're trying to dodge them.

Crossing the road was impossible so he turned down a quiet side alley. Earlier on he'd noticed the streets were in a grid pattern, so two right turns would take him back to the square and past the drunks. He tried an archway on his right. As he'd hoped, there was a junction ahead. Another corner and he'd be out of the back alleys. But for Roger, few things were that simple. Before he could reach it a figure turned the corner and came in his direction. His heart lurched. Was there no escape from this man? The hunched shoulders, the chin stuck forward like the prow of a destroyer. No one but Kropp walked like that.

He ducked into a doorway, walking straight into a bead curtain that dragged back over his face then became hopelessly tangled in the camera strap. Slipping this from his shoulder he took a quick glance up the street. The man was running towards him and raising a hand as if to detain him. So this was where his life would end. Some hole-in-the-wall dive in a foreign port. A punch from a heavyweight like Kropp would kill him. His neck would snap like a wrung chicken's. As he entered and backed away from the entrance, the bead curtain jerked open and he nearly fainted with relief. It wasn't Kropp but a similar looking stranger.

"Pardon please." A French accent, he thought. The man ducked his head. "Pardon. I make a mistake."

"Me too," said Roger and the Frenchman departed. Outside again, he read the name of the establishment over the door. "Ziggi Bar. Cocktails." There were other people about now. Setting off he saw more *Garvie* faces. A few yards on he remembered the camera left twisted in the curtain. Back he trailed. The curtain now hung straight, untangled and camera-less. Growing accustomed to the ill-lit interior, he made out a small bar and half a dozen men at marble tables. A flight of steps led to a shadowy landing.

"Here you are – I've got it," said an English voice. At one of the tables sat a man in a singlet and grubby white trousers. There was an air of the sea about him. A kind of breeziness, as though he'd just shinned down one of *Victory's* foretops.

"Thanks," said Roger, taking back the camera. He wanted to get on but it seemed churlish to dash off. Left where it was the camera could have been stolen by any passer-by.

"You're off that troopship," said the seaman. "Am I right?"

"Yes, having a look round before we go down the canal at six."

"Bit of korey too I suppose?" That word again. Like so many that were new to him it came up all the time now. He noticed the man was drinking Coca Cola, the first soft drink he'd seen anyone with since leaving home. Behind the bar a youth was reading a paper. Now he sauntered over and stood by Roger, indicating with a lift of one eyebrow that he might be prepared to accept an order.

"A Coke please," said Roger. "Is English money OK?" The youth shrugged. Roger passed over what he would have paid at home and took a seat opposite the seaman.

"No. No korey. Just taking a few snaps." They might have been in Lyme Regis.

The man was watching him with faint amusement. "And what was all the fuss about just now? You shot in here like the devil was after you." The inevitable cigarettes appeared and Roger accepted one. They must be a local brand, he decided shrewdly, noticing the picture of a camel on the pack. Then he was startled by a sound like a spitting cat right next to his head. The young bartender had opened his bottle of Coke.

"Kropp," mused the seaman when Roger explained.

"Rings a bell. I once sailed with a Scot had a name like that. Quick tempered character, bit mental; nearly killed a man once who climbed in the wrong bunk by mistake."

"That's him, I'm sure." Roger longed to leave. He didn't need to know more about Kropp's nightmare personality. Common courtesy held him. But the cigarette was rather strong, the Coke too sweet and teeth-settingly cold. And time was getting on.

"I'm off a tanker," said the seaman. "*Esso Forester*. We're waiting for a canal convoy. So are you till you leave. If you're going at six you'll be with us on the evening convoy."

"How long does it take to Suez?"

"Twelve hours. Sometimes you stop halfway. There's three lakes you cross. Hundred miles in all."

The bead curtain rattled as someone entered, a burly man in a brown suit. The youth dropped his paper and bustled about as if busy. Obviously the owner, the man went behind the bar and spoke to him. Money changed hands, then the owner came over and pointed upstairs.

"Other man not pay right price. Not price agreed. Ten piastres more."

The seaman glanced at Roger. "I'll pay it or he'll take it out on the boy. The whole amount's only about five bob, average for a short time." The money was paid and the owner left. The seaman must have seen something in Roger's face.

"They're not to blame. We are. These places didn't exist before we came. The British, the French, the Romans, and all the rest of us, coming here with our armies over the centuries. Blame them if you disapprove." A bearded man came down the stairs. The seaman finished his Coke and stood up.

"I must say you took your own sweet time. And you owe me ten piastres." He turned to Roger. "So long. See you in Suez." The bead curtain swished and they were gone.

Roger drank a little more of the sweet icy Coke, drew on his Camel and considered the kind of place he was in. What was he *doing* here? He jumped to his feet and left, striding up the alley for nearly a block before slowing down. It had to be faced; there would be no naughty nights for him. Paying for it was too sordid, too quick, his whole being refused the notion. At the corner he re-entered Ahmed Square, grateful for the noise and light, the lively babble of many tongues. For another hour he wandered happily, taking random shots with the Ful-Vue and marvelling at the variety of scenes. An elegant mosque, gleaming with blue and white tiles. Pavement cafés with huge canopies and buzzing tunnel-like interiors that seemed to go on forever. Handsome, mahogany-skinned men sipping hot mint tea from tiny tumblers as they talked and gestured.

Next came a small courtyard with a slender obelisk in the centre. As he walked the blistering streets he had the uneasy sensation that the place was engulfing him. The tide of noise and colour and motion seemed to have an undertow pulling him along. And the square was now some way back, the geometry of the streets breaking up so that he could no longer place his whereabouts by noting blocks and corners. There were no more European faces to be seen, a sure sign perhaps he was a long way from the centre.

It was now eleven, time to start back. He paused and took stock of his surroundings. On the ship someone was sure to ask where he'd been. And there on a wall was a name, Avenue Clermont. Where, he wondered, was the Boundary Club? No matter. He'd seen one house of ill repute today and had no wish to see another. Even if it did come recommended. Retracing his route, he drew level with the courtyard again and saw that the obelisk had turned itself into a circular column he'd never seen before. He felt the first stirrings of unease. Right, now he must have gone the wrong way after seeing the sign. Back he went and the sign had vanished. There was no need to worry of course. It was only eleven. As long as he was back by twelve it was OK. But what if he was late?

Bill's voice leapt into his ear. "First time the Lodger goes ashore – and the jerk only gets fuggin' lost!" He quickened his pace. Here was a café he clearly recalled seeing earlier. There had been an orange canopy and round wooden tables. Yes, there was an orange canopy, but the tables were square metal ones. Roger took a deep breath. Now let him think. Ahmed Square had one side parallel to the waterfront. After dodging the drunks and the French Kropp, he'd found his way back to it. But if it had been some other square? Unbelievably it was now 11.15. His watch seemed to jump five minutes each time he checked it.

Up ahead he spied a blue and white building. It must be that same mosque. Approaching it he had more flutters of alarm. The façade was quite different. He'd never been in this spot in his life. Where was he? And then someone came out of the mosque. Tall, white-haired and clad in black robes and a white turban. Immensely dignified, the man stood watching him. Roger by now had resigned himself to asking the way. For all his liberal views, Roger was not quite free of the English tendency to mistrust foreigners. And Egypt, in common with much of the earth's surface, had been under the influence of Britain or France for years. He recalled the five men stumbling and bawling through the square. Ambassadors all. What an example to set. Why should they love us?

The tall man still stood there. How about asking him? No – too stern looking. And he might need an interpreter. Yet this august figure spoke to him.

"You have lost your way?" They might have been nomads meeting in the empty desert.

"Yes, I went wrong somewhere. What I thought —"

"I shall guide you. Where are you bound?" The deep voice was cultured, compassionate.

"Ship. *Empire Garvie*." The man took his arm and gently turned him round. That was all. There was nothing as vulgar as a pointing finger.

"We stand before the Amin Mosque, in the street called Alexandria. Your way lies before you. There, where the merchant stands. That path will bring you to your destination." What would be the proper response? A handshake seemed a liberty, a slight bow perhaps.

"Thank you. You are very kind."

"Not at all. Go safely." Once again Roger was back in the shadows. The alley was the longest and narrowest yet. Ahead was a blank wall. Either he'd gone wrong again or the man had misled him. If he had to return to the mosque and start again he'd be hopelessly late back. And he'd never hear the last of it. But fate was kind to him. The wall was one half of a sharp right-angled turn. Before him lay the entire waterfront. A broad, palm-edged boulevard thronged with people ran alongside. Nearby, an elegant building, the Casino Palace Hotel, stood smugly aloof. But the fairest sight of all was the *Empire Garvie*. He hurried over the snake and up the gangway.

At the top the MAA asked, "What did you think of Port Said?"

"I got lost."

"We've all done that. At least you came back sober."

In the cabin he got mocking cheers. "Here he is," said Bill. "Back from his you-know-what."

"No I didn't, honestly."

"Get away," said Martin. "We know your game, all goody-goody on the outside and inside, the same as the rest of us."

Toddy said, "Dark horse."

Jack asked, "Where did you go?" The expected question.

"Oh – let's see. Ahmed Square. Different places. Clermont Avenue. I never saw the Boundary Club though." The implication that he'd been looking for it triggered a gratifying chorus of "Crafty bugger", "Told you so" and similar knowing cackles. Sooner or later his bluff would be called, but for now his embarrassing innocence was nicely tarnished.

Bill and Martin returned from their afternoon jaunt at five o'clock. They'd been drinking, but showed an odd reluctance to talk, merely listing a number of drinking places. A bar-crawl, thought Roger, unable to call anywhere he'd seen today a "pub" as he knew it.

"Did you do anything else?" asked Pat darkly.

"Course we did," laughed Bill with forced jollity. "Had a quick bunk up. Why not?"

"Where was this?" asked Jack.

Bill glanced at Martin. "Where was it we went? Did you see?"

Martin floundered. "Oh – er – some place. Didn't know what they called it." They were lying. But to admit this after a week of lewd boasting would be an intolerable loss of face.

Bill saw the need to elaborate. "Only cost us – um – a pound – no, ten shillings each it was. You should have come with us Roger. Might make a man of you." He wished they hadn't said that. Now he would have to shoot them down in flames.

"Ten shillings! They saw you coming. You could have got it for five bob in the Ziggi Bar." They were still gaping as he went to fetch the bread.

By the time he was free to go on deck, the *Garvie* was entering the canal. Afterwards he would always remember his first sight of de Lesseps' masterwork. More than anything he was struck by the closeness of the land on either side. The smallest error must see the ship ram her nose into the sand. At first the town kept pace with them, but soon the clustering houses petered out, leaving a straggle of life along the banks. Trucks and buses speeding along a road, further off a train, all overtaking the ship. Men with donkeys or camels plodding the dusty verge and beyond it all the Delta spread westward, becoming greener and wetter as it neared Cairo and the world's longest river.

"From here on," said Jack. "It'll be really, really hot." That night he slept on deck again, the joy of privacy now enhanced by the nearness of the scenery. Once he awoke and the picture had changed. They were crossing Lake Timsah, a smooth expanse shimmering in the starlight and dotted with slender white triangles, the lateen sails of the graceful local boats of Arabia. Then the desert closed in again as they re-entered the waterway. The troopship was only one of a line of vessels strung along the canal, each with a powerful light lashed forward to avoid collision. How strange it was to be on the moving ship yet miles from the sea! Next time he opened his eyes they were on another lake and stopped. It was just on daybreak.

"Morning Roger." Jack was on his way below. "Sleep OK?"

"Fine. Where are we? Suez? I thought it took twelve hours."

"This ain't Suez. This is the Great Bitter Lake, got to wait here for some reason. See you below." All around in the growing light, the lake lay as if cowed into submission by the heat to come. Other ships were widely scattered around them. Roger fished in his bedding for the binoculars kept hidden during the dark hours. To starboard a Liberty ship hung on her anchor, still as a tethered ox. Orange and red dribbles of rust ran down her nose like dried tears. Along her flanks every gap had its telltale streak where paint had surrendered to salt water. Mass produced in wartime along with thousands of others, she would pass from hand to hand till one holding a cutting torch took her apart for scrap. For the moment she called herself *Valencia* and flew the flag of Spain. There was a large tanker with a boxy bridge the wings of which resembled horns. She had no flag. *Esso Forester*? Raising the glasses once more he focused on her stern. *Gulf Splendor*. *New Orleans*. And all the others were too far off to read their names. After breakfast they got under way again and he lost no time getting back on deck to top up his tan and take more photos. The lake was smaller. Someone informed him they were now in Little Bitter Lake. Then as they slipped in the final section of canal, he saw Clay approaching. He wasn't sure where Clay and his cronies stood in the matter of whoring. There'd been little mention of it in Cabin 21. And what of the light-hearted threat to take away his innocence? On this ship it could mean anything. There'd been Penny and Nelson. The latter had been mortally afraid to break off the liaison. But there was also Kropp, a fire-breathing paragon of manhood able to sniff out perversion a mile away. With him in the cabin they would all be heterosexual to a fault. Clay touched his arm.

"Go anywhere in Port Said?"

"Yes – did you?"

"Oh sure. We ended up at the Casino Palace, me, Batten and Smith."

Roger couldn't think how to put his next query. "Did you – you know?"

"Korey you mean? Won't need to. Come over here, I've something to tell you." They crossed to the hatch and sat on it with knees drawn up.

"I've got a date," said Clay smugly.

"A date! Who with?"

Clay put a warning finger to his lips. "Wait till he's gone."

Shuffling along the deck came Batten, now resembling the Outcast Of The Islands. Everything about the man was frayed, the worn rope sandals, the grey shorts made of cut down trousers and the floppy straw hat, the brim of which kept snapping up and down in the breeze. His shirt was a wondrous thing of whiskery short sleeves in a pattern of blue and yellow now fading and running together into a bilious green. It might be an idea, thought Roger, to visit the dining saloon where Batten was on duty. Just to see him in conventional clothing.

"Don't tell him," said Clay, "what I just told you. Don't want everyone to know."

Up close in broad daylight, Batten had the visual attraction of condemned veal. By now everyone, even Roger, had taken on some kind of colour. Batten's pear-shaped torso was morgue white, beaded with tiny globules of sweat that never seemed to run together and with hair in all the wrong places. But the man's unfailing humour was compensation. As he came up he began to sing, "Oh, a life on the ocean wave … is better than going to sea. But where the difference is … I'm buggered if I can see." Sitting on the hatch he patted his pockets.

"Clay my boy. I would be willing to accept one of your cigarettes."

"Sorry, left them below."

"That was extremely thoughtless of you."

"No cigar today?" said Roger.

"No, had the last one in the Casino Palace. They're pretty awful I know." He cupped a hand to his mouth and exhaled. "God, that breath would open a bank vault. Still, could be worse. I could be queer."

"I thought maybe you were," said Clay.

"No – I'm not. My husband is." A harmless joke often used, yet to Roger unnerving. Sometimes he felt he was on a tightrope. Made up of the two strands of sex everyone talked about. The one he knew and the other kind. With a thread of dangerous humour that could rebound at any time. All pickled in alcohol with an abyss of violence on either side. Oh he had to stop drawing these over-ripe analogies. There were around twenty-thousand miles to cover before he got home. If he didn't learn how to relax and fit in soon he never would.

A pause came in the talk and they watched the scenery. Away from the rail, the canal itself could not be seen, only the flat pan of the desert gliding past. On this, the last leg of the canal, the land either side was as featureless as an ocean. To port the Sinai wilderness marched all the way to Israel. To starboard, the ship's shadow moved with them, the surface of the sand so smooth the dark profile showed every structural detail. Batten pointed west.

"See that out there? That's the desert, your actual desert, Beau Geste and all that stuff. If you went out from here, first you'd come to the Nile, then nothing but sand, miles and miles of it till you hit the Atlantic w-a-a-y over on the other side of Africa."

Roger was suddenly taken with a strange thought. There was something about the way the three of them were grouped, two young men sitting with their knees up to their chins; an older man in a straw hat pointing into the distance. Somewhere he'd seen this tableau before. As he thought about it he lay back and half listened to them talking. What had Clay meant? A date? Stewardesses had no work this far aft and passengers stayed amidships. Clay of course was a steward. His work entailed meeting passengers. Roger sat up and saw two things that hadn't been there before. In the west, far out over Batten's desert an aircraft skimmed along at low altitude, heading north east. And closer to hand Bill was coming along the deck. He collected himself, ready for whatever came next.

"Oh here you are then," said Bill sourly. "Jack wants us in the mess a bit earlier than usual, about eleven. We got to get some lime juice up."

"OK."

Bill noticed the others, and Roger wondered if he knew them. They didn't eat in the mess.

"They're stewards," said Bill. "From No 21. That's where you been going ain't it, mixing with 'em?" It dawned on him that Bill regarded stewards and the like as a lesser breed. Not real seamen. Even though his friend Martin had once tried it.

"What if I have? They're alright, most of them."

"Do they know you're a Brylcreem Boy?" Roger at first didn't see the relevance of this but soon guessed where Bill was going with it, and was suddenly irritated by the whole thing.

"I don't know. Let's ask them shall we? I say ..." Clay looked round. Batten took off his tatty hat and fanned himself with it.

"This is Bill Vincent. Bill wonders if you know I was in the RAF."

Clay said, "I know because you told me. I'm an army man myself. Eighteen months of it." Batten replaced his hat.

"I had the honour, or possibly misfortune, to serve in the Royal Navy. And I never knew why they called you the Brylcreem Boys. We used that head-lard as much as anyone."

Batten's flippancy threw Bill into confusion.

"Yeah, well. I never had any time for the Raff myself. I was in the army too and the Raff always seemed to get the best of everything before us." Roger gave the others a despairing glance and looked aft. The plane was nearer the canal now, some way off and well astern. While he watched, the tiny dark dot changed to a cruciform shape as it banked into a turn. And he knew then what plane it was. The wings were unmistakable.

Bill was making the best job he could of getting at Roger through others. But it was the wrong audience.

"Seems to me the army had to do it all. Look at this ship, all army. No Raff sweating away below decks. Not now the war's over. Same in Port Said. No sign of 'em. Know why? They're all in Alex or Cairo, living it up while the army guards the canal." Batten caught Roger's eye.

"He's right Roger. I can't think how you ever confessed to being in it." If Bill saw he was being humoured he gave no indication. Probably he was too intent on Roger's face as he tried to provoke him. But Roger had seen what no one else had. The plane had turned towards them and levelled out. And he knew what was about to happen. Perhaps the pilot was bored, saw the ship and thought he would give them a thrill. This could be the point-score to end them all. So long as Bill kept going. And Bill obliged.

"You got the canal zone garrisons haven't you? Port Said and Ismalia, and Suez what we're coming to. Soldiers everywhere. Where's the Raff? Not a smell of them this far down the canal —" With an explosion of sound the Spitfire was upon them. Barely clearing the telephone poles, the plane bellowed along the canal road, the pilot waving a gloved hand from his slid-back canopy. The RAF roundels were bright in the sun, the whole machine a thing of vibrant life in a dead landscape. It sang a song as it passed, that roaring, whistling song unique to the Merlin engine, echoing up and down the canal with its line of plodding ships and bringing eager faces to the rail.

At most, four seconds. Then it was gone, soaring with the grace of a kestrel before executing a faultless barrel roll and vanishing over Sinai. Clay and Batten watched Roger.

"Er, you were saying Bill?" What *could* he say?

"Of all the stupid things to do. Joy riding, flying low like that – dangerous. In the mess eleven o'clock, right?" He stalked off.

"Mr Vincent doesn't seem too fond of you," remarked Clay.

"Cat-and-mouse game," said Roger. "Most of the time."

"There's always one," said Batten sadly. "You've got him, we've got Kropp. Why can't people just get along? You're a long time dead."

"What does Kropp do?" asked Roger. "What's his actual job?"

"Assistant Pantry man," said Clay. "Up in First Class. Our friend here had to work with him."

"He shouldn't really be with us," said Batten. "Last trip he had a dust-up with someone in his own cabin. Josephine. Yes, honestly. That was the name. Kropp was hauled to the bridge and charged with assault. They let him off but had to put him somewhere else. So, for our sins we got him. What possessed Josephine to make a pass at him we'll never know."

Roger joked, "I suppose Kropp said 'not tonight'." Batten slid off the hatch.

"The only Napoleonic thing about Kropp is an eagerness for battle. Now I need a ciggie. Clay?"

"Alright, you know where they are." Batten hurried off below.

"At last," said Roger. "OK, now what's this about a date?"

"Well, I got these eight bloods in the saloon; a six table and a two. Women and kids, the NCOs' families. And on the two table I got these girls. About – oh, I don't know – nineteen, twenty or so. They're Southampton girls. Or used to be. And I tell you, one of 'em is real friendly. I thinks she fancies me, I'm sure of it. I mean she suggested we meet tonight, up on B Deck. I reckon if I —"

"Take it easy," said Roger. "Don't get too excited." Two girls, and Clay had a date with one. This held promise. "I wouldn't tell too many people."

"I haven't, only you. Keep it to yourself. B Deck accommodation is strictly out of bounds unless you work there."

"Is it worth the risk?"

"You've not met Pauline. That's her name."

"Where will you go?" Clay this time was stuck for an answer.

The vision was of himself and the girl and like all the best visions the background was dramatically misty.

"Go? Well it's only a first date, a chat, a snog somewhere, by the rail or on some corner. Maybe I can slip a few shillings to a bedroom steward. There's some empty cabins since we left Port Said."

"Sounds hopeful. Oh, about that business with Kropp. Did anyone try to explain to him? About me and the tattoo?"

"Batten tried, but you know by now what he is. It's when he's drunk, that's all."

It was 11.50.

Roger said, "Got to go. Let me know how you get on."

"I get on the same way you do, first one leg, then the other." Going below, Roger considered the latest development. If he was to be Clay's confidant the man might be willing to fix something for him once he'd made some progress himself. A double date. At the mess he joined Bill and Martin as they went to the galley for the lime juice. This was in cartons of twelve bottles. As they struggled back with them he wondered what lime juice was like, never having had it before. Same as lemonade, he supposed, or orangeade. They stacked the boxes in the pantry and Bill took out a bottle.

"What do we do?" asked Roger. "Give them one bottle each?"

Perhaps he was tired or still basking in the glow of the Spitfire. Whatever the reason, he failed to see the knowing look that passed between them.

"That's right," said Bill. "Come lunchtime we hand these out to the queue, one each, no more. They love the stuff. Ever tried it?"

"No." Bill unscrewed the top and put the bottle to his own mouth. Tilting his head back, his Adam's apple bobbed happily up and down.

"Beautiful," he remarked. "Finish this one off before Jack comes. We're going down for the spuds." They left him alone. The bottle stood in cool splendour on the counter. A sudden thirst seized him, induced by all the talk on deck while staring at hot sand. Taking his mug from a shelf he poured some out. The smell alone was refreshing. He took a good swig and his tongue caught fire. Something akin to curry powder and battery acid swilled agonizingly around his mouth.

"My God!" he croaked. Eyes streaming, he rushed to the pantry sink and put his mouth under a jet of tap water.

"What's up?" said Martin. "Too strong for you?" They had remained outside the door.

"Sorry," said Bill. "Should have told you." Now they really left him and he heard their laughter echoing down the corridor. He looked at the juice in the mug. Bill's pretence at drinking it had fooled him completely or the deep colour and strong smell might have told him. Belatedly he read the label. "Massey Fruit Corp. USA. Warning: highly concentrated. Dilute well before use." Jack arrived. "Good. You got the juice up. By the way, I wouldn't try drinking that. There's enough in one bottle to make four gallons."

Later than expected they came to the Gulf of Suez. Roger's erratic attempts at a sun tan had resulted in the early pink's replacement with a deeper, if patchy shade. And the peeling had begun, starting with numerous ragged circles reminiscent of a moon map. That evening the jibes were almost up to standard. Bill still smarted over the Spitfire episode and the lime juice trick had done little to mollify him.

"Last time I saw skin like that," he said, "it was on a rice pudding."

Martin offered, "If Isobel saw him now she'd think he had the pox."

Weary of their voices he sought solace on deck. The Gulf was dotted with ships. Some, like the *Garvie*, headed south. Others came up to join the next convoy north. And the Red Sea of course was blue. That sublime, flawless blue that would always enchant those who know only northern seas.

As usual it was not long before somebody engaged him in conversation. It may have been because he was by nature a patient listener. Frank Seymour was a loner. Rat-like, he darted across open spaces, avoiding groups and sidling along the rail to Roger.

"You're the one Kropp's going to beat up aren't you?" The bald statement was disconcerting to say the least.

"Hope not. He's got me all wrong."

"They got me all wrong too. They say I'm nuts. They don't believe I caught four Jerry airmen once with a toy gun, when they made a forced landing near my place. I did you know. Go on, laugh at me."

"No," said Roger hastily. "I believe you – honestly."

"They say I made it up. But it's true. The police said I was brave. It was in the paper, and — and only the year before that I rescued some kid from drowning. Winter it was, freezing cold."

Seymour, it was plain to see, lived in his own world. One in which he was a hero performing daring deeds to the acclaim of all. Not a friendless middle-aged man drifting through a boring life. Roger cast about for a suitable reply. "I must say you've had some adventures, something to tell your grandchildren." He should have done more casting.

"I got no grandchildren." Seymour's voice was low and filled with some ancient hurt. "I got nobody, have I?" Roger opened his mouth to apologise but Seymour was gone. Turning back to the sea Roger watched an Arab *dhow* elegant as a Cowes yacht, come scudding past on its way to Suez. So Seymour was another touchy character, along with Kropp. And Batten too, he suspected, had another side to his dotty humour. Weird but decent had been Clay's assessment of them all. And he'd hardly spoken with Smith or Nelson yet. At eleven that night he was still awake. His place this time was further aft, near enough to hear the propellers rumbling.

His name was called. What now? But it was Clay in his white jacket who squatted down beside him.

"Roger, I'm off to B Deck. Have you got any money on you?"

"What for?"

Clay lowered his voice. "In case I get lucky and need to bribe the steward for an empty cabin. I'm OK for connies but I'm skint till I get another sub. Ten bob. I'll pay you back."

"What are connies?"

Clay dipped into his back pocket and held out his hand. "These."

In the gloom Roger just made out what he saw there. "Contraceptives you mean? I might have known they'd have a different name on this ship." He fished in his own pocket and produced the note.

"Look, you needn't pay me back if you do me a favour. Fix up a double date."

"Alright I'll try but I can't promise anything. They share a cabin you see and the other one's not too chatty." Clay stuffed the money into his breast pocket and departed.

Roger wondered if he was being too ambitious, trying to start an affair on a ship. On a forbidden deck with a girl he'd yet to meet. He didn't even know her name. What if she had strict parents with her? They were afloat on the ocean. If it all went wrong there was nowhere to run. Her army family could chase him all over the ship. Yet if Clay could do it, why not him? As for her name, he didn't mind what it was. But he sincerely hoped it wasn't Connie.

Chapter 5

Between midday and late afternoon, time slows down. Each hour becomes a dragged-out ordeal of never-ending heat. The sun is a blowtorch nailed to the sky. From the air, high in the midday silence, the troopship *Empire Garvie* is nothing more than a tiny splinter of white on the blue table of the sea, smaller than a child's toy, and as lifeless. But only descend, draw near and we see that she is a living community packed tight into a sweltering metal box. Throbbing with all the emotions and yearnings humanity is heir to. Move closer and now we see individual people. A team of soldiers in green shorts and red singlets are performing PT. Above on the bridge, officers in starched white uniforms converse as they pace the scrubbed deck. Elsewhere wives are strolling, calling to errant children or thinking of the life to come in some distant garrison that will be nothing like Aldershot. In the galley a clattering, shouting chaos reigns as always.

And further aft down in the crew mess the Lodger stands with a pair of alloy tongs, placing two pork sausages on every plate thrust towards him. The routine is so familiar he can do it without thought, oblivious to the clamour and the hot edge of the counter pressing into his thighs. By now he knew most of their names and faces; the ones who took their meal with an amiable nod, the ones who looked askance at it, muttering or frowning. It was all part of the game. Depending who it was, he would respond with a jocular oath selected from his rapidly growing vocabulary.

"Don't complain to me, I didn't cook the fuggin' stuff. Go and see the chef." His circle of acquaintances was growing too. The lugubrious Seymour, he of the heroic fantasies, had caught him again this morning, enthralling him once more with the tale of the toy gun. Roger had listened patiently, knowing that by so doing he was condemned to more of the same in the future.

"What sort of plane was it Frank?"

"Er — a Heinkel. Yes, that was it. A Heinkel." There had been a bad moment when he met Kropp in the glory hole, but the man was sober. His hatred of seemingly everyone was off the boil and settled into a venomous pool none dare disturb. Roger had flattened against the bulkhead so the man could pass without even accidental contact. Kropp had contented himself with a glance of calm loathing. As far as he was aware, Roger's mess-room colleagues knew nothing of his troubles with Kropp and he decided against telling them. He mistrusted Martin for one, believing him not above tricking Kropp into a fresh grievance. What he found alluring was the prospect of getting away from them all for an hour or two up to B Deck with Clay and these two girls; if possible with a grand physical finale. But Clay was nowhere to be found. A quick call at No 21 only deepened the mystery.

"We don't know where he went last night," said Nelson. "The bugger came back about midnight as sick as a parrot. Spent the rest of the night in and out of the bogs. Don't know where he is now."

"And he wouldn't say where he'd been?"

"My Clayton was closely interrogated," said Batten majestically. "But the information was not forthcoming."

That afternoon Roger stretched out on the after hatch, knowing Clay would seek him out. In five minutes he was proved right. Clay climbed up beside him.

"I made a hash of it. I had this part bottle of liqueur I lifted from the saloon. And I took it up there with me. You know, help things along. So anyway I met Pauline and we went straight to this cabin she shares with the other one."

"Are you saying you had the two of them to yourself?"

"Yes but you see you couldn't expect the other one to leave 'cos of us. And Pauline told her to stay. They took one sip of the Cointreau and said they hated it, asked if I had any gin. Most of the time they talked among themselves or Pauline did. The other one didn't say much. And they had this great box of chocolates somebody bought them in Port Said. What with stuffing myself with them and the liqueur I just overdid it."

"So you never —?"

"No. In the end I got fed up and started feeling queer, if you'll pardon the expression. So I left them to it. Got back here and was bad all night; most of the morning I was at the quack's. All I got from him was two pills and a temperance lecture. The nurse told me he's a teetotaller. God knows how I got through lunch."

"So that's the end of that."

"Not yet." Clay smiled weakly. "I wasn't too sick to think ahead. It's on again tonight, double date, and I can get some gin."

"You're doing all the work for this. What with fixing it up and supplying the gin and the connies."

"That's alright. We're both first trippers. If we can't help each other no one else will. And don't forget you're paying for the spare room, if it goes that far." True; and he couldn't help reflecting that ten shillings was about what it would have cost the pair of them in the Ziggi Bar. But surely there was a world of difference. It was a pity they had to take gin along. He would need all his wits about him for this.

"What goes with gin?"

Clay shrugged. "Water, I suppose, or lime."

"I can get some lime juice." There was a silence as they considered the coming event. Clay, for all his breezy assurance, was not really that accomplished. Last night's debacle had shown that, and Roger? Roger only knew this opportunity had to be seized come what may.

"I'm in the crew mess. What if somebody asks what I'm doing on B Deck?"

"That's a point. I'll lend you one of my white jackets. Pretend you work up there. Meet me here tonight about 10.30. That's the earliest I can get away from the saloon. I'm off now. I'm doing afternoon teas in the lounge. What a chore! See you tonight. Oh – no, connies you said? Here you are." It wasn't the first one he'd held. On optimistic dates he'd always been prepared and always brought it back unused.

He watched Clay climb the stairs to B Deck. So here it was at last. It had to be. Two girls fond of gin who let men in their room late at night? This wasn't a "good bet". This was a cast iron certainty. That night as he gathered up his things it took an effort of will not to tell the others where he was going later. Only Pat and Toddy still slept below. Everyone else spent the nights on deck.

"I'm really worried about you Roger," said Bill. "All alone, up there in the dark, aren't you afraid you'll get six from someone?" Roger knew what "get six" meant. The figure referred to inches.

The necessary secrecy made things difficult. There was his bedding. Leaving it on deck could mean losing it. Left on his bunk they'd want to know why. For a wildly tempting moment he almost blurted it out: "I'm off to B Deck with a friend. We got these two girls." No – not yet.

The entire thing might be a fiasco. He waited at the stern. Stuffed in the waistband of his trousers was a bottle of lime juice, smuggled from the mess and hidden in his locker ever since. Clay arrived with a white jacket and something in a canvas bag.

"It's the gramophone and a few records. Break the ice a bit. But I'm not leaving it there. I don't want it lifted by some cabin steward. It must come back with me afterwards."

"They'll miss it in your cabin."

"Yes, but it's my gramophone. Trouble is I had to tell them where I was going with it. They all know now, except Kropp."

Roger said, "I've not told anyone, and I'm wondering what to do with these blankets."

"Pick them up and follow me." They made their way along the ghostly deck. Clay stopped at a large wooden chest against the bulkhead.

"Life jackets, it's where I stowed mine last night." They put Roger's things inside with lifejackets on top. Clay furtively closed the lid.

"They'll be alright. I see you've brought the lime."

"Yes, you got the gin?"

"I have. Come on, let's go."

They came to the companionway. "OK, slip into this," said Clay. "If anyone asks, you're a bedroom steward." The white jacket was a good fit. He remembered the last time he'd had brass buttons, so long ago, another life. As they mounted the steps he felt a surge of excitement. B Deck was forbidden territory for them both. And this of course was what gave it that extra thrill.

At the top of the steps they went through a door into a spotlessly clean corridor. Hushed and orderly, the very feel of the place was different. Here were dark wood veneers and polished brass, waxed floors shining underfoot. No sound, save the soft creak of woodwork. No angry voices raised in argument, no slamming doors or breaking bottles. This part was as different from the glory hole as a palace from a slum. They took a cross-passage to the port side. Another long corridor stretched fore-and-aft.

Clay paused. "God, I've forgotten exactly where it was."

"I hope you know the number."

"Yes. B126. We're on the correct side. Even numbers to port, odd ones to starboard."

"Alright, let's find it before we're seen." There were short side alleys branching off the main one, each giving access to four cabins. Clay darted along one to check the numbers. Roger felt horribly exposed.

"Steward!" The voice was loud and feminine. He froze. A few yards ahead a figure beckoned. Clay hung back in the side alley.

"I can't go. She might recognise me from the saloon."

"Steward – did you hear me?"

"Bluff it out," whispered Clay. Roger approached the passenger. He'd known this would happen. Caught trespassing – a DR on his first trip. The woman was around thirty-five, dark haired and wearing a black dressing gown embroidered with a red dragon.

"I've been pressing my buzzer for ages. Hold on, you're not my steward." He fought an urge to turn and run all the way back to the cosy squalor of the glory hole, away from this gilded trap.

"Er – no madam. I normally work elsewhere. I'm only up here for tonight." At least that was true.

"Very well then, I'd like my window open." She led the way to a cabin and he followed her in, noticing that it was B98. The room was very small, with a single bed directly under a porthole.

"I had it closed coming down the canal. One never knows what might come through it there. Now I'm sweating like a trooper and I'd like it open please." Unhappily he knelt on the bed and reached over to the port. The three clamps in the form of large brass wing nuts were hideously tight and as he strained at them the lime juice bottle slipped and dug into his groin.

From the corner of his eye he saw a camera on the bed. It was a Leica, the sort of thing he couldn't afford. "Are you interested in photography, steward?"

"Only in an amateur way."

"What do you use?"

"Ensign Ful-Vue. It's my first camera. Kind of glorified Box Brownie."

"Can't say I know that one, I've always used one of these; thirty-five mil." She picked up her camera. "I've taken hundreds of shots all over the Far East. See; with this you've got a good range of F-stops and exposure times. What you need in the tropics where you get a lot of light variation." It was new to him, hearing a woman talk in this assured way on such a subject. The more so as he wasn't himself too sure what an F-stop was.

Two of the clamps came undone. In the porthole glass he saw her face over his shoulder. It was an interesting face. "I don't know where Farley my own steward's got to. Half the time he's nowhere to be seen and when he is he can be rather unpleasant. He propositioned me a couple of times in such a revolting way I nearly reported him. Do any of your passengers play mahjong? I can't find any partners." He remembered he was supposed to be a bedroom steward.

"Er, mahjong?"

"It's a Chinese game. You have all these ivory pieces, or tiles we call them."

"No, I don't think so." The remaining clamp shifted slightly. His wrists felt near breaking. Then the lime juice slipped again, threatening to plummet down his trouser leg and emerge at the end. God – what a pickle to be in. Any minute the real steward might turn up.

"Quite nice and slim aren't you?" she said thoughtfully. It may have been the first time his thinness got a favourable comment.

"How old are you, steward?"

"Nineteen."

"Incredible. You look much younger." The clamp yielded at last and he raised and secured the port. A breeze rushed into the tiny room. The woman pulled open her gown as far as decency would permit, flapping the lapels up and down in rapture.

"Oh, that's a lot better. Would you care for a drink after all that effort?"

"No thank you. I must go. We're very busy." He read the unspoken message that hung in the air between them.

"I must say you didn't *look* busy. You were only standing there." Some instinct told him it was a moment for kindness, not cold formality.

"I'm supposed to be somewhere else – really. Otherwise I'd be only too glad." Again the silence that said so much. She stood aside.

"What's your name?"

"Roger. What's yours?" he said without thinking and was shocked at his own temerity. Her laugh had a touch of self mockery.

"It's Gina, and I'd like to thank you, Roger, for making me a *bit* more contented." He stepped out of the cabin and she laughed again as the door closed. Now he had to find B126 and get out of sight before he ran into anyone else. There was no sign of Clay. Hitching up the lime juice he hurried along the corridor checking the side alleys. Here it was, a small brass plate on the corner stating B124-B130. The cabin was going to be another one with a porthole. A discreet knock and the door opened half an inch. A brown eye showed in the gap.

"Who is it? What do you want?" For a truly dreadful moment he thought it might be the wrong cabin. A different eye appeared.

"Let him in. It's Roger," said Clay.

The cabin was not much larger than the solitary Gina's. Simple furniture consisted of two chairs and a small table, wardrobes of barely adequate size and a small wash basin. There were two bunks one above the other and a dressing table, every square inch of which was taken up by cosmetics of one kind or another. Now, finally he met the two girls who were the object of all the subterfuge.

"This is Pauline Fletcher," said Clay. The girl who let him in was slim, dark haired and wore a yellow frock with a wide red belt.

"Hello Roger," she greeted him with a dazzling smile. "Welcome to the party."

"And this is Ruth," said Clay. The second girl stood gazing out of the open port, one hand grasping an upper clamp like a strap hanger on a bus. "Hello." The voice was flat, devoid of interest.

Clay produced his Lucky Strikes and they all lit up. "Now then," said he. "Let's get cosy. Roger, where did you disappear to?"

"Yes," said Pauline. "We hear you were called away by a lady wanting some service."

"That's right. Only I think it wasn't so much service she wanted as *servicing*. If you know what I mean." Clay gave an up-from-the-depths belly laugh and the girls exchanged sly grins. And Roger had a pang of conscience. Lonesome Gina "sweating like a trooper" in her airless cell, and no one to play mahjong with. Who was he to toss out flippant remarks about sex? Wasn't it what they'd come up here for?

"Don't look so worried," said Pauline. "We won't let her catch you."

"What cabin number was she?" asked Clay.

"I never noticed." The lie was instinctive. Something made him defensive about her, possessive almost.

"She wanted me to open her porthole."

Clay said, "I bet she did!" and Pauline gave a silvery laugh. The white jackets were gratefully shed and the bottles produced. They used the ice water carafe from the wash basin to make up the diluted juice and soon had their gin and limes. Where the four tumblers came from he never saw. Clay wound up his gramophone and set it on the floor.

"Better keep the noise down," said Roger. "The last thing we want is complaints from the neighbours." Pauline and Clay were in two chairs which they had placed together. This left Roger with the lower bunk where he settled as best he could. The edge of the top bunk was level with the nape of his neck so that he had to either crouch forward and be constantly peering up or lean back on his elbows which put him rather at a distance. It was not the most comfortable setting. The cramped space, the need for low voices, the clandestine nature of the whole thing did not at first produce a torrent of conversation. Ruth sat on the bunk with Roger. Like Pauline she was quite pretty, but somewhat less animated. Her blonde hair lacked the carefree look of the other girl's and her trim figure was encased in a severely cut skirt and white blouse. Taking her drink without a word she leaned casually against the bunk support. Roger took a sip of his own glass, resolved to make it last as long as he could. He *had* to stay sober.

Clay put on a record. "This is nice, you'll like this," he assured them. Another sentimental air drifted up, another male voice and fluent lyrics.

"One has my heart, the other has my name. With one I'll remain, that's when my heartaches start."

They were all so young, so far from England and home, and intensely aware of the invisible threads of curiosity, desire and love of intrigue passing between them across the short space. The small talk began, haltingly at first then easily as the gin oiled their tongues and the seductive tones of the crooner smoothed away their inhibitions. He learned they were both eighteen, bound for Singapore with their respective parents. Like him they were Southampton born but had moved to Aldershot some time ago. Their fathers were sergeants, regular career soldiers to whom the army was everything.

Clay asked, "Do they ever come here?"

"Not this time of night," said Pauline. "After nine o'clock this deck's out of bounds even to them. This ship's got rules like a nunnery."

"My dad's so mean," said Ruth. "Keeps a tight hold over money; me and mum have to go to him for every penny. See these?" The infamous box of chocolates appeared. "We didn't pay for these. Some woman we went ashore with bought them. We don't have hardly any spending money. Not much fun ashore. And we got Aden yet, and Colombo."

"What about your mothers?" said Roger. Pauline poured herself another drink.

"Don't worry. They were in bed hours ago." The chocolates circulated. Roger tried one.

"These are good. Who is this generous lady?"

"Mrs Morrell," said Pauline. "She's over on the right-hand side of the ship in one of those inside rooms where you get no window. It must be awful for her."

"And she took you ashore in Port Said?"

"Yes. Our parents *generously* allowed us off with her taking care of us. Anybody'd think we were kids. She didn't mind, seems to prefer the company of younger people. We did think of having her round here one day."

"Not tonight though," said Clay.

Ruth said, "Where do you work on the ship Roger?" He thought quickly. As an occupation, skivvying for the crew was seriously lacking in glamour. He jerked a casual thumb.

"Oh not up here; down aft; more to do with the actual running of the ship." It was 11.30. The gin trickled again, the record was restarted and arms began to steal round waists. Roger was coping with the accustomed gin quite well, confining himself to sips that might have been taken by a canary. One that wasn't really thirsty. So far, once the door had shut on the outside dangers the evening had been similar to others in his life. Drinks and girls, a friend who liked to organise it all. The earnest attempts at conversation, the search for that elusive Something in Common. But there was very little. He seized what there was.

"Oh you like Ingrid Bergman? So do I. Did you ever see *Casablanca*?" Yes, she had seen *Casablanca,* more than once. And yes she'd loved it. The atmosphere was changing rapidly. Clay and Pauline were very close. They were necking now; quite wantonly he saw with a rush of envy. He tightened his grip on Ruth's waist and pulled cautiously. To his surprise she instantly turned and put her arm round his neck. He kissed her hesitantly, just a touch at first then longer as he felt her respond. Disconcertingly, her blue eyes stayed open for the duration of the kiss, looking into his with frank curiosity. It was now plain to him he could be the only virgin soul in the room. These girls, these *women* knew precisely what they were doing and what happened would be by their design.

"Roger," she said. "You've been overdoing the sunbathing." She pulled one side of his collar down. "Look at you." His skin had quietened down a bit, the pink patches had linked up into an acceptable browny-pink and the peeling was past the confetti stage. Her fingers played on his chest and the nearness of her made his head swim. It tended to do that at such times.

"What have you been putting on it?"

"Nothing." She reached across to the dressing table, not even needing to get up.

"This is what we use." The label on the jar said Medoline Crème. "We get a touch of the sun, me and Pauline, and this stuff is marvellous. It goes on before and after. I shall put some on tonight before we go to bed." The "we" seemed quite natural. This time his head did half a length before he realised she could have meant herself and Pauline.

Clay put on his jacket.

"Won't be long." A glance at Roger and he slipped out of the cabin. A balmy breeze danced in at the port. They toyed with their drinks, made trivial talk and somehow filled the triangular silence. The closing words of the record made them smile. "One has brown eyes; the other's eyes are blue. To one I am tied, to the other I am true."

Holding a key, Clay returned.

"Almost next door – 130." Pauline joined him and the door closed soundlessly behind them.

"Time for my shower," said Ruth. Her brisk manner conveyed no hint that this was other than an ordinary night or whether she knew what a turned on state he was in. Carrying a sponge bag and what seemed to be a large white towel she left the cabin without another word. The minutes went by as he sat holding the lid down on his feelings. In the nick of time he remembered the connie in his back pocket.

Of course it wouldn't happen. Something would spoil it. Something always did. She might simply turn him out, shocked at the very idea. One of the parents could pay a surprise visit, checking on the daughters. It would be a father-sergeant with a bullet shaped head and a face like a bag of chisels. Or the ship might collide with something. This night of all nights would see another *Titanic*. No, even his frantic imagination couldn't put an iceberg in the Red Sea.

The girl returned, now carrying her clothes over her arm. The "towel" had in fact been a bathrobe which she now wore. The blonde hair, untouched by the shower, was yellow gold against the white robe.

"That was quick," he said.

"Oh it's not far. Down the corridor a little way." Cleaning her teeth at the sink she said, "Why not take off your shirt and we'll have a go at the sunburn."

There was a curiously domestic flavour about what was going on. While he folded his shirt and placed it on a chair she was at the sink rinsing her mouth and replacing the glass. It was almost as if they were married. There should have been striped pyjamas and a cup of Horlicks.

The Medoline was cool and colourless with the scent of pine and with her fingertips on his hot skin the intimacy of it all was like nothing he had ever known. All this on a first meeting. It was indeed another world. The unreal setting of a ship at sea, where people met and fought or made love with complete strangers. Like the voyage itself everything was transient. In the heat-racked boredom every pleasure was eagerly seized, savoured and discarded for the next one; for who knew what the future held?

"How does it feel?" she asked.

"Wonderful. You should have been a masseuse."

"I was once. Trainee. Dad made me pack it in."

Smoothly, without either suggesting it, they changed places. She pulled the robe out towards her shoulders.

"See where I caught it yesterday?" Her skin was reddish with two pale lines where shoulder straps had been. Gently he rubbed the back of her neck. Her head tilted back, rolling in response to his touch. His voice sounded hoarse.

"Any other areas require treatment?"

"Yes, but turn out the light first." He crossed the cabin. It was only four paces. Turning, he looked across at her in the feeble light of the port, and his heart seemed to give one tremendous thump as if trying to send half an hour's blood round in one delivery. She stood naked with her back to him. As he went over she put her hands on the edge of the top bunk and leaned forward.

"The back," she murmured. "All over the back." He'd never in his life been so aroused. Taking a second dab of Medoline he applied it between her shoulder blades, moving his hands in small semi-circles, his fingers massaging each side and his thumbs riding down the just visible knobs of her vertebrae. This went on till neither could keep up the charade any longer. As she turned to face him he kissed her with all the starved passion he'd bottled up for so long.

"I hope you're prepared," she said coolly, and lay back on the lower bunk.

"Of course," he replied, surprising himself with the matter-of-fact tone of his voice.

She said nothing more, raising her slim arms to grip the bunk supports at each side, a vaguely sacrificial posture that sent a fresh charge through him. At first he was clumsy, but she had the sense (and possibly experience) to make no comment. Somewhere deep in his brain he knew this bolting horse that was his body had to be reined in before the high jump that would end it all. Even now, at such a moment, there was still that isolated corner of his mind assessing the situation. Then this detachment was blown to pieces.

Reaching up, she linked her hands behind his head and pulled him closer for another of her unique open-eyed kisses. At the same moment she arched her back so that her breasts pushed harder. And he was lost then. There was no more trotting but the full gallop. His body seemed to turn itself inside out. Words tumbled out of him, meaningless phrases barely audible in this crushed mouth. When they stopped, his first sexual encounter had lasted all of forty seconds. And still she hadn't spoken. He rolled onto his back. This was just possible to do without falling out, but he put a foot to the floor as a precaution.

"That was really something," he said. This seemed a feeble comment on an event of such magnitude, but some of his newly acquired instinct advised against anything more. Any kind of gushing gratitude would belittle him in her eyes. Of that he felt sure. Somewhere he'd seen a photo of a Liberator bomber with a slogan painted on its nose. *Wham – Bam, Thank You Ma'am*. Well, he couldn't say *that*. He put an arm round her and kissed her tenderly.

"Ruth, you're terrific."

"I don't normally do this on a first date you know." It was hard to believe her. From the start her demeanour had shown a practised flair unlike that of any other girl he'd met. And she'd hardly said a word.

Perhaps she regarded sex as a thing to be sampled as casually as anything else. But for him it was anything but casual. The great divide was crossed, the long jinx broken. Yet he still didn't really know her.

"What's your name — your full name?"

"Ruth Newbury."

"Mine's Roger Wren." It wasn't easy to gauge what she was thinking. "We've made a shambles of this bunk," he joked.

"There won't be any complaints I shouldn't think."

"Complaints?"

"From Pauline. It's her bunk."

Totally relaxed, they lay in the half light, listening for imagined noises. Gradually they began to really talk. He learned that she too was away from home for the first time.

"We don't know for sure how long Dad's posting to Malaya is for. I only hope he and Mum get along better now we've left England."

"Trouble at home?"

"Oh yes. Arguing over money." She sighed. "Roger, take me ashore in Aden. Mum won't go and *he* won't let me off the ship alone or even with Pauline. And we haven't seen Mrs Morrell again."

"Sure – I'd love to."

There came a faint sound. "They're coming back," she hissed. They hastily sorted themselves out, throwing on clothes and robe as the door was discreetly tapped. He turned on the light and opened the door, realizing with a shock he'd completely forgotten to lock it before the main event. They crept in. Pauline's hair was even more carefree now. It was 12.35 and the party was definitely over.

Clay sounded confident. "Same time tomorrow?"

"Maybe," said Pauline. "There's a dance we're supposed to go to with the other families. We'll keep the drink till next time." They donned the white jackets and Roger blew Ruth a farewell kiss, but she'd turned away to tidy the lower bunk. Strange girl, he thought. On and off like a tap. Outside, the long corridor stretched to infinity.

"What's that pong on you?" asked Clay.

"Tell you later. Let's get off this deck."

Thieves in the night, they hurried through the sleeping ship, certain the next corner would bring them face to face with authority. Their luck held. Back where they belonged, the crew deck resembled a seal colony, dark shapes pointing all ways and giving the odd twitch in the quest for comfort. His bedding was retrieved and they went to the stern for a jubilant debriefing. Every detail was described.

"How did you get the other room?" Roger asked.

"Found the steward, crafty looking devil. Wanted more money at first, I said I couldn't pay any more now but I may be back again. He thinks it's only me. With luck we can keep the key and use it twice without him knowing." Talk of keys reminded Roger of his own carelessness. Clay was appalled.

"Do you realise anybody could have come along? One of the fathers – anybody?"

"I know ... I know. Must have been too worked up, too excited." Clay gave him an indulgent smile.

"It was your first time?"

"I wouldn't tell you if it was, would I?"

"Oh that's OK. I can understand. Only natural. Makes you forget things." He yawned luxuriously.

"What a night. See you tomorrow."

"That was a good job you did, fixing it all up. By the way, about forgetting things, you left your gramophone up there."

"Oh God, so I did. That's shown me up hasn't it? It's been Amateur Night tonight. But at least I wasn't sick. It could only have been the Cointreau before. I'll have my jacket back now too."

Finally alone, Roger undressed. What a night indeed. No longer putting on an act, he could look people like Bill in the eye, knowing he had joined their strutting species. But even as this pleasing picture formed, he knew it was not really for him. Ruth Newbury. An ordinary girl, but possessed of a face and figure a man might leave home for. He wouldn't sully the picture; reduce it to a randy story to tell others. He stretched out on his blankets. Everything seemed different now, even the ship itself. One last look at the scenery, empty, no lights anywhere. Only the *Empire Garvie* moving all alone over a placid sea. Heading, as he was himself, into ever-deepening and mysterious waters.

In the morning the memory of it all was disturbingly vivid. So was the piney smell of Medoline. A shower was urgently needed. Clutching his bedding, he stumbled to the deckhouse door. In his creative mind the feverish half minute copulation had already become something more; a romantic union of two young lovers in a faraway place. This colouring-in of what was really a monochrome image was quite involuntary, and he knew he was doing it. The fall to earth was abrupt.

"Roger!" bawled Bill the moment he appeared. "You look a fuggin' wreck. What you been doing all night?" He sniffed. "Hey, he's only got bloody *scent* on him!"

"Linda found him," said Martin. "The poor bugger got six before he knew what was happening."

Later that day he had a further talk with his co-conspirator at the very end of the stern. "Nothing doing tonight," said Clay. "They've got that social do with their parents. Did you say you were taking Ruth ashore tomorrow?"

"Yes, if we stay long enough. Can't we all go?"

"Depends if I can get out of doing afternoon teas, we don't arrive till around eleven." They decided to meet on D Deck square at 2.30. If Clay didn't make it Pauline would go without him. A threesome, thought Roger, and saw himself stepping ashore with two girls. What would Bill make of that?

At Port Said the early arrival had meant having no time for more than a hurried once over before going below to work. Aden was different. Coming in late morning offered a chance to view the scene at leisure. His first thought was how small it was. Against a backdrop of barren hills a tiny collection of buildings lay huddled at the water's edge as if the town itself was stooping down to drink. There were few trees and its status as a bunkering port was revealed by a cluster of oil storage tanks off to one side. Again Roger got a letter from home and dashed off a reply. By 11.30 they were moored to buoys in the middle of the harbour.

"We take a boat here," said Jack.

In the mess they had the usual discussion on the port's offerings compared with others.

"This here is called Steamer Point," said Jack. "Aden itself is further in. This is what they call the Aden Protectorate, part of Yemen."

Roger couldn't decide whether to enjoy his secret till they actually saw him with Ruth or to casually drop it in conversation. What the reaction might be he couldn't be sure. Martin had an unpleasant streak in him. At lunch Pat announced that he was going ashore with Bill and Martin.

"Any korey?" asked Roger. He was going to drop his bombshell. But first the targets must be led into range.

"Any korey?" mimicked Martin with his donkey laugh. "Why don't you stop kidding us? You couldn't do it if you tried 'cos you're scared of it."

"Keeping himself pure," said Bill. "For darling Isobel back home."

Jack sighed. "Leave the laddie be."

"Well, he shouldn't talk about it," snapped Bill, "if he's not man enough to do it!" Roger felt again that wild body writhing under his, the cornflower eyes in that open gaze as they kissed. Now, now, they would know!

"Bill, when did you last do it?"

Taken by surprise, Bill glanced at Martin, who stared back with treacherous unconcern. "When did I —" he began. "When — well, back in Port Said. We told you. When did you last do it? That's the point, if you ever have."

It was more than a good moment. It was victory cake. A great sweet wedge of it set in icing sugar and studded with flakes of chocolate. Compelling – irresistible. So much for his vow, not to make a salacious story of it.

"The other night. Wednesday."

Knives and forks stopped. The silence deafened. An assortment of reactions went round the table. Toddy paused with a match one inch from a cigarette. Martin dropped his fork. Pat smiled broadly. Jack paused a second after a mouthful of food, his mouth tight shut and one cheek bulging forward. His face was an asymmetric parody of Louis Armstrong in mid-session.

Bill lifted his chin defensively and braced his shoulders as if his own virility was a garment Roger was about to snatch away to try on for himself.

"Oh yeah, I'm sure you did. Where would you get your korey? We were at sea Wednesday —" He stopped as the truth loomed.

"That's right," said Roger. "Me and a friend in No 21 got these two girls up on B Deck, army girls, eighteen years old." Rub it in, why not? "Smashing; absolute knockouts both of 'em. Better than anything ashore, and free too." He wouldn't mention the squaring of the cabin steward. Martin had lost the power of speech.

Bill recovered a little. "What's her name then?"

Roger said, "Before I tell you any more I want to be sure you won't let on to anyone. It's not only me, there's this other man, the girls too. Trouble all around if it gets out." They assured him the secret was safe.

Martin found his voice. "Sneaking up on B Deck, if you please. Now we know about this you better watch your lip Roger. Otherwise we might shop you to Candy or the Chief Steward. Don't think we wouldn't if you get too smart." Jack got up and came ambling round the table. One hand went slowly round Martin's neck, while the other grasped his chin, pinching his mouth sideways so that it popped open like a hungry fledgling's. Then he leaned down till his face was alongside Martin's. His voice was gentle, almost sad.

"If you *should* do that, Martin, I would'na like it at all. I would squeeze your balls together so hard you'll think you've only got one." A bizarre threat. To a part of human anatomy that would be mentioned more than once on Roger's voyage.

"So you won't do it will you Martin? Do tell me you won't?" Gagging like a dental patient in mid-treatment, Martin affirmed that he would not. Jack released him, gave Bill a cold glance and returned to his lunch. Martin fingered his jaw and avoided everyone's eye.

"So," said Pat. "When did you meet these girls?" He told them, trying very hard not to exaggerate. But he didn't omit the Medoline sequence.

"Oh," said Bill. "So that's why you stank like a Turkish knocking shop."

"Dark horse," said Toddy. "Dark horse, Roger is."

Bill and Martin were in a quandary. Consumed with lusting curiosity, not to say envy, they still had to appear unconcerned. This upstart in their midst must not think he'd achieved any more than they could if they chose. They were in need of a face-saving loophole. Ever kind, he gave them one.

"I was really fortunate. This steward, Clay, I knew him years ago. He met them in his saloon job and fixed it all up. I couldn't have done it otherwise." There was a visible easing of tension. So the Lodger had a special connection with that rarified world of the upper decks where all the korey was. A unique advantage denied to them. No wonder the jammy swine got lucky.

"When will you see them again?" asked Bill almost cheerily.

"Today. Taking them ashore."

"Fuggin' 'ell," sulked Martin, then caught Jack's eye and smiled limply.

Roger was on D Deck square at 2.15.

"More expense," said Clay. "I had to pay somebody to do my afternoon shift. Worth it though, I hope." The sunlit harbour twinkled invitingly. One of their own motor launches came to the foot of the gangway hung down the side. As yet there was no sign of their female companions.

"Too soon," said Clay. "We said 2.30. They won't be here a second before." But Bill, Pat and Martin appeared.

"Stood you up Roger?" said Bill. "She's tired of you already. Once was enough. Go back to Isobel." Pat gave him a wink as the three men left and joined the people making a click-clacking progress down the open metal steps. Only half filled, the launch sped away from the ship. They waited on the square. Clay leaned out and peered fore and aft.

"You'd think they'd lay on more than one boat." More people gathered on the square. At the head of the gangway, a young sailor of the deck department leaned perilously on a safety rope. If anyone should stumble at the top step it was his task to prevent them falling sixty feet into the harbour. Today the chalked board had a sterner message, warning not only that they would sail at 1830 hours but that the last launch would leave shore promptly at 1800.

"The last launch?" said Clay. "The only launch they mean."

"No we don't," said the sailor curtly. "We're using both. The other one had engine trouble. Here it is now." The second launch appeared, chugging furtively round under the stern as if ashamed of its belated arrival.

"Brought plenty of cash with you?" asked Clay.

"Yes. English will do here I was told. I'm not going boozing."

"No, not for that. We'll have to buy them things, the girls. Trinkets – some kind of junk. Keep 'em sweet till we lose 'em at Singapore." New to the game, Roger found it difficult to take the same ruttish, throwaway attitude. They would indeed say goodbye before very long but for a blissful period Ruth was His Girl. Any money spent on her would be out of affection and respect, not merely to buy her favours.

They arrived ten minutes late. Pauline wore a crisp white skirt, a blue blouse and the same red belt he'd seen before. Whether she'd dressed like the Union Jack on purpose was unclear, but the sailor came off his rope for a closer look. Somewhat disappointingly, Ruth was in brown slacks but this was offset by a low-necked pink top that revealed quite a lot to the casual eye; and even more to the keen one. Both were bare-headed.

"No hats?" said Clay.

Pauline replied, "I'm hoping somebody might buy us some."

Ruth said, "I've had a lecture from Dad. We can only go with you if there's no getting tipsy."

"As if we would," protested Clay. At the base of the gangway a small platform hung a foot or so above the water. Alongside lay the launch, its exhaust alternately popping or gurgling as it dipped above or below the surface. The two man crew stood one at each end pulling on the platform ropes, endeavouring to narrow the gap to one that could be crossed without doing the splits.

Roger sat by the gunwale with Ruth on the inside, which seemed proper. A nautical variant of the gent-next-to-kerb rule. This time the boat was full.

"Right – that's all!" shouted one of the men to the sailor above and the next batch was halted on the square. The throttle was shoved open and they surged away from the side, emerging from the ship's shadow into the brassy beam of the sun. Pauline stood up and waved at the receding ship.

"Isn't this *fun*?"

"Sit down or you'll fall in," growled the helmsman. They passed a Royal Navy destroyer whose crew whistled and waved at them. Always the quieter one, Ruth kept her eyes on the people in front, not the water swishing by, nor the arms of the harbour curving round on each side. Crossing the wake of another craft the launch curtsied once or twice as they hit the ripples. Her jaw tightened and he thought she seemed tense.

"Are you alright? Not seasick?"

"No, of course not. I don't like boats much that's all."

He put an arm round her and it seemed she moved away slightly. The shore trip had been her idea. Perhaps it was only the boat that bothered her. But he thought a little of the sunshine had gone from the day. And he'd forgotten the camera. They were heading for the quay at an alarming speed, till at the last minute the engine note rose to a whine as it was thrown into reverse. The forward momentum of the boat and the braking effect of the screw now balanced out so precisely they coasted to a halt right at the feet of an Arab waiting to grab the painter.

"Been overseas before, Roger?" asked Pauline.

"Only the Isle of Wight."

"That's not overseas."

"Isn't it? You try walking there." This earned him a welcome peal of laughter from Ruth.

The British abroad can be an intimidating sight. A chattering tide of loud-tongued women in floral prints and ill-chosen hats, clutching handbags and children with equal tenacity and accompanied by sweating men in long shorts. And mingled with the army families were crew members, unattached males with shirts open to show their tans and flaunting Port Said bargain watches.

"Where are the shops?" said Ruth. The rest of the party made for a gap in the quayside buildings.

"Follow them," Roger suggested. Before long they emerged onto the Crescent, an extensive arc of colonnaded stores. There was little traffic here aside from the odd military vehicle or elderly taxi. The shops were of the "colonial" school of design, with plenty of cast iron filigree work. Upper storeys were supported on iron pillars set at the pavement edge while ground floors lay well back in cool darkness, offering escape from the blazing street.

Roger was happy. For a while the *Garvie* and all his cares were on one side. True, the ship was still glaringly visible, an iron-studded symbol of empire lording it over the modest anchorage and its brown circlet of hills. But she was a boat ride away. Open water lay between him and Kropp, the clamouring mess-room, the crushed cabin and all the rest of it. He was well and truly ashore, with good friends for company. Holding hands with a girl who had led him from the darkness of his empty existence into bright meadows. Who walked the baking street with a balletic grace and whose blonde hair bounced and sparkled in the harsh sunlight. Progressing down the Crescent, the girls lingered over every trinket-strewn display, discussing and discarding, while their escorts found more interest in the passing scene.

Ruth, her attention caught by some article at the back of a trestle table, reached across to it. This action turned her body into an alluring right-angle, of which her bottom formed the apex.

"God, look at that," muttered Roger. "I wonder if we'll be lucky again tonight."

Ruth held up what she'd seen.

"Roger." The wheedling note in her voice told him the time of reckoning was at hand.

"Get your money out," said Clay. It was a wide bracelet made of some bright metal and marked with a pattern of stylised falcon heads.

Ruth slipped it on her arm where it shone against her tan. She just *had* to have it. But her mean father never gave her money for things like this, did he? Hadn't she told him that only the other night? Her winsome Cinderella act wasn't needed. He would have got it for her anyway. She deserved it for having such a miserly father. The prices were all in rupees.

"How much in English money?" he asked in an offhand manner that deceived no one, least of all the vendor.

"Very cheap," purred the man. "For you very cheap price I make no money. Is last one left, special price for you and your lady."

"Alright, but how much?"

"Is real silver, very fine for cheap price. Is only one left."

"How much?" said Roger patiently.

The vendor judged he'd played them long enough. Time to reel them in.

"For you, three poun'." Roger wanted to say "Fuggin' 'ell" but the girls were too near. And he knew by now the first figure is only the starting point. This was the Middle East. Here you negotiated.

"Too dear."

"OK – OK, so how much you pay?"

"Ten bob," said Clay, butting in.

The vendor sucked his teeth and gazed into the distance, contriving to look both noble and deeply hurt.

Clay said, "Now put it back and walk away."

"It's silver and the last one," said Ruth peevishly.

"And it's really beautiful," added a wistful Pauline. They began to leave as the vendor watched from the corner of his eye.

"OK – OK. Two poun' ten. Last price. I lose money." Roger picked up the bracelet. Two days' pay!

"I doubt if it's real silver."

"Don't you want me to have it?" said Ruth in a small, tight voice. He saw the danger.

"One pound ten."

Now the vendor clutched his forehead and let out a sigh. A doomed, stricken sigh, having in it something of the oven-hot wind off the sands, or the dying gasp of the traveller peering down a dry water hole.

"OK." The money changed hands, they resumed their walk and Ruth put the bracelet back on.

"We beat him down to half price," crowed Clay joyfully. "It's haggling. Everybody does it."

Behind them another group approached the stall. The vendor took an identical bracelet from a box under the table and put it on show. If only they were all as easy. Perhaps he might start at four pounds.

"What I really need," said Ruth, "is a hat." An hour had slipped by since that first purchase. They'd left the rather sedate Crescent and drifted into a much livelier area, a labyrinth of small shops and keen salesmen. Anything of feminine appeal was thrust to the fore. Bracelets slid up unresisting arms, rings onto fingers. Only the simple formality of payment remained. In this way, Ruth had acquired a rather fine silk scarf, now knotted elegantly round her neck

"Sun bad for lady sir, must cover!" – while another bracelet adorned her other arm. No less acquisitive, Pauline had a ring and a really exquisite necklace that would not have disgraced a Bond Street shop window.

"We got a couple of magpies here," Clay decided when they were out of earshot.

Roger said, "Let's hope they come across for us again." He was still surprised to hear himself talking thus. As if he'd been "doing it" for years. Both he and Clay were well aware of the position their young appetites had put them in. Driven by the implied promise of further late night couplings, they were in a time-honoured spot. Pay through the nose, or haggle over everything and appear to be cheapskates. Or refuse to spend any more and be banished to a celibate wilderness of uncertain duration. He realised Ruth had called him.

"Sorry, what did you say?"

She fingered her bracelets and said coldly, "A hat. You know what that is, don't you? A thing people put on their heads." Her words stung him. The sarcasm was undeserved. She hadn't done badly. Their stop-go safari had cost him a week's pay so far.

"Alright, let's get you one, shall we?" In his irritation he took a few strides up the street, obliging her to scamper after him. The others grimaced and followed. They turned into an ever busier thoroughfare, with food stalls and a number of shoe-shine boys. Traffic hurtled by with scant regard for the people spilling across the road.

The pleasure of buying gifts for a pretty girl was diminishing with each outlay. Her earlier appreciation had been dropped a long way back. The assumption now seemed to be that she could have anything; he was merely there to foot the bill. Pauline, on the other hand, never let go of Clay's arm and received each gift with whoops of joy, planting a kiss on Clay's cheek. If it was an act it was a good one to see. They got their hats. Pauline settled for a straw boater which she wore tilted back like a saucy Edwardian at Bognor. Ruth's choice was a wide brimmed affair with a turned down front edge.

"I've got Ingrid Bergman's hat in *Casablanca,* remember?" The hat delighted her. Honey coloured, it had a silk band round the crown and a very small ribbon inside for the owner's name. The shopkeeper passed Roger a pen and nodded eagerly. She gave him the hat.

"What would you like to write?"

"You think of something. Bit boring just putting my name."

"Put something," said Pauline. "Even if it's only her initials." There wasn't room to write much. It was a tree and penknife sort of moment. He put "R loves R true" and handed it back. She read it out.

"We don't know who loves who."

"No," he said pointedly. "We don't – do we?"

She kissed him then. "Has naughty Ruth been taking her Roger for granted?" she cooed.

"Not made of money you know." However he said it the words sounded mean and he tried to soften them.

"Don't forget we'll go ashore in Colombo."

Pauline clapped her hands. "That's good to hear. They've got some really wonderful things there, I've been told."

He tried to ignore the mask of consternation that was Clay's face and glanced at his watch.

"I don't know about you but I've got to be back about 4.30." As usual the girls had drawn ahead, enabling them to talk freely.

"Sooner the better at this rate," said Clay. "Now you've gone and promised them another day like this one. I suppose you're aware in Colombo they specialise in uncut gems. Rubies and amethysts, stuff like that." A taxi shot past, missing them by inches.

"Christ!" said Clay. "That was a near one. You're right of course. We've got 'em for about five days after we leave here. We can't *not* treat 'em in Colombo but after that they won't want to know us – you see. They're getting off at the next place remember."

They watched their two companions. Pauline in her pert boater and Ruth, bracelets flashing like the smile she bestowed on Roger each time she turned her head.

"I think I've seen enough of Aden," he said flatly. They'd explored Steamer Point, visited shops and markets; they'd seen the town beyond the waterfront and declined a taxi driver's offer to take them to Zinjibar. To their relief the girls agreed it was time to go back. Throughout the walk Roger had expected to run into Bill and the others. They'd passed several bars, but heard no chorus of catcalls or comments. So they still hadn't seen him with her. They paused yet again. The girls were inspecting brass ornaments laid out dangerously near the road. Clay stood before a rotating postcard display, turning it as they waited to go on. And for some reason Roger felt uneasy. There was no way he could have explained this. They weren't lost. He wasn't repeating the errors of Port Said. The Crescent and the ship's launch were just two blocks away. Ten minutes' walk. But *something* was wrong.

Across the street the angular buildings threw their garish colours back at him – ochre and white, pink and yellow. A hotel in flaky sky blue with palm trees either side. Windows shuttered or staring blackly out of sun-drenched façades. Another taxi fussed up the street, a raucous modern intrusion in a time-worn setting. And that's what it was, what bothered him – the traffic, an incessant orchestra of off-key hooters and a swirl of dust, through which the endless figures paraded. He wanted to get away from here, back to the gentle, near-empty Crescent before something happened. And then one of the figures stopped and spoke to him.

"Shoe-shine sah? Very good. Haji give very good shoe-shine sah."

Haji was perhaps eleven or twelve, and wearing a kind of candy-striped nightshirt.

"No. No thanks. Don't need one." Undeterred, the boy knelt and placed a small wooden box on the ground. From this he produced brushes, polish and a rag. Then he inverted the box and tried to place Roger's right foot on it. The feel of the hands on him, the cringing servility of the kneeling boy repelled him and he jerked free. Haji turned to Clay.

"Shoe-shine sah? Your shoes *very* dusty sah. Need Haji to clean." Clay raised a hand.

"Cheeky little monkey. I'll box your ears." It was all in jest. Everybody smiled.

"OK sah." Haji stepped into the street.

What happened next had a kind of evil haste to it. As if fate was ashamed of what it intended and needed to get the obscene cruelty over before anyone saw it coming. But some saw it. And all heard it, a pop and a thud. The pop was the shoe box imploding to matchwood under the wheel of a truck. And the thud was a nearside fender hitting Haji in the back and tossing him aside like a broken doll. The truck slowed. A face peered back from the cab then the vehicle accelerated away to be swallowed up in the maelstrom of traffic.

Roger was the nearest. He knelt beside the boy. Haji lay on his back, eyes bright with shock. There appeared to be no blood as yet. Very gently he moved the boy's arms to his sides and his legs together, feeling creepily like an undertaker. The traffic made a grudging detour around them. More people came to form a murmuring circle. Already in the strange way of these things he seemed to have acquired some kind of vague authority. They were clustering round yet not coming *too* near, looking from him to the boy and back again. Waiting to see what he would do. Clay thrust his way forward.

"Somebody's gone for an ambulance I think – or phoned, I'm not sure which. But I believe something's on the way. The girls are in a state, or Pauline is. What shall we do?"

"I don't know. Can't just walk away. I think his back could be broken."

Two men suddenly made to grab the boy at each end. Roger pushed their hands away.

"Leave him alone. You can't lift him like that. His back could be gone. Wait for an ambulance." The men protested vehemently in Arabic and appealed to the crowd. Voices were raised and the circle tightened.

Clay said, "We'd better go. Leave them to it." Now somebody grasped the boy's feet and tried to drag him away. Roger stopped him.

"Don't do that. You got to wait. Keep him still. *Don't you understand*? His back!" He pointed to his own back and grimaced.

"They only want to get him off the road and into the shade," said Clay nervously.

"Well they can't. Until the ambulance gets here he's not moving." Roger was going through another of his fits of rebellion. When the cloak of timidity befitting his slight build got too wearisome and had to be cast off for awhile.

Clay said, "What about the traffic?"

"Sod the traffic. They can go round us. I'm keeping him still and straight till they get here. Pull him or pick him up the wrong way now and he could end up paralyzed. Someone should have got that bastard's number." Clay glanced around, oddly secretive.

"Someone did. Me. It was 30."

"Only that? 30? Nothing else?"

"I never saw the proper number, if there was one. This was on the side. A white circle with 30 in it."

The crowd pressed closed, voices high and excited. The injured boy rocked his head from side to side. A thin trickle of blood now emerged from under him. A murmur of sympathy rippled among the stony faces. Sympathy and something else. More and more they were glaring and pointing at the two Englishmen; the two pink-faced intruders who seemed to be at the centre of it all and now claimed all rights over the boy's fate.

Clay said, "It's well gone four. Let's go now, they'll see to him."

The boy was conscious but mute, his eyes rolling miserably. His fingers opened and closed, and one arm semaphored flatly on the road, making a quadrant of smoothed dust. There was no movement whatever from his legs. And Roger knew then that he would stay.

"No, I'll just see him onto the ambulance as I'm here. You go on. Get the girls back or we'll have the fathers after us. Drop in at the mess and tell them where I am."

"Alright then, if you're sure, I mean. I got off one shift. I can't be absent again. If I lose the saloon job we won't see the girls again. Wouldn't want that, would we?" Clay gave a jittery laugh which the crowd heard and promptly misunderstood. A new wave of anger rolled out and around them. Very unwillingly the circle allowed Clay to leave. Before the gap closed again he saw him rejoin the girls as they hurried away. None of them looked back.

Alone now, he felt the stirrings of genuine fear. The hostility was quite tangible. And where was this ambulance? It could be one of those instances when everybody thinks someone else has sent for one. In the meantime Haji would die while he crouched there like a buzzard over a kill, driving away all comers. Any time now they would forcibly separate him from the boy, who would then be dragged and bundled to "safety", his battered bones grinding, the spinal cord parting forever. The notion made him feel physically sick. And then a heavy hand fell on his shoulder.

Chapter 6

"What happened here, then?" It was a recruiting poster come to life. The British sailor was all in white, glowed with health and stood as straight and strong as a dreadnought's mainmast. His hat was tilted jauntily on one side and on each sleeve various service and trade badges proclaimed his sturdy reliability. Roger underwent the most immense relief. With this pillar of empire beside him he was safe.

"Shoe-shine boy," he replied. "Got run over. I'm waiting to see he gets attended to alright."

The sailor barely glanced at Haji. "Off the *Garvie* ain't you? Destroyer me. The *Portland*. Got in today from Durban. Where can you get a drink around here?"

"There are some places. Back along this street." His champion was proving less than godlike.

"I dunno why you want to hang about," said the sailor. "I wouldn't waste my time on them. He'll be OK. Theses street kids are tough as nails." With that he elbowed his way through the group and was gone.

Roger was alone again. The man's callous unconcern and his utterly crass parting words filled him with despair deeper than the ocean. The one he now longed to be back on. His nose tickled as a bead of sweat ran down it. He felt the menace closing in again. Where were the other *Garvie* people? His watch began to speed up, the same illusion he'd noticed in Port Said. It was 4.50. About an hour before the last boat left. His self-imposed vigil must end soon or he'd be marooned in the Aden Protectorate. There was a new buzz of interest among the spectators. Someone or something had arrived. Heads were turning to where that universal symbol of authority, a peaked cap, moved through the crush towards him. The law was here. Now he could say his piece and go.

The Arab police sergeant studied Haji's face.

"I believe an ambulance is coming," said Roger. "I can tell you what occurred. This lorry —" He was talking to himself. The man was questioning the people in the crowd. Again he saw much emphatic nodding and pointing at him. A sudden trilling sound announced the arrival of the ambulance. Even now he felt he had to watch the boy's treatment. He mimed a back injury and pointed. The two orderlies nodded and spoke gravely in Arabic. Tenderly, expertly, they lifted Haji, keeping him straight and supported along his whole body. On the stretcher he looked more fragile then ever. Roger became uncomfortably aware of the police sergeant very close behind him. The man was around thirty, with a thin moustache and high cheekbones.

The ambulance departed and the traffic roared again over the scuffed patch where little Haji had lain. The remains of his box were scattered, the brushes had disappeared and only the polish tin remained, already flattened into a black star by the heedless wheels. Roger confronted the sergeant.

"I can't tell you much about the lorry except —"

"Where are the others?" said the man sharply. "I have been told there were three other persons with you. Where are they?"

"Well, to the ship. We sail at six. Now if I can tell you what happened I'd like to be going —" The man shook his head.

"That is not possible. You must come with me. A statement must be made."

"I can do that here." The face hardened.

"No. You must come with me." They set off along the street. The sickening inevitability of it all, the overpowering heat and the mounting panic at the time being used up made his head throb. And it was all his own doing. He should have said "Poor kid" and walked on. Like Clay, the British matelot and everyone else with a grain of sense. Now he would miss the ship. His great voyage would end here.

They walked and walked, turned up a side street and mounted a flight of steps. The room was large, cool and quiet. A young police clerk sat typing at a modern machine.

"Wait here," said the sergeant and slipped into an inner office. Roger sat on a long wooden bench and tried not to look at his watch. Perhaps if he just looked to his front. He did, and found himself admiring what hung on the opposite wall. A beautiful antique clock whose beautiful antique face told him he had fifty minutes left. The sergeant emerged and beckoned him into the inner room. There were two desks, a large one before the window and a small one to the side. Waving him into a cane chair before the larger desk, the sergeant settled himself into a wide leather one behind it.

"I am Sergeant Fouad. The commander of this post is away at present and I am in charge until his return. Tell me your name — one moment." He scanned the desk top for paper, tried to open several locked drawers and went over to the small desk for a note pad. Then he did all this over again for pen and ink. There was little doubt whose desk was which, and that the commander liked to leave his tidy and secure.

"Your name," rapped Fouad, annoyed by his unimpressive start. Roger told him, and the girls' names, and the ship's, and Clay's. Down it all went on the pad.

"And what is your occupation on the ship?" He described his work.

"Would you mind if I told you in my own words what occurred?"

"Proceed." He gave all the details he could, including the number 30 in the white circle and how the perpetrator had driven off. Fouad finished writing and looked up.

"Why did the boy run into the road?"

"He didn't run. He simply stepped back into the path of the lorry. It came far too close to the edge."

"But this child made his living on the street and was wise to the dangers. Why would he be so foolish?" There seemed no answer to this. Fouad leaned back in the commander's chair.

"Mr Wren. I'll tell you what others have told me. You or somebody in your party struck the boy. Or threatened to strike him; causing him to run away in fear." Roger got to his feet.

"No, that is not true. It didn't happen that way at all!"

"Please stay where you are." He sank back on the chair. No wonder the mob had been angry, if that was the story going round. It was 5.30. The ship could be forgotten now. There was no earthly way he could be on that launch by six. Trying to keep his voice steady, he told of Haji's saucy remark, Clay's joking gesture and the general good humour of the whole incident.

"It may have appeared to be a threat, from a distance. But really it wasn't. There was an accident, pure and simple. And I did stay with him all the time till help came."

"Because you felt guilty – responsible for it."

"No, because his back was hurt. They were trying to drag him along. That's not right."

"Are you a doctor?"

His patience ran out. "No – I'm not! But — well I just *know* that. Why don't you go after that driver?" Too late he saw his error. The sergeant bridled, snapping the pad shut.

"That will do! You may be sure we will find him. I have your statement. Now you will wait here while I get it typed out."

Roger was left alone to contemplate the large hand of his watch in its rapid ascent from the six to the twelve. Before him the window offered a spread of flat roofs and dusty trees. But there was another thing he could see. With a furtive glance at the door he crossed to the window. Yes – blue water. That long walk from the scene of the accident had actually brought him nearer the harbour. Maybe there was a short cut. One thing was sure. He wasn't going through this again. There was something about him. Places seemed to lock onto him. In Port Said he'd got lost, seduced by his first foreign excursion. Now he'd got himself more or less arrested. Never again; for the rest of his time he would stay on the ship. Get home with most of his wages intact, the enduring memory of Ruth to console him, and the father and mother of all suntans. But it wasn't going to happen. Not while he was in the hands of the Middle East's very own Robb Wilton. He scuttled back to his chair.

Sergeant Fouad returned and took up his throne again. Roger wondered if he ever took his cap off. The typed sheet was pushed over to him, along with the pen and ink. Resisting the urge to scribble his name and beg to go, he read it carefully. Quite short, it was not so much a statement as a good summary of what he'd told the man. There was no mention of the alleged striking. Relieved, he signed it and stood up.

"May I go now?"

The sergeant pulled a telephone towards him. "Presently. First I must inform the commander. Wait in the outer office, and please ask the clerk to come in here." Outside, he passed on the message and the clerk joined Fouad.

Back on the wooden bench he gazed longingly at the sunlit rectangle of the doorway; anywhere but at his watch or that smug-faced Victorian clock. Through the office door he heard their voices droning on. Perhaps the commander would want to hear Haji's version of the events. They might decide to hold Roger. "Pending further inquiries" as Fouad would surely phrase it. What if he just walked out right now? Would they chase him? Sorry Sergeant, I thought you'd finished – yes this cell will do fine. Dear God, it was 5.45. They'd forgotten about him. Without a backward glance he hurried out into the sunlight, down the steps and along the side of the police station.

Running now, he found a long fence with spikes along the top. More steps down and he was on a path that led to an enclosed yard. Heart pounding, he dashed in the opposite direction. His eyes ached with the constant switch from dazzling glare to dark shadow and back again. Now came a ten foot wall that went on and on. Which way – which way? Try left. A high iron gate was next and through it a view of the water, a hundred yards away. But the gate had a chain twisted round it. Please God, he thought. Be kind; remember how all this started. Blessedly unsecured, the chain lifted free and he was through. Public spirited as ever, he rewound the chain and hurried in a kind of running walk towards the quayside. It was five to six.

"Cut it fine, didn't you?" said the *Garvie* seaman at the head of the steps.

"I got held up."

He cast an anxious eye back the way he'd come. As yet there was no Sergeant Fouad pounding along the quay. Virtually full, the launch rocked gently, its engine dead to the world.

"We'll be off now, I suppose?" he remarked tensely to the helmsman as he stepped aboard.

"Not yet. Not till six."

A new agony began. He hadn't cut it fine enough. The longest five minutes of his life now had to be endured. What is it that gives time the ability to speed up or slow down according to circumstances? His watch now clung possessively to every sluggish second. His inner voice yelled in a silent scream – "Oh come on – let's go!" Around him people chatted, comparing purchases, reliving best moments. But Roger sat alone, his eyes drawn to the edge of the quay high above him. They'd ordered him to wait and he'd run away. Quite distinctly he pictured Fouad's hawkish face narrowed in fury. And then he saw somebody talking to the seaman on the quay. Two foreshortened figures silhouetted against the sun and one had a peaked cap. So it had all been for nought, his scurrying flight through the alleys.

The seaman came to the top step and looked down at the

passengers. Roger shrank inside, willing himself lost to sight among the others. The man put out an arm and he waited for the "Hey you!" But the action had only been to expose a wristwatch which the man now consulted. Still they lingered. Six o'clock. What the *hell* were they waiting for? The seaman looked up and down the quay, shrugged and nodded to his colleague in the boat. The starter whirred and the engine burst into a delicious, music-to-the-ear growl. Roger offered up a silent prayer. The seaman said goodbye to his friend in the cap, a Petty Officer from the *Portland*, ran down and jumped into the launch, which streaked away on an arrow-straight course for the ship.

He had to look back. The quayside was deserted. And as the scene shrank in size it took on the aspect of a painted picture. Like Port Said and the sterile beauty of the canal it no longer seemed real. He must put from his mind the memory of Haji the shoe-shine boy and Sergeant Fouad enjoying a spell of borrowed power at his chief's desk. They were vanished brushstrokes in the artwork receding astern. In half an hour the *Garvie* would be gone. Unless Fouad got an order they surely wouldn't send a boat after him or detain the ship. A more pressing interest would be turning up in the mess late and explaining why; and later – of course – Ruth. But where he was concerned fate never believed in half measures. For the second time that day he felt a hand on his shoulder.

"Roger, why are you ignoring me?"

The woman from B98, she of the closed port and open invitation sat right behind him. In his distracted state he'd completely failed to notice her. Gina wore a small white beret, white slacks and a cotton top in green and white stripes. The Leica, in a smart case, hung at her shoulder. A pair of densely black sunglasses gave her an enigmatic touch. For a few seconds he wasn't sure what to say.

"Hullo Gina, have you been ashore?" An idiotic question.

"No. I've been going back and forth in this boat all day."

"Sorry – wasn't thinking. I had a little unpleasantness in Aden." He wondered if he was blushing and if it would even show if he was, given his patchy complexion.

"I thought you were bothered over something," she said thoughtfully. "I didn't like to speak until we were settled. What happened?" Flattered by the interest, he told his story, deciding at the last minute not to mention Ruth or Pauline.

"How dreadful." When he reached the later events she smiled.

"Oh dear. The Aden police. They can be almost too efficient. My husband had some dealings with them once."

She was perhaps fifteen years older than him yet he now felt less inferior. When they had first met she'd been a passenger, he an uncertain trespasser in a humble white jacket. But here they were quite literally in the same boat, crouched together on the same wooden seats with the same odd teardrop of spray touching their cheeks. He saw that she was actually rather attractive. Too old for him of course, yet she had something. The word he was groping for was quite simply – style.

"Your husband?"

"Yes. John was Deputy Supervisor of Purchasing for the Hong Kong garrisons. We called here once on our way home." John sounded important.

"Ah, an army man."

"No, civilian. We both worked in the same office in Central. That's a district of Hong Kong on the island. We lived in a villa at Wei Ho Bay. I still do." Her constant use of the past tense did not escape him. And there was that tiny single cabin of hers.

"I forgot my camera but I see you've got yours."

"Yes. I'm never without it. I'm hoping to get some work on show in a gallery." She must be good. He tried to sound like a photographer.

"I took some good ones in Port Said, in Ahmed Square; diagonally from a corner. Plenty of contrast – light and shade." Perhaps she saw through him. But she was of a breed that was courteous to everyone.

"Did you? I went exploring too but I missed that part. Let me see them one day. They sound promising."

A ragged series of wolf-whistles told them they were passing the anchored *Portland*. Some ratings waved from the destroyer's foredeck.

"Could you love a sailor?" he asked teasingly. She took off the dark glasses as if to study him.

"You mean as in – all the nice girls? Maybe I don't qualify. Of course it would depend on the sailor. Are you bright and breezy?" He had to see her again somehow.

"Not always. I can be free and easy."

The glasses went back. "Yes. I think we've used enough of that song now don't you?"

The *Garvie* drew near. "Ship ahoy?" he murmured drily. Her elbow dug him in playful reproach. As the engine was throttled back, a flicker of disquiet ran through him. It was the thought of going down to the mess to face them all. Fifteen minutes ago he'd been desperate to get back to it. Now he wanted to stay on the launch and enjoy this woman's company a while longer, before they returned to their poles-apart stations in the ship's community. The momentous events of Wednesday night had wrought a change in Roger. Gina, at the first meeting, had frankly alarmed him. For a start he'd had no right to be there – an impostor from the lower decks. As for her advances, her broad hints, what could he make of that? He was hardly anyone's ideal. Younger than nineteen she said he looked. Perhaps that was the appeal. He looked so damn *young*.

After parting on D Deck square his mood was noticed by the gangway sailor.

"Quite a lad you are, ain't you? Go ashore with one piece of korey and come rolling back with another." As a neat postscript to his day it could hardly be bettered. The evening meal was over but he was in time to have some food and play his part in the strap-up.

"Sorry I'm late everyone."

"Oh, here's the Lodger at last," said Bill. "Now most of the work's done."

"Get your meal," said Jack. "Then tell us why you're an hour and a half late."

Martin still seethed with envy over Roger's good fortune so early in the voyage. While they were still talking about it, this bugger actually had it available on the ship; a jerk like him. It rankled so much he took refuge in a lofty disapproval, which in his mouth sounded laughable.

"Roger, it's all very well you getting —" he choked "— your end away on B Deck, but you're here to do a job. Don't forget that."

"I wasn't on B Deck today. I was ashore. You saw me waiting for her."

"Yeah – then you came back and went topsides with her." He realised Clay had told them nothing.

"Alright, here's the story. There was a road accident and I got the blame. I was nearly lynched by a mob. The police took me in. Then I ran away and just made it back."

Again that day he brought the meal to a startled halt. "Dark horse, Roger," said Toddy. Pat leaned forward.

"I'm getting to quite enjoy his adventures – by land or sea. Fire away my son." They were sceptical.

"We were in town too," said Bill. "Didn't see no accident or crowd; or you or this marvellous tart we hear so much about. Sure you didn't just get lost?"

When he'd convinced them of the truth they routinely got some fun out of it. The plight of the shoe-shine boy was of no great interest.

"Really in it, you are then," gloated Martin. "If they don't come for you now they will when we get back homeward bound. Escaped suspect you are. Next time we're here you'll have to hide down in the engine room."

"Daft I call it," said Toddy. "Worrying about that. Weeks to go. Case'll be over."

They didn't come for him. And as the ship began to move Roger couldn't wait to go on deck. He had to see he was putting distance between himself and Sergeant Fouad. As he came to the rail they were passing the breakwater at the harbour mouth. Aden was but a memory. Soon it was gone – devoured by the sunset. There were other waters to cross now, the Indian Ocean, the Malacca Straits and the South China Sea. This was where the eager dolphin sprang. Here fish could leave the water and fly on silver wings. There would be fluorescent waves to light the tropical darkness and distant waterspouts to hang like black snakes from the clouds. Barely sampled yet, this alluring world awaited. And parallel to it the other world, also but fleetingly tasted. Forbidden love had beckoned and absorbed him, sweet in novelty and rendered even more piquant by secrecy. In Cabin 21 he found only Batten and Clay.

"Come in young Roger," called the older man. "We've heard all about it."

"Not everything. Clay, I thought you were going to tell the mess I would be late?"

"Sorry, no time. I had to tear up to the saloon."

"Where's Kropp?"

"Fear not my son," said Batten. "In company with similar gentlemen he is in the Pig pouring alcohol down his throat while considering who to hit. Now what became of this unfortunate shoeshine boy?" This time the narrative got a more serious reception. Batten shook his head sadly.

"Sounds in a bad way. I imagine you'll be staying aboard next time we call. Defying the police like that."

"Talk about injustice," said Clay. "I was joking – raised my hand to him, that's all."

Roger asked, "What's the position re the girls?" Clay looked grave.

"We can forget about tonight. Pauline was upset about the accident. Ruth's seeing to her. She's OK." He'd guessed as much, that Ruth would be unaffected. There had been signs, a touch of hardness beneath the surface charm. Almost by reaction he thought of Gina and felt guilty for doing so.

"I met the porthole woman again, coming back on the boat. She was good company. I think she might be a widow." Batten was in the high-backed chair regarding him with some amusement.

"Roger, I have to say you are becoming a lecher of the first order. It breaks my heart when I think of you on sailing day. A tweed-clad angel on his first day at prep school; all that sweet innocence!" Batten put his head in his hands and staged a dramatic sob. "Another soiled dove!"

"Come off it," said Clay. "You only wish it was you." Batten sat up and beamed.

"Of course, but don't worry. My time will come. I'm already negotiating. There's a certain party. Up in first class of course. No rubbish, me." Roger tried to picture him in the act.

"What is it Roger? Can't you see me on the job? You'd be surprised. I've entertained more women than you've had hot dinners. And notice I say women. I refuse to say korey. Detest that word." Roger's new buoyancy had strayed a little close to cockiness. And Batten he felt sure would make a bad enemy.

"Sorry, I wasn't thinking anything like that."

"Oh yes you were. It's alright, I'm not offended. I'm no Adonis. My body is not calculated to excite all female minds. But, if you'll forgive my candour, neither is yours. By all means enjoy yourself on B Deck but remember it's thanks to us, or to Clay that you're getting anything at all. In the normal way you'd be trawling the red light districts ashore, as your chums in the mess will doubtless be doing. And I'm supplying the connies. Or didn't you know that? Clay gets them off me."

Somewhat chastened, Roger said, "Of course you're right. I do realise that."

"Another thing," Batten went on. "You want to be careful prowling around up there at night. Last trip one of the barmen was actually caught in flagrante with a Warrant Officer's wife and got a black eye and the sack to go with the DR. They're all at it. I know for a fact one of the senior deck officers had a piece on the side. Some party in first class. I won't tell you his name; but he's got a wife and kids back in Southampton. The real crime is getting caught. Then they have to set an example. Something to put in the log."

In the ensuing silence Roger thought about the ship around him. An almost imperceptible tremor of the engines seemed to convey the physical and emotional energy coursing through it. The daily toil on every level and the off duty quest for some kind of outlet. And he was part of it now. Joy and fear; adventure and drudgery. A crash course in life for a man still recovering from adolescence. His own boldness surprised him.

"I'll have some more connies off you if I may. How much do you want for them?" The price seemed high. "That's a bit steep isn't it? Timothy Whites in our High Street are cheaper."

Batten rummaged in his locker. "Very true. But we're not in your High Street. We're in the Indian Ocean. And I had to buy them in the first place. Still, if you'd prefer to wait, I'm sure the enterprising Timothy White has an outpost somewhere between here and Southeast Asia."

"Sorry," he had to say again. Batten gave him two packets.

"I should think so." The assumed note of severity could not hide the humour shining behind it. "Any more impertinence and I'll find Kropp and tell him you desire his body. That should be interesting. I've never seen anyone beaten to death." Something about these men made the badinage a pleasure. There was no self-promoting malice in it. The levity was a communal comfort, softening the drab reality of their lives.

"I'd like to straighten myself out with Kropp, any suggestions?"

"That's difficult," said Batten. "Once you're in his bad books there's little you can do. Only keep out of his way."

"I don't know why he's like this. I mean he only *thinks* I'm one. The others make no secret of it."

"Well he can't attack them all. You're an easy target Roger. It's not only you. He's threatened quite a few people. Sooner or later he'll be on the bridge again ... one more complaint."

"Don't worry," said Clay. "Relax and have a ciggie. That's another one you owe me."

"Thanks. I'm going on deck now for a read." Returning to his own cabin for a book, the cigarette caused a minor sensation.

"Whatever next?" said Bill. "What with boozing and being unfaithful to Isobel, now he's smoking!"

"Ah, pay no heed," said Pat. "Smoke keeps the bugs away when we get further east."

"Liquor, fags and korey," said Jack. "These things make life bearable. Everywhere, all over the world at this very moment people are supping, smoking or shagging. Think about that." Roger did think about that; often. He also wondered whether to tell them the truth about Isobel; that their affair had more or less petered out some time ago. According to the lies he'd felt obliged to tell at the outset he was now cast as either a two-timing brute or a wicked rascal who liked his korey. Depending how they saw it.

Up top once more he found a spot on the hatch where he could settle with his book or think about things while he watched the flat sea go silently past. The dying sun still touched this end of the ship, throwing long, slowly moving shadows across the deck. He glanced about at the men he shared this idyllic evening with. Penny was in conversation with a young chef who was still in his work clothes.

"Oh no. Never again. I've finished with Mike Nelson and Freddie Bates too. I wouldn't see Freddie again if he was the last homie on earth; ever since that time in Wanchai when the beast stuck one on me. Made me nose bleed he did. Absolutely *ruined* that bona Canton blouse I'd only just bought." Still bewildered by hearing this sort of thing in a male voice, Roger stared up at B Deck. Somewhere up there was a real girl. One he would meet again; God willing.

Music again. An accordion, in the skilled hands of someone out of sight on the starboard side. The sound was not loud, coming and going as the breeze played tricks about the cluttered deck. Yet enough came his way for him to recognise *Lily Marlene*. What a ship this was for contrasts! Violence and sweet melodies – hatred and amity. All lumped together so that you never knew where you were. Pinching out the Lucky Strike he thought again of Ruth. For all he knew she could be with someone else right now. But he hoped they weren't using Medoline.

Over at the rail he noticed Seymour, leaning with his head sunk onto his arms. He watched him, hoping he would give some indication of being alive. At such a moment the man struck a false note. This was a gentle time. An evening of oyster pink clouds and air like warmed wine, a time for human contact. Roger closed his book and walked over, knowing it was the Aden thing again. Somebody needed solace.

"Cheer up Frank. Worse things happen at sea." The saying tumbled from his lips, the feeble joke therein sounding quite asinine. Seymour lifted his head.

"Hullo Roger, how's your love life?" For him, it was almost jocular. But the eyes were cold, the face joyless.

"It's OK." What could you say to a man so locked in himself? "Sorry if I upset you the other time. About your grandchildren. I didn't know – never thought –"

Semour lifted a limp hand. "Doesn't matter. We're all on borrowed time anyway. Did you know that? Borrowed time, every one of us."

Knowing he'd regret it, Roger asked, "Why do you say that?" The man studied Roger's face as if deciding whether his level of intelligence merited an answer.

"I'll tell you. This ship is going to a war zone; carrying troops, and the North Koreans will get jet planes off the Russians. Have you ever seen what high explosive can do? Were you even in the Blitz or were you sent somewhere safe where the nasty Germans couldn't kill you?"

Roger was annoyed. "No I wasn't. I spent the whole war in Southampton. We got our share of bombs."

"Alright, alright. But did you ever see any actual Germans face to face?" Resigned, he prepared to hear the story again. True or not, the picture came to life as Seymour described it. The damaged plane slithering to a halt (it was a Dornier now; at the last telling it had been a Heinkel), the quartet of Germans tumbling out to be confronted by the intrepid Seymour brandishing his younger son's toy revolver.

"Hero of the hour, that was me. After that my luck ran out. You never want to believe what they told you in Sunday School, Roger. Good always wins over evil. Bollocks. I was always Good' and where did it get me? On this thing with a bunch of piss artists and queers; and with a chance of being shot at again in somebody else's quarrel."

The litany of woe went on, the sackings from a string of jobs; the drinking.

"I beat the bottle in the end. For about six months. Now I come on here where they do nothing else." Roger nodded in sympathy.

"What about —?" he began and stopped. He'd been about to ask after Seymour's wife and children but thought better of it. They may have left him when he was impossible to live with.

Seymour said,

"I suppose you reckon I'm a nut. That nut Seymour babbling on again. I know what they say about me."

This was a man pursued by demons; shutting out reality to retreat into a fantasy past. Or indulge in dire prophecies. Again he felt inadequate.

"Well I'm sorry to hear you had a such a bad time of it." How could he comfort this man? "If you like we could go ashore together one day. Get off this ship for a few hours." Seymour's face lightened a little.

"That's quite good of you." The surprise in his voice was unmistakable. Perhaps it was the first time his story had been listened to with any patience, any compassion. "Not a bad sort are you, Roger, for a youngster? At least you lend an ear to someone. I might take you up on that. We could go ashore in Japan, that's a new place to me." Roger now changed his mind about the atom city. Maybe he would go, in the right company.

"Fine. And if you fancied it we could make the trip to Hiroshima."

At once Seymour changed. A trap seemed to come down on his face. "Hiroshima! What the hell you want to go there for? Trying to be funny aren't you? I might have known!"

"No – I just thought —" But Seymour had turned back to the rail, head down and staring at the water. Roger wondered if any sustained contact with this man was possible. Returning to the hatch he found Linda.

"I've been watching you Roger. If you're trying to be a Good Samaritan with Seymour you're wasting your time." Roger glanced uneasily about the deck and Linda smiled.

"Oh don't worry about Kropp seeing us together."

"You heard about that?"

"Yes. He's butch, that one. Or thinks he is. Kropp's all mouth and trousers. I'd sort him out if I wasn't such a peace loving type." Roger must have appeared sceptical. "I see you don't believe me. Listen, you've only just begun to learn. I know about you upsetting Penny. Not normal! The silly cat's too sensitive, that's her trouble. But the thing is you got to watch yourself, Roger. Steer clear of Penny for a start. Know your friends, as I told you at the beginning. You look at us and you think we're just raving queens good for a laugh."

"No I don't really."

"Yes, you and any first tripper. Well, it may surprise you to know I was the battalion boxing champ three years running, when I was in the REME in Germany. And I once knocked a guy out in Cape Town; knocked him out, just like you see in the films. There was me sashaying down Adderley Street with my friend when this big Yarpie has a go at us."

"Yarpie?" Linda sighed and shook his head.

"Don't know a thing do you? Afrikaner – white South African; dockyard boss with a gutful of Kommando brandy inside him; came at us with a stevedore's hook in his mitt."

"Why did he want to attack you?"

"Oh, Lord knows. There'd been a big bundle outside the Delmonico. I think he wanted to carry on with it. Go for the first English bods he found."

"The Delmonico," said Roger. "That's a nightclub I imagine."

"Yes in Van Riebeek Street. Lovely place it is too. Good as you'll see anywhere. A lot like Bernie's in New York only cheaper. Bona cabaret they do. Go there if you're ever in Cape Town." Such easy appraisal of cities, thousands of miles apart. These people spoke of the world as a pleasure resort, using ships as he would hop on a bus.

"I must say this hook you mention sounds pretty lethal."

"Can be. They use them in the docks to shift bales and stuff. When he swung it at me I nipped under and grabbed his wrist, my friend kicked him in the nuts and I poked him in the jaw. Down he went and my friend gave him another kick for good measure. Then a pack of his mates turned up and chased us all the way to the *Athlone Castle*." Roger tried in vain to match this brutal activity with the man's camp and affected manner. Linda folded his arms and regarded him with a devilish grin. "Learning a lot these days aren't you? You know what it is. Positively virginal, that's you. You look about sixteen but you're really nineteen so that makes it OK. Everybody likes 'em young. They want to have a go at you. Beat you up or shag you or take the piss out of you according to taste. I fancied you myself as you may recall. Sorry about that. Blame the drink. I'd just had a simply *ghastly* quarrel with a very dear friend in Southampton." Linda paused at the memory.

The dulcet tones of the accordion drifted about the deck. Shapes and faces were becoming indistinct in the deepening dusk.

"As for friend Seymour, try and buck him up if you wish. But be careful. Something happened to him in the Blitz. Then he turned funny and started making up these fairy tales about him and the Germans, and rescuing people. We never hear about his wife and kids. They walked out on him when he hit the booze, though he won't admit it." The line of men at the rail thinned out till only Seymour remained. Eventually he too straightened up and passed them, gazing dully ahead as if approaching a scaffold.

"Poor sod," said Roger. "Someone told me if you stare at the sea too long you want to jump in."

"No fear of that with him. All he wants is someone to listen to him. Then you end up buying him drinks."

"He hasn't touched it in six months."

Linda scoffed. "Don't believe all that polari. Wait till you see him ashore."

"Actually I offered to visit Hiroshima with him."

"Big mistake Roger. If you want to spend your money on anyone stick to this tart you got topside." So even he knew about Ruth.

"She's getting off at Singapore, but who told you about her?"

"Friend of a friend. You know how it is. I forgot you don't know, do you love? We're all getting our oats on this ship, in our *infinitely* varied ways." The whole deck was in shadow now as the last light died behind them and the ship ploughed on through the night. Since Gibraltar they had been in enclosed seas, guarded on every hand by the landmasses of three continents. Now they had broken free, and were crossing water that was wide open. Nothing but a thin scatter of islands lay between them and the endless empty miles of wind-stung waves that marched all the way to Antarctica, far away at the bottom of the globe. And he was sitting on a hatch cover conversing with a boxer named Linda who called him "love" and once carnally desired him. Maybe still did.

There was a new word for his collection.

"What's a bundle? You said there was a bundle in Cape Town."

"A big fight, usually a running fight in the street. Ooh I've seen some I can tell you. Brits versus Aussies, or Yanks, or Irish. Jocks versus — well anybody. And we're all supposed to be allies. How we won the war I'll never know. They get liquored up, some silly homie says the wrong thing and it starts. Then one lot gets outnumbered and needs help. I've been in a bar and somebody comes and shouts Bundle' and they all rush out to join in. Army, Navy – anyone. With sailors you can get rivalry between ships as well." Roger tried and failed to see himself running about shouting "Bundle". Such ridiculous antics were beyond his understanding. But by now he knew better than to say so.

It was time to go. "Don't forget your book," said Linda. "What are you reading?"

"Robert Service."

"Oh him. I prefer Somerset Maugham myself. She's one of us too you know."

"Surely not!"

"Ooh yes, and Noel Coward; camp as a row of tents." His arm got a friendly squeeze. "Nighty-night Roger. Keep your buttocks crossed." The man gave a throaty chuckle. Roger cast a wistful eye up at the lights on B Deck. When he thought of Ruth she was a distant figure, in every sense above him as he slunk about down here in his dank underworld of strange people and stranger practices. Ruth represented normality. The outside world, where all things were as they seemed to be. A place he came from.

"There he goes," said Bill as he collected his bedding. "What do you want blankets for? Ain't she got a bed in her cabin?"

"I shan't go there tonight," he replied, skilfully implying he had a choice. "I might toddle up there before Colombo."

At the stern he stretched out and listened to the murmur of the wake. Drifting off to sleep the salient points of the day did their usual march through his mind. And each time he thought of Ruth a disquieting thing happened, Gina swam into his picture. How foolish. As if he would fall for someone so much older. And this reminded him of another landmark, one that had crept up almost forgotten in this breathless week. Tomorrow was his twentieth birthday.

In the morning he lay for a while enjoying the early morning breeze. Twenty years old, surely a magic figure. Why was twenty-one considered the big turning-point? Key-of-the-Door – Coming of Age – A Man my Son – all that stuff? He was a man now, of sorts. Later on he told Clay.

"Many happy returns then. Quite a week you've had. Christmas also came early for you the other night didn't it? We must try and get up there again soon. They were a bit quiet at breakfast. I'll sound them out later today. See if it's on again."

But it wasn't on again. Not then or the next two days. Pauline was feeling better but Ruth's mother was said to have a stomach upset and needed personal care, Sergeant Newbury being too busy with shipboard duties. The suspicion grew that they were being fobbed off. Unlike Clay, who saw the girls every meal time, Roger could only drift about the after deck, peering at passing vessels with his binoculars or watching in vain for the fabled dolphins or flying fish. One afternoon he took a pencil and pad up with him and made a belated start on "Trade Winds" as he decided to call his poem. After one verse he ran out of ideas and returned to the cabin, remembering to conceal the pad. Better they shouldn't know about such soppy interests. The ribbing of late had been relentless, especially from Bill.

"No more korey for the Lodger. Quick stab and that's it. It'll take him another three weeks to get it up again. By then she'll be in Kuala Lumpur being seen to by her dad's CO." Bill was in his element, but Martin rather subdued. His threat to betray Roger had damaged his standing somewhat. For now he was content to watch as Bill piled it on.

"I reckon she didn't like your style. Did you ride bareback?" Roger's now practised mind guessed the likely meaning of this.

"No, I had a connie."

"Just as well, imagine if she had a baby. They'd make you marry her and join the army to keep her. Left, right – left, right. Roger in the army, fuggin' 'ell! They wouldn't need a pull through on rifle cleaning. Tie the four-by-two on his foot and he could crawl down the barrel."

There was some respite to be had in Cabin 21. Smith, who he'd since learned was happily married, thought they were lucky to have had one night of it.

"I mean, I'm not after it myself but if I was I wouldn't count on more than once. They got you to spend money on them, now you get the push." But another voice was ready to reassure them. Against all the rules of nature Batten had by now made his own conquest. Nobody could explain what it was Batten had, the gift of the gab maybe. Something had worked the miracle. A love-starved lady of his own age had succumbed to his sump oil charm, to the extent of slipping away for a midnight rendezvous with the podgy ex-Cunarder.

Batten gleefully took the role of ancient patriarch, one willing to advise his eager juniors.

"Draw close my children. Heed my words, for verily I speak unto you with the wisdom of years. Now, I think I know where you're going wrong. You're doing the wasp round the jam pot thing. Never appear too eager. Be offhand. Say casually you're thinking of having a birthday party for Roger, with some special cakes and stuff from first class. And some wine. I'll get all that for you. Tell them it's expensive. They'll jump at it."

They didn't jump, but the idea of a really special party did have some allure. Pauline had got over the shock of the accident and as she fingered her Aden necklace she thought of Ceylon and its fame as a gem centre. As for Ruth, her whole existence was a fight against boredom. Her father had always seen his home as a mere extension of the barrack square. Her mother had a range of ailments, every one of which would vanish the moment she got some attention from someone. And the prospect of being dumped in Malaya to set up home in some dreary married quarter was depressing. If her father had to busy himself dealing with communist insurgents he'd have even less time for his family. She'd been told as much.

"See here my girl. I got a job to do, me and the rest of the lads. What we been sent out here for. Your job is to help your mother. At least till you're older and more grown up."

Her only escape might be marriage, but not to a soldier, or anyone in any kind of "service". The truth was that both girls were beginning to feel the imminent break with England. Perhaps it wasn't such a bad country after all despite its faults. The smoking trains and tiny cars, fog and rain and rotten films and all the things they claimed to despise. And the boys! Boys with awful hair, in awful clothes; leaning on the milk bar counter and sucking Woodbines as they ogled the passing talent. But how about this one? Roger Wren? Green as grass but decent enough. Thin certainly but at least he was clean. Showered often, he said. Unlike some she'd been close to in the heat. The sex – well, not bad she supposed, while it lasted. And she could screw money out of him with little effort. Yes, a proper party. Who knew when there would be another? After Colombo they'd be preparing for Singapore and the big arrival.

Clay was jubilant when the idea was given the nod.

"Oh and we'd like to invite another guest," said Ruth as they rose from the lunch table. Clay had cleared his section and had time to put down his steward's tray and absorb this bombshell. An intruder, a fifth person at the feast would spoil the vital symmetry on which so much depended.

"A guest? Who?"

"Mrs Morrell," said Pauline. "We haven't really spoken to her since Port Said. Real nice to us she was then. Those chocolates cost a lot."

"How old is she?" asked Clay with a sinking feeling.

"About – oh – forty-ish. It's alright, she won't want to stay long. She'll want to get to her bed."

When Clay brought Roger the great tidings he said nothing about the extra guest. Later would do for that.

"I talked them round. Said I would didn't I?" At 10.30 that night Clay called at No 17 and gave Roger his white jacket in front of everyone. Setting off for B Deck had been easier the first time. Now they all knew about it and had comments.

"Don't be late in the morning or we'll come and chuck a bucket of water over you."

"Bring 'em down here and let 'em see how it should be done."

"Shove it out the port if you get overheated."

He shut the door on their grinning faces and hurried after Clay to No 21. Batten handed over the promised extras swag-fashion in a knotted cloth.

"Thanks," said Roger. "What's in it?"

"Things they'd never get in second class. The best part of the Beaujolais we didn't finish when Kropp broke us up. Plus some *petit fours* and a jar of *Marrons de Lozere*. Something special, you'll see. Don't anyone say I don't take care of my friends."

This time the night was quite dark as the padded across the deck among the sleeping bodies. Mounting the steps Clay knocked the bundle against the ironwork, triggering a *clonk* that seemed as loud as a gunshot.

"What the hell's in this?"

"The wine and some other French stuff, something in a jar." He wondered what to do if they met Gina. Keen as he was to see Ruth again, he felt an inexplicable need to please the older woman. Gina got to him somehow. She talked to him as if they were the same age. Only a friendship, that's all it was. But he didn't want it spoiled. He wouldn't ever tell her about Ruth. Otherwise he'd be just another youngster panting for sex. Not a man she could confide in about

F-stops and shutter speeds and villas at Wei Ho Bay. Up ahead two people approached; a woman in a green frock and a man in a white tuxedo. As they drew near the man hung back, waiting shiftily as his companion fumbled with her handbag.

"Evening sir, madam," chirped Clay boldly. The pair nodded cautiously, waiting to them to go by. "Army officer from first class," whispered Clay. "Slumming it in second. Batten's right. Ship's a regular Sodom and Gomorrah." A door closed and the corridor was empty again.

"Why do you say slumming?" asked Roger.

"Because it is. First class sneak down here for a bit of rough when they want a change from their own kind."

"And I suppose second class —?"

"That's right. They turn to the next level down – us. They know we're keen and they won't have to see us again when they leave. We're the bottom of the barrel. We can only go up. Unless you want to snog a shark."

"How do you know all this if it's your first trip?"

"Batten. The man's a mass of information."

They came to B126. "Before we go in," said Clay, "we've got a fifth person coming; the woman who bought them the Port Said chocolates. Yes, I know what you're thinking, but I couldn't very well prevent it. She'll soon go."

"Let's hope you're right." But Mrs Morrell was not there yet, so for the moment they put her from their minds.

"Happy Birthday Roger," said Pauline warmly.

"Thank you." He wished Ruth had been the one who'd said it. But she was full of questions about his brush with the police.

"They might have come on the ship after you. What if my dad had found out I was there? He'd have gone mad." Not a word about the injured boy. And she wasn't wearing any of her Aden things. Oh what did it matter? They weren't *engaged* for heaven's sake. They all sat where they'd been before, Roger being too late to claim the chairs, obliging him and Ruth to take the lower bunk again. Clay put the swag bag on the table.

"Let's see what we've got here. First class this is you know." The Beaujolais took its place beside the gin. Then came a large flat tin that had once contained Sharp's Toffees. Batten had packed in the *petit fours* with loving care. Tiny iced cakes of such perfection they might have been made by Fabergé. But what of the jar? They passed it among them. Clay read the label. *Marrons de Lozere*. "Save them till later. They look like pickled onions."

Pauline poured a little of the wine. "This looks expensive. Who paid for it?" Clay laughed.

"Best not to ask! Probably someone who doesn't know they paid for it. They can afford it in first class. When they're half cut they'll sign anything."

Roger said, "Is this other woman still coming?"

"Yes," said Ruth. "She promised she would."

"Did you tell her about us?"

"Not your names, only that it was someone's birthday."

Roger recalled that other time when he'd awaited the arrival of a new face. And that had turned out to be Kropp. Now they had to meet this motherly old dear. Until she'd been and gone the party could not really start. But as the minutes slipped by the wine worked its magic and nibbling the scrumptious little cakes gave a sense of wicked indulgence. Across the ridiculously small room they looked at each other, mouths full of sugar icing and longing. As before they paired off, the kissing began and the real world faded away. Then came a knock at the door. They all sprang apart.

"She's here," said Clay in a voice of doom. "Let her in Roger."

He opened the door. Gina stood there. Surprise was mutual, but she recovered first.

"I believe I'm expected. Mrs Morrell."

"Yes, come in." Once more, chance and his own inept attempts at flirtation had placed him in a spot. Who knew what and about whom? He'd never named his "porthole woman". But the way he'd spoken of her that first night! What if they'd repeated that story to her, including the "servicing" joke? What if Ruth had told her about —? Head whirling, he stood aside. During the introduction it became clear how she wanted to play it.

"This is Archie Clayton," said Pauline.

"Hullo Archie."

"Pleased to meet you Mrs Morrell. But don't call me that, call me Clay."

"As you wish. And who is this young man?"

"That's Roger Wren. It's his birthday party."

"Many happy returns Roger."

"Thank you." He shook her hand, searching her face for the spark that had jumped between them on the launch. There was something there. What, he couldn't tell. But she was pretending they'd never met. So they can't have passed on his smirking porthole story. Then he remembered. According to Pauline, Mrs Morrell had *no porthole*. Gina, he knew only too well, did. At this point his brain rebelled. Perhaps the riddle would explain itself in due course. For now he would simply go along with her.

They were short of a chair. Pauline gave Clay a meaningful glance.

"Why don't you fetch one from Cabin 130? Didn't you once have the key to that?" When at last they were all settled the atmosphere was initially somewhat strained. Mrs Morrell's extra years were enough to give her an edge over the girls but not enough to make her seem old. It was the men's presence that did it. Ashore in Port Said they'd been three girls together. Now she seemed, not a threat exactly, but a very clear example of the sophistication they still aspired to. Her traveller's poise and faultless manner made them feel like puppies in a basket.

Clay said, "I understand you are going to Hong Kong."

"Yes. I've been in UK for a while on vacation and clearing up some business. Now I'm off home." As Roger had guessed, she was a widow, had been for a year. But her work had been so integrated with her husband's the department had kept her on with a salary increase and the same free travel to England for vacations.

"I've never travelled on a troopship before but I had to get back somehow. This trouble in Korea's thrown the normal services into confusion. But I've always gone second class. I prefer it. A better sort of people here I think, more honest and straightforward. We used to mingle with the colonial crowd when John was alive. Happy Valley – Britannia Society and so on, but we only made a few friends there. John called them the Bamboo People, hard but hollow and found all over the Far East."

Round the little table they crouched, sharing the *petit fours* and sipping the wine. Gina talked, but never dominated the conversation. Her voice was cultured, but by no means "cut glass". And she made many jokes against herself.

"Ex-pats they call us. Sometimes I think I've been there long enough. I'm only thirty-six but I'm told you age fast out there. Another fifteen years and I may be getting around slung on a pole between two coolies." For the girls it wasn't turning out quite as they'd expected.

Mrs Morrell had hidden depths. The men were captivated, Clay in particular. Roger remembered to pay heed to Ruth. Rather more than Pauline, she was holding her own quite well, countering each story with one of her own. Tales of garrison towns, late night dances and darkened army trucks in quiet country lanes. Told with a clinical detachment frightening in one so young.

But his attention was always drawn back to Gina. Mrs Morrell had sent him signals at their first meeting and again at their second. Now she was at it again. Glancing from one face to another she seemed to linger fractionally longer on his. She'd pretended not to know him. It was a special personal game they were playing that excluded the others, and the temptation to tease her was too strong.

"We can't keep calling you Mrs Morrell. May I ask your first name?" She was too smart for him.

"See if you can guess. It begins with a G." Now he was in a corner.

"Begins with a G. Hm —"

If playing games with one woman, don't invite another one to join in. A lesson Roger had to learn at some time. Tumbling head first into the trap he said,

"What to you think it could be, Ruth?"

Her voice was a wet scalpel dipped in sugar. "I honestly don't know. Why don't you open up this French jar and see what's in it? I would like to know that!" A brief silence and a few darting glances. In Gina's face he saw mischief and a touch of contrition. The lid of the jar was tight and she watched as he struggled with it.

When he finally succeeded she said, "Well done," adding drily, "I had a feeling you'd be good at undoing things. My name's Gina."

Pauline wondered what *marrons* were. Gina knew.

"Chestnuts. If they come from Lozere they'll be pickled in syrup." They each sampled one, spearing them from the jar with Clay's penknife.

"These are really good," said Roger. "I don't know how Batten smuggled them past the head waiter."

By now the party had taken on the aspect of a garden picnic hurriedly moved into a potting shed when it rained. Despite their care, in such a confined space some crumbs had escaped to pepper the table and chairs. At least one cake had plunged to colourful destruction on the floor and the chestnuts dripped stickily on their journey from jar to mouth. The empty wine bottle and still untouched gin stood ready to fall the first time somebody bumped the table. Roger discreetly checked his watch. Midnight. Three women full of wine and cake might talk all night.

"Now let's have a quick slurp of gin," said Ruth elegantly.

Gina stood up.

"Oh no, thank you but I really must go now."

Then Pauline said brightly.

"Hey, we haven't told you what happened in Aden." Gina sat again and Roger had to watch as she listened to a repeat of the story he'd hold her. Only now it was a picture of four close young people abroad for the first time. And she would be remembering the night he'd come to her days ago, reluctant to stay. She would guess where he'd gone afterwards, his reason for being there at all.

They omitted nothing, telling of the ham-fisted bargaining with wily traders, showing her the baubles and fripperies they'd come back with. Gina admired it all. Not once did she hint that in her travels she must have seen such things many times before. When she was told of the accident and Roger's lone vigil the game re-started.

"Oh dear, the Aden police can be very strict. My husband had dealings with them once." He didn't need the oblique look she gave him to know she was at it again; reminding him of their talk in the launch, repeating her words almost exactly, and inviting him to go on acting. Very well, he would.

"Yes. Somebody else told me that. Somebody I met on the boat. Don't know who it was. Charming person."

Again she prepared to leave. "Be careful Roger. There are some scheming females on this ship on the lookout for innocent young men. Still, you're twenty now aren't you?"

Everyone laughed except Ruth. Gina said, "It's late. Thank you for inviting me."

"Are you going ashore tomorrow?" asked Pauline.

"I may do. Actually I'm not all that keen on Colombo. I prefer Singapore. I know that place well. We lived there before going to Hong Kong. There's a temple in Singapore I've yet to visit. I've studied eastern theology. It's not everybody's cup of tea but it can be fascinating. This particular temple is dedicated to Shiva's wife or a manifestation of her. It's got a marvellous gateway I want to photograph, a sort of big carved tower. Afternoon's the best time I find. The light's better then. That's when I'll be going, right after lunch."

The details seemed over-precise. They hadn't seen Colombo yet and here she was telling them – or him – when and what she was doing in Singapore. When Ruth would be out of the running. Almost like making a date. He took another pickled chestnut. This woman would send him crazy if he didn't stop fantasizing.

CHAPTER 7

AFTER SHE'D GONE AND THEY SETTLED down her presence was still felt.

"I wonder why she's so pally with us?" said Pauline. They'd got the lime juice made up to go with the gin. The dubious wisdom of topping up with spirit what they'd already consumed did not seem to occur to anyone. They were young weren't they? They could do anything. They had lives to fill; a mine of pleasure to plunder, and an eternity of years in which to do "sensible" things.

"I've seen her in the saloon," said Clay. "Misses her old man I think. We heard her say they didn't know many of the posh ones in Hong Kong. You girls remind her of when she was younger. Who's for a gin and lime?" So Gina was dismissed; at least for now.

The girls partook freely of the gin, Ruth especially becoming almost maudlin. In fact the contrast between this Ruth and the coolly composed nymphet of the other night was disconcerting. He had a nagging worry she might pass out on him. Throughout the last hour and a half he'd again kept his own intake to a minimum. Now they were back on gin he'd have to be even more sparing. And he wished never in his life to see another *petit four*. They didn't use the gramophone this time. Not only were they running late but there was no ice to break now.

He glanced around for something to talk about. "How do you manage to climb up into your bunk?" Ruth pointed.

"I get that ladder down – see?" It hung on a wall bracket, a lightweight creation in alloy tubing.

"That's handy," he said. "We don't get those where we are, do we Clay?"

Pauline asked,

"Where exactly do you sleep?"

Clay shook his head and assumed a hangdog face. "Oh, a long way down. So deep; bottom of the ship. We can hear the sharks talking!"

Ruth wasn't fooled. "Don't believe that. Nobody is that far down. Not seen any sharks anyway. Mus' think we're daft." She was slurring her words slightly and cropping her sentences in a Toddy-esque way he found endearing. He pulled her towards him and kissed her slowly. This time she closed her eyes in a melting sort of way. Or it may have been the gin. Clay got to his feet.

"Who's going where then?"

"Very romantic I must say," complained Pauline.

Ruth said, "I'm staying here," and gripped Roger's arm. His ego preened itself for an instant till she said, "Too hot for me that other room'll be. No window. Too damn hot." Never mind Pauline, he thought. Never mind her best friend being uncomfortable. The gin didn't soften that side of her.

"What are we doing tomorrow, all of us?" she asked. "When do we arrive?"

"Five in the morning," said Clay. "And we leave at five in the evening, so I was told. And it's another boat trip I'm afraid. Only one boat too. The other one's broken down again." They told each other what a bind that was. Ruth grumbled.

"Don't this ship go *anywhere* that's got a wall thing they can tie it on to?"

"I can get off about seven-thirty," said Roger. "We can work something out in the morning after we're in, depends when you finish in the saloon, Clay." For a while they were all self-conscious again, covering the awkward parting with coy jokes and affected *sang-froid*. Finally they were gone. The door was closed and this time, locked.

"Let's sit in these chairs for a change," said Ruth. This wasn't right. What about the shower – the Medoline? She took a gulp of gin. It astonished him how anybody so young could take almost neat spirit so easily.

"Like your gin don't you?"

"Only if someone else is paying for it. Dad wouldn't have it in the house. Pauline's people are the same. Only time we had a drink or any fun was at the dances at the camp. Sometimes we'd go to Southampton and meet boys off the ships. At the Guildhall dances, and swimming at the Lido. We're good swimmers, me and Pauline. Even then Dad used to crozz-crozz-kweshon me when I came home. An' now — an' now we're going to some horrid dump in the jungle where it's hot and — and they got big spiders an' things — an' nowhere to go of an evening —"

The tears began, silently at first then in a hiccuping stream. And as she sobbed, her bosom shook, stretching a taut line across her dress front and stoking him up to boiling point. He felt hugely sorry for her and protective, hugging her as she laid her head on his chest.

"Come on now. I'm certain it won't be like that. They won't put you up in the jungle. They got proper homes for army families. In Singapore, nice modern places. And there'll be dances and shows. And swimming – lots of swimming. Same as England, only more sunshine." She gave a long, wet sniff.

"How do you know that?" How indeed, he thought, improvising feverishly.

"Well, it stands to reason. The British Army's been there for years. Like India and —" (a rapid global scan) "the Khyber Pass, and er — Gibraltar and places. We've got camps and bases all over the world." The weeping had stopped.

"You know a lot don't you?"

"I've read too many books." They were quiet for a while.

"No Medoline rub tonight – no shower?"

Without replying she came unsteadily upright, took down the ladder and placed it against the middle of the top bunk. Ruth, it seemed, was turning in. Either they were doing it on the top bunk or they weren't doing it. Boiling over though he was, the notion of climbing to a bed five feet up for it was less than enticing. Not to say hazardous. If he rolled off the bunk, forgetting in the heat of the moment where he was! Already she had a foot on the bottom rung, apparently intending to retire fully dressed and shod.

"Ruth," he said quietly. She swung round and staggered, grabbing the edge of the bunk. It seemed she'd forgotten he was there. And was well sozzled. No, it wasn't going to happen. Not with her in this condition. Then she looked intently across at him, clinging to the ladder as she began taking off her things. "Well turn out the damn light then."

Roger's second visit to the valley of delight was rather less smooth than his first. What happened resembled an under-rehearsed play; one of those repertory productions wherein lights and trousers go off together amid wobbly scenery. And tonight the world outside was as black as Indian ink, devoid of any celestial glimmer. When he turned the switch the room became an instant obstacle course of invisible corners and hard edges. That she always preferred to disrobe in the dark he understood, but the will-we-won't-we preliminaries had given no time to clear the field, as it were. He had the connie to deal with, and the ladder where she'd placed it barred easy access to Pauline's bunk. So the eager fumbling union took place, as and where they collided. With Ruth draped against the ladder like a Florentine statue, and Roger shedding garments as fast as he could kick free of them.

Oblivious to his barked shins and stubbed toes he was propelled by a passion that was part physical and part something else. The tears and her new vulnerability sowed special feelings within him and an extra something was added by the peculiar way it was happening. His arms encircled her, joined up behind the ladder and enhanced the sense of possession. At the same time the irreverent side of his mind searched for the word that described this particular way of copulating. There was one, he knew.

When it was over they relaxed, supported by the ladder which towards the end had begun a series of plaintive squeaks at such improper use. In the hot darkness she spoke softly in his ear.

"Tired out Roger. Bloody gin – sorry."

"Want to turn in now?" he asked tenderly. Their cheeks rubbed together as she nodded. Her knees buckled and she began to slide down between him and the ladder. He tightened his grip and she came to a halt with her head lolling back between two rungs. Carefully he reached one hand up to her bunk and pulled off one of her blankets. This he wrapped round her, rolling her sideways to tuck it in while still keeping her vertical. Now he was able to sit her on Pauline's bed, move the ladder and lay her out full length. Pauline would have a bed swap tonight.

Somewhat breathless, he dropped into a chair. A drunken, tearful Ruth had been an unexpected development. He had a creeping feeling he'd taken unfair advantage of her. Then his head spun. First a little, then a lot. This helped his conscience. They were *both* drunk, so there. The others were at it. And she'd given him the nod. A tiny knock came at the door. Up to this point, he'd moved silently, respecting her wish for darkness, collecting a few knocks from the fittings and managing all this time to avoid the table. But now, right at the end he bumped into it.

The cake tin, bottles and glasses didn't just fall. They came together in a hideous, jangling racket that went on and on. It was the most sordid, shameless, Bacchanalian noise he'd ever heard. Ruth stirred and mumbled.

"Tired – tired out." Hurriedly he put on some clothes, switched on the light and let them in. Clay and Pauline surveyed the wilderness. Garments male and female lay scattered among the debris. Ruth sprawled with one leg fully exposed and her head drooping upside down over the bunk edge. Her second blanket hung down in a long triangle where he'd pulled at the first one. On the floor the two bottles clanked together in a happy duet with every roll of the ship. Only the chestnuts stood smugly unmoved, unspilled.

"There's a word for this," said Clay. "I believe it's orgy."

"Is she alright?" asked Pauline. Roger assured her she was.

"It was the gin. Taking it almost neat she was." They cleared up the mess as quietly as they could, stowing the remainder of the food in the bottom of the wardrobe. Miraculously nothing had broken. Clay returned the third chair to B130. Pauline made a closer examination of Ruth.

"I've seen her like this before, a couple of days after leaving Southampton."

"You had a party?" said Clay.

"Yes alright, a party. So what? Do you think we never had one till we met you?" It was the first irritation Pauline had shown to anyone. Clearly it was time to go.

Safety back on the after deck they talked things over. "A ladder?" said Clay. "Whatever next?"

"It just happened that way. You can sense the end coming can't you? Pauline's getting shirty. And can you imagine the state Ruth'll be in tomorrow – the hangover she'll have?" He sprang his surprise.

"The porthole woman on that first night. It was Gina. Mrs Morrell"

"In that case you'll be OK then. Korey all the way to China." He hadn't expected the sudden bluntness.

"Oh come on, you must be joking. Gina?"

"Why not? Good looking woman. I saw you took a shine to her. Never mind pretending to be strangers, I could tell she knew you. How did she know you were twenty? I never told anyone. Did you tell the girls your age before tonight?"

"No, only Gina."

Clay chuckled cruelly. "There you are then. Now you'd better pray Ruth don't remember that in the morning."

Creeping back like an errant son to his own quarters he was glad to find Bill and Martin still bedding down on deck. Without their presence he was comfortable enough in the unpretentious cell they called the glory hole.

"Roger," called Jack softly. "How did it go tonight?" Keeping his own voice down, he told it all including the ladder. "Now Roger. It all sounds a bit rough and ready to me. Are you sure she was willing this time?" He told himself Jack was a naturally cautious type.

"Oh yes."

"Well then, if you're sure. Only I've known some women swear blind they were raped after being plied with drink." This was a new troubling thought.

"She wasn't plied with it. She poured it down happily, more than any of us." Nevertheless, he wondered exactly how Ruth would recall events. That she would be in a foul mood he didn't doubt.

He slept well. The drink he'd had and the comfort after the hard deck were enough to send him off. The only thing to spoil it was a shocking dream he had just before dawn. Wrapped in a blanket, he was running around the well-deck hotly pursued by Sergeants Fouad and Newbury, while Ruth, clothed all in white, clung sobbing to the after mast. At five he awoke. The ship was stopped. Carefully he sat up. God he'd never survive many more of these parties. His entire body reminded him of the previous night. Gin and Beaujolais! In a kind of intestinal Agincourt, English juniper berries and French grapes fought for possession of his stomach and brain. Cakes and chestnuts, and the odd chocolate added their support on the sidelines while a buzzing head competed with the now remembered leg bruises.

Pat beamed at him. "Roger my lad. Let's hear it. Must have been something unusual – always is. Did you get your oats?" Jack answered him.

"Oh aye. He did that. On a ladder." And as Pat's jaw dropped he added wryly,

"What did you expect?" Toddy stirred himself. They awaited the familiar comment.

"Dark horse, Roger." Outside, another scene would be appearing. Before Bill and Martin returned, he dashed on deck with his binoculars.

"Hang on, I'll come with you," said Jack. Strange he should want to share his interest. The man had been here many times before.

"Yes but I always like to see us arrive. A grand sight Colombo is. 'Specially first thing in the morning as it is now." Another surprise, the pragmatic Scot waxing lyrical. Jack pointed.

"What do you think of that?"

It was more than another scene. It was another continent. Up to now there had only been the desert. Along the African coast and down that narrow gap the biblical desolation had always been there, watching them pass. Hard and shadeless. But here all was green. A lush, spicy, tropical green that spread in every direction, tumbling and swaying in a variety of shapes and shades all the way back to a hazy blue-grey skyline. Ceylon hung like an emerald from the necklace that was India.

And Colombo the town was different too. The Middle East's flat-roofed cubic simplicity was gone. Here were the Victorian styles favoured by decades of Empire builders. Hotels, department stores and offices stood confidently in their livery of dull brick and sandstone, the sun-loving soft pastels of Arabia replaced by municipal grey. And then he realised that these were merely the most prominent things in a brilliant garden of tawny roof tiles, leafy parks and gilded domes. They took turns with the glasses, the veteran and the novice.

"There's Cargill's," said Jack. "See it? Big store when you can buy anything. That other place is the Grand Oriental Hotel." With them in the harbour were two other large vessels, one of which seemed to be a copy of their own. The same two buff funnels, white hull and blue line. In the glasses her name swam into focus. *Empire Windrush.*

"Another trooper same as us," said Jack. "Going home. Good thing too."

"Why?"

"You'll find out if you run into any of 'em. It's over something happened a long time back in Hong Kong. We had a lifeboat race in the harbour, us and the *Windrush* and a Clan Line ship. There was a money prize put up by some hotel."

"Who won?"

"We did, but there was trouble over it. We were well in the lead, nine or ten yards ahead of the *Windrush* crew. The Clan boat was nowhere. Then we ran into something, some flotsam or other bits of timber. Our helmsman claimed he never saw it in time. Slowed us down and the *Windrush* got in first. Bad luck, nobody's fault really. But the idiots running things decided we were the winners as we'd been ahead and would have won but for the stuff in the water. None of us were happy about it but there you are. We had to go and receive this cheque at the hotel. Five pound each for the boat crew. The *Windrush* men were mad as hell over it. And then the story got round that one of the organisers was related to our Captain. Not true, but the harm was done. Next day there was a big fight in Hanni Lu's place in Kowloon. Worst bundle I've ever seen. Police got called. Booze of course. And it's been daggers drawn ever since. So watch it when you're ashore today."

More violence. In the midst of so much beauty. To take his mind off it he made another sweep with the glasses. Across on their other side was a graceful ship painted in several shades of green. This time her name rang a bell. His father had mentioned *Caronia* many times.

"That's what you want to get yourself on," said Jack. "Ship like that. Cruising all over the place. Folk on there tip for everything. Come home rich you would." Yes, he thought. But in a way I'm already rich. I'm travelling the world with a cross section of humanity that would take a lifetime to meet anywhere else. People whose skewed brand of humour could lift him out of the blackest melancholy. Others whose mere presence was enough to disturb or scare him,

"I see that's got you thinking," said Jack. "But you got this voyage to do yet. Come on, time to get below and start slaving."

Breakfast was something of a trial. As he worked amid the sweaty clamour of the mess the heat pouring up from the hotplate and mixing with the smell of food brought on a wave of nausea. To relieve it he recalled more ecstatic moments, in the heady darkness of a tiny chamber far away from all this. Ruth whispering her fears and clinging to her silver ladder as she waited for him. But then everything was shattered, cut down to the crude reality it actually was. Bill dropped a tray of finnan haddock on the hotplate with a jarring crash.

"Heard all about it Roger. You're a bloody lucky sod – that's all I can say!" Martin entered the pantry and Bill passed him the news at the top of his voice.

"Hey! Guess what? The fuggin' Lodger, he only had a *knee trembler* that's all!" There it was, the word that had eluded him. Better that it had – such moments of rapture hardly needed the intrusion of locker room slang, however physically accurate.

"Bully for him," said Martin sourly. "When are we going to actually see this korey of his?" They would see her that day, though none knew it yet. A hastily arranged plan saw Clay and Roger once more fretting on D Deck square.

"How do you feel?" said Clay.

"Alright now, bad at first. And you?"

"Recovering. I have to be back in the saloon before twelve. It's 7.30 now. We got about four hours, allowing for the boat back."

The girls showed in their different ways how they were coping with the heavy night before. Pauline had rather too much make-up, and a smile that was quick to vanish. Now and then her eyes would close and jerk open if someone spoke to her. This time she was the one in slacks, but with the same blue top and Edwardian boater. Ruth, as expected, made no bones about how she felt.

"Never again. Never, never again." Which particular activity she meant was not apparent. Only the drink, he hoped.

Across another shimmering turquoise harbour they sped, but their thoughts were on more mundane things. Ruth had a hangover, and she wanted them to understand it was the worst one ever suffered by anyone in history.

"Why you had to bring along that French plonk I do not know." In a wide green skirt, matching blouse and the Bergman hat she was undeniably attractive. But he rather wished she'd shut up. At least till she felt better.

"As for that other stuff; chestnuts – I ask you! My guts are churning round like a damn cement mixer." A down to earth sort of girl, he told himself desperately. Charming frankness, that's good in a person surely. He sought solace by watching her figure as she tried to settle on the hard wooden seat. Gripping the front edge she lifted herself slightly, taking the weight off her bottom as she jiggled it around for comfort. Once she stopped fidgeting she folded her arms across her chest in a line as grimly set as her mouth. It seemed impossible this was the same person who had wept on his shoulder a few hours back.

He said gently, "Perhaps if you feel that bad we shouldn't go ashore."

"Oh I suppose I'll stick it out. You and the others want to go so I'll have to drag myself along." The ungracious words jarred with his idealised view of her. Some asperity crept into his voice.

"You weren't too reluctant about putting it away. I've never seen anybody swill it down the way you did."

"Oh really? Maybe I was fed up watching you two listening to darling Gina." Staring skyward, she sighed long and miserably. Unlike Pauline, she wore none of her Aden trinkets. To leave room for more new ones, he thought with a touch of new-found cynicism.

"Take it easy Ruth. We all overdid it. That's the trouble with birthday parties." Vaguely he knew there was something about Ruth and his birthday he was supposed to worry about. There was no time to pursue it. They were at another flight of steps and scrambling out of the boat.

"So here we are," said Clay. "Where do we go now?" Innocents abroad, they moved by instinct to what seemed familiar; the wider street, the English type of façade beckoning from beyond the hurly-burly of the waterfront. Roger took a look back at the harbour. Already it was nearly lost to sight behind the criss-crossing wheels and legs of the local population.

"We ought to plan what we're going to do," he said. "Keep together and remember the way back. And we don't want to spend too long in any one shop."

"Amen to that," said Clay under his breath.

"OK then," said Ruth. "Lead on."

He felt again that inner thrill of curiosity and "newness" that comes with the first steps into a totally strange place. And yet in a way he'd already been here. For years he'd fed his hungry mind on the stuff of empire; bejewelled Rajahs sitting in fairy tale palaces; perspiring Tommies in pipeclayed itchy splendour. Stomping round dusty squares and dreaming of Blighty. *Pukka sahibs* in their "Bombay bowlers", reposing with parasolled ladies and watching cricket under an alien sky. He knew this great bursting sub-continent that Kipling had loved and written of. But India had been independent for two years now, and Ceylon? That too he supposed. Above the Grand Oriental Hotel the Union Jack still flew, albeit as one of several flags.

Standing at the kerb, they waited for the traffic. "Remember," said Pauline, "any accidents – we don't stop. We keep going."

"And another thing," said Roger, "I've been warned not to tangle with any *Windrush* crew. They don't like us apparently."

There was a greater mix of people now, truly cosmopolitan. A kaleidoscope of linen suits, turbans and *dhotis*, or any of a dozen or so uniforms. They saw their first rickshaws, high-wheeled and bouncing behind the barefoot human engine that pulled them. Holding hands like four children on an outing, they crossed Church Street and turned the corner of the hotel. York Street. The English names abounded, a homely sound in the midst of so much that was strange. Cargill's was a red-brick edifice with a long colonnaded frontage. Inside, a thousand and one glittering articles, rich fabrics and ornate piles of expensive novelties vied for their attention. But it was the gems that drew them, the local industry. Johannesburg had its gold, Meissen its porcelain. And Colombo had precious stones. Spellbound, the two girls pored over the multi-coloured rows of cut and uncut mineral fragments under the glass-topped counters.

"Look at these," breathed Pauline. "These blue and white ones." Cunningly lit, the stones took the light and threw it back in a rainbow.

"Sapphires," said Roger, reading the little plates at the end of each line.

"Seen how much they want for them?" muttered Clay. The prices, all in rupees, were staggering. As if from nowhere, a dark, elegant man in pinstripes appeared and began a description of it all, taking out some stones to show them.

"We have this group, chrysoberyls, that includes alexandrites too of course – magnificent I'm sure you'll agree. See, they're olive-green by natural light, and then —" he switched on a lamp obviously there for the purpose "— they turn red in artificial light." They were suitably impressed. "Also they come in honey-yellow and apple-green."

"It's all too dear," said Clay.

Unstoppable, the man paraded his endless collection. Golden amethysts; star rubies giving six separate rays when moved in the light; garnets, aquamarines, moonstones and tourmalines; Zircons, spinels and the warm glow of topaz. The sight of this geological banquet set Ruth's taste-buds tingling.

"Oh but it must be cheaper than England. I mean, they dig them up here don't they? Here in Ceylon."

With startling calmness, Pauline asked,

"How much is two hundred rupees? Do we know the exchange rate?" Roger had had the foresight to find out earlier.

"Thirteen point three eight to the pound."

"Oh good," trilled Ruth. "That makes it crystal clear."

"Two weeks' pay for the likes of us," said Clay. About fourteen pounds sterling for a pretty pebble. More than they even had on them.

"What a shame," said Pauline. Ruth was alarmingly quiet. He put an arm round her and gave a cautious squeeze.

"Never mind. We'll find something." In her reply was a hint of the person he'd known before this uncomfortable morning.

"I would have liked just one stone. *Something* to get cut for a ring or a brooch, or *something*." Her voice sank to a little-girl whisper.

"I feel so rotten. What with last night and Mum not really well, and Dad forever going on about reaching Singapore." It was the two-way sensation he'd come to know; the sight of her peachy lips in the upturned face, his body responding instantly to the touch of hers. And the leaden hand of common sense that told him it was all a sham.

His body won. If there was *any* chance of visiting B Deck again; he turned to the others.

"Let's find a cheaper place. A shop this size is bound to charge more." The pinstripes heard this.

"Excuse me sir. Cargill's are not in the habit of over-pricing any of our goods."

"No, I didn't mean —"

"We have been trading here for many years. Our name is a byword for quality and value."

"Yes of course. I wasn't implying —"

"By all means visit other establishments if you wish. Most of them are quite reputable. But I must tell you they do not *all* conform to our high standards. There are some dealers who offer stones at a lower price, but these may well be flawed – not of the highest order of purity."

"Thank you," said Clay with feeling. "We'll bear that in mind." Emerging into the sun they continued up York Street. Clay was somewhat relieved. "I suggest we have a drink. Now we know. The whole thing's a racket. He gave us fair warning." But Ruth was not to be deterred.

"Yes – well. He would say that wouldn't he? So we'd buy his gems and not some other shop's." Disappointment over the stones weighed on everyone, with the possible exception of Clay. Roger meanwhile was keeping track of their route. They were heading back towards the waterfront. He was determined not to stray too far from it. Nothing was going to go wrong this time. They would find a bargain-basement type of place where he would buy some reasonably priced bauble for Ruth, have a drink and make their leisurely way back. Sometime before Singapore a final happy pilgrimage to B Deck would wind up the whole episode.

Back in Church Street they went left and discovered a public park. A short conference and they entered it, learning that it was called Gordon Gardens. Ruth said,

"I thought we were going to find another gem shop."

"We will, we will," Roger assured her. "If we'd turned right we'd be back at the quayside. We'll see what's at the end of this place." Walking on, they came to an imposing statue ringed by park benches. Roger read the inscription on the plinth: "Governor Barnes".

Clay said, "I bet he shopped at Cargill's." Pauline suddenly announced that she was footsore.

"Let's sit here for a while. It's only nine o'clock."

They rested there in the shadow of Governor Barnes and watched the few people going by on the gravel path. And as they watched, a man of about forty years of age turned off the path and approached them.

"Hullo there!" he called.

"Do we know him?" asked Clay. No-one did. The stranger wore white shoes, a pink shirt and an oatmeal-shade linen suit. A striped tie and a panama hat completed his outfit.

"Pardon me," he said raising the hat. "I knew I'd seen you before." His voice was cultured, fruity and very English. "Please don't think me rude, but I saw you all in Cargill's. Did you get what you were after?"

"No, we didn't," said Ruth. "Too expensive, for some, apparently."

The man chuckled. "Yes but you mustn't judge too harshly. Things are rather dear at Cargill's. Are you all from the *Caronia*?"

"*Empire Garvie*," said Pauline.

"Ah – the old *Krugersdorp* as it once was. Of course it's P&O that serves Colombo and all points east. I came here some years ago on one of their ships." There was something not right about him. Too smooth,

Roger thought. He felt a need to catch this man out if he could.

"Which one?" he asked.

"*Strathmore*." His father had once told him all about this ship.

"I know that one. Three funnel job."

"Er — no. When I last saw it there was only one. I believe the *Strathaird* once had three." Whether the man had noticed the attempt to trip him up he couldn't tell. But it was the right answer. Why couldn't he trust people? Had life aboard ship soured his judgement that much?

"Yes," the man continued. "I remember that voyage well. We missed the UK a lot at first, but Colombo is a wonderful place to live. My wife and I have been very happy here."

Ruth said, "We're on our way to Singapore with the army."

"Are you really? Well, I can't say I envy you, although Malaya does have its points." He laughed. "Plenty of rubber. With Ceylon of course it's tea and precious stones." By chance or design the favourite topic returned. "The gentleman in the fine shop was right about crooked dealers. But that doesn't mean you have to pay Cargill's prices. Not if you know where to go."

"Do you know?" asked Pauline. The man waved a modest hand.

"Oh, but I wouldn't presume to advise you on that."

"No of course not," said Clay. "Let's get on shall we? Have ourselves a drink."

But it was a losing battle. The girls had taken to the cultured expatriate who looked a lot like David Niven and raised his hat to ladies.

"No," said Ruth. "We ought to hear what he has to tell us."

So they listened as the man in the panama hat described how to find the bargain gems. Into Flagstaff Street beyond the park and then into Galle Buck Road. They must find the Star Hotel then turn left along Madras Road.

"I can recommend this shop. We've been there often. My wife swears by it, tells all our friends to go there."

Roger said, "Let's hope we can find it." Deep down he wanted to drop the whole idea. He saw disaster looming again.

"Oh you'll find it alright; up Madras Road on the left; R D Lachant. Don't be deterred by the look of the place. It's nothing fancy. But he'll give you a good deal on gems. And he'll take English money." They talked a while longer then the goodbyes and handshakes were exchanged. The man had greatly enjoyed chatting to them and was only too glad to be of help to fellow-Britons.

"Young people abroad for the first time 'ave to be careful. When you get 'ome spare a thought for us blokes soldierin' on in the far-flung corners." The hat rose again as he returned to the path.

"Now there's what you call a gentleman," said Pauline. Roger wondered why a gentleman, after sounding like the Duke of Windsor for ten minutes, would start losing aitches towards the end. Or why, when at first he'd been walking in one direction, would now walk off the other way. Again he told himself not to be so suspicious.

Galle Buck Road, when they found it, was another teeming corridor of trade, with a large number of barbers' shops. They couldn't miss the turn-off point. A crumbling confection of peeling pink shutters and patchy lemon stucco, the Star Hotel slumped on the corner like a dropped birthday cake. Over the open doorway a sign in the shape of a bottle carried the name in reflecting glass studs. They heard a piano and lusty voices.

"There's an old mill by the stream NELLIE DEAN!" The bawled words rolled out of the shadowed interior into the street and the bewildered ears of the local citizenry.

"I bet it's full of our people," said Clay.

"Or the *Windrush*," said Roger. "But not both." Madras Road was a quieter side-alley with only a few traders' stalls. As promised, here was the establishment of "R D Lachant. Purveyor of Fine Quality Precious Stones. Also Supplier of Travel Goods and Every Requisite for Comfortable Journeys". This information was scrawled in steadily diminishing letters on a board hung over a dark and narrow doorway.

Portly and balding Mr Lachant came out of a back room.

"Good morning ladies and gentlemen. What can I do for you?" Mr Lachant was a long way from his birthplace. His voice carried a harsh undertone, and a vaguely East European accent that suggested jackboots on wet cobblestones, or the growl of half-tracks in the night. Out came more stones in shallow wood trays. Here there was no subtle lighting, no dark velvet backing. But they shone just the same, winking on and off as passers-by obscured the doorway. Ruth held up one stone, and the needles of colour fell across her hand like spilled wine.

"Topaz," said Lachant. "One hundred and sixty rupees."

"That's around thirteen quid," said Clay the mathematician. "No different to Cargill's."

Lachant took back the stone. "I'm afraid topaz does not come cheap, perhaps if you shared the cost, between you?"

"What about me?" came a spirited protest from Pauline. "She gets her topaz – what do I get?"

"What ship are you on?" asked Lachant. They told him. "Ah, so you will be gone by five o'clock I believe. I'll tell you what I'll do. If the girls really want topaz and you boys are willing to pay a reasonable figure I can offer you something really special. Let me show you." Roger noticed how soon they had been demoted from ladies and gentlemen. He would have liked to get her a stone. The truth had been obvious for some time now; sex for gifts. It had been costly but he wasn't too aggrieved by it. They each got what they craved. And surely better (and healthier) than following the sordid paths of Bill and Co. Coldly appraised, he'd spent more entertaining Isobel for less result.

Lachant produced another selection.

"This is what is known as smoky topaz. Rather less expensive because it is found nearer the surface, easier to extract. As you can see it has its own unique quality. Many people prefer this to the other kind." Certainly the stones had charm. Faint reddish-brown tints could be seen through the uncut surface, a promise of splendour to come when cut and polished. And as they gazed at them Ruth's left hand found its way round Roger's waist and under his shirt. He was reminded of the time she'd fingered his pie-bald tan. And he underwent the same reaction. Especially when she reached round to tickle his stomach. With her other hand she picked up one of the stones and slowly rotated it.

"That's so lovely," she murmured. "It would be a memento of us I could always keep." The left hand continued exploring. "Really fine isn't it Roger? Too good to miss wouldn't you say?"

"Yes," he replied, trying to steady his voice. "And even better after a little work. A good rubbing to bring out the best of it." He could almost smell the Medoline. "What's your price?" he asked Lachant and the fingers stopped. Four pairs of ears awaited the reply.

"One hundred." His hopes plummeted. The fingers withdrew. Clay, who may or may not have had a similar vamping from Pauline, seemed ready to haggle. For haggle they must.

"Mr Lachant," Clay began. "We came to you because we were told you didn't overcharge; now a hundred rupees is seven pound ten. More than any of us have with us. It's a week's wages. We can't pay that for one stone. And we need two. So unless you can come down quite a bit we must walk out of here and you've lost a sale." It was a masterly speech. Lachant carefully marshalled his stones, lining them up in files of three like twinkling toy soldiers.

"So make me an offer,"

Roger said "We'll have to get the stones cut." Lachant shook his head.

"You won't get that done anywhere by five o'clock. Where is your next port of call – Singapore? There are places there to get it done quite cheaply." The wrangle began, the initial price soon forgotten, being only the opening shot. Before long they were swinging between sixty and forty per stone, till the obvious figure of fifty was proposed.

"What do you say Roger?" asked Clay. His gaze strayed to the open doorway. Across the street two workmen were placing a bamboo ladder against a wall, a narrow, bouncy type of ladder. "Yes OK, fifty rupees." He and Clay paid out four pounds each and the two stones were each packed into a tiny box lined with cotton-wool.

"Right, that's that," said Clay as they passed down Madras Road and back among the Galle Buck hairdressers. Ruth said little. As at Aden, Pauline at least made a show of appreciation, linking arms with Clay and talking about the gems. Smoky topaz; having an adjective in front gave it extra appeal. Like dusty-pink or shot-silk.

"I'm hungry," said Ruth. What about her monster hangover? Her cement-mixer tummy?

"Oh I'm a little better now." Four quid better, he thought and hated the way they'd become. His own fault he knew. Building it up into something it could never be. "I had no breakfast," she added. At the end of Galle Buck Road they found a café where they could sit at a window and see the waterfront reassuringly close by and beyond that the waiting trio of ships. At a nearby table a party of tourists chattered away. Casually dressed, but smart. Now and then they glanced over at the four by the window, those young people obviously from one of the troopers sharing the harbour with the *Caronia*.

Only Ruth wanted food. Omelette, tomatoes and toast with Cooper's Marmalade. A large pot of tea shared by all and a bill that wasn't. Roger did the honours. He watched her tucking in, saw her fork with its goodly portion of tomato enter her mouth and emerge clean as her lips came together in a puckering motion as they had in their first open-eyed kiss. God she even ate sexily. Not for the first time that day he thought of Gina Morrell. He wondered how she kissed.

"Roger!" exclaimed Clay. "Wake up. I said you pour the tea, I've put the milk in." They could have been in England; the spotless cloth, the bone china; an aspidistra-type plant in a brass urn by the window. And the two young Englishwomen in their contrasting hats. Pauline turning to peer across the harbour, Ruth with one brown arm draped over the chair-back waiting for her tea to be poured.

"Let's have another look at our gems," said Clay. The stones were laid out on the table. Maybe it was the proximity of gleaming cutlery, or the whiteness of the cloth, but it seemed to Roger some of their inner fire was gone. The sugar-bowl was empty.

"I'll borrow theirs," said Clay. They saw him approach the other table, talk for a while and return with the sugar.

"They wanted to know what ship we're on," Ruth said. "Why does *everyone* we meet ask us that?" Roger picked up the sugar-cubes with the silver tongs. A genteel touch after the crew mess free-for-all.

"There's three British ships in. The town's full of us." Outside the window a straggle of *Garvie* crewmen passed by and he saw Bill among them. Could Martin be far away? No, there he was trotting along behind. The endless talk of "bag-offs" now seemed to have been empty boasting; to impress him or frighten the life out of him. But there were other, more notorious places yet to be visited.

"Someone's coming over," said Pauline. "One of the posh tourists." The man was grey-haired and ruddy-faced.

"I understand you are all from the *Garvie*."

"That's right," said Roger. "And you're from the *Caronia* I expect."

"Yes. We're leaving first thing in the morning for Australia then across to Los Angeles. But what I came over to see you for was this. I've got a nephew on your ship. Young chap name of Tony Davis, works in the galley as an assistant fish-cook. Do you know him? You are in the crew?"

"Yes," Clay replied. "Afraid we don't know any fish-cooks though, not by name."

"Oh sorry. Bit of a cheek to ask really. Only we tried to see him and they wouldn't let us on. Troopship you see."

"We could find him in the galley," said Roger.

"Well, if you could get word to him. Tell him we're here in Colombo, Uncle Harry and Aunt Sophie. If there's time they might let him on the *Caronia*. Would you mind?"

"No, not at all. Glad to oblige."

"Thanks a lot." The man noticed the gems. "I see you've been shopping. What are they, if you don't mind me asking?"

"Topaz," said Ruth. "We went all over the place for them."

"Four pound each, they were," said Clay. "They were a hundred rupees each at first but we beat 'em down to fifty. Easy when you know how."

"Good for you. How far are you going?"

"Japan," said Roger with some satisfaction. It sounded more exotic that Los Angeles.

"Really, Japan! Sounds exciting. Thanks again. Nice meeting you all. Have a safe trip."

Back with his own party, they saw him telling what had transpired. His wife beamed across at them. Pauline said,

"I think we've made Aunt Sophie happy."

Ruth was growing restive. It was agreed they'd seen enough of Colombo. Twenty yards away the ship's motor-launch lay at the quay wall, filling up with passengers. All they had to do was walk over to it. No panic this time. It is possible Roger believed the gods were smiling down on him from some Sinhalese heaven. Or perhaps these things are not pre-ordained at all but really are dictated solely by chance. If they had not run out of sugar; if nephew Tony had plied his trade on the *Windrush* instead; even if they'd left the café by a route that didn't pass the *Caronia* table. They were almost outside when Uncle Harry called them over and introduced them to a man in his party.

"Mr Emerson here is very interested in your gemstones. Would you mind if he saw them?"

Mr Emerson did not have the appearance of a man on holiday. Pasty-faced, he wore a bow-tie, "cruel" glasses and a suit of Bible-black. They all waited while he examined the stones.

"Mr Emerson is something of an expert," said Uncle Harry. "Knows all about gems he does; runs a shop in Eastbourne." Emerson tightened his thin lips at being said to "run a shop". He preferred to think of himself as the proprietor and managing director of a select retail establishment. Now he put down the stones and removed his glasses.

"My reason for asking to see them was basically curiosity—why topaz was being offered at such a relatively low price."

"They're a bargain then," said Roger.

"They would be if they were topaz." He felt the room closing in on him. *Please no. B Deck. One more visit to B Deck, please.*

"They are topaz," he said. "It was a recommended dealer we saw. The man told us. They're not the usual kind. These are smoky topaz. That's why they're cheaper." Emerson polished his glasses, held them up to the light, gave another rub and finally put them on using only his finger-tips. Roger decided that he hated everything about Mr Emerson.

"There is no such thing as smoky topaz. It's a very common trick. What we have here is low-grade quartz." Aunt Sophie was upset.

"Oh, what a shame. How awful for you after all your searching. Goes to show you can never be too careful. I've always said —"

"So what *are* they worth?" said Clay. The Eastbourne Expert put the stones back in their cute little boxes and handed them over.

"In sterling, about seven-and-six. That's if they can be safely cut, which I doubt." They made their farewells. A grim silence gripped each of them till they were out on the street. Here the storm broke.

"Seven-and-six!" Ruth's face contorted into an unlovely travesty of the one he knew. "Fine travellers you turned out to be, you *and* Clay. All that bargaining — and — and traipsing about and you pay four quid apiece for — a — a — damn bit of — I don't know what, worth seven-and-six!" True to form, she was devastated at not having the coveted topaz and quite unmoved by his own loss.

"I'm sorry," he said, and was amazed to find himself apologizing, when he was as much a victim of the fraud. Pauline took it a touch better.

"It's not really their fault."

Clay stood holding the stones. "Time's getting on. Are we going back to that place or not?"

But Ruth was making a meal of it. "I wasn't all that keen on coming ashore today, the way I felt. Then I thought if I have to endure it I would —" It seemed she was about to say "make it worth my while" but even Ruth saw this wouldn't go down well "— I would maybe look for something special. I really fancied a nice stone, something that might fetch a bit more in the future." So much for it being a "memento of us", he thought; and the last of his delusions blew away. Under the rampant sex-appeal she was utterly selfish. And yet was he really any better? Any less of a hypocrite?

"Let's go and get our money back," said Clay.

"Then what?" snapped Ruth. "Run about after gems again? There won't be time now if you've both got to be back."

"I'm inclined to forget it," said Pauline. "Put it down to experience."

"Never mind experience," said Clay. "I want our money back. And if I ever meet that smarmy gent in the park again —"

"I didn't really trust him," said Roger.

Ruth exploded. "Oh you didn't really trust him. Yet you went along with him and ended up being done. Very clever. With all your book-reading and knowing all about the empire and stuff you still get taken in. What a twerp!" Her voice was gratingly shrill, her mouth pouting in and out like a spoiled child's. He felt actually repelled. This he knew was the end of it. Whatever they'd had was gone, borne away on the same waterfront breeze that carried the sweet smell of sandalwood and coriander. Patiently he pointed out that *she* had insisted on following the park man's advice.

"And don't forget you fell in love with those stones, begged me to get one."

But Roger was learning lessons, almost daily. To some the idea of shared blame is quite foreign. To Ruth it was positively Martian. Quite cynically, she and Pauline had decided to dump the two men well before Singapore, having first got them to spend money at the preceding ports. But Roger and Clay had proved not to be the free-spenders of legend. Not quite the tip-laden imitation Yanks who came down gangways at Southampton looking for girls to spoil. And now they were going back to the ship with nothing. After last night! It was somebody's fault, and certainly not Ruth's. She grumbled on.

"We should have walked around Cargills' a bit more. Got something decent instead of going to back-alley places. That man in Cargill's told us about cheap stones. Well, he was right. These are not of the 'first order of purity' are they?"

His control went at last. "No. But neither are you." The Bergman hat tipped forward, hiding her face. The words had stunned him as much as her. Never in his life had he insulted a female, and in such a way. Slowly she looked up.

"Go and get your sodding money back. I'm going on the ship." Turning on her heel she walked off.

"Anyway, thanks for the tea," said Pauline drily and followed her.

"That's that," said Clay calmly. "I said it would be over in Colombo didn't I? And we've missed the boat. Now we've all got to wait till it comes back. That'll be nice." So they stood there on the noisy quayside, each hugging an aching resentment at the morning's outcome. Talk was as laboured as it was pointless. The four-cornered affair was over, as they had known it would be. But not like this! Robbed of both his money and what it might have won for him, Roger now had a visit from the perky little spirit of rebellion that now and again fired him.

"Clay, give me those stones. I'm going back to Madras Road. Stay here and see the girls on board." He left them staring, swiftly crossed Church Street and hurried to Cargill's, dodging the taxis and rickshaws as if he'd lived there all his life. A quick check to make sure of his case. The pinstripes man took one disdainful look.

"Quartz. Five and a half rupees. Maybe six. Aren't you the gentleman who was in here earlier?" But Roger had gone. Back to Gordon Gardens, striding like a man possessed through the scented shadows, past the banks of oleander, the statue and the circle of seats where the whole deception had begun. No wonder everyone asked what ship they were on. The best dupes are those soon safely out of the way. And it was obvious now why they were told to postpone the cutting work.

At the Star Hotel the piano still pumped out old favourites. Nearing the entrance, a short figure lurched across the road and cannoned blindly into him. A pair of beery eyes focused up at him.

"Why don't you look where you're goin' pal?"

He said "Sorry" and tried to walk on.

"Just a fuggin' minute." Two hands grabbed his clothing and swung him round to face his diminutive challenger. "Wha' ship you from?" That *question* again! And never had the answer been so important. His powers of observation heightened by danger, he saw clearly every detail of the man before him; the bull-neck, the sweat-darkened collar of the red shirt, and the obligatory tattoos on each arm. And he noticed too a couple of paper slips peeping from a breast pocket. They could have been anything. Raffle tickets, laundry labels? The lettering on one was partly obscured by the other. All he could see was "IRE". And beneath that "USH". It was enough to save him.

"I'm off the *Empire Windrush*." His back received a pat that rattled his teeth.

"OK pal, as long as you're not one of them bastards off the *Garvie*." The man released a Richter-scale burp and stumbled into the hotel. Roger hastened up Madras Road, realizing belatedly he could have simply said *Caronia*. The shop was quiet. Behind the counter this time stood a young Sinhalese woman, dark eyes gleaming in a face of extraordinary beauty.

"These stones," he said, putting them down before her. "We were told they were topaz. They're not. We'd like our money returned."

"I will fetch Mr Lachant." She vanished behind a curtain. Voices murmured and she returned. At another time her sing-sing accent would have delighted him. "Mr Lachant cannot see you now. Can you be coming back later?"

"No I'm afraid I can't. And he knows that. Please tell him I simply want to return the stones and he can give the eight pounds back. That will be the end of it."

Back she went. The voices rumbled on. It sounded as if two men were back there. Unwillingly he looked at this watch. 10.30. He had to be back at twelve. They only had to stall him long enough and he'd have to concede defeat. Scurry back to the ship as he seemed fated to do at every port. Again she returned alone.

"Mr Lachant sees no point in discussing it. You wanted the stones and the price was agreed on. The transaction is final." He saw himself back at the quay, lamely admitting he'd not even spoken to Lachant. And he thought of the hundreds of greasy plates he'd washed to earn his miserable four pounds. Quite calmly, but quaking inside, he skirted the counter and drew back the curtain. Lachant and a companion were at a table engrossed in some eastern board game with a great many small counters. The other player was no stranger. The pink shirt, jacket and tie were gone, but the man in the grimy vest had retained his panama hat, now pushed to the back of his head. Lachant jumped up.

"What you do here?" In his agitation his grasp of English began to slip. "To come in here you have no right."

"It was quartz you sold us."

"No, is topaz. You leave now. I wish no trouble."

"I want the eight pounds back," insisted Roger doggedly. Lachant hustled him out to the front of the counter again.

"Is topaz. Please to go, otherwise much trouble." Somewhere in the back he heard a door slam. The gentleman of the park had made a tactical retreat.

"No. Here are the stones. Eight pounds please."

Lachant drew the woman aside and whispered an instruction. She slipped out of the street door. All smiles now, Lachant took out the tray of "smoky topaz".

"Please you take another stone. No charge. You have three for price of two." Roger was losing the game. Time was against him.

"No I'm sorry. I insist you pay me back. This is only quartz. Two experts have said so." The woman returned, gave Lachant a nod and passed behind the curtain. The narrow shop suddenly became crowded. Three men had entered, and he knew fear again.

Dacoits, Thugs, Badmashes, the Indian words sprang into his mind from the books he'd soaked up all his life. Probably they were none of these, but no less menacing. They were local men, quite young with unkempt hair and shabby clothes; drifters of the kind to be found in any large city. Lachant put away the tray and pushed Roger's two boxes towards him.

"Take your stones and leave right now. These friends of mine do not like the way you have accused me. They are of a mind to punish you." Inwardly raging, Roger picked up his wretched stones.

"I will go to the police," he said, not even believing it himself.

"Then you will miss your ship. The law in Ceylon moves very slowly." They all grinned at him then, eyes and teeth gleaming whitely in the dim light.

Only as he went back along Madras Road did he realise he was trembling from head to foot. He'd lost Ruth, been humiliated, physically threatened and finally seen off the premises by a quartet of smirking villains. And he'd paid four pounds to bring all this about. No, it had not been a good morning for the Lodger. And it wasn't over yet. The three street ruffians were following him. Passing a trader's stall one of them picked up a thick length of bamboo. Clearly they had expected a spot of mayhem, a little assault and battery to enliven the day. His early surrender had robbed them of this. He stuffed the stones into his pocket and speeded up; so did they. The quick walk became a trot.

The Star Hotel was near. An obvious refuge, but he could be trapped in there; staring at the clock while they laid siege. Fortunately, his pursuers were somewhat inept at pursuing. The one with the bamboo club tripped over it and fell, bringing down the others. His lead increased slightly while they picked themselves up and resumed the chase, now spurred on by the embarrassing loss of face. And then a number of men spilled out of the hotel, having among them the back-slapping *Windrush* man of recent memory. This group milled about for a second or two and began to pass from sight round the corner. A wild idea seized him. Only days ago he'd thought himself above this sort of thing.

Cupping his hands to his mouth he bawled, "*Empire Windrush* BUNDLE!" and gestured despairingly at his pursuers. The hotel men, five in number, caught on quickly and strode towards him. Faced with an abrupt change of odds, his would-be assailants decided the mayhem could await a better time. The bamboo was half-heartedly thrown and they took off, back up the alley as fast as they'd come down it. The *Windrush* men gathered around Roger, led incongruously by the red-shirted one who was shorter than any of them. Somebody retrieved the bamboo club.

"What's up pal? Those guys after you?"

"Yes but it's alright now. You scared them off. Thanks."

"Come on, let's get 'em," said Red Shirt, who seemed to have sobered up at the promise of combat.

"I doubt if you'll catch them now," said Roger, rather alarmed at what he'd started.

"I say they're asking for it," said the one with the bamboo. "Three of them against one of our people? They're not getting away with that, come on!" Roger, after some hesitation followed. The degree of protection he now had was almost embarrassing especially as he was getting it under false pretences. Perhaps he could sneak away once his private army was fully engaged. Up ahead he saw the five casting about like foxhounds on the scent. The few stallholders took scant notice of them, merely clutching their wares and flimsy stalls together in case they were sent flying. When it was apparent the foe had vanished, Roger realised he had a chance to retrieve something from the wreckage of the morning. The shop was nearby, and he was now the one with friends, albeit very temporary ones. Disconsolate, the *Windrush* detachment returned.

"Lost them," said one. "Why were they after you anyway?"

He showed them the stones. "Had an argument in that shop. I got done over these things. Now his mates are away I might get my money back if he saw you chasing them. Thanks again." The bamboo man tapped the club thoughtfully against his thigh.

"Done you did they? Can't allow that can we lads?" Shuffling feet and a murmur of assent. Pack-like, they'd caught the scent of trouble again, and he regretted telling them so much. Someone said,

"Right that's it. Let's get your money back. We'll come in with you." This again was not quite what he'd intended. They were supposed to be a sort of vague background presence Lachant would think he could whistle up when required. He hadn't meant to march into the place at the head of his own Praetorian Guard.

Summoned by the frightened young woman, Mr Lachant paled at the sight of six men lined up at his counter, all scowling and one with a blunt instrument.

"Mr Lachant," said Roger. "These are my friends. Yours are gone." The much-travelled stones came out for the last time. "Two lumps of quartz for you, eight pounds for me." There was no argument. Muttering about a "terrible mistake", the man took back the stones and gave him the notes passed over so long ago. Red Shirt, deprived of his battle, shook a fist at Lachant.

"And don't you try it again pal. Not with the *Windrush*. We take care of our own we do." The woman cowered behind her employer, and Roger deplored what they were doing. The whole thing was uglier than he wished. Constantly appalled at his countrymen's overseas conduct, today he'd been part of it himself.

As they were leaving Lachant with some nerve said, "I do hope you find what you're after sir. Perhaps at Singapore? Your next port of call?" From habit he gave a polite response.

"Yes, thank you. I'll try again when we get there." He realised his error when the first man stopped in the doorway and the others bumped together like freight wagons.

"Singapore?" said one. "What are you talking about? It's Aden next."

"Yeah well. The jerk don't know that, I suppose. I was just kidding him along. Let's get out of here." They filed out of the narrow entrance and down the road, Roger contriving to gradually drop back so that the gap between them increased.

As the truth dawned, the strung-out line of men halted. Red Shirt looked back at him.

"He's not one of our blokes at all, he's off the bloody *Empire Garvie*!" Roger turned and fled. Back up this wretched back-alley he was clearly doomed never to leave. But there was nowhere to go.

Nowhere that might not become a trap, except Lachant's. That had a back door, he'd heard it slam. For the fourth time that day he entered the gloomy little shop. The woman gave a cry of alarm.

"Sorry, it's alright," he said. "Only taking a short cut. Excuse me." At the curtain he collided with Lachant, too startled to do more than gape as he hurtled through. In his haste he bumped against the unfinished board game, still awaiting the return of Lachant's partner. It didn't fall, but the knock was so slight and quick that inertia kept the counters still as the board moved under them. Apparently undisturbed, every piece was in fact now on a different square. It gave him huge satisfaction to think of the two men trying to make sense of it.

The rear door led to a dusty courtyard with a bicycle against a high wall. There was no other exit. "David Niven" must have stayed here till he'd gone then slipped out the front. Voices from the shop drove him on. Standing on the bike's cross-bar he got one leg on the top of the wall and pulled himself up. The bike fell over with a clatter. On the other side was a wide thoroughfare he didn't recognise. Immediately below, hard against the wall, a long row of trestle tables carried an assortment of vegetables and spices. The nearest stall's owner and a number of customers watched him expectantly. He brought his other leg over and indicated he wished very much to be on their side of the wall. After a debate they pulled one of the tables away. Roger dropped to the ground, falling against the vegetables as he did so.

"Thank you. Sorry about the inconvenience. Would you mind telling me the name of this street?" They didn't at first understand. But he thought – why should they understand anything about the English? They consider us all mad. When we're not boozing we're shouting the odds and running up and down streets at the hottest time of day. As yet no heads had appeared at the top of the wall. A few inquiries and he learned he was in Chandler Street. Mingling with shoppers, he found a kiosk where he bought matches and a packet of Camel cigarettes. Well he wasn't a boozer, a brawler or a gambler. One vice out of four wasn't bad going, given his current way of life. He'd sponged off Clay long enough and the odd cigarette did calm him. The pound note did not faze the man for a second.

"I give you change in rupees OK?" The handful of notes and coins added up to about twelve and a half rupees. It looked a lot.

Chapter 8

Camels were American, he knew that now. Not Egyptian, despite the picture on the pack. He lit one and walked on. Up ahead was another seedy bar with another disorderly collection of seamen outside. No, he wasn't going through that again. How did one hire a rickshaw? They didn't have For Hire signs and with the canopy up you couldn't readily see if anyone was in the back. He put out a hand and one stopped. The vehicle resembled a large pram with only two, admittedly large, wheels. Between the shafts was a bony, hairless man who seemed too old for the task. Quite small, he wore overlong shorts and a singlet that was also too big for him. Lowering the shafts to the road, he waved a hand at the rickshaw and flashed a smile, showing such an array of gold teeth the rest of his face seemed to disappear.

"Where you want sir?"

"The waterfront please, I want the *Garvie* boat." He climbed in and settled on the padded seat. His first sensation was one of alarm. When the man picked up the shafts the rickshaw abruptly tilted back like a ducking-stool, giving him a sudden view of the sky and his own feet.

"How much will it be?" he asked.

"Not worry sir. Not cost much. I take you. Be OK sir." They rolled along smoothly enough, now and then porpoising over a rough patch, and the man keeping up a steady jog-trot with his loose singlet ballooning out in the slipstream.

There is something about a rickshaw. In no other mode of transport is the divide between master and lackey so marked. The man between the shafts, back bent and feet pattering, is the very essence of servitude, while his fare, lounging far back in the canted-up carriage, has to look down his nose just to see where they are going. Turning a corner, he recognised Gordon Gardens and caught a sight of Governor Barnes peering through the trees. Not long now.

The awful row with Ruth came back to him. One blessing, it had not been observed by Bill or Martin. His newly-minted personality was undamaged, saving him from a repeat of those terrible early days. His non-return to B Deck he would cover with some face-saving story.

"She's not well, nervous about Singapore." That was the truth anyway.

His intention in taking the rickshaw had been to save time and avoid meeting any hostile elements – of whatever race. Somewhere near the end he would have stopped and walked the rest of the way. But he hadn't paid attention. They suddenly rounded a corner and pulled up with a grand flourish right in front of the *Garvie* crowd on the quayside including Bill, Martin and in mauve shirt and lime-green slacks, Penny. There was no immediate sign of his own party.

"Vada!" shrilled Penny. "Get him if you please! Lord Muck has arrived. It's that silly homi who likes to say he's *normal*." Bill's comments were almost benign.

"Where you been this time? Anybody else just goes ashore, has a few bevvies, enjoys himself and comes back. Not you. You stay sober, don't do anything and still turn up late looking a total fuggin' mess."

"Have you been stabbed?" asked Martin oddly. Somebody touched his arm. The rickshaw man smiled his Fort Knox smile and asked for two rupees. Roger gave him three and watched the curious vehicle bounce away into the traffic. The little man with the gilded grin was the most honest and likeable character he'd met in Colombo.

He found them sitting on a low parapet at the rear of the group. Clay sounded relieved.

"Roger, there you are at last." They had missed the boat more than once already, Clay persuading the girls to wait.

"What a state you're in," said Pauline. Now he discovered the reason for Martin's strange question. During his escape from the courtyard he'd not only picked up dust on his knees and elbows but another more dramatic memento. His fall against the trader's table had caused something to be squashed against his chest. Something very juicy and very red that left an ominous stain over his heart.

"It's a long story," he said. "I've been threatened, chased by a grand total of eight multi-national bully-boys and climbed a seven-foot wall. Here's your four quid back."

The atmosphere was still frosty. They heard how he'd got the money, and the "bloodstain". None of this would repair the rift with Ruth, he knew that. Hardly to be expected after his shattering remark to her. The best thing was to call it quits. They'd had some good moments, exchanged joys and insults with the same degree of warmth. Experience? Of course it was. And he wasn't halfway into the voyage yet. But he hoped they might part amicably. Sitting beside her he made a start.

"Ruth, what I said to you earlier —" Her head turned slowly to face him. Governor Barnes had shown more recognition. "I shouldn't have said it. Sorry." Somebody was watching them.

"So this is the girlfriend is it?" Across the harbour the launch was returning, a welcome sight.

"Yes, this is Ruth Newbury. Ruth – Bill and Martin, my shipmates." The bold, semi-formal introduction caught them out, as did the quaint term "shipmates".

"Pleased to — er — meet you," said Bill. Ruth favoured them with a smile, the first seen for a long while. He felt a jealous twinge, quite forgetting he'd just written the whole thing off.

"I hope Roger's been treating you right," said Bill. "You know he's a devil on the quiet. Got a bit of — got a girl in every port he has — like they say." This was so obviously untrue of Roger she was amused, widening the smile into the one he knew. She took off the Bergman hat, smoothed her glowing hair and replaced the hat at a slight angle, affecting not to notice the attention of the four men, or Pauline's amusement. There was no doubt she loved that hat.

With a nudge to Martin, Bill blundered on. "We all wondered what a girl saw in him, a pretty thing like you. No oil-painting Roger, is he?"

"Oh, I don't know. Some might say he was *fairly* good-looking." This surprised everyone, most of all Roger. Was that all it took, an apology and a thrilling account of his derring-do in the back-alleys of Colombo? He was back in favour. Hitherto silent, now Martin decided it was time he said something so witty she would turn those blue eyes on *him*.

"Good-looking you say? Who? Roger? You might think so darlin'. But what's underneath, that's what counts. There's an old saying. Beauty only goes skin-deep." Martin got his first and only blue stare.

"So who peeled you?" Roger didn't join in the guffawing chorus that greeted this. Clay took him aside.

"Listen. We met Gina Morrell. She did come ashore after all, took the earlier boat back. Sounded worried when we told her where you were."

"How did Ruth react to that?"

"Dunno. Who can tell with Ruth, the way she's been all morning? And don't forget what you said to her; what you more or less called her."

The launch arrived. "I've apologised for that. It's alright now. I'm in her good books again." Settling into the boat it did seem that all was forgiven. Today's fiasco had not really been his fault. He'd seen suitably contrite over his remark, even though she'd goaded him into making it. Added to that she'd pronounced him good-looking before witnesses. Her thug-defying, wall-scaling hero perhaps. Thus he took the fatal third step. From despair to hope to conceit. They were about halfway across the harbour when his world fell apart again.

On this occasion they sat opposite each other and some distance from the others. It was amusing about Gina; just as well though she wasn't in the boat with them. Facing forward everything in sight pleased him; his girl smiling at him from under her prized hat. To make it perfect she ought to be trailing a delicate hand over the side, like girls did in punts. The water sparkled and hissed as they sped along, and up ahead the three ships waited for their respective boats to come alongside. The moment seemed suspended in time. As if a memory was being formed. It was. The last one before the mould was smashed.

"Roger," she said, leaning forward confidentially. He came closer too. Studying his face she spoke calmly. "I don't want to see you anymore." He felt the breeze still on his cheeks, heard the slap of water against the side and the murmur of voices around them. Everything seemed the same, yet suddenly nothing was.

"Why?" he heard himself say. "Was it what I said?" She shrugged and leaned back on the gunwale, watching as they passed the *Empire Windrush*.

"Yes, that. And partly —" He could see she was hunting for more reasons. It occurred to him now that the apparent thawing had been a ruse so that the brush-off when it came was more savage.

"Look, I said I was sorry and I am. And I'm sorry you never got your topaz. But I got you other things, didn't I?" Too late he noticed a pleading note that he never meant to be there. She rounded on him.

"Oh yeah? Only 'cos of what you hoped to get out of it."

"If that's true then it goes for both of us. OK, if you say it's over, it's over. I hope everything's alright for you in Singapore and your parents." His easy acceptance annoyed her. Ruth's "affairs" were not always to her liking or as gainful as expected. This could lead her to take brutal pleasure in the act of rejection and it showed.

"Yes well. I can tell you, you got more out of it than I did." She was no longer whispering. "And you'll be alright anyway. You got Gina." This did shake him.

"Gina, Mrs Morrell? What about her?"

"You know damn well. We met her just now. Oh, she was *very* concerned about you. It was her cabin you went to that first night wasn't it? When she came on to you, opening her window you called it and you've been back there since."

"No, not true." He rather wished it was. "I have *not* been back. And I did open her porthole, had to unscrew the clamps."

"Liar! She's got – what do they call it – an inside cabin. I've been there and seen it that day in Port Said. There is *no* porthole. It wasn't *unscrewing* she wanted you for. And that party last night. Both of you pretending you'd never met. What a fool I was not to catch on sooner. How did she know you were twenty unless you'd met before and told her?"

They were nearing the ship. His head ached with his ever-changing fortunes, trying to follow her words against the hiss of the wind and babble of other voices. And he still wondered how the same cabin could be both with and without a porthole.

Another boat overtook theirs, a *Caronia* launch as green as the water she rode and going at a fair rate of knots. Now as the *Garvie* towered over them he tried to placate her before they parted for good.

"Listen Ruth, I only went along with her game at the party because she seemed to want to. Maybe she wanted to spare your feelings." It wasn't the wisest way to put it.

"Roger I'm fed up with you, and Clay and Colombo; and going about in *boats*." With a toss of her head she stood up.

"No standing please," ordered the man at the helm. Ruth, however, was feeling dramatic.

"I want to be the first off this boat. I can't wait to get off the thing." Having made this pronouncement she placed a foot on the starboard gunwale and stood erect with folded arms. Cleopatra at Luxor must have waited thus to alight from her golden barge. But as they approached the platform something else arrived first. The bow-wave set up by the *Caronia's* speeding launch. It wasn't much, but enough. A smooth undulation rippled unseen beneath their own boat, inducing a brief, drunken see-saw. No Cleopatra, Ruth jack-knifed, straightened up and flailed the air. The boatman stared, and the sailor on the platform, and everyone else.

Ruth was indeed first off the boat. She entered Colombo harbour bottom first, her arms and legs coming together in the splash as if she were trying to touch her toes as she went in. Several people began to shout at once. The boat drifted. Nobody seemed inclined to jump in after her.

"Stay where you are all of you," yelled the boatman. "I'll bring us in again. Don't worry, we'll get her out." She was a strong swimmer. A few easy strokes took her back to the boat. Here she trod water, glaring at them while her skirt floated up and formed a flat green disc around her. With her livid face in the centre she resembled an irate water-lily. Behind her the Bergman hat surfaced and drifted sadly away.

"Come on then," she bawled. "Get me out if you're going to!" Several hands reached down to her, one of them Roger's which she pushed away, an action seen and relished by Bill. Trying to haul her aboard was difficult. The gunwale was high. Fingers slipped on wet limbs. And the task was not rendered any easier by the stream of invective she felt obliged to send upward each time they failed. The boatman meanwhile, by judicious work with throttle and rudder, had got the boat closer to the ship. This gave Ruth, who by this time was plainly in no danger of drowning, a simpler option.

"Over here," called the platform sailor. "Swim over here." Turning, she struck out for the ship, straight as a torpedo. High above at the ship's rail a growing number of spectators shouted encouragement. At the gangway platform the sailor stooped and began to heave her out. Suddenly she shrieked, so startling the man he lost his grip. Ruth renewed her acquaintance with the harbour, the splash this time getting a ribald cheer from the audience. It was her skirt. Now water-logged and heavy, it had begun to come off as she came up. Ruth Newbury, whatever else she may have been, was not one for a public striptease. Particularly when soaked to the skin. There now followed the spectacle of her treading water again while clawing under the surface to get the wayward skirt back where it belonged, all the while watched avidly by the personnel of both ship and boat.

When she was finally pulled out she elbowed the sailor aside and flew up the steps pursued by applause and whistling.

This very public finale to their Colombo visit left Roger shaken. Thank God she'd been able to swim. Clay and Pauline were beside him. Still wearing her straw hat and with her Aden trinkets on show, Pauline was taking Ruth's side.

"Her dad'll go berserk when he hears about this. She'll blame you for it Roger. Too upset to think, she was. First you give her a stone which turns out to be junk. Then you call her — you know what you called her." He didn't want to argue with Pauline or anyone else. Whatever he did, whatever fine intentions he had it was obvious some scrape or disaster was going to befall him at every port. On D Deck square Pauline bade them a crisp farewell and set off after Ruth, following a trail of wet footprints up the main staircase.

"Quite a morning," said Roger. Clay shrugged.

"I got the elbow too, before you did in fact, while we were waiting for you. They've done alright from us. Gold-diggers both of 'em." Martin passed them without a word. Bill came up the gangway next and gave them his views.

"Real sorry about your girl Roger." His beaming face belied this. "Heard the two of you fighting before she fell in. Shame. Nice piece of stuff too. I bet she's mad at losing that hat." Next aboard was Penny.

"What a bold one you are! Trolling about town in a rickshaw, while your tart hangs around with rough sailors; then you come back and pick a fight with her. Perhaps you're not cut out for girls. Perhaps you're not as 'normal' as you like to boast. Could be you're secretly queer, are you?" Batten's joke came handily to mind.

"No I'm not. My husband is." Penny gave a squawk of delight.

"Ooh go and jump in the knife-box. You're too sharp for me." They watched him tripping lightly down the corridor.

"Makes you wonder don't it?" said Clay. "How we ever built the empire."

The entire lunch period was a prolonged post-mortem on the story of the gems and his shattered affair with the erratic, and indeed aquatic, Ruth Newbury.

"Never mind my son," said Pat. "At least you're getting korey. We're still waiting for Singapore and Hong Kong."

Belatedly he remembered he had a promise to keep. Roger always found the galley fascinating. Placed between the first and second class saloons, it was double-ended, with long "presses" or heated counters running athwartships. Stewards queued here to pile their trays with food passed over to them. The cooks stood on duckboards which added five inches or so to their height, increasing the somewhat menacing look already bestowed by their tall hats. The non-stop noise, the bright utensils and wicked carving-knives wielded by scowling figures in starchy white gave the place an air of some mad surgical hospital in a constant state of emergency.

His nose told him where the fish department was. At a table two cooks were breaking up blocks of frozen cod.

"I'm looking for Tony Davis." For some reason this caused amusement.

"Oh are you? *Tony Davis* is it? Well *Tony* is off duty now. Try his cabin. No 25. Make them promise to let you out again. Better keep the door open." As he left them they were still chuckling. Now what? Something about the name Tony. And Cabin 25 he felt sure was the one Martin had slipped into on sailing night to set up the stunt with Linda. The misgivings grew as he neared the open door of the room. Somebody yelled:

"Not like that you fool, turn the edge first then tack it. I thought you knew how to do this."

"Alright, alright. Keep you knickers on." Roger halted, undecided. It was probably OK. He would stay near the door.

There were four men in the room. Linda sat drinking tea from an Orient Line cup. Another man was standing on a stool. A third knelt on the floor beside him. And Penny, still in the lime-green slacks, was sorting through a mass of clothing on a bunk. But it wasn't meeting four of them all at once that unnerved him. Or the row of pins in the mouth of the kneeling man. Or even the lace curtains at the porthole and male pin-ups on every vertical surface. No, it was the man on the stool. He was wearing a strapless white satin wedding-dress. They all stared at Roger.

"Who the hell are you?" inquired the one on his knees. "If Carol sent you for that cat-and-dog brooch you can go straight back and tell her she's not having it. I told her that ten minutes ago. Rupert gave it to Linda and she gave it to me. It's mine and its stays mine."

"I'm not from Carol," said Roger. "I've got a message for Tony Davis." Again the Christian name brought smiles.

Linda said,

"This man is Roger Wren. And he's not as innocent as he sounds, believe me."

"I'm Davis," said the one in the dress. "And if you don't mind the name's Antonia. What's the message?" He was in a whirl again. Just when he thought he'd seen everything.

"What are you staring at?" said Antonia. "It's the dress isn't it? You don't like it do you?"

"Why does it matter what he thinks?" snapped the dress-maker.

"Because he's the first one outside of this cabin to see it, we're all familiar with the wretched thing. He's coming to it with a fresh eye. You get an unbiased opinion. Now Roger or whatever your name is, what do you really think of it?"

"I don't know — I mean I'm not — it looks, well I guess it's very pretty."

Antonia sighed. "I knew it. He hates it. And after all these alterations. Of course, it would help if a *certain person* knew what they were doing!" The kneeling man stood up and took the pins from his mouth.

"Right, I've had it. Get some other mug to do this. I've had enough of you complaining." Antonia was instantly contrite.

"Oh I'm sorry Doreen. Really I am. I didn't mean it, honest. It's a *bona* dress. Please don't go, I need you." Muttering darkly, Doreen resumed work on the dress. During this diversion Roger had composed his face and thoughts. He passed on the message.

"They're thinking you might get over and see them. They couldn't get on here."

Antonia was peeved. "Damn. I knew they were doing a cruise. I didn't know it was this year. I'll have to go, if I can get a boat to take me. Perhaps I can bum some cash off my uncle." He began to remove the dress, whereupon Doreen protested.

"Sorry again pet, must change now if I'm to get on *Caronia* before we sail." Roger, his promise kept, turned to go and saw something hung on a locker door.

"That hat. It looks like the one my girlfriend lost today."

"Told you, Penny," said Linda. "I said you'd be found out didn't I?" Penny gave Roger the hat.

"A friend in the boat rescued it and gave it to me. It's quite clean, been washed and dried in the galley. I wasn't going to keep it."

"Oh no! Not much you weren't," said Linda. It was still legible, what he'd written back in Aden. While Antonia put on his shore-going clothes, the other three read his dedication.

"R loves R true," said Doreen. "We've been wondering what the other R stood for." He told them.

"Lovely lady," said Linda. "I saw her fall in. Now you can give her the hat back and make it up with her again." This was unlikely, but he would get it to her somehow. As he was leaving, Linda spoke to him at the door.

"More surprises for you, eh Roger?" A backward tilt of the head to show what he meant.

"You'll see plenty of that from now on. What we call drag."

He thought he saw the light. "Oh, dressing up same as on the stage. The Ugly Sisters, Widow Twankey." The ghastly silence told him he'd done it again. There was a squeal of rage from Penny.

"Did you hear that? Ugly Sisters! Shut the door and get hold of him, we'll have his drawers down." He was grabbed by Penny and Doreen. Dropping the hat he struggled helplessly in their grip. They wouldn't stop at de-bagging; there would be more to it than that. The stories he'd heard.

"Let's make him up first shall we?" said Doreen. With his arms pinioned behind him he was held in a grip like a gorilla's. Why were they all so *strong*? Giggling insanely, Penny fetched a lipstick and tried to apply it to Roger's mouth as he sought to avoid it by twisting his face from side to side.

"Should have heard him that night," said Penny. "Typical of his kind. Oh we're all normal in our cabin says he with his fuggin' nose in the air. I know, we'll black his balls for him." At this Linda came to his rescue.

"Alright that's enough. Leave him alone." Strong arms; boxer's arms pulled him free.

"He's the one who upset me that time in Mike Nelson's cabin," said Penny petulantly.

"Yes and you know why. It's his first time at sea."

"That's no reason to be disrespectful," growled Doreen, now sounding not the least effeminate. Hands on hips, Penny glared at Linda.

"Being a first-timer didn't save him from your clutches did it? I heard about your game. Not above a bit of cradle-snatching yourself are you?" Linda's face turned scarlet.

"Who told you that?"

"Ah, that struck home didn't it madam?" The trio began a general debate on each other's morals, enlivened by the most grisly physical threats he'd yet heard. During all this, Antonia had quietly finished changing. Now he took Roger's arm and pulled him outside, shutting the door on the argument.

"You've done it now, upsetting Penny again. I'm off to the *Caronia*. Here's your girl's hat."

"Thank you. I — er — I didn't intend to be insulting. It was just — you know — seeing you —" Antonia nodded.

"I know. That dress. It's hideous."

"Yes, but why a *wedding* dress?" The man looked him up and down.

"Why do you think? Because I'm getting married of course."

Baffled, Roger headed for the washroom. All it needed now was for Kropp to emerge from No 21 and see him. Smeared with lipstick and carrying a girl's hat. But only one person, a stranger, passed him as he hurried to the washroom, which was empty. Here he snatched a yard of toilet paper and rubbed away the lipstick. What kind of *asylum* was he in? A man getting wed in a dress! Who would conduct the service? And where? No sooner had he reached his own cabin and finished explaining the hat and his second escape of the day when Jack came in looking grim. It was a day of messages.

"Roger you're wanted on the bridge." Would it *never* end? "First Officer Quinn sent word down to the galley. Three o'clock, his office on Sun Deck."

"Now the Lodger's well in it," said Bill. "Up before Captain Baskerville on a charge. Left right - left, right. Prisoner and escort - halt! Caps off."

"It's Quinn he's seeing, not the Captain," said Jack.

"Asked for it you did Roger," said Pat. "Fornicating in the passengers' quarters."

Martin was almost hugging himself. "She's shopped him, dropped him right in it. What'll he get I wonder? Two hundred lashes I reckon, or slung in the brig on bread and water."

"Alright," said Jack wearily. "We've all seen *Mutiny on the Bounty*. Give it a rest. Roger you got to be there in ten minutes. Put on a decent pair of trews and a better shirt than that one. And call him sir. Don't worry, they're not allowed to hang you nowadays."

"Quiet life," said Toddy from his bunk. "Quiet life I go for."

Five sets of stairs later, Roger stepped out onto the Sun Deck. A number of seagulls or at any rate some species of seabirds were in evidence, waddling confidently about the deck or exploring the superstructure. He tried not to dwell on what might be coming. Awaiting him was some modern equivalent of the eighteenth-century cruelties Martin had drooled over. Demotion? But he could hardly go lower than his present job. They might dock his pay and give him a DR. Well, at least he'll have done his world trip. The First Officer's quarters were on the starboard side near the forward funnel. Shooing a path through the seabirds he reached the door, knocked and was told to enter.

Quinn was a tall, handsome individual, who wore his uniform with great elegance as if starched white was the very best thing to be seen in. Few men look good in shorts. Mr Quinn did, and he knew it, leaning back on the front of his desk with one lean, languid leg crossed over the other.

"Ah!" he began, pleasantly enough. "Now we're all here. All present and I hope, correct." On a sofa to one side were Ruth and her father. Opposite stood a sailor Roger recognised as the boat helmsman.

"Are you Wren?" asked Quinn.

"Yes sir." Should he salute? They were both hatless. In the RAF you didn't salute unless ...

"That would be Wren, Roger, employed in the crew mess, Article No 361?"

"Yes sir."

Demurely posed, Ruth sat with her hands in her lap and eyes downcast, a portrait of innocence. Sergeant Newbury was short and stocky, looking in his black beret and dark uniform totally out of place in a room full of things brassy and white and nautical. The man was woefully ill at ease, as if he'd rather be stood to attention on a frosty parade-ground, than perched sweating on a chintz-covered sofa, but protocol had to be observed. Passengers sat, crewmen stood. For an outraged father, Newbury barely glanced at Roger, seeming more intent on the sailor.

"Right," said Quinn. "The purpose of this meeting is to discover how this young lady came to fall into the water this morning." So it was a meeting, no more. Not a carpeting or a court martial or whatever they called it in the Merchant Navy. He might as well own up. A touch less worried now, he tried to catch her eye, but she avoided his glance and looked uneasily at her father. Sergeant Newbury folded his arms and sat back.

"There's no mystery about it. I know damn well what happened. This man in charge of the boat couldn't handle it properly. Rocking all over the shop it was. My poor girl got tossed out and very nearly drowned."

"That's not how it was," said the sailor. "I had control. The lady stood up and fell in when we pitched a bit. *Caronia's* launch went by much too fast." Newbury snorted.

"It's not good enough. She could have died. Somebody should be made to pay for this." Quinn turned to her.

"Is that correct? You were standing at the time?"

"Never," growled Newbury before she could reply. "She'd never do a stupid thing like that. Not her. Sensible she is. Way she's been brought up. Knows the rules and keeps to 'em. Knows what she'll get if she don't. That goes for everything."

Roger recalled the wild moments in that pokey cabin, when just about every rule her father knew was joyfully broken. And her tales of army trucks and late dances. The short secret escapes from her barracks-like home life. It struck him then that this hide-bound martinet of a father had made her come here. Probably she feared telling him the truth. So the whole thing was to be dumped on the boatman's head. Quinn asked Newbury,

"Did you see what occurred?"

"Not exactly, not myself personally. But I heard about it and knowing my daughter it's obvious. I mean the water wasn't rough or anything. Why else would she fall?"

"Perhaps she can tell us," said Quinn. "Were you standing at the moment you fell?"

Again her father spoke for her. "Course she wasn't. It was him; the boatman, sheer incompetence." The sailor began a new protest and Quinn held up a hand.

"If you please, both of you. I'd like to hear what this young man has to say. Mr Wren, by the way, how old *are* you?"

"Nineteen — twenty sir."

"That's your age? Not the year you were born?" Quinn gave a snicker of amusement which died when no-one else responded.

"I had a very recent birthday"

"Quite so. Now then, I've been told Miss Newbury was on shore in your company today. What did you do?"

"We went shopping."

"That's all you did? You didn't go in other places, pubs and bars? Anywhere like that?"

"My daughter does not drink," said Newbury sternly. "I may allow her a small sherry at Christmas or Easter, no more."

At this Roger just had to take another peek at Ruth. She stared back deadpan.

"Mr Wren?" prompted Quinn.

"We had a pot of tea in a café."

"I see," said Quinn, who did not see at all. In his experience, British seamen did not go on shore for pots of tea. Even in Ceylon.

"I tell you she was not drunk," snapped Newbury.

"No I'm not saying she was," said Quinn smoothly. "I was only thinking she might have been feeling – not quite herself."

"Not herself? What does that mean?"

Quinn addressed Roger.

"How well do you know Miss Newbury?" Without moving his head Roger sensed what was on the other faces. The sailor's prurient interest and relief that someone else was on the spot. The sergeant's sudden suspicion there could be a new culprit. And the girl. Oh Ruth, he thought. What a dance you've led us all. And here she was in her victim's role again. He felt the silent entreaty coming across the room at him. *Don't tell – don't tell*! She'd driven him half-mad with her changing moods, on-off affections and inverted logic. And he thought of the rest of it, the two eventful nights, her wonderful put-down of Martin. No. Sod Newbury. And sod Quinn. He would confess nothing. This called for white lies; white as Quinn's shorts.

"We don't really know each other at all. We met on the boat at Aden and again today. That's all." It may have been his fancy, but she seemed to relax. A slight droop of her shoulders; a backwards sag of her head.

"Very well," said Quinn. "So anyone who says you were quarrelling is mistaken."

"We did have a lively chat about about some gems we saw."

"Alright then," said Newbury angrily. "If she wasn't upset about anything and the boatman did his job, how did she come to fall in and nearly died? Tell me that!"

Now, at last she spoke. "Because I stood up!" They were all startled. "I was never going to drown. I can swim like a flaming fish as well you know, Dad. I stood up. Like this." Getting to her feet she sent a withering gaze round the group. "I ignored what the man said. *I stood up*. OK? The boat moved and in I went. That's how it happened. Sorry for all the trouble. Can we go now?"

Sergeant Newbury floundered among the ruins of his case. "What made you go and do something so silly?"

"I've been silly all day," she retorted crisply. "And sick and ratty. Women's trouble I expect you would call it." Her father rose from the sofa, red-faced. It was possibly the first time she'd got the better of him. He took off his black beret, turned it over twice and put it back on.

"Yes, well then. That's — no more to be said then, just a simple accident after all. These things happen." Ruth was already out of the door. They could be heard arguing as they crossed the Sun Deck.

"Give me strength," said Quinn clutching his brow.

A telephone rang and he snatched it up. "Yes, what is it? Mr Hewitt, what's *your* trouble? Very well, I'll be there shortly." He replaced the receiver. "Duty calls." A nod to the boatman. "Alright Cardwell, that'll be all. Next time they mess you about *make* them sit still and keep their bums on seats. Threaten to stop the boat till they do. Bawl 'em out if you have to. In the politest way of course."

"I will sir." The door closed. Quinn went to where his cap hung and put it on very carefully, using a mirror specially fixed alongside the hook. Waiting to be dismissed, Roger noticed a memo-pad on the desk and managed to read the upside-down writing on it. There were two entries. The first read Newbury comp. 1500. The second was Prentice comp. 2000. He wondered who Prentice might be and what his complaint was.

Only when Quinn felt smart enough to appear on deck did he confront Roger again.

"How old did you say you were? Twenty? And she's what, about eighteen?"

"I couldn't say sir."

"Oh no? Butter wouldn't melt would it?" His voice was quiet but firm. "Listen to me Roger Wren. I don't know how long you've been at sea —"

"First trip sir."

"Really? And already at it! Making use of your boyish charm. You look about sixteen. I suppose you're always being told that. And I saw every look you and this girl passed between you. You're on much better terms than you both make out." Roger tried to remember what DR stood for.

Quinn continued relentlessly. "It so happens I spoke to Cardwell earlier. And the Fourth Officer who was also in the launch. It was rather more than a 'lively chat' wasn't it? She was hopping mad. I think she stood up to get away from you. What you had was an all-out, up-and-down stinker of a row. A lovers' quarrel it sounds to me. Do you hear what I'm saying?" Behind Quinn was a square window, outside that the rail. And on this, one of the seabirds floated down and settled; a mean sort of creature, bone-ash grey with a murderous beak and Stuka wings. The Angel of Doom, he thought, bang on cue.

"Yes sir. We did have an argument."

"Very well then, I'll tell you what I think. I think you've been seeing this person, visiting her cabin quite improperly on the passenger decks after dark. I know she shares with another female, which suggests a further liaison. Possibly with an acquaintance of yours." Quinn paused, waited for a denial, and went on. "My job, or one of my jobs, is to maintain a firm but friendly separation between the crew and the military authorities aboard *Empire Garvie*. We simply can't have people in places they don't belong. There'd be a breakdown in discipline and good order, the very things safety at sea depends on. Now I won't ask you to confirm or deny what I've said. For one thing I'm too busy with other matters at present. It would mean calling in all the others involved and I've got another complaint to deal with after dinner. Also …" the official tone softened "… that young madam has enough on her plate already. Her father's been made to look a fool, not a difficult task, I grant you, but I dread to think what he's putting her through at this moment. Or how he'd react if he knew the whole story. They're getting off at Singapore. So I don't intend adding to her misery. Anyone with a father like that deserves kindness."

The seabird had gone from the rail. There was now only a bright blue rectangle of water and sky.

"However —" Quinn seemed to like the word. "How – ever, I want you to know that if any more of this comes to my notice, I shall descend upon you from a very great height, understood?"

"Sir." They left the room together.

"What you get up to ashore is your own business, but keep off the passenger decks. You'll find what you want where we're going. Hong Kong or Japan. This place Kure. If it's anything like Yokohama. Some of them might even give you a cup of tea." Not knowing what else to say Roger simply smiled. Quinn called to a passing seaman.

"Where's the Second Officer?"

"For'ard well-deck sir."

"Very well. Go and ask him to meet me in the chartroom. Mr Hewitt has a problem." The First Officer set off for the bridge and Roger started on the first of all the stairways that took him down, down, ever downward to where he lived. A day of escapes. How long could this kind of luck last? What a blessing, the cabin was empty except for Toddy.

"Hello Roger. What happened?"

"He knew about it. It was supposed to be about her falling in but the First Officer knew about her and me. I was let off with a warning."

"Lucky it was him. Randiest one of the lot, Quinn. Different woman every voyage. Known for it. Married man too." So that explained it. Quinn was a philandering rascal. And a hypocrite, giving him that lecture, but it was his job after all. The old dictum. Do as I say, not as I do. Batten had mentioned a senior deck officer who played around. Mr Quinn's shorts, it seemed, were the only spotless things about him. The thought made him chuckle.

"Don't get cocky," said Toddy. "Too sure of yourself. Fatal, that."

"I won't." He could see Colombo through the porthole. His binoculars brought it closer. The trees of Gordon Gardens where they'd talked of gems. The flags of the Grand Oriental and the café where the day that promised so much began to go so wrong. Framed by the relative darkness of the cabin, the circular picture had the crystal clarity of an Edwardian lantern-slide.

On impulse he got out the Ful-Vue and took a photo of it. Something to show Gina. A round picture. Pity the camera got left behind today. Ruth had looked good in that hat. Oh Lord, he remembered. "Toddy, I saw one of the fish-cooks today in a wedding-dress!"

"So what?"

"Seems strange, that's all. Seeing a man in it."

"Why strange? She's getting married. Bound to want a dress for that."

Perhaps it's only me, he thought. Perhaps I'm the one who's mad and everybody else is perfectly sane. He asked where the others were.

"On deck. Watching the other trooper go."

"That feud between them and us. I had a taste of it today." Toddy summarised the *Windrush* crew in a short burst of verbal shorthand.

"It's not all of them, few hotheads, boozers. Can't let it die. Daft I call it." Booze. It always came back to that. While it was quiet he began a letter to his father. There was a lot to tell.

A sudden glow filled the cabin. The *Windrush* was passing, and the sunlight bounced off her snowy flanks and into the porthole. She moved in stately silence, blocking the view for half a minute till the town reappeared. Colombo would join his swelling collection of people and places and memories. Along with little Haji, stretched in the dust with his smashed belongings. And Sergeant Fouad, like Newbury a walking rule-book. Not forgetting "David Niven", a tout for a shady dealer picking up gullible tourists, and Ruth. All these people had entered his life, turned him inside out and vanished again.

The others returned to hear of his brush with authority.

"The Lodger does it again," said Bill. "You must be the jammiest bastard on this ship bar none. Anybody else would have got a DR. Not you. No, you get to see Quinn of all people. That bugger spends more time sniffing around A and B Deck then he ever does on the bridge." Bravely, Martin hid his disappointment.

"Roger'll come unstuck sooner or later."

"That'll be the day," said Jack. "Be happy then won't you, Martin? Roger, can't you or your steward friend fix him up with someone? Before he dies of jealousy!"

They laughed then, all of them. Laughed with him, for him. For the first time he knew some kind of rapport with the whole cabinful at once. His moments of achievement; the korey triumphs that were his ticket to ride in their company had been tempered by failures and close shaves. And this he also knew was right for him. They were following his progress, the fumbling ascent of his own personal Everest. So if he took a few tumbles on the way they could enjoy that too. Stop the Lodger getting big-headed.

"What will you do for korey now?" said Pat. "You can't go up there again."

Gina, he thought, and the idea seemed madder than ever. On a whim, he said,

"Let's all go on deck this evening. Just for a change, as a bunch."

"Why not?" said Jack.

But first he sought out Clay and Batten, making his usual Kropp-check after entering No 21.

"Don't know where Kropp is," said Smith. He went off somewhere right after dinner. It's too early for the Pig so he may well be sober. Don't worry over him. If he's not pie-eyed he'll only threaten." Only threaten. So that was alright. Anything short of murder wasn't worth getting upset over.

Batten summed it up. "Life on the *Empire Garvie*. Drink, depravity, hard work and boredom. Relieved by occasional violence. A cross between Dickensian London and the Guards Depot at Caterham."

"I hear you were on the bridge," said Clay. He told his story. Clay was relieved at their narrow escape.

"And I've got Ruth's hat back." His ordeal in No 25 brought hoots of merriment from all.

"At your own risk going in there," said Nelson. "That's how Penny got her claws in me."

"About the hat," said Clay. "There's no way I can get it to her now. People got off at Colombo and there's been some shifting around. They're not in my show any more, and they turn their backs if I go near them. The mothers keep going to the cabin now too. I barely got in to retrieve the gramophone." So he was stuck with the hat. Singapore, he would try and catch her at the gangway.

"How's Ruth's mother now?"

"Nothing wrong with her. When I last saw her she was scoffing our chestnuts." Next he called on a man who developed films for the crew, a barman named Byfield who had turned part of his workplace into a darkroom.

"Only the one film is it? I'm a bit choc-a-block but as it's only a 120 roll I might do that first. Give me a few days." Back in the cabin he finished his letter and took it to the mailbox on D Deck square. He resolved to write home as often as he could and enclose picture-postcards of places visited.

That evening a remarkable gathering took place. Up to now he'd never seen all five of them together on deck. But now sure enough they came sauntering over to the hatch where he was. Colombo had passed from sight but the lovely green island still showed on the port quarter.

"Gathering of the clan," said Jack. "Men of the mess taking the evening air." They all settled down, sitting or stretching out on the rough tarpaulin covers. Perhaps the off-duty life below decks, the sprawling, swearing, tummy-scratching squalor of it had begun to pall. Or they simply needed somewhere else to do it. Up here was a kind of beauty only the most obtuse could fail to see. Even Bill was moved to comment.

"See that? Looks like a fuggin' great *picture*, dunnit?"

In the west the Old Master Painter had done his daily work. The sunset amazed Roger, as it always did. So much colour visible at one instant. As if a vast explosion had been stopped halfway through. At the horizon the sea and sky were virtually the same startling orange-red. Over this stretched a multitude of puffy cloudlets, each with its two-tone scheme of apricot and lavender. And this whole assembly thinned at the edges through indigo and purple into the deepest blue-black. The orb of the sun itself was lost to sight, seemingly swallowed by its own fire – smashed and smeared along the earth's rim like an overturned furnace.

"That's a special thing you're seeing there," said Jack. "I mean with the times we're living in. What with India gone, and soon Malaya. That'll be the next place to go. The Japs showed we could be beaten. Now the Malays won't want us back again in a hurry." Martin scratched his head.

"What's the sun got to do with it?" Jack rolled his eyes.

"Well – it's kind of –"

"Symbolic?" said Roger.

"Yes, that's the word I want. They said the sun would never set on the British Empire. They're wrong. It is setting a wee bit at a time all over the shop. Bit by bit we're giving it back or they're taking it. Good thing too. The war's changed things. We'll spend the next ten years or so handing over all the other parts what we've been clinging to for centuries."

"Blimey," said Martin, eloquently enough for everyone.

So the little group on the after deck watched the splendour in the sky, the sun sinking into the sea. And the Lodger was the most moved of all, for he knew well this empire, these pink patches strewn across the globe. It was not the last sunset, but it was one of the last, and the more poignant to him for that.

"The Lodger's still upset at losing his tart," said Bill. "Don't worry boy. Where we're going you'll soon forget her, take it from one who knows." Away from the confines of the glory hole he felt less intimidated by the weight of their combined knowledge. As ever, the impossibly huge ocean-world reduced both them and the ship itself to their true microscopic size.

That first evening out of Colombo was memorable in other ways.

"Flying-fish!" came a cry. Roger darted to the rail in time to see disturbed water but no fish.

"Wait," said Pat. "They'll come up again." Nothing happened, and nothing went on happening for quite a while, till Pat and the others departed for the Pig and he was left alone again with his recollections of this crowded day. Always partial to solitude, these days it was increasingly hard to come by. Clay was hurrying along the deck.

"Roger I've been looking everywhere for you."

"What's up?"

"It's Kropp." His heart froze.

"Go on."

"He was on the bridge today too. Eight o'clock, right after dinner for a bollocking. Threatening behaviour they accused him of."

"I'm not surprised. Kropp's always threatening people. Batten told me –"

"Yes but –" Clay glanced around.

"The thing is, he's convinced it was you who reported him when you saw Quinn today." Seymour-like, Roger leaned with his head in his hands.

"But it was way back in the Med I had that set-to with him. Why would I wait till now to report him? I hope you told him the truth."

"We did, but he said we're lying to protect you. They wouldn't tell him who made the complaint and he's sure it was you. You been seen with Linda. And you were in one of the queers' cabins today. They're suffered a lot of abuse and threats from Kropp so he thinks they put you up to it. Someone's been goading him about it. They saw you coming out of 25 and later on joking with the First Officer."

He'd had enough today, more than enough. He didn't want any more ugliness right now at the first tranquil moment of the day.

"So whoever really made the complaint is safe as long as I'm on the spot. God I'm so sick of Kropp. I've half a mind to just let him bash me and be done with it. Otherwise I'll have him on my back the whole trip."

Suddenly, at that moment the water burst into life, a score or more of glittering cigar-shapes appeared. Flashing coppery-gold in the dying light, each one skimmed the surface in a dead-straight line, cutting a thin furrow with its tail as it went. First one shoal popped into the daylight, then another and another; each group following its own path, criss-crossing but never once colliding. And as quickly as they came, they were gone. A last set of splashes and the surface was empty again. He was glad to have seen them after watching for days. It got him thinking about his projected poem once more. He would definitely persevere with it if he was permitted to live that long. The following morning he did something he'd hesitated over for a long time. He told his cabin about Kropp.

The news was received with the mixture of jokes, predictions and advice he'd come to expect.

"How did you come to fall foul of him?" asked Pat. They heard about the shower incident, the moment in No 21 and now this latest peril. Pat said,

"It's when he's had too many. That's when he's dangerous."

"Poor old Lodger," said Bill. "What a voyage he's having." Martin relished the moment.

"If Kropp's after you there's nothing left to do except jump over the side. That's what he's like, holds a grudge for — well forever. He's crazy. He'll bide his time then pounce when you've forgotten about him."

"But I've done nothing!" said Roger. He waited for Jack's comments.

"First of all laddie, don't panic. I think if he intended to get you he would have done it by now."

"Suppose I confronted him? Pleaded my innocence?"

"Where do you think we are?" said Bill. "In court?"

"That's where he would be," said Roger heatedly. "If we were back home where you've got proper law and order." He'd forgotten how swiftly the mood of the cabin could change. The unnatural pause was the sign of another *faux pas*.

"So it's a jungle then is it?" said Bill. "What you decided to grace with your presence; all us horrible villains scaring the crap out of you. And not a policeman for miles you can run to. I can't see you lasting this trip. You're too green. At sea or ashore you invite trouble. I reckon you should have stayed in the poncey Raff where they're all the same as you. God knows what'll happen to you in Singapore, never mind Hong Kong."

Martin gave a ghoulish chuckle. "He'll end up somewhere in Chinatown. Face down in a monsoon ditch with a knife in his back and the alley-dogs sniffing him." While they considered this picture, Toddy cleared his throat. They watched and waited but nothing came. Not even "Dark horse". Unexpectedly the cabin gave a slight heave. Enough to remind them they were on a ship. Pat stuck his head out of the port.

"We'd best shut this thing. Do the clamps up and all. You ought to see what's ahead of us. Sky's as black as O'Leary's beard."

Next day Roger came face-to-face with Kropp in the shower-room. There was no point in running. He felt only a kind of terrified calm. The man could bash him and the business would be over where it began, in the shower. There would even be somewhere for the blood to drain. Kropp, however, was quite sober.

"So you went to the First Officer about me?"

Roger was glad of the chance to speak. "No I didn't. I mean I did go but not about you. We didn't mention you at all."

"Who's 'we'? You and your friend Quinn?"

"No – well – he was there of course but there was the boatman too – and – and – other people." Kropp frowned.

"Boatman? Why a boatman? What was his name?" Oh God, what was it? Quinn had mentioned the name. What was it?

"I can't remember. He was there though, honestly." Kropp reached out and clutched Roger's hair as he had the first time. On this occasion, by way of a change he did not wave a fist but wriggled Roger's head violently from side to side, giving him a painful scalp and a crick in the neck.

"I don't care how young you are, you're a lying, snivelling, perverted wee bastard, hanging around with the queers and running up to the bridge for them. I got your number, Jimmy, make no mistake. I think it was you. Keep out of my way if I see you ashore, that's all." With a he-man flourish he cast off his towel and entered the shower, hounds and horses wetly gleaming. Roger left. His own shower could wait till later. Somehow he couldn't put his mind to it now.

For the time being, the days of merciless sunshine were ending. Now the burning rays were thwarted by a mass of cumulo-nimbus that daily filled the skies. There came instead a new discomfort. As they drew near the top end of Sumatra they met the dank, gluey humidity of South-East Asia. But Roger had additional concerns. Kropp's parting words had stayed with him. Ashore, not on the ship? Was he safe then till he went down a gangway? Batten, when they met on the hatch, was optimistic.

"As I see it, by now he's had enough warnings. Unless he curbs that violent streak he'll be off the ship at Southampton. There was that thing about Josephine. And Henrietta. Actually that wasn't Kropp. A mate of his did that. Stabbing that was." Wonderful. Kropp had a friend who stabbed people.

"I didn't know that, and I wish I still didn't." He gave Batten a Camel and a light for it. It was high time. He'd had a few of theirs.

"Thank you dear boy. No, I think you may be alright now with Mr Kropp of Glasgow. He could lose his job. One more assault, that's all."

"Yes. But I don't want the 'one more' to be me."

"Well, look out for him ashore. Trouble is, they're all after the same thing, drink and sex. Both of which are usually found within a quarter-mile radius of the ship. Add to that the fact that most people only get a few hours off and you see how easy it is to run into anyone, friend or foe." The ship had begun to roll heavily and men were leaving the deck.

Over to starboard the sky had taken on the face of nightmare. Tumbling banks of gun-metal clouds boiled and seethed together. Vague, ghostly lights darted and flickered along the undersides.

"Listen," said Batten. "Hear that?" Until now, Roger's new world had spoken in two voices. The wind and the water had whispered to him all these long sea-miles. Now came a third voice. Far off and high-hidden but slowly making itself heard.

"Yes, I hear it." The thunder was hesitant but unmistakeable. "We'd better get below," he said. "It's going to come down in buckets any minute."

"I don't care. I love the rain. What better than a tropical storm to wash away the sweat? Here, do me a favour, will you? Stow my gear in the deckhouse." Batten peeled off his clothes, revealing a pair of swimming-trunks *circa* 1930. Lightning scratched the sky and the thunder rolled again.

"Will you be OK staying out in this?"

"Roger, I'll be as happy as a butcher's dog. I'm an eccentric. So I've been informed. We're always alright, us eccentrics."

The storm finally broke as Roger reached the deckhouse. A multi-million-volt flash that illuminated everything in sight; a thunderclap so loud he jumped. And a sudden deluge unlike anything he could have imagined. Roaring and drumming on every surface, trying to batter the ship down by sheer weight. He folded the clothes, stowed them away from the door, and took a last look out. Batten was standing on the hatch in the midst of the downpour, head tilted back in ecstasy.

The weather was bad for three days, during which they passed the Nicobar Islands and started down the Malacca Straits. Many were sick, the troops suffering most. The work was more difficult but Roger coped, and was spared the agonies of the dreaded *mal de mer*. Thank God he had his sea-legs. Yet he knew there was something else. Perhaps it was too much Conrad, too many windjammer films. He enjoyed the sea, it was as simple as that. In the occasional lull, when the storm paused for breath he'd gone up to the drenched deck to watch it. Even below, the creak of steel and the "whump" as a ton of water struck it had a drama all its own. In a smaller vessel he knew it would be quite another story or if he had to work on deck.

"Of course this is nothing," said Jack. "I've seen waves higher than the bridge on cargo boats. Bent the rails and smashed windows in. I've seen men washed overboard. Gone. Not even time to call out." Yes, a different story altogether. He would keep his peculiar thrills to himself. The violent rolling produced strange effects. The bunks were fitted abeam, so heads pointed to port and feet to starboard. This meant that as the ship tilted left or right his body tended to slide up or down the bed. He tried having a folded blanket at the bottom and the pillow stood against the frame. This helped, although the pressure switching between the soles of his feet and the top of his head gave the eerie illusion that he'd sampled one of Alice's "Drink Me" bottles and was outgrowing his own bed. Typically, no-one else seemed affected.

They would reach Singapore next day at dawn.

"And we're staying overnight," said Jack. Martin chuckled.

"Hear that Roger? All night. That'll sort the men from the boys."

"Look out Malaya," said Bill. "The Lodger's coming to town." Jack waited for the crowing to stop and continued.

"We lose about a third of the troops here. They go first then the families." So he might get to see her one last time. The hat was in his locker, causing comment every time they caught sight of it. He hadn't let them see what was written inside or told of the other gifts.

"What makes you think she wants it back?" asked Bill.

"I'm sure she does. And I paid around ten shillings for it."

"Fuggin' 'ell," sniffed Martin. "Ten bob for a hat."

"Keep it," said Bill. "Give it to a geisha girl in Japan. They'll treat you to the whole works for that."

"No they won't," said Jack quietly.

"What do you mean?" Bill sounded like a child whose promised treat had been cancelled. "You told us. Yokohama. You said—"

"I was talking about prostitutes. Geishas aren't prostitutes. And they're expensive. They're educated, well-mannered and smart. Geishas are not for the likes of you. And we're not going to Yokohama. We're going to Kure." Educated, well-mannered and smart; yes, thought Roger. I already know someone like that. He recalled his first sight of Gina Morrell in her dragon dressing gown. And it wasn't a great effort of fantasy to see her as his personal geisha if he played his cards right. Or his mahjong tiles.

Chapter 9

There is an unearthly feel about a harbour approached in the dark. With no clear horizon for reference you have less sense of being on the sea. Strange half-lit shapes appear and pass silently, or circle like wary phantoms. Leaning on the rail, he experienced again that sensation of entering the unknown, the suppressed excitement of a new place, a fresh flood of sights and sounds. As at Colombo, he was joined by Jack Cutler, who seemed to have a taste for Asian landfalls.

"Where do we go Jack?"

"Keppel Harbour. We go alongside here. Gangway for a change." That was good. No more hastening to catch the boat.

"And when do we sail again?"

"Ten in the morning. You want to be back by six though, to do breakfast." The assumption that he would stay ashore the entire night was a bit startling. Would they all be doing it? He saw himself alone in the cabin when they came breezing back at dawn, in his proper place as a korey-starved loner.

"Will you be –?" He couldn't bring himself to say 'out all night." Not to Mr Cutler. Tact was needed. "Will you be – late back?"

In the darkness he could not see the man's face clearly. But he could tell there was a smile on it.

"Don't be afraid to say it Roger. If you're asking am I after korey the answer's no. I'm going ashore but not for that. Hong Kong's my place and Pat's. The two young ones will stagger back in tomorrow full of liquor and stories. I don't know about Toddy. Nobody knows where he goes and we don't ask."

A tugboat hooted and was answered by another. The ship shuddered as the screws were reversed.

"Do we stay overnight in Hong Kong too?"

"Overnight? It was four days last time. Now you're going to ask about time off, right?" In fact he'd been wondering where Wei Ho Bay was and how long it took to get there. If he saw her again and got invited. You never knew.

"Yes. We do get some I hope."

"Oh, sure. We each get a day off. There's these Chinese come aboard and do the strap-up and other jobs. Empty the bins. In exchange they get all the leftovers. They take it home in cans. They get free food, we get time off. But that's Hong Kong. Let's get though this place first."

By the time breakfast was done it was light, they were tied up at the quay and he was free to take in the latest scene. Another Asian port, but there were differences: rather more red or green-tiled roofs, more oriental faces peering up at the ship. The imperial presence was everywhere, from the ubiquitous pith helmets and flapping service shorts to the olive-green Leyland trucks filling up with conscripts. Watching these youngsters stepping ashore he imagined their predecessors. Any time in the past hundred and fifty-odd years this picture might have been seen somewhere in the world. Then they may have worn ludicrously high shakoes on their heads, had black leather bandoliers and vivid scarlet tunics; carried spiky muskets taller than they were. Now it was the squat beret, dark-green battledress and the faithful Lee-Enfield he'd once shouldered himself.

At ten most of the troops had disembarked, and he was on D

Deck square with the hat.

"Roger!" He wished they weren't so fond of sidling up in this way.

"Hullo Linda." It still seemed strange using these names to address men. "I'm waiting to see Ruth and give her the hat."

"So am I," said Linda. "Waiting I mean, to say goodbye to somebody." The square was packed with people, mostly mothers with fretful offspring in tow. Army officers and NCOs helped them towards the gangway where papers were checked and they finally parted company with the *Empire Garvie*. Ruth was nowhere to be seen. Linda waved.

"There's my friend!" A young corporal came over, looking uneasily at Roger and the hat.

"Don't worry about Roger," said Linda. "He's seeing someone off too." They moved a little away from him. And then he spotted Ruth and her mother on the main staircase.

There was no way to reach her. A solid tide of people kept them apart and she didn't see him wave. Her mother was as he'd expected, a meek, harassed sort of person, subdued by an overbearing husband and rebellious daughter. But the Sergeant wasn't with them.

"Ruth!" As he called her name he wondered if Quinn was about and realised he didn't give a damn, not at this moment.

"Ruth!" It was no use, she glanced in every direction but the right one. The Corporal had seen him waving.

"Do you know the Newbury family?"

"He knows the daughter very well," said Linda. Roger called again but they had moved nearer the exit. Linda and the friend were parting. The sight reminded him of Nelson and Penny. But here discretion ruled. Men saying farewell in public shook hands or slapped backs, said hearty things. Yet there were the other subtler signs he could now recognise. How small the difference was between shaking hands and *holding* hands.

"Roger, what about the hat?"

"Too late, I can't pass it to her now unless I can catch her on the quay."

"Impossible," said the corporal. "They won't let you off yet. Army personnel only. Is this hat important?"

"To her it is."

"Give it to me. What's your name? Roger? I'll see her before she gets on the coach for Gillman Barracks."

"Thanks." The corporal merged into the crowd, holding the hat up to avoid damage.

"God, I'll miss that boy," came a muffled voice. Linda had a handkerchief to his face.

"Cedric his name is. I've never known anyone called Cedric before." A quick sniffle, a sneeze and the usual control was restored. "Life goes on. Let's go up a deck Roger. See better from there."

Roger asked, "Have you had many friends?"

"I certainly have, proper mixed bag. Two years ago I had an affair with an airline pilot."

"What was that like?"

Linda thought, and replied, "Turbulent."

From C Deck they had a grandstand view. In single file the families were shuffling down the narrow gangway and forming a queue to a line of motor-coaches. Cranes swung rope nets full of baggage down to be put into vans by Malay dockers.

"This part will be full of traders soon," said Linda. But where was Ruth? Looking first at the coach currently loading, he ran his eye back along the queue. There she was, almost on the coach with Pauline just ahead of her. Forced to move at a snail's pace, Cedric inched down the gangway, holding the hat above him like a leaf-cutter ant.

"That thing gets around doesn't it?" said Linda. "What's the betting he'll catch her in time?"

Cedric triumphed. The celebrated Bergman hat changed hands. Cedric spoke to her, pointed up at the ship and went to join his men. Even at this distance her pleasure was obvious. And she wore her Aden bracelets now. She scanned the ship as if trying to see him, and gave a vigorous two-handed wave. It was surely a reconciliation of sorts, something that may have begun with the little conspiracy in Quinn's office. Her mother chivvied her on to the coach and they drove away.

"She was only the Sergeant's daughter," quoted Linda. "But she knew what Reggie meant." A pun or a quip for every situation – that was the way to survive life. Draw a line under it and turn the page.

Later there was the customary debate about where to go, what to do and how to stretch their meagre finances. Merely seeing the sights and using a camera was considered outlandishly dull.

"The Lodger got to get fixed up here," said Bill. "Now his own private korey's gone. Tonight you're coming with us Roger. We're going to Custard Lane." He wasn't going with them. Not even to a place with such an intriguing name.

"Thanks all the same. I'll be alright on my own. There's someone I'm hoping to meet." Martin sensed further amusement.

"Oh, who might that be?"

"Mind your own business," said Jack. "I keep telling you. Roger's OK without your help. He seemed able to scrape along quite well on his own." Roger allowed himself to enjoy this accolade. No, he surely wasn't a drip now with what he'd been through, and his korey record. Even the bridge summons and his subsequent "acquittal" bestowed some measure of roguish glory. And there were his proven sea-legs and a decent tan. Put all this together and you had a passable facsimile of a Merchant Seaman.

There was the question of currency.

"Dollars," said Pat. "Malayan dollars. Eight and a half to a quid." He decided to change six pounds' worth. At the purser's office he met Batten.

"Roger my son. I thought you spent all your money on the NCO's daughter. Now I find you clutching a wad of notes that would choke a horse. They'll take our money here you know."

"Yes, but I'm fed up with trying to work it out in my head every time. Clay can do it but I'm going on my own today."

"I hear she's older than you."

"Who?" said Roger, knowing quite well who.

"Your widow friend. Clay says she's going in town today. Planning to meet her?" He felt the defensive irritation he always got when asked about her.

"What if I am? She's only thirty-odd." Only! What was he thinking of? Barely out of his teens and running after …

"Take it easy," said Batten. "I've heard about her from Clay. From what I gather she seems a most agreeable person." Yes, that was Gina, someone to spend an afternoon with. Taking photos of temples and things. Where could the harm be in that?

"I'm not especially planning to meet her, just hoping I might."

"Yes of course. Only, please don't take this the wrong way – I've had some experience with widows. They can be unpredictable. Hope you don't mind me telling you this." Roger counted out his dollars.

"Not at all, I know what you mean. Sex. They're supposed to think of nothing else, widows."

"Exactly. They can turn funny if they think you've insulted them. Or rejected them, come to that. You can't win sometimes. You've been on the bridge once. If in doubt anytime, try to make them laugh. Humour's a wonderful thing between a man and a woman." As soon as he could he was down the gangway and threading a way through the traders and souvenir sellers. This time he took the camera. It was 1.30. If she'd hurried her lunch or even skipped it she could be already in town. So it was pointless to loiter on the quay in the faint hope of seeing her.

"Hullo sir, you want taxi?" The man had a moustache like Jerry Colonna's.

"No, no thanks. Not just now."

"Yes, I take you. Low price. More better than foot. Long way for foot."

"No. not now." The man returned to his car, a thirties Chrysler in canary yellow. Roger made for the exit. Still he had no clear plan. If she hadn't left yet she might use a taxi. Maybe stop and invite him along.

A sign told him he was on Tanjong Pagar Road. Ahead of him were a number of crew members while behind him a further group straggled along the verge. He saw the taxi pause by them and then come his way. The driver leaned out of his window and slowed down so abruptly it was as if the moustache had acted as an air brake.

"Hullo sir – you want taxi now? Town very long way. Taxi much better." If it was so far why was everybody in sight walking?

"No. No taxi. Go away." The car slowed again, dropping back to a point a few yards behind him. He wondered how many temples there were in Singapore and which one she was visiting. Some name – some eastern name she'd mentioned.

The Chrysler continued to stalk him, staying at the same distance and matching his pace exactly. As if he were a millionaire taking a walk with his chauffeur cruising nearby in case he got tired. Temples, who would know the temples? There was no need to beckon. The taxi hurtled up to him the moment he looked back.

"What temples are there here?" The driver was taken aback. Here was a young British seaman, straight off a ship, not asking for a woman, a bar or a dance hall.

"Temples?"

He remembered more of her words. "Yes. I want one with a carved tower." The man stroked his moustache, starting at his nose and sliding his finger tips pleasurably out to each end. It was that kind of moustache.

"Many temples in town. What is name?"

"I don't know. Tell me a few; I'm hoping one may ring a bell." That explained it. This oddball was a campanologist pursuing his hobby. With luck he could make a day of this. Pulling in the dollars while his fare gleefully tried out all the bells in Singapore.

"Get in please. I take you."

"No, tell me some names first." He hadn't taken many taxis in his life but he wasn't going to be whizzed all over a strange town till his dollars ran out.

The driver switched off his engine, took a deep breath and began to reel off names.

"Tell me the ones with a carved tower."

"Many have towers, but some no bells."

"Bells? I'm not interested in bells." The other walkers drew level.

"Taxi?" called the driver with a certain desperation in his voice. Everyone declined. Roger entered the car.

"Alright, take me to the nearest one." Once clear of the docks the scenery was mostly neat, green tiled bungalows and a profusion of tropical blooms. All too soon they came to the town.

"Your first time come to Singapore sir?"

"Yes." There was no sense denying the obvious, best to keep an eye on the meter and not get the run-around. Go up to five dollars say. The first temple was Chinese and had two towers, woefully plain ones.

"No good sir? OK we see more better one." Next came the Sultan Mosque with its many minarets, all smooth. It became apparent that every creed in the world was catered for here. There were synagogues and churches, mosques and shrines. But none of them had what could be called a "carved tower".

Eight dollars. He hadn't been watching. "Stop here please." The driver protested.

"Many more to see. I take you to Nagore Shrine. More better. Amoy Street. Very close. We go there now." His religious tour could take hours. And he would still need the taxi fare back. He suspected the man knew the temple in question and was saving it till he'd seen all the others.

"No, this will do thanks." The moustache drooped.

"OK." Roger paid him.

"Where exactly are we?"

"Chinatown. Hokkien Street." The Chrysler departed and Roger was alone. Eight thousand miles from England, looking for a temple and a woman who took pictures and knew the French for chestnuts. The choice was to seek this elusive building or forget Gina and the remote chance of running into her. See what he could of the area, take his snaps and have a leisurely, dollar-saving stroll down – what was it called? Tanjong Pagar Road, if he could find it again. Roger chose the latter course. He had to be back by five, she didn't.

Which way – left or right? As at Colombo, he was in the hands of the gods. And here there were many, many gods. Which one propelled him to the left and thence into nasal range of Tommy Wang's Treasure House? It was his first encounter with the unforgettable aroma of joss sticks. The shop was large, with vertical lines of Chinese lettering on every outside surface. Inside, it was hung about with mysterious ornaments, toys and strings of objects twinkling and tinkling wherever he looked. Here was the treasure. Where was Tommy Wang? From behind a stack of varnished boxes the shopkeeper popped up like one of his own novelties, wearing the black, pyjama style garment he would see everywhere in the east. Tommy was extremely old, yet darted about his shop like an eager child.

"Hullo sir. Good afternoon sir. Come in please. Have souvenirs sir. Have also silks and jewellery, many fine things. Please to examine. Very reasonable sir." The gushing welcome no longer surprised him. This was not England. As he moved around the man followed.

"What you want, sir? You want souvenirs?"

"I'm only browsing." The shop was like the town itself. No faith went unrepresented. Many-limbed gods and goddesses smiled or frowned down at him. In jade, ivory or flesh pink porcelain, Buddhas large and small squatted in beaming groups, flat eyes half closed as if against the aromatic smoke issuing from the little brass pots in their laps. Ikons and crucifixes stood with fearsome dragons and ruby-eyed tigers. A row of ebony elephants with silver tusks and diamond toes waved their trunks at him begging to be purchased. The place was well named. A treasure house, presided over by a wizened husk of a man more fragile than anything on display.

"What is it you wish for sir?" There was no time to explore this Aladdin's Cave, much as he'd like to. The name Gina had mentioned came to him at last.

"I'm looking for the Shiva Temple." Tommy shook his small white head.

"No temple that name sir. Not in Singapore."

"It's got a carved tower." The old face lit up.

"Ah yes. Sri Mariamman. Not tower sir. *Gopuram* gateway. Oldest temple in Singapore. South Bridge Road, sir. Very fine Hindu place." He had to buy something so he picked up a porcelain Buddha about five inches high. The loose ticket under it said three dollars. A present for somebody, or a keepsake. Tommy took his three dollars and gave back one.

"Only cost two dollars sir. Ticket wrong."

"I see, thank you," he said, impressed by the aged one's honesty. Along with the Port Said priest and the amicable rickshaw man of Colombo, Roger's respect for other races increased further in about the same proportion by which he was becoming disillusioned with his own. Tommy gave him the Buddha wrapped in tissue paper.

"South Bridge Road, sir. Up Hokkien Street and then to the left. Sri Mariamman is other side. Not long way."

Turning into South Bridge Road he experienced the full impact of the place. A thousand different odours wafted in and out among the stalls and displays. There were rickshaws, trishaws and ravishingly beautiful bar girls with easy smiles and glossy hair parading or posing in skin-tight *cheongsams*. Everywhere he saw the up and down oriental wording, the black clad workers supporting huge loads on bamboo shoulder yokes. There were old, crumbling shop-houses patched and repaired with whatever came to hand. Ancient façades of peeling plaster leaned mouldily towards each other. Here he saw monsoon gullies deep and wide enough to break a careless ankle, and still half filled with sludge and litter from the recent rains.

Five noisy blocks down he found the Sri Mariamman Temple. He decided to wait for say, fifteen minutes. If she didn't appear he had time for more wanderings. The *gopuram* was an immense five part structure covered on all sides with innumerable carved animals and humans. A Hindu temple in the middle of Chinatown! Maybe he should keep the Buddha well wrapped up, rather than put religious tolerance even further in the test. And then, as he was admiring the sculptures he saw her – sunglasses on and as smartly turned out as before. The Leica was up to her eye as she slowly panned around choosing her shot. He kept still, waiting till she saw him in the viewfinder.

"Roger!" She looked past the camera. "No, stay there. I'll get you in this." They might have been on holiday together. "That'll be a good one," she said adjusting her camera.

"Hullo Gina, fancy meeting you here. What an *amazing* coincidence."

"Yes it is isn't it? Who would have *thought* it?" Games again, only now they could be open about it.

He told her about Colombo, omitting any mention of Ruth's mishap or his summons to the bridge. Maybe later.

"How did you get on in the storm?" he asked.

"Oh, I was fine. It doesn't bother me, a spell of rough weather. Rather exciting in fact." Gina, he felt, would be at home on a raft so long as she had her camera and decent clothes. They admired the carvings, and the Leica and Ful-vue blinked in unison.

"Shall we go inside?" she said brightly. The interior was sweetly cool, a huge relief from the sticky heat. They weren't alone. Small groups of worshippers moved along the side chambers where statues and painted images stood eternally on guard. Gina seemed different, subdued. And she looked different. In the light of so many candles her face had a burnished hue. It was the atmosphere of the place. Too much imagining, too much incense in his nostrils. He had to get a hold on himself. Talk to her!

"Didn't you mention someone called Shiva?"

"That's right Shiva the Destroyer." Instinctively they spoke in whispers. "And his wife is called Parvati, also known as Kali. This temple is actually devoted to Sri Mariamman, who is a manifestation of Parvati." His bemused face made her smile. "I know it's complicated. But it's a lovely religion. So all-embracing. They have a god or goddess for everyone. Somebody once wrote that if they were all counted there'd be three hundred thousand million of them; because everyone on earth has his own conception of God. Isn't that a wonderful idea?"

Roger was far from ignorant. For the better part of his two decades the joy of books had loomed large. But Eastern theology? Somehow he'd missed that.

"Certainly is. Makes the old C of E appear rather impoverished." She emitted a little choked-back sound and he realised he'd nearly made her giggle out loud. Progress. If he could tickle her funny bone ...? He pretended to be shocked.

"Mrs Morrell – really! Laughing – here of all places!" Her shoulders heaved in suppressed mirth and her elbow dug him as it had on the Aden boat. How strange that he, the junior partner so to speak, should be the one doing the leg-pulling. And stranger still for it to be here. Sealed off from the strident world outside, moving quietly through this holy place. Overhead, a splendid frieze ran round the ceiling, in line with a row of Sanskrit lettering. There was a host of carved and painted figures in vibrant pastel colours, each one with a different expression and all watching these intruders from another continent.

Serious again, she told him who they were.

"That's Brahma the Protector and Shiva the Destroyer. And that one there is Vishnu the Preserver."

"I must say you're well up on all these characters." There was no answer and he feared he may have been too flippant. Quite obviously she was keen on all this so a measure of respect of his part would not come amiss.

"The power of prayer," he said wisely. "I imagine it can teach every one of us something." She nodded and walked on. So far no mention of Ruth or the awkward end of that party.

Gold, precious stones, Spanish and Italian tiles. The grandeur took their breath away. But eventually they'd seen their fill of it. Outside, the gateway soared above them.

"I know the right name for this," he said.

"Do you now, and what might that be?"

"It's a *gopuram*."

"That's right." She sounded pleased. "Have you been studying?"

"No. An old Chinaman told me today. In Hokkien Street – a shopkeeper." The Leica was busy again. Another one of the gateway and a long shot down the street captured the whole lively medley of it.

"I bet it was Tommy Wang," she said.

"It was and I got this there." The Buddha came out of its wrapping to be duly admired and assessed.

"Two dollars? That's a bargain Roger. It's a good place to go, the Treasure House. I've got things there in the past. He knows a lot, old Tommy Wang. He once gave me a long lecture on Asian beliefs plus a lot of stuff on Confucius. Did he tell you anything else?"

"No and Confucius wasn't mentioned. Mind you, when I first met him I thought he *was* Confucius!" He could have bitten his tongue off. The effect however was gratifying. The camera wobbled as she tried to contain herself. Then she gave up and lowered it, giggling like a schoolgirl.

"Oh Roger what am I going to do with you?"

"What did you have in mind?" An error. She turned away, ostensibly for another shot but behind the now rock steady camera her face had straightened grimly. Would he never learn?

"Me and my mouth," he offered cautiously.

The shutter clicked, she wound on the film and turned to him. "I like you Roger. But remember I'm not Ruth Newbury." Lightly said, but the message was there. Keep your distance unless I give you the nod.

"What would you like to do now?" he asked. "Another temple?"

"No, I've done them all. It was only this one. They were restoring it when I was here before. There is somewhere else I want to go, if you don't mind tagging along."

"Not at all. Lead on."

The breathless humidity hung about them like an itchy cloak. It was a heat that appeared not to need sunlight. The dark shop-houses that hemmed them in, the very walls around them seemed to generate and pour forth the ever-present cloying dampness. Passing down South Bridge Road the fascination of everything kept them walking.

"I love Singapore," she said. "I once knew it so well, Chinatown especially." No further mention of Ruth. His fling with her seemed to count for nothing with Gina. Maybe if he – enough, he told himself. Ruth was gone. Nobody belongs to anybody. Take it as it comes. Same as everyone else was doing, from Quinn downwards.

The heat was getting to him, although she seemed unaffected. As cool as ever, she wore a white shirt much like his own, and a pair of khaki drill slacks. No hat this time but a polka dot headscarf of which even the knot was elegantly tied. Presently she turned right. Sago Street. The name jogged his memory.

"Is there a Custard Lane hereabouts?"

"Next turning."

"What's after that? Rhubarb Crescent?" It wasn't that funny. Yet her head went back and a peal of laughter rang out over the vendors' cries; over the hooting trishaws and the squawking of a nearby radio. An utterly carefree sound, sweeter than birdsong and as inspiring.

Gina, I want you. The words flew round in his head. But all that came out was, "I'd like to buy you a drink if I may. Go somewhere cool."

"I know the very place – where we're going." Custard Lane, he thought. We'll meet Bill and Martin, pie-eyed and festooned with harlots.

"Gina, I've heard about this area. Why are we coming here?"

"You'll see." They passed the end of Custard Lane and continued up Sago Street.

Outwardly the Jade Palace and Bar was much the same as any other eating place in a long, pungent line of them. Vivid Chinese signs marched up and down square columns framing the entrance, over which the name was painted in a flamboyant swirling script with a curled end to every letter.

"I want to pay a call on somebody," she said and pushed through the doors. Inside was a noisy mixture of all races, busily chomping and chattering their way through the most diverse selection of food he'd ever seen. She led him through the packed mass of diners to a flight of marble steps. These led to a second, upper restaurant. Here the tables were well spaced, each having snowy napkins, gleaming silver and a centre display of carnations. There were only a few patrons, people ready to spend extra to escape the gorging masses below. There were wide windows half shaded with rattan blinds, and the ceiling fans he'd always known were a feature of these places. They were impressive affairs with brass centres and squared off wooden blades like the airscrews of early flying machines, revolving at precisely the right speed to cool everyone. She spoke to a waiter who hurried away.

Roger picked up a menu and read, "Goose in soy sauce with fried goose blood and garlic", "Roast pigeon and braised eels with bamboo shoots", "Baby squid and rice". When he came to sharks fin soup and neck of giant clam he couldn't go on and put the menu back, hoping fervently she wasn't hungry.

"Let's sit here," she said, choosing a table by a window. "My friends will be along in a minute." From here they could look out over the enclosing shop-houses, a jumbled roofscape of steep gables or flat tops with a whole forest of potted plants. A lurid sign read Miranda Beers. And everywhere the fluttering flags of laundry on long bamboo poles thrust out from windows and balconies. "There's the temple," she said. Three blocks away the Hindu building soared over its neighbours. To the right of it across the buzzing commercial heart Keppel Harbour sparkled.

"I can't see the *Garvie,*" he said lightly. "I hope she hasn't gone."

"Who cares? I'm going to jump ship Roger. Settle again here in Malaya. Buy my old bungalow back. Want to come with me?" An enticing notion, even though he knew it was impossible. What about money, immigration papers, luggage? Of course she was kidding – wasn't she? He tried to think of a way to decline that didn't sound stodgy or, heaven forbid, unadventurous.

"Thanks for the offer but I want to see Hong Kong and Japan." Inspired, he added, "I'm dead-set on getting pictures of those arches they have. You know, with the ends turned up."

"They call it a *torii,*" she said eagerly. "That particular arch. That's another one you've learned today, to go with your *gopuram.*"

"Gina!" somebody called. The man was tall and bearded, wearing the oatmeal linen suit so favoured by expatriates.

"Gina my love. How wonderful to see you again." He bent down and kissed her.

"Roger," she said. "This is Neville Pickard – Roger Wren." They shook hands.

Roger said, "How do you do?" wishing he could think of something sophisticated to say. In truth he was a mite put out having to share her company. There was never enough time.

"May I?" said Neville and took a seat. "I hope you haven't ordered yet. Gina – I know your favourite, Singapore Sling. Roger?"

A waiter hovered. His mind raced. He had no idea what a Singapore sling was.

"Try one," said Neville. "We do a great Sling here at the Jade, even if I do say it myself. Better than you'd get at the Raffles even." The beard swung away from him towards her. "Gina, we should have kept in touch more. How long is it now, a year?"

"Yes, I'm getting over it more now. I've sold the boat."

"We'll miss John. We were devastated when we heard. Me and Yingsu." Gina glanced around.

"Where is Yingsu?"

"Trouble in the kitchen – new staff, she'll be along. Did you notice I've squeezed in more tables downstairs? And I've extended this room another fifteen feet." Roger realised he was sitting with the owner of the restaurant. The drinks came and they raised their glasses.

"Cheers," said Neville. The Sling was very agreeable. Tangy and cool with a delightful kick to it.

It was depressingly obvious they were old friends. Gina, this man and his wife. While they chatted and told each other how Singapore was changing he studied the view again. Of course he had no right to feel miffed. Perhaps she had hinted vaguely at a sort of date. Back in Ruth's cabin when they'd all had a fair measure of drink. But it was no more than a friendly gesture. Clicking away with their cameras for a while till she went to see Neville and who was it, Yingsu? She would probably spend the day with them while he had to crawl back to his skivvying job. A familiar word came his way. Ful-Vue.

"Sorry. I was admiring this lovely view of your town."

Neville was holding the camera. "Ful-Vue. Funny shaped thing. Get good results with it?"

"Oh yes. Not big though, only two and a quarter inch square. But they usually come out well. It's a good lens."

"When am I going to see them?" asked Gina. "Roger's quite handy with portholes. I'm still waiting to discover his other talents." He couldn't look at her face when she said things like that.

"Actually I took a film in the other day." He told them about the Colombo porthole shot and was surprised by the reception this got.

"That sounds a novelty," she said thoughtfully. "A round view inside a black surrounding."

"Couldn't you use a shot like that?" said Neville.

"For the gallery you mean? If it's sharp enough to blow up. Graininess can be a problem."

Gina, he now recalled, was hoping to show her work in an exhibition. "I want to see your pictures Roger – OK? That one in particular; as soon as you get the prints back. Who's doing them?"

"One of the crew."

"Well I hope he knows his business. A good negative is vital. I'm getting mine done in Hong Kong." His snaps on public display. Good going for scullion. He wondered how he might get the prints to her. Going to her cabin was too risky now.

Neville said, "I'll go and see where Yingsu's got to. I know she'll love to see you again."

When he'd gone Roger said,

"How did you come to know them?"

"Through John. They were in the army together and got captured; ended up in Changi."

"That's the prison camp."

"Yes. Unlike many POWs they were kept on there, never left the island. Then when the liberation came Neville met this Chinese girl employed by the Allied Commission. Her father owned this place. When he died Neville married her and they took it over. This was after months in hospital recovering from the four years in Changi.

Roger revised his estimate of jolly Neville. The shallow front hid a deeper pain, buried in a too recent past. "The restaurant was in a terrible state at the war's end. Smashed and looted. Now look at it. They both worked their socks off to make it what it is today. His army friends helped."

Neville returned with his wife. Yingsu was unusually tall for an oriental and seemed a good match for her lanky husband. Wearing a *cheongsam* of shimmering purple silk, she carried herself with the same easy grace as the younger bar girls he'd seen down on South Bridge Road. If I remember anything at all of this, he thought, it'll be the stunning women. The *cheongsam* fitted her like a second skin, from the high tunic collar down to the daring split at each side. But she wasn't smiling. Something was amiss and they soon heard what. "I'm really sorry," said Neville.

"We've had a telephone call. It's Yingsu's mother. Taken ill. Might be serious. We must go to her. Now, I'm afraid."

"Nothing we can do?" asked Gina.

"No, really I'm sorry about this. I'll leave Ali my restaurant manager in charge. I pay him enough and it won't be the first time he's done it. You both stay. Have a meal. On the house of course. I'll leave word with Ali."

There were more handshakes and comforting words; a sudden end to an agreeable thirty minutes. Roger asked Yingsu, "Have you got far to go?"

"Oh yes." Her voice was low and husky. "On the mainland. A long drive. Two hundred miles. To Kuantan."

"Do write," said Gina. "Let me know how things go. I'm still at the villa." Neville downed the last of his Sling.

"We will. Sorry again about this. 'Bye Roger, nice to have met you. Take care of Gina won't you?"

As they hurried away Roger said, "They seem a good couple."

"Yes. These mixed marriages don't always work but that one does. I know another couple like them in Hong Kong, neighbours of mine. Neville's one of these types who just naturally adapt to a country like Malaya. Despite what he went through here. Europeans either hate it or fall in love with it. There's something about the Far East that affects people."

This was true. Never mind the paralyzing heat, the frenetic trading and the avalanche of odours. There was something and he was beginning to feel it. He could see and hear the street life below them in the heaving stews of Chinatown, the ceaseless ant-like activity, the spirals of pungent smoke from the little cooking stoves along the sidewalks and he marvelled at the benign muddle of it all. She said, "I don't want anything to eat. Do you?"

"No. I'm afraid I've got to return aboard." The Buddha was retrieved from under the flowers of the table display. He hadn't wanted to flaunt it. Too "touristy" for people of Neville's background.

Up till today his shore visits had been fraught affairs. Always with a thread of unease to speed him back to the *Garvie's* steel bosom. Now he wanted to stay in this high, cool room with its "colonial" fans, enjoy his Singapore Sling and go on talking with the erudite woman who seemed to have so many hobbies.

"Are you doing anything tonight?" he asked her. "If not we could come ashore again. Go uptown. I'm sure there must be an uptown."

"There is. It's *very* uptown." Possibly implying he couldn't afford to take her there. Almost certainly true, but it piqued him nonetheless. "Roger, please don't misunderstand me. I was going to come back here tonight. We could have made an evening of it, the four of us; free meal and transport. Neville would have done the honours. Now ..." A hand lifted and dropped in resignation. "Now I've put a damper on your afternoon. You wish now you'd gone off with your friend Clay."

"No I don't, really. I'm not one for boozing, you know that." The abrupt and sad departure of the Pickards had upset her, he saw that.

She said, "I'll be staying aboard after dinner. The ship will be quiet with so many ashore. Good chance of an early night; shower and bed, with no one to disturb the peace." He glanced at her, but she'd turned away as if to study the party of shark-faced businessmen in Hawaiian shirts at the next table. So it would have been another foursome, but nothing like Aden or Colombo. But now it was off. His first night in a foreign port would be spent alone. And yet, her last remarks had again been ambiguous. Empty ship. No disturbance. And she wanted so much to view his pathetic snaps. That was a pretext if he ever heard one.

"But Mr Quinn sir, the lady invited me." No it would be insane. Gina liked to tease him, that was all. Wishful thinking did the rest.

"Would you care for a cigarette?" he asked her.

"Thank you. I do have an occasional one." They lit up and sat there quietly, with the ceiling fans going *wish – wish – wish* and the street song of Singapore drifting up from below.

"Tell me something," he said. "Your cabin has a porthole. Yet someone I know swears it hasn't."

"The someone being Ruth Newbury – and she didn't believe you went there to open it. Is that anything to do with her dip in Colombo Harbour? Oh, don't look surprised Roger. Everyone knows about the blonde mermaid of No 2 boat. I'm only glad it wasn't Pauline. Much nicer girl I thought. Did you have words with Ruth?"

"Yes. I was called a twerp and a liar. The last thing she said to me was that she would be the first off the boat. At that point she fell overboard." Gina did it again. Head back and that contagious laugh that made even the Hawaiian shirts look up from their Peking duck.

He told her about the Colombo caper and some of the other startling things that had come his way. Even his RAF service and poetic leanings got a mention.

"I'm doing a poem now about the sea." She enjoyed it all, taking in her stride the tale of Linda's visit and Antonia's impending nuptials.

Unexpectedly she said, "Where do you work on the ship?"

"I'm not a bedroom steward."

"No, I had a suspicion you weren't. So what do you do?" In spite of himself he couldn't keep a defensive note from his voice.

"It's not a bad job. I'm in the crew mess. Fetching the food and strapping – washing up afterwards."

Pensively, she toyed with her drink. "Carrying food and washing up. What an exciting occupation. I know because it's exactly what I did myself. For three years before I met John. While I was studying."

"Really?"

"Yes, really. In a place in London, not a smart one like this either. A real working girl I was even though my father ran a shipping agency." Would she ever stop springing surprises?

A waiter appeared. "Would you care to order now sir? There will be no bill." What a novelty. The Lodger was in an exclusive restaurant with a female companion, and he could order anything they liked, on the house. The only snag being the menu. Everything on it turned his craven English stomach. And there was little time anyway.

"Are you sure you're not hungry?" To his relief she shook her head.

"I had a very good lunch on board. If it's fine with you I'd like to go back. Didn't you say you were due on board too?"

"Afraid so, but I'm hoping for a day off in Hong Kong."

Down on the street he said, "Let's have a taxi."

"No need. Save your Malay dollars for homeward bound. When do you have to be back?"

"Half four at least."

"Plenty of time, come along, Roger, it's not far. A good stretch of the legs."

So they went back to the corner, took a last look at the Hindu temple and trudged the rest of the way to the junction with Tanjong Pagar Road. As he'd suspected, the taxi driver had taken him all over Chinatown. He could have walked straight to Sri Mariamman. But then he wouldn't have got his Buddha or made a Confucius joke for her to double up over and think him a proper caution.

The moist heat still gripped everything and the dismal overcast threatened another storm. But the ever-changing backdrop of unusual buildings and monsoon-fresh tropical blooms were a pleasant distraction.

"I'll try to get the photos to you," he said, without knowing how.

Still there was no direct invite, she merely said,

"Do that Roger. I'll look forward to it." On D Deck square there was a brief uncertainty between them. "Well ... thank you Roger, for the company. I enjoyed our little excursion no end."

"But you've seen it all before."

"No matter. It's always good to have a companion to share it with." The gangway sailor was watching them. She took off the sunglasses. "Don't forget the prints will you?"

"Trust me."

"I do Roger – I do." Slipping the camera case from her shoulder she wound the strap slowly round the case.

"My father always said to me, there can't be much wrong with a man who loves the sea." Another of her waggish elbow-prods and she was gone. The sailor turned back to his work. Stewards – always getting the best korey.

Before going below Roger called on Byfield, the man with the makeshift darkroom.

"All done my son. Five bob to you."

"I've only dollars on me."

"Couple of bucks then." Byfield was ex-Cunard. Roger paid. The hand stayed out. "And another dollar for getting 'em done so soon." An envelope was passed over. Roger never checked his photos the moment he got them back. Even at home he liked to settle down in private to view the results. And this time the results were crucial. If they were good he would have to visit B Deck. There would be no yellow-bellied excuse not to. Yes he did want to go. But – widows. Imagine her in Quinn's office. If she turned against him he'd be for the high jump, no question.

Jack liked the Buddha but everyone else reproved him for spending good beer money on a lump of porcelain.

One of their heaviest chores was emptying the two gash-bins, great riveted iron tubs with handles. Depending how full they were, these had to be dealt with twice daily. Upended over a galley chute, a stream of discarded food would be shot into the passing sea. Generations of seabirds and fish had reaped this bounty for years. But in port bins had to be manfully lugged ashore to be emptied by local labour and retrieved later. Tonight it was Jack and Roger's turn. The first bin was only half-full, but the other overflowed with semi-liquid waste and weighed a ton – it seemed.

"Keep your legs together and your back straight," warned Jack. "Otherwise you'll get a hernia."

Down the galley they struggled, past the now closed chute, through the shell door and across the short working gangplank to the quay. Here they placed the bins in a line of others, all marked EG. (There were other ships doing the same, and gash-bins rules forbade mixing with neighbours!)

"Take a breather," said Jack, and sat on a bollard. "I saw you today. Coming back aboard with a woman – a different woman." There was concern in his voice, not the nudging tone the others would have used.

"Yes. It's someone I met some time ago before the other one. When I first went to B Deck she called me over. Then later on—" Jack interrupted.

"Don't tell me any more. It's your life. Are you expecting to get away with it a third time?"

Behind Jack, Roger could see the main gangway; a small group were piling into a taxi. One of them was the First Officer escorting a lady. And this man was the only denizen of the upper decks who could recognise him as a trespasser, white jacket or not. The man was going ashore. For the evening probably – or all night, given his reputation.

"I just saw Quinn going off in a taxi."

"Then I guess that answers my question. As long as you know what you're doing. Be careful that's all. Me – I'll keep my trap shut." They returned aboard.

Work over, the other five got ready to descend on Singapore. It was the first overnight stay of the voyage. And everyone harangued Roger for staying aboard, except of course Jack. Said he slyly, "Perhaps the Lodger's got more secret korey up top somewhere."

"Too soon," said Bill. "Even for a randy sod like him." When he was finally alone he took Byfield's envelope over to the rusty table under the porthole. Another of his Moments. What if they were no good?

He could hardly rap on her door and say, "The snaps were awful but I came anyway because you've been dropping hints." And if they had come out well he still didn't *have* to go. He could get someone to deliver them. But then she'd have to send back her answer and – oh it was all too involved. Impulsively he tore open the envelope. The twelve prints and their negatives were far and away the best he'd ever taken. And the porthole shot was exceptional. Holding the negative up to the light only confirmed this alarming fact. Very well then, so be it.

Later, shaved and showered, he donned Clay's jacket and crossed the after well-deck. It was eight o'clock. A huge wall of black cloud was coming in from the north, rolling down the Malay Peninsula as if to cut him off before he could reach B Deck. And he could hear more thunder somewhere. He was on the brink of another experience, he could sense it. Gina's whole family of gods was watching him, he could feel that too.

B Deck was deathly quiet. Unlike when at sea the motionless ship made no noise now that the usual movements had ceased. The port side corridor was deserted save for a steward and stewardess outside the small pantry at the forward end. Soon they went inside and shut the pantry door. A woman passenger came out of a cabin and walked away from him. He found B98 and gave a cautious tap. There was no response. The woman returned, passing the end of his side-alley without glancing down it. In the main corridor a voice called,

"I say, Janet. Have you seen our steward anywhere?" His nerves shrieking, he knocked again.

"No I haven't," said Janet.

"Seems we're expected to fend for ourselves tonight." His white jacket felt like a shining beacon. The first speaker went on.

"I thought I saw one a moment ago then he disappeared." He screamed silently inside his head.

"They're in the pantry! Why don't you look in the bloody pantry?"

At last her door opened. "Roger, so soon." Once inside with the door shut he breathed again. Somewhat unexpectedly she was in the black dressing-gown he'd first seen her wearing. An early night she'd said. Eight o'clock?

"I've got the photos."

"Splendid. Take a seat Roger. I get the impression you had a scare on your way here." He took out the envelope.

"It's the white jacket. Part of the disguise but it carries the risk of being called on for things."

"Disguise?" He remembered he'd never told her of the out-of-bounds rule, or even the bridge summons. So he did so now.

"Roger, I didn't realise."

"Oh yes, when you called me in about this porthole that was my first transgression."

"No wonder you had a worried expression that time. On the way to cabin 126 weren't you? I'm sorry I teased you." So it was only that, he thought – teasing. And since …

"Fancy you being on the bridge over Ruth and her mishap. Thank goodness you didn't get the sack for that." It hadn't only been "for that" but she needn't hear what Quinn had really accused him of. She must already know anyway, or suspect. "Then you shouldn't really be here now."

"No, but I wanted to get the photos to you. There was no other way, unless you came down the glory hole."

"The what?"

"The crew quarters. That's what they're called – the glory hole, though I can't think why. Certainly it's a hole but there's no glory attached to it."

This made her laugh, as he'd known it would. Something was lessening by the minute the gap of age and status between them. He was young, with the innocence of his years yet possessed knowledge and understanding enough to converse with her on a number of things. In the Jade Palace talk he'd known what the infamous Changi was. He'd taken a genuine interest in the artifacts and painted effigies she so loved. And now there were the photographs.

"These are terrific," she said. "That lens of yours is good, as you said. I love the ones of Port Said and the Bitter Lake. And as for this —" She held up the porthole shot negative. "This is going on display next to my offerings in the gallery."

"I'm glad you like it." If nothing else, he would share a wall with her.

"I'll have this blown up," she went on. "Say, eighteen by eighteen. We'll call it — um — let's see now; 'Landfall'. Yes, or perhaps 'Harbour'. Funny, all the ones I've taken, I never thought to simply aim at a window. It's the round black framing makes it stand out. And you can see a faint shine of brass at the edge of the circle. It's wonderful." The outpouring of praise left him a touch cynical; all this about his picture being so special. Gina had a better camera, her own cabin and all the time in the world to take porthole shots before her gallery event.

They chatted on, while the *Empire Garvie* lay grave-quiet at her moorings. Outside the porthole the light was fading. He listened with unfeigned interest as she described life in colonial service. Like Neville, John Morrell had been released from Changi and also stayed in the Far East, getting more government work and moving to Hong Kong.

"It was good, our time there." She told how they would take a boat round the island, visiting captivating small bays with names like Big Wave and Shek O, Polly's Bay and Tai Tam Bay. He heard about the Nine Dragons, the line of hills over Kowloon, and the curiously named Tiger Balm Gardens. It was as though she yearned to tell someone of times once known and still missed; someone who would really listen. Someone like – who else? – Roger Wren.

He wondered if there were any young Morrells. "And you married when? Before the war?"

"Just before. 1939. You're thinking … any kids?"

"No — I —"

"That's alright. No, after Changi John was — no – we never

had any children. As it was we only managed a few years together anyway. When the Pacific War began I was in Australia on a work assignment. Well, his work too. And of course when Yamashita and his boys started down the peninsula there was no getting back here. Everything was going the other way." Through the port came a muttering of thunder, distant but full of menace. Like the guns of that advancing army nine years ago.

"Is there a Hindu god of thunder?" he asked.

"Probably, but I can't think of him. There's the Scandinavian one, Thor. Good name, Thor. He'll do.

Inevitably she was offering a drink. "I'm afraid I can't run to a Singapore Sling. How about sherry?" He didn't want a drink, he wanted her.

"Fine, thanks."

"Roger do take off that white jacket. You look like one of Neville's employees." He did so. "I'm glad to see you've got a better tan now."

"Yes. I remember that early one. I resembled badly fired terracotta." This time she forgot the need for caution and burst into a guffaw loud enough for the whole of B Deck to hear.

"Roger you must be the star turn down the glory hole."

"I'm not, quite the reverse. They thought I was green. Still do. But the main thing that gets them is I'm rather thin." He took a sip of sherry, convinced he'd said too much.

"What if you are? Most women don't care about that. It's a sense of humour they value."

"I guess so. There's a funny side to most things if you can find it."

"Stand up," she said. Half-expecting to be ordered to strip, he obeyed. There was little doubt what was happening. The business with the photos, her ready appreciation of every second-hand quip he made, and now this physical appraisal.

"Turn around. Hm. Slim that's all you are. Frank Sinatra's the same, and look at the fans he's got." He sat again.

"I'm sure he's never been likened to a matchstick with the wood scraped off." Another bulls-eye. As she choked on her drink he lobbed in one more. "They said if I took a shower I'd have to run about in it to get wet." By now she was wiping away helpless tears. He found her hugely intriguing. Where Ruth's appeal had been there from the start, entirely physical and shallow as tinsel, Gina's came in a plainer wrapping. A blend of slightly mannish humour and the broad bit-of-everything knowledge of a traveller, but presented in a lighthearted and challenging way that was purely feminine.

"Pity about Yingsu's mother," he said while he cast about for more jokes.

"Yes, it would have been a super evening."

"Never mind, perhaps I can get us invites to Antonia's wedding. I wonder who'll be the best man, the bride or groom." She began chuckling again so he went on. "When you think of it; a thing like that gives new meaning to the term 'bottom drawer'." For an instant he feared he'd gone too far. No – banging down her glass she snatched a handkerchief and spluttered into it, gagging with mirth.

"Roger, I must say you're a change from most of the crew I've met. They only seem to want to brag about their travels and achievements. Or they keep making lewd suggestions. My conversation bores them. I'd begun to think you were all the same. Instead I've laughed more in the course of today than I have in weeks. You're not all the same – you've proved that."

"Well, I've travelled nowhere and achieved nothing. So thank you. We do aim to please and proof is very important."

In the dim light he could just make out the dragon on her gown, coiled round her body like a live pet, moving when she did and glaring at him bug-eyed from her left shoulder. He wondered if she wore anything under it.

"Precisely how good is your aim to please?" she said quietly. Remembering the value of humour he said,

"Only one girl has gone overboard for me." Her smile now was a shade mechanical. As though there had been enough dalliance. "Gina, I find you intensely attractive." For a second she seemed less sure of herself, teetering on the brink.

"That's an easy thing to say."

"Do you believe me?"

"What if I said no to that?"

He waited till she put down her sherry. "I would have to prove it."

Now one small word remained to be said. And after an electrifying pause she chose to utter it.

"How?"

He'd never so much as kissed her. Yet when he took her in his arms it was as if they'd met years ago. And the physical allurement was only part of it. Yes, her body seemed to mould itself to him and yes, her sherry-sweet mouth was a joy to join with his. But there was so much more to it than this. All his wants came together as he held her. Throughout the voyage he'd ached for something like a kindred spirit. Ruth had satisfied one craving, at some emotional cost. And some of the men he shared the glory hole with were agreeable companions. But Gina, she had it all. Gina was happy with him as he was, revelled in his attempts at humour and talked of the world. The world he wanted to see and meet – the far-off pavilions of empire and the Kiplingesque colonial tribe who still ran them. And now one of them had stepped from the shifting scenery and joined him.

As they kissed again he found the dressing-gown cord in his hand.

"I seem to be holding the end of a cord." Her reply came as soft as the breeze rippling the port curtains.

"There's only one thing you can do with cords." Vanquished, the dragon died a silken death at their feet. No, there was nothing on underneath. Unexpectedly, she pulled away and sat on her bed. "Roger this is madness."

"We're both adults, and who's to know?" Now she uncoiled onto the bed and decorously turned away as he struggled with connie and clothes, trying to keep his movements calm and deliberate.

Facing the bulkhead she murmured,

"Did you — have you got —?"

"Yes, it's OK." So it was here, on a clammy Singapore night in 1950 that fortune smiled again on the Lodger. It would not be the last time. Or even the strangest.

CHAPTER 10

THE CLANDESTINE NATURE OF IT WAS both a check and a spur. Yet after all the hints, the vamping and giving him the clear go-ahead she was at first oddly nervous, talking in little bursts as they made love in the gloom and showing an uncertainty that was light-years away from Ruth's up-front sexuality. They were both grown-up yet the awful hallowed stillness of the ship made every movement and whispered word a guilty act that must bring a raging Quinn to bang on the door. But gradually they came down from the razor-edge of tension and the quick take-it-now urgency.

"Ever since I first saw you," he said, "I pictured this." They rolled sideways and she became a naked silhouette against the white bulkhead.

"Did you now?" Her poise had returned. She adopted an impossibly upper-crust manner. "And what made you imagine I'd be interested in a mere servant?"

"Well lady," playing along, he spoke in a rough "sailor-man" voice, "when we join the ship they sez to us, don't let the people get bored – keep 'em 'appy – so I sez to meself it's this or mahjong and I dunno that at all." The humour didn't always work. Her words were deadly quiet.

"So you think it's boredom, why I'm doing this."

"Steady on now. Don't forget you started with the funny voices."

"Yes, but that is my privilege Wren. Kindly remember your place." Startled, he realised she was still play-acting, taking the lady/servant pretence further. "Otherwise I'm afraid I'll have to punish you." She accompanied this with a sudden smack on his backside, stimulating him beyond all control.

"Yes madam – sorry madam." With no more ado he resumed his ecstatic duty, knowing even as he did so that someday, somehow he would pay dearly for this.

"You're quiet," she said when they paused. Before he could reply the thunder spoke again. Louder now, it seemed to target the ship, circling like a restless, unseen presence.

He squeezed her close and said, "My mother when I was a kid used to tell me that was the sound of God re-arranging his furniture."

"More likely showing disapproval of what we're doing." That was a jolt, after such a tremendous half-hour. By now he'd assumed her initial unease had long gone.

"Gina it's alright. We both wanted this."

"I know, but it's a risk. What if you get the sack for being here?" The nagging thunder and her sudden fretting had broken the thread somewhat. He wanted to recapture the earlier fantasy when she'd played the vamp to his deferential youth. But now came another intrusion, the patter of rain outside; gentle at first, then swelling to a roar as the heavens opened again. Unexpectedly she knelt up and looked out, whistling at the sight. He joined her and they put an arm round each other like toddlers in a cot.

"Like storms don't you?" With anyone else he would have felt foolish for asking.

"Not if I'm on the street in it or a small boat. But if you're somewhere safe a tropical storm can be exciting." There wasn't quite room at the porthole for two heads so they had to share the view, one eye each. The quay was covered in a moving, glassy sheet churned by the millions of heavy drops lashing down. Further back a corrugated warehouse roof shuddered under the weight, its row of lights dimmed under the cataract pouring off the edge. Lightning flared, and the universal wetness flung it back, lighting up the entire dockyard in glistening white.

"We used to do this. John and me, watch the rain."

"Is it the actual monsoon?" He wanted it to be. It was one of those things that made up his vision of the Orient along with joss-sticks, rickshaws and so much else.

"Not yet I think. When it does come it can go on for days. It's easing off already."

The weather seemed an incongruous topic. But with Gina, even conversing could be sensual. When she was so close and her breath was on his cheek.

"Have you been lonely since ..." he baulked at John's death, but she seemed in a mood for nostalgia "... you were left on your own?"

"Yes. When we were here before the war we thought we had everything. We both agreed, no children at first. Then the war turned it all upside-down. I spent the whole five years in Freemantle. Answering the phone and checking invoices while John —" she faltered "— John was in Changi." With freakish suddenness the rain stopped and the humid silence clamped down again. "Yes it has been lonely since he passed away. That God-awful Changi camp, that's what finished him. Neville got over it but John was — he could no longer — it wasn't the same as before." Slowly he grasped what she was trying to tell him. The "good times" in Hong Kong had been overshadowed by the cruellest deprivation of all. Gina and John, with their mahjong parties and island trips had lived since 1945 without that which sustains a man and woman in any happy partnership.

"I've never told anyone all this before. I don't know why I am now." He knew. Good listener. It was proving a useful attribute. "And if you're going to ask me Roger – yes. You are the first. There's been no-one since he went."

"Why me?"

"Because — oh I don't know — because you're rather like him I suppose. That kid in Aden, John would have done the same. Stayed with him as you did, nearly missing the ship. And faced that crowd." While he comforted her, Roger tried to work out her life in his head. They'd been split up by the invasion and when he got back her husband had been so ill, he was — what was the word? Then he'd died a year ago. No sex since 1942 – a woman like this? Incredible. Ah, but she'd said he was the first *since John went*. So maybe, in Freemantle and the four years between Changi and his death — maybe there were other games played after the mahjong sessions broke up and poor John was elsewhere.

There came a sound at the door. A small bump as though from an incautious elbow, followed by retreating footsteps. They waited but heard no more.

"I bet that was Farley," she said disgustedly.

"Who?"

"Farley my cabin steward – nasty piece of work. Made a few passes at me in a way I didn't much care for. I told you that night we met." He wondered if her cabin came under the same section as Ruth's further along. Farley could be the one paid by Clay for the use of the vacant B130. Perhaps he should have approached the man before coming here.

"Don't worry Roger. It'll be our word against his." He thought, not when Quinn hears I'm involved. And what about her?

"It would be embarrassing for you."

"Kind of you Roger to think of that but I wouldn't get the sack would I? When I get off in four days time this ship'll never see me again." Neither will I, he thought, and the thunder rolled again, underlining his mood.

Presently they made love again, if anything more ardently than before. He felt now an inner desperation, as if Farley and the ship and the leering, stodgy hypocrisy all around them were closing in, hastening the end of this special time.

"Roger, it's 10.40." They both knew he must leave soon. "Before they start coming back," she said. "This deck will come alive with them." As they dressed he tried to figure out where this relationship might be going. And there was the matter of the gallery exhibit.

"What about the photos?" he asked, switching on the light. She put on her gown and her reptilian protector resumed its watch on him.

Picking up the porthole negative she said, "This one's got to be enlarged as soon as I get back. Leave it with me. The exhibition's on the twenty-fifth."

"I'll be away before then."

"Yes, but you're going on to Japan so you're bound to call again on the way back. They'll still be on show." Outside on the dock they heard voices, shouting and running feet. "There are prizes for the pictures," she went on. "The best one gets 600 dollars, and then there are other amounts down to 100 dollars for each runner-up." There were more disturbances on the quay and people were shouting in alarm.

"We get there in four days," she said. "Come and see Wei Ho Bay." His spirits soared, then levelled off when she went on. "Bring a couple of friends. Ask your friend Clay to come."

"I'd like that very much." She wrote down an address.

"Here, this is the place and my telephone number. Call and let me know when you can make it. If you like I'll introduce you to somebody at Wei Ho who's absolutely mad about poetry." There was a hint of briskness in her manner and she realised this. Softening, she put her arms around his neck and kissed him slowly. "It's been nice Roger, knowing you. But we can't go on with it. They'll catch you and I'll never forgive myself."

"You said it didn't matter; his word against ours."

"I know I did, but all the same —" She was distracted by a fresh row on the quay and what sounded like two dustbin-lids being banged together. For the first time he saw her really angry.

"What in hell's going on out there?"

Roger peered out of the port, unsure of what he might see. A party of drunks quarrelling; one of the legendary "bundles" he was forever hearing of. But it wasn't that, or anything like it.

On the puddled concrete facing the ship was a half-circle of assorted passengers and crew. All were absorbed in a drama taking place near the edge of the dock. Here stood a man with a pair of gash-bin covers, now and then bringing them together with a clang. Twenty feet or so away two other men each held out a bamboo pole with a large fishing-net slung between them. As if on a stage they were all harshly illuminated by the dockyard lights. And in the middle of it was an animal.

"Gina, come and see this." He moved aside from the port, allowing her to put her face fully in the brass circle.

"Heavens, what's that? A leopard?" The animal was about five feet long from nose to hips with a smallish head and a sleek body that appeared to be composed entirely of muscle. Moving with a leisurely grace and defying all attempts of capture, it roamed at will, padding languidly about the quay, avoiding the pools of rainwater and blithely ignoring the "beater". As it moved, the shoulder blades behind its head poked alternately up and down, and the long curving tail just cleared the ground.

"He must have escaped from somewhere," said Roger. "Could be from a crate in that warehouse, on his way to a zoo."

She said, "Don't they have wild leopards in Malaya? I ought to know but I must confess I don't."

"I'm not sure he is a leopard. Let's have another peek out." The creature had spots alright but there was a difference, he knew. Needless to say, he'd read about it somewhere. The World again. So much to see, so much to relish. Spots. Yes, solid spots. Not the hollow ones of a leopard. And those long sooty streaks down each side of the nose. As if it was wearing mascara that had run in the rain.

"It's a cheetah. No doubt about it. And they don't have them in Malaya."

"Thank you Dr Livingstone. What's it doing now?" The scene was being enacted immediately below them.

"Making fools of everyone. Each time they get him under the net he nips out before they can drop it."

"Let's get some pictures." The Leica clicked and clicked again. "I don't have any flash equipment but we could be lucky. The dockyard lights might be enough." The cheetah was outnumbered. Egged on by the net-men, the bystanders closed in till the animal was trapped at the edge of the dock. Here it loped sadly back and forth, stopped and contemplated the murky water.

"Jump," said Gina. "Get away from them my beauty." They both wanted it to escape, this exquisite golden creature turning a disdainful back on the chattering mob around it.

"He won't jump," said Roger. "Not down there. He can't see where he'd land. And he's a cat. We know about cats and water."

They found they were thinking for the cheetah, willing it to stay free. It could have charged the crowd and they would have scattered like chickens. But the brain behind that handsome mask was not attuned to mere theatrical displays. The cheetah could stalk its prey, or chase it at seventy miles an hour over baking plains. It was not equipped to deal with weird beings that went about on two legs, made clanging noises and smelled strange.

"He's had it," said Roger. The cheetah raised its noble head and stared straight at them, as if their porthole might have been a last refuge. A little too far to jump. Now for the first and only time it gave voice. The ears went back, the whiskers turned up like a Prussian moustache and the wide mouth opened in a long snarl of despair. The net descended, to be swiftly drawn together and secured. They watched the cheetah carried off, its captors crowing with triumph and receiving the plaudits of the crowd.

"Roger please, you must go." Because of the cheetah a fair number of people had been gathered on the quay and these were now pouring aboard. Putting on Clay's coat and grabbing the remaining photos he took this bewitching woman in a last embrace and thought of the amazing string of events that had brought them together. Here on a rain-slick dockyard at the tail-end of Malaya. The place had even managed to lay on a wild and exotic animal for them, a fitting end to an evening, itself wild and not a little exotic.

"Gina, I must see you again."

"You will, at Hong Kong, the villa."

At the door he said,

"Bye, thanks for everything." God, was that the best he could do? They heard a rush of footsteps in the main corridor.

"Go now Roger. Before they all see you leaving. And Roger ..." she grinned a schoolgirl grin "... stay slim."

Outside, people were drifting along the corridor discussing the cheetah or their impressions of Singapore. Among them was an officer in a white uniform, as yet too far off to recognise. Quick as he was, he got caught.

"Steward!" A woman taller than he was cut off his escape. On her nose was a large strip of sticking-plaster, as though she'd lately walked into something.

"Steward, what can I do with these silly dollars now?" The officer got nearer, alternately shadowed or lit as he passed each side alley. "Can I get my English pounds back? I didn't spend as much as I expected." Neither did I, he thought, but I'll be back in a few weeks.

"We'll be here till ten tomorrow," he said, trying not to look at her nose. "There may be stuff for sale on the quay till then. If not I expect the purser will change them back." Released, he snatched open the exit door, crossed the open deck and shot down the companionway with the alacrity of powder-monkey at Trafalgar. At the bottom he glanced back, half expecting Quinn would be on the top step. But there was only the Nose Lady watching him.

"You want to be more careful," she called, pointing to her injury. "Going downstairs, that's how I got this." In the glory hole, he paused at No 21. There was no sound from within. Very cautiously be peeped around the door.

"Enter!" boomed Batten from the dark cavern of his corner bunk. It was like their first meeting and again they were alone. "Roger Wren, you have the insufferably smug expression of one who has been to Arcadia and back. Approach fair youth and speak unto me of the widow Morrell." Batten's habit of giving his words a theatrical spin seemed to make him easier to confide in. As though nothing could ever faze or offend the man.

"How do you know I've seen her?"

"Roger, I'm sure you are aware there was an escaped cheetah on the loose a while ago, causing quite a gathering of natives and returning colonials, myself included. And in the course of this I chanced to look up at the ship while all about me were studying the animal. Need I say more?"

"You saw us at the port."

"I saw you and a female person I took to be the celebrated widow. That is, I saw first you, then her, then you again as you took turns at the porthole. It was not dissimilar to watching a Punch and Judy show. I expected you to state loudly that was the way to do it. I trust the union did take place?" Roger put the white jacket on Clay's bunk.

"Oh yes, it certainly did. Is everyone else still ashore?"

"Everyone, Seymour too. Kropp I can assure you always returns late. About two o'clock he'll come barging in. Now, I will hear your progress report. Did you make her laugh as I advised?"

"I did, and it worked like a dream." As he described events it was clear Batten was impressed.

"No ladder though, Roger, and no kinky massage. Alongside your other couplings this one sounds almost conventional, apart from the wildlife prowling about. I must say you've been extremely lucky, what with that and this photographic fame coming your way in Hong Kong. My own inamorata got off today but unlike you I have to at least get my breath back before leaping on to somebody else. I wish I had your daring – not to say stamina. So you went to the Treasure House?"

"Yes and a temple, and the Jade Palace. The swanky part upstairs; had a Singapore Sling. And I met the owner and his Chinese wife. Given more time we could have had a free meal, only to tell the truth I didn't fancy anything on offer."

"You should have eaten downstairs, English food there. Fish and chips if you want it. I saw Kropp there last trip. Did you buy anything in Tommy Wang's?" Hearing of the purchase, Batten became more serious.

"A porcelain Buddha for two dollars? What make is it? What does it say on the bottom?"

"I don't know. I'm sure it's not an antique."

Batten got up and searched in his locker. "Doesn't have to be, it can be brand new. Where was it made – that's the thing I did have a book here on porcelain. Now I need it of course I can't find it." Roger heard footsteps and checked outside. "Your people coming back I think, supporting someone between them."

"Probably Seymour. I'd advise you to go now unless you want to spend the rest of the night hearing his troubles. We can talk about the Buddha at some more peaceful moment."

His own cabin was still empty. Retrieving the Buddha he examined the ideograms on the underside. They meant nothing to him. He thought of the woman he'd so recently lain with and how she'd confided so much of her life to him. And he thought of the shallow way he'd discussed her with Batten. "Worked like a dream – what a way to talk of her! As if she was Ruth. But she wasn't Ruth. Gina wanted nothing from him but a few laughs and some enlightening talk. Giving herself to him had seemed a natural thing; a progression – a sort of topping to round off their day.

Feeling vaguely on edge he glanced out of the port. Here on the starboard side there was nothing to see but the inky depths of Keppel

Harbour and the riding-lights of anchored ships. Yes, he'd been so lucky. That was the unnerving part. Martin could be right. Sooner or later – he heard a sound, turned and nearly dropped the Buddha. A stranger sat on Pat's bunk.

"So, we meet at last. Where's your white jacket? Finished with it for tonight have you?" On the surface a friendly enough voice but there was something unsettling in it; a hint of secret knowledge. The man was about forty, had rather shabby steward's clothes and a face as pale as his own once was.

Roger said,

"I don't own a white jacket."

"No, don't need it in your job do you? Only for getting your korey up on B Deck where you got no fuggin' right to be, I seen you. We weren't all on deck watching the tiger." Still holding the Buddha, Roger drew up a chair and sat down. There was only one person this could be.

"It was a cheetah. Are you Farley?"

"Never mind my name. I know yours. I seen you up on my section twice now. First you went for a sniff round. That was in the Red Sea. Then tonight you were with her. That Morrell bitch." The word burned into his ears.

"Don't call her that!"

"Why not? What will you do about it? Have a go at me? I'll knock you through that bulkhead my son." Roger found he was clutching the Buddha tightly, as if he might absorb for himself some of that beatific calm. So this was the repellent Farley she'd told him of. No wonder he was peeved – seeing Roger succeed where he'd failed.

"Roger Wren's your name right? Been up before Quinn for fighting on the shore boat at Colombo and half-drowning that blonde party, so I heard. That young tart you pushed in was one of my bloods. By the time she'd sorted herself out the cabin carpet was soaked, and guess who had to see to that? Now you got this little game on with the widow. I reckon you owe me. I can drop you in it any time I want."

"There was no fight," said Roger. "And I didn't push anyone in. What is it you want with me?"

Farley crossed his legs and clasped one knee, rocking comfortably to and fro and clearly enjoying the situation. "This must be your first trip my son or you'd know the way of these things. You want korey? You pay for it. That woman's on my section so you must get me to look the other way. Otherwise I talk to the Chief Steward or in your case, Quinn. Save on introductions." Twice – the man had seen him twice; each time entering Gina's cabin, nothing about seeing Ruth. So he couldn't know about that. Of course! Clay had paid him for the spare room so he'd left them to it. Not knowing of Roger. Or even the second visit. Luck again, pure luck.

"Why did you call her that name just now?"

"Because she is one. Stuck-up and lah-de-dah. Even after what I did for her she wouldn't come across for me." Frustrated, eavesdropping Farley, beaten to the prize by a plate-washer half his age. It must be galling. As was his way, he had a pang of sympathy, even for an adversary.

"What did you do for her?" Farley stopped rocking.

"I got her that cabin didn't I? Before Port Said she was over to starboard in B83. Too hot she said. So after we started down the canal I had B98 going spare and I told her steward there'd be something in it for him if he agreed. Then I saw the purser and fixed the swap. And what did I get out of it? Sod all. Thank you very much steward and I'll see you at the end of the trip."

Roger was reluctant to put down the Buddha. It gave his hands something to do while he tried to think how to deal with this man. One way might be to establish some kind of rapport. Farley had a right to feel aggrieved.

"Yes, I can see you must be annoyed. Perhaps you went about it the wrong way. She did mention —" Farley's face darkened.

"Oh she told you I tried it on did she? Very nice. What a chuckle you must have had, both of you."

"No honestly. She hardly —"

"Shut up!" Farley leaned towards him. "Now you listen to me, and for God's sake put that thing down. You been hugging it like bloody Aladdin's lamp. It won't bring no genie to help you so put it down and listen to me." Roger placed the Buddha on Pat's bunk as Farley got to the point of his visit. "I want a fiver for tonight and a fiver to cover any future visits." Roger nearly passed out.

"A fiver! You can't possibly mean that! Alright I admit I should have spoken to you first. I'm sorry. But it wasn't actually planned. I never really believed – look, ten bob is the going rate isn't it?" He couldn't believe he was doing this. Bargaining over rights of access to Gina.

"Ten bob?" scoffed Farley. "Think again my son. This one's special. And she turned me down. Because of that you are paying over the odds. I'm kind of mean that way."

"I've only been with her the once."

"I don't care. Pay up or Quinn hears about it in the morning."

Money taken before the event is a bribe. Demanded afterwards, it's blackmail. The only difference was in the amount. He tried again.

"Have a heart. We all need spending money. I can't afford a fiver. There's weeks to go yet. And I don't get any tips."

"Too bad, should have thought of that before. And don't plead poverty. Not when you go buying stuff like this." Farley took the Buddha and tossed it to Roger who by a sheer fluke managed to catch it. "Well caught. Now give him another rub for luck. Go on; see if a genie does come to your rescue." The door opened. There was no drum-roll and puff of smoke as Batten entered, but there really should have been.

"Here you are, Roger. I found that book. Hullo Farley, what are you doing here? Putting the bite on someone I suppose, as usual."

"None of your business; this is a private talk between me and — and Roger. So if you don't mind —" Farley broke off in irritation as Batten sat on the bunk next to him and took the Buddha from Roger.

"Let's have a butcher's at this. H'mm, as I thought, cheap tourist junk. They saw you coming Roger. This is rubbish."

Roger was reminded of Emerson, the *Caronia*-borne merchant of misery whose expertise ruined his chances with Ruth. But Batten's words were strangely abrupt and coarse for him. Almost deliberately so, he thought.

Farley said, "Turning out an expensive day for you my son, one way and another. Remember what I said. I'll expect to see you later." Batten got up first and edged him back onto the bunk.

"Don't go. Finish your business with Roger. Perhaps I can help in some way. Would I be correct in thinking money is involved?"

"No, nothing. Look, I'm off." Again Farley tried to leave but Batten pressed him gently back.

"Yes, I'm sure this concerns money. Presumably fun and games on your section of B Deck."

"What if it is?" protested Farley. "I'm not the only one doing it."

"Of course you aren't. What sort of sums are we talking about here?"

Roger said, "He wants a fiver now and a fiver on spec."

Batten tut-tutted. "Oh Mr Farley, that is so unkind."

"No, it's not. It's only fair I get something for turning a blind eye."

"Yes, but for second-class BRs an attack of Nelsonian vision normally costs ten shillings. A fiver a throw smacks of extortion." Farley shifted uncomfortably.

"He can pay it. For this woman he's going to."

"Ah, someone special. Would that be —?" Batten glanced at Roger who nodded. "I thought so. The widow. But nevertheless —" Farley made his third vain attempt to escape and Batten leaned against him.

"Please, I shan't sleep tonight unless this is resolved. I'm wondering what the outcome will be should Roger fail to meet your demands." Silence. "Well?"

Farley squirmed. "I'd — have to — I'd —" The man was trying to put a respectable gloss on what he would do. "I'd — well I'd have to inform the Chief Steward. We're duty bound to report all these improper goings-on. Can't let it happen. More than my job's worth." Batten nodded understandingly.

"Yes, I can quite see your point. And this bounden duty, do you have to do it very often?"

"No. Alright maybe I did once or twice, long time back." Farley strove to regain the initiative he'd come in with. "Look, he pays up or takes the consequences. That's it. I'm saying no more. I mean, nobody likes having to — ah — shop people but if they won't play the game I can't just ignore it can I?"

"No," said Batten. "That would never do — er — these other times, when you had to report people, was Kropp one of them?" Farley was startled.

"Kropp? Not likely! What could I say about him? I've only spoken to him a couple of times and then he called me all kinds of names. Thinks all BRs are queer. Listen, I've had enough of this. You explain to this greenhorn what the score is."

"Certainly," said Batten. "But what do I tell Kropp?"

There was a momentary disturbance up the alleyway, violence – ugly and close. A voice screaming abuse, and a thrown bottle smashing against steel plating. Footsteps pattering rat-like into silence. Farley made a huge effort to appear unconcerned.

"I don't get you. Where does he come into it?" Batten put on a grave face.

"Kropp was called to the bridge in Colombo. Somebody made a serious complaint against him. Poor man, he received such a bollocking. They accused him of behaving badly. Not playing the game as you put it. As a result his constantly expressed wish is to meet the person responsible and rearrange the structure of his face and body. I would dearly like to help in his quest, put an end to his mental anguish."

By now Farley had lost all bravado. "It wasn't me — fuggin' 'ell – it wasn't me! I would never cross that mad bastard – nobody would. He's not normal!"

Batten's face became even more solemn. "Well, *somebody* did. And you have already stated your willingness to report anyone not adhering to the rules."

"Yes, but not him. I wouldn't dare."

"We have heard how Kropp so unkindly insulted you simply for being a bedroom steward, an honourable profession deserving of respect. No wonder you felt obliged to make an official protest."

"But I didn't – I didn't! I've never said a word about him to anyone. If he gets the idea I did there's no telling —"

"Calm yourself. Kropp at present suspects anyone he doesn't like the look of. That's a lot of people and he persists in asking my help in the matter. At this very moment even as we speak he is weaving his way down the dock road in an advanced state of alcoholic confusion, carrying more grievances and hate than he knows what to do with. The first thing he'll do is ask me how my inquiries are going. You can appreciate my problem. I could be *forced* to give him a name just to make him leave me alone." Farley shot to his feet.

"Well for God's sake don't give him mine. Fuggin' 'ell – tell him you don't know of anyone. You know what he's like. A joke's a joke but you can't go giving my name to Kropp." He appealed to Roger. "Tell him not to do it!"

Batten said, "Roger can't help matters I'm afraid, concerned as he is with how to raise your ten pounds."

Farley went through a charade of thinking deeply. "Oh, that. I reckon, on second thoughts that was a bit high. Let's forget that. Have that one on me Roger."

"No," said Batten. "Roger, give this man ten shillings." The note was pressed into Farley's trembling hand. "Rate for the job," said Batten. "And there will be no more extortion. Funny things – second thoughts. I'm thinking now I might give Kropp some other name." Farley gave a sickly smile and left, closing the door timidly behind him. Batten sighed and flopped out on Pat's bunk. "Oh what a tangled web we weave, when we first we practise to deceive. Any ciggies?" The Camels were produced.

"Thanks for seeing him off," said Roger. "That was good timing."

"I saw him come in here and guessed what he was up to. So I listened till it was the right moment to materialise. You've done very well, you and Clay. You've actually had five nights for the price of two, between you. Now then, this —" Batten picked up the Buddha again.

"Is it really rubbish?" asked Roger.

"No, that was for Farley's benefit. I didn't want him knowing what you had. See this?" The Buddha was inverted to expose the marks. "That's the sign of the pottery that made it. And when it was made." They consulted Batten's book. "There, I knew I'd seen it before. The Chokai factory right here in Malaya. It was made a couple of years ago. They turn out some of the finest porcelain outside of China. And you paid what? About four and eight pence?"

"Whatever two dollars is – yes."

Batten put the Buddha on the bunk and switched on Pat's light. Thrown into sharp relief the placid features with the faint Mona Lisa smile seemed more knowing and amiable than ever.

"He's brought me luck today," said Roger. "But why did Tommy Wang let me have it for only two dollars?"

"Perhaps he just liked your face. He's like that, old Tommy. Very unusual kind of shopkeeper. One minute driving a hard bargain, next he'll give something away to a passing stranger. I expect he gets these straight from Chokai. It's only up the east coast from here. You can get stuff here would cost a fortune in England. Jade, ivory, everything. By the time the wholesaler's been paid and the shippers and retailers and all the rest it gets dearer every mile it travels. This'll be worth three or four quid at home, in the Lanes of Brighton say. Trouble is, His Majesty's Customs and Excise might have ideas on it. Whack a big duty on. Stow it away somewhere. I'm off now. Cabin 21 will be bracing itself for Kropp's return after seven hours' drinking. Heads down, lights off and don't even look at him the wrong way. What a life."

"Thanks again. By the way, do you happen to know if Cabin B83 is inside or outside?"

"Funny question. I'm pretty sure it's inside. Why?"

"Mrs Morrell. That's how it all began. Between her and Ruth and that missing porthole."

"Please Roger. Some other time, forgive me but I must get my head down."

After he'd gone, Roger took a shower and climbed up into his bunk. There was of course no possibility of sleep. Not yet, after a day like this. His body was a compressed spring, still tensed and tingling from the passions and alarms of the twelve hours since he set foot in Singapore. Outside in the alleyway came the sounds of men returning from their first prolonged run ashore. The glory hole that had enjoyed a virtual peace all evening became a bedlam of chattering and light. One by one the cabins came to life as men told each other where they'd been and what they'd done. Toddy returned cold sober and offering little news of where he'd been.

"Few Mirandas in the Royal. Called on somebody. Old friend." The friend's sex and occupation were not divulged.

Jack and Pat were more forthcoming, describing a run of places. "Ended up at the Universal Club," said Jack. "On Battery Road. Stuck in there owing to the rain." This was the drill, he thought. You went ashore; you moved around then you "ended up" somewhere. We are autumn leaves, drifting among the remains of empire and taking it all in with a kind of languid thoroughness that is essentially British. They were waiting for him to speak.

"Me? I stayed aboard."

"You disappoint me Roger," said Pat.

It was no use. They were decent men, these three. Good men. From them he'd had only kindness. He would have no secrets, no happiness they could not share, if only vicariously. "There's this woman I met on B Deck."

What a strange reversal of roles it was; seasoned seamen listening to the escapades of a raw youngster, but then much was reversed on the *Empire Garvie*. The sexual inclinations of a number of her crew, an attitude to violence that was, to say the least, relaxed. And himself a late adolescent becoming embroiled with a female who might not have even noticed him anywhere else.

"I'm sure it's all true," Jack assured the others. "I saw him come aboard with her."

Pat said, "And with Roger there's always something extra. I heard there was some animal running around."

"Tiger," said Jack

"Leopard," said Toddy.

"Cheetah," said Roger. "Yes but that was nothing to do with me. Although watching it from her cabin —" Pat broke in.

"Ah now Roger, don't go betraying any more about your fine lady. I only hope you'll not be letting it go to your head."

"Fatal," said Toddy. He hadn't mentioned Farley or the Buddha valuation or the party at Hong Kong. That could still fall through.

"I wouldn't tell the young 'uns about her," said Jack. "Not yet anyway." About three o'clock when he'd managed about an hour of fitful slumber the other two arrived. Snapping on the main light, they exploded into the cabin with all the subtlety of Pamplona bulls.

"Roger!" yelled Martin, falling dozily against his bunk. "Still here then? What you been doing aboard all this time?"

"I'll tell you what he's been doing," said Bill. "Sod all, that's what. He's been lying there since we left him at — at seven o'clock last night." Another half-hour had to be endured as they prepared for bed, all the time pausing to talk at length on their doings ashore. A slurred, oath-filled account of how much drink consumed and how many women paid for and used. If but a fraction of it was true they shouldn't have been still upright.

"Custard Lane we ended up," said Martin. "Cor, Custard Lane. What a — what a —" He struggled, trying to trawl enough words from his addled brain to form a sentence.

"Korey everywhere," said Bill. "More than last time. Navy ships in. Must be this war in Korea. Of course you need your wits about you. Some of them try to roll you; half-inch your wallet. Best give them a smack in the mouth if they try it." On this edifying note the story ended.

Breakfast was hectic, and noisier than usual as the hungry throng regaled each other with tales of the night in town. When it was all done he called on Clay and they went on deck. Clay's visit to Singapore had been uneventful.

"The rainstorm was a nuisance. Crossing the street you got drowned. Nelson and some others went after korey. Me, I didn't fancy the ones I saw. I ended up in the Flying Angel, a sailor's club. Had a couple of Miranda beers, watched a film and came back. I never saw the leopard."

"Cheetah," said Roger automatically. "Did you see Kropp?"

"I did. Watch out for yourself. And what's this about you and Mrs Morrell?"

Retelling the remarkable hours yet again it seemed to have taken place on some other planet. B Deck swam above the glory hole like some misty Shangri-La.

"And we're going to a party in Hong Kong, me, you and I don't know who else to invite. She left it up to me."

"Are you seeing her again before then?"

"No, too risky now, and the steward's being difficult."

Down on the quayside the vendors were busy. He was pleased to see the Nose Lady, fresh plaster aglow, spending her spare dollars with happy abandon.

"Someone's coming," said Clay.

Antonia was flushed and excited. "Roger, I've been meaning to see you for days but that storm laid me up. God, what a morning I've had, to say nothing of last night. But I think we'll draw a veil over that. I know me and Steve won't be let back in the Raffles again. Legless we were by the end. Now, Roger. My messenger boy. What can I say? Thanks to you my worries are over."

"What do you mean?"

"The *Caronia*. I just managed to get on her before we sailed. Remember you braved facing Penny to tell me about my uncle? I hoped to squeeze a tenner off him. Instead I got enough to buy a decent outfit ashore instead of that abortion you saw me in. And I still had enough left for a simply *bona* party at the Raffles. All 'cos you got the message to me so quickly. So now you're invited, see? Ten o'clock tonight in the after storeroom. The bedding store."

"Can I bring a passenger – a lady friend?"

"Good God no! Definitely not! No women. But if you don't come I'll be very — very hurt indeed." Antonia patted his arm and hurried away.

Clay said, "You'll have to go. If not she'll turn nasty and come after you with accomplices. You know what they're like if you cross them. This comes from being too helpful and obliging. What with that Aden kid and the police. Seymour too. Cheer him up and he bites your head off. Now with this one and Linda you're the queers' favourite. And who's Steve?"

"I've no idea. Antonia's intended I suppose."

"Just be careful. Keep your pants on and your mouth shut. Of course, as a favoured guest," Clay made a heroic effort to keep a straight face, "you'll be expected to kiss the bride."

Chapter 11

Singapore was gone, with so much else he would never forget. Sri Mariamman's sculptures; the high cool room where a purple-clad Yingsu breathed "Kuantan" in his ear as though it were a lover's name; the teeming warrens of Chinatown, where another woman had talked of life and love before it all came true for him. And now they were at sea again. Back in the twilit madhouse of the glory hole, where Kropp stalked and Farley schemed, and where he now had to watch two *men* get married.

Jack was missing from the cabin that evening.

"Where's Jack?"

"Jack?" said Martin innocently. "Jack's away on his part-time job. Where are you off to?"

"Antonia's wedding. I got an invite." They didn't appear too surprised.

"Always thought you were one of them," said Martin.

"I can't be," he replied and mumbled something else.

"What?"

"I said, because I'm not hard of hearing." Reborn, the old gag still served. This time they mocked Martin.

The after storeroom lay deep, in part of the ship that had never known breeze or daylight, and whose shadow-crossed alleyways were half-lit by a few grimy bulbs. Here was a door stout enough for a castle, painted an "institutional" shade somewhere between rat-hide and Thames mud. He recalled coming here for his blankets. Why couldn't he just walk away from the whole idea? So he'd done the fish-cook a favour, so what? There was no need to attend this Alice-in-Wonderland ceremony. What would they do? He knew very well what they would do. They'd already manhandled him once. Strong as oxen, and probably in drag, they would come to his cabin and bawl him out. Then drag him below like trap-door spiders. He'd never hear the end of it in the mess. No, get it over with. Sneak in, wish Antonia well and be gone before anyone knew he'd been there. He tried the door. It wouldn't budge. The speakeasy-type panel slid open.

"Who are you?" said a face.

"Roger Wren."

"Never heard of you – piss off." The panel banged shut. Fair enough. If they wouldn't let him in he couldn't attend. Relieved, he hurried back to the stairway he'd come down by; glad to head for the stars and fresh air. Half-way up the sound of click-clacking feet made him pause. Now stairs, particularly if narrow and ill-lit, are not an ideal place to meet head-on. And when the person descending is in high heels and a flouncy frock wider than the stairs retreat is unavoidable. The frock was being lifted by the wearer to avoid contact with the dust on the steps, an action that revealed a pair of long legs so shapely he stopped in wonder.

"Young man, when you have quite finished clocking my lallies I want to get past."

The masculine voice was a shock. Back-tracking to the deck again he tried not to stare. This was drag, Merchant Navy style. Here was no pantomime dame, no concert-party parody. Clothes, hair and make-up might have been created by someone who worked in Paris and charged a lot. Only the deep voice and Adam's apple gave the game away. But it was a piece of jewellery that caught his attention first. Pinned to a shoulder was a small sparkly thing in the shape of a puppy and a kitten embracing. He knew then who this was.

"You're Carol."

"I am. And you're the Lodger."

"It's the cat and dog brooch that told me. Doreen had it and wouldn't return it."

Carol touched the brooch fondly. "That's right. Cute isn't it? It was mine in the first place. My friend Rupert gave it me in Southampton. But we had this awful fight and he took it back. So he starts going with Linda and she's wearing it. Then she's out of favour and before you can turn round it's pinned on Doreen's left tit. I don't know. Really super guy that Rupert was before he walked out on me, sort of cuddly you know? Like a big friendly Alsatian. Now I think of it he had all the best qualities of a dog. Except loyalty."

"How did you get the brooch back?" Carol licked a finger and rubbed at a smudge on the frock.

"Damn. Will you look at that? Ship's the filthiest I've ever been stuck on. Oh, it was all because of last night. Antonia's come into some money and we got her a new outfit at Hadley's in Singapore, spent the afternoon traipsing round the shops. After which we all ended up at the Raffles. Doreen of course was quite *livid* over the new dress 'cos the one she'd worked on wouldn't now be wanted. Silly whore got legless and insulted the manager. I had to literally *pour* her into a taxi. Ooh, what a performance. Then the driver overcharged us and called his mates over when I argued with him. In the end I had to pay it all *and* promise to sell the old dress for her when we get home. I've got this friend on the *Arundel* who'll snap it up. But I'm getting commission on it, oh yes, ten percent and this." Again the brooch was lovingly fingered.

Slightly dazed by all this, Roger said, "And are you going to the wedding?"

"Sweetie, why else would I put on my best gear and come down to this boghole? What about you? Why are you leaving? She invited you special." He saw what was coming and there was no way out. Not without more risk.

"They wouldn't let me in."

Carol grabbed his arm. "Is that so? We'll see about that. Come on." There was no hope now of low-key visit. The door received an energetic thumping on the panel, which caused it to jam in its grooves. The guardian had to open the door to see them. "Oh it's you Carol. So he's your friend."

Ignoring him, Carol swept in; shrieking salutations at the gathered company and towing Roger behind him like a fashion accessory. He was introduced to a group of men wearing all manner of female apparel.

"This is Roger."

"Hullo Roger, I'm Trixie." They were not all as well turned out as Carol. Trixie had overdone the lipstick, wore a gown that was less than immaculate and a curly wig of a style (and condition) that might have dated from the court of Louis XVI. The general effect was of an underpaid extra from *A Tale Of Two Cities*.

He saw the store man emerge from a small office. Presumably he'd been bribed for the use of his workplace. There were several "ordinary" people here who must have come for free drink and the spectacle of men dressed as women. There was a cloth-covered table with unopened bottles and an accordion on a chair. Antonia was not present, evidently intending to make the traditional entrance at the right moment. With one obvious exception, the inmates of Cabin 21 were also in attendance, including Seymour, wrapped in soundless melancholy,

"Surprise, Roger," said Clay. "You worried it was only you. We're all here."

"I wouldn't have got in without Carol. They shut me out."

"Antonia's fault," said Batten. "Forgot to tell the one on the door; there's a certain few being kept out, trouble-makers. We had a do like this last time. They love any excuse to camp it up and prance about. Everyone knows it goes on. As long as it's out of sight they say nothing. Some of the things that go on you'd be arrested for on shore but here ..."

Smith said, "This is nothing to what you get on Cunard or Union-Castle. I don't mind them but there's so many." Nelson was quiet but as fidgety as ever.

Batten said, "He wants any ale that's going, but he doesn't want Penny lusting after him again – right Mike?"

"Never mind me, when's this crazy business going to start?"

In answer came the sound of the accordion. Dah-dah-de-DAH! The first notes of the Wedding March blared forth around the stuffy chamber. He couldn't see who was playing it. Antonia's new dress was similar to the old one except for a halter neck and much better stitching. The "groom", Steve, he recognised as another fish-cook. The accordion stopped as the pair came together. A hush fell as even those who came to mock waited expectantly.

"Different world isn't it?" said Clay.

Roger said, "I'm waiting to see the priest. Is it one of the army chaplains?" They were looking at him again. Maybe his naivety was simply something that had to surface now and again. Like hayfever.

"Roger," said Batten slowly. "None of this is real. It's all a game. To us anyway. To them it's sort of real. The nearest they'll get to it till the law changes." The "priest" appeared. Wearing a dark suit and an ordinary collar turned back to front, he stepped forward and beamed at the couple. Roger got another surprise. The man in the dog-collar was Jack Cutler.

"I know the priest," he said weakly. "I'm in his cabin – I work with him."

"Nothing unusual," said Batten. "Cutler did this last time. They slip him a quid to do his act. Must look the part I suppose. Or they like his accent. Doctors or engineers always sound more convincing if they're Scots, same with clergymen." Jack had a book in his hands as he questioned the pair and glanced from one to the other. A ring was produced but there appeared to be no best man. What impressed Roger was the lack of any buffoonery on the part of the principals. Antonia, Steve and Jack conducted themselves with a gravity that shamed any would-be wags into tongue-tied respect. In a few minutes Jack closed the book and made the customary pronouncement. The happy couple linked arms. Roger hoped they wouldn't kiss – they didn't. The chattering assembly descended on the booze table. Here there was something of a crisis. Not everyone got a drink. This and a certain fading of the novelty caused some to leave, including Nelson, Clay and Smith. Soon the numbers were down to around twenty-five. Jack joined them, pulling off the dog-collar with evident relief.

"Phew – that's enough of that."

"Did you get a drink?" Roger asked.

"No but I will. The party's no' started yet." This sounded optimistic. It was past eleven and the drink seemed to be finished.

"It appears to be already over. What else is there to stay for?"

Jack murmured, "Oh, brother," and shook his head.

Batten said, "If you have to ask the question you're too young to hear the answer."

"Go to bed Roger," said Jack. "While you can." They heard a metallic rasp.

"Too late now," said Seymour. A second door-bolt had been slammed into place along with the first. Some of the lights were turned off. Antonia tapped two bottles together for attention, stood on a beer-crate and addressed the company.

"Boys and girls, homi-polones and anyone who may be on the turn. And all so-called men, of whom I can't see very many except my good friend Roger there. Nice boy. Don't hide away honey, show yourself." He longed to be invisible.

"All I did was take a message," he muttered to Batten. "And what are polones, homes or whatever they are?"

"Homi means man, Polone means woman. So a homi-polone – work it out."

Jack said, "Listen to the speech."

"First," said Antonia, "I want to thank Linda Reynolds and Penny Prentice for their efforts in setting things up and getting the drink in. By fair means and foul we have something for everybody stowed away here – now the company's down to a select few." Roger tried to recall where he'd seen the name Prentice before. "Secondly I'm indebted to Doreen Whittaker for helping me choose my *bona* new outfit yesterday. I have to say she wasn't too pleased at first but I believe she's now come round to it like the true pal she is. Also Carol Thomas for her support when things got out of hand at Raffles. Mr Cutler did his stuff as usual tonight. We are also grateful to Dave Gilray for getting such super music from his accordion. So thank you all for coming down here in this dreadful heat. Now do help yourselves to drinks."

From their hiding place under the table came gin, brandy and spirits of all kinds. There was more bottled beer and glasses of every size, evidently borrowed from the public rooms above. The musician moved into the foreground. It was the Master-at-Arms. Roger might have been surprised by this once. Not anymore. He'd seen it all now hadn't he? Wrong again. As the accordion wheezed out the strains of *Besame Mucho* he saw men pairing up with the ones in drag and doing a shuffling, giggling dance round the storeroom. Arms held waists, lips touched, conventions crumbled.

"Relax Roger," said Batten. "It's not real remember." But it was real. Men were dancing with men.

"Takes all kinds," said Jack. "Everybody does things their own way. Back door – front door — know what I mean? As long as they're happy and no-one's hurt, how is that a sin?" Seymour watched the dancers as though they were simply a part of the world he no longer lived in. The sadness on his face got to Roger again and he considered another attempt to console him. Being twice rebuffed was not encouraging.

Not far away was Farley, on his own and tapping his foot to the music. There must be several loners on this ship. Even, he ventured to tell himself, Gina. With her daunting intellect and outlandish interests she might well deter the average fellow traveller with only sex in mind. Not him of course. A little seed of conceit took root and he hastily stamped on it. He'd been as confident of Ruth before his hopes sank in Colombo harbour.

Batten fetched drinks for all four of them.

"Whisky for you Jack – right? Same for you Frank. Roger, can you guess what this is? A drop of brandy and gin, fruit juice and smidgeon of Cointreau. Oh and Angostura Bitters. Sorry no slice of pineapple."

Roger took a sip. "Singapore Sling! Thanks. Very thoughtful of you."

"Now you can imagine you're back in the Jade Palace with you know who." The dance came to a ragged finish and Gilray played a long chord. Linda, in surprisingly ordinary clothing, stepped onto the beer-crate.

"Cabaret time! Now, what can I say about our first artiste? Take a gorgeous figure, a winning personality and a sweet singing voice. Throw them all away and who's left – Penny Prentice!" Another chord, a ripple of applause and Penny stepped forward.

"Good God," said Roger quietly.

Penny wore a black wig, a swirling scarlet dress and a colossal hat sprouting wax flowers and fruit.

"Marie Lloyd," said Jack. "Same turn she did last time. They always bring some gear with them. Some were in ENSA during the war." Penny gave Linda a glacial smile and bowed.

"Thank you dear for that kind introduction. What a pity though you're not in drag yourself tonight. Anything would be an improvement on that. I've seen *wounds* that were better dressed." The audience brayed with delight.

"Start singing," said Linda. "Before that hat ferments." The patter may have been entertaining, but in their voices he detected the same spiteful edge he'd heard in Cabin 25. He took a fearless swig at his Sling. The musician hitched up his instrument and played again, swaying like a Rumanian gypsy. Penny struck a pose and began to sing. Except for a faked Cockney accent the voice was his normal one, with no attempt to sound feminine. "The Boy I Love is up in the gallery – the Boy I Love is lookin' dahn at me …"

A man in a dress; an old-time female song. It should have been ludicrous. There should have been howls of derision. But the sniggers petered out in a second. Prentice could sing. Fixing his gaze at a point somewhere over their heads he poured into the words all the defiance and pathos that were the stock-in-trade of his outcast society.

"There 'e is, can't yer see – a wavin' of 'is 'ankerchief – as merry as a robin what sings in a tree." By the second verse they were hooked, watching the rouged face under the cartwheel hat. This was the same man who had held him captive in Cabin 25. Streaked his face with lipstick and threatened the traditional torture of genital-blacking. A cruel punishment of which he'd once been a witness but never (as yet) a victim.

"Enjoying the show Roger?" asked Batten. Here and there men were embracing, even necking. He realised that "straight" people were a minority here; Jack, Batten and Seymour. Farley and a few others.

"Not what I expected. Certainly this one knows how to belt out a song. It's the audience I'm not sure about."

"You ain't seen nothing yet," said Jack, with a knowing glance at Batten. At the song's end there was a roar of approval and calls for more. Penny blew kisses and took another bow.

"Come along darling," said Linda. "Time to get off and give somebody with talent a chance."

Penny appealed to the crowd. "Do you want me to go, or would you like some more?"

"Another one Pen – give us another song." Linda threw up his hands.

"That wasn't a song, that was a *crime*! What do they see in you, that's the big question?" The watchers switched from face to face, following the dialogue.

"No dear," said Penny. "The big question is what's a dump like you doing in a beautiful place like this?"

"Ooh, don't be a bitch all your life. Take a day off occasionally. Very well then good people – on your own heads be it. Penny is about to *commit* another song." Gilroy played the introductory notes as Penny strutted to and fro then launched into another Edwardian number.

"My Old Man said foller the van, an' don't dilly-dally on the way." Roger quaffed his Sling and allowed himself to be spellbound. The figure in the outrageous get-up gave this song all the lusty treatment it demanded, bawling out the lyrics as the original singer had done; a vivid contrast to the sad sentiment of the previous effort. "Orf went the van wiv me 'ome packed in it, I follered on wiv me old cock-linnet ..." Penny had one more offering, *Mad About The Boy*, which if out of period was at least relevant to that company. For this they got a drawling, Cowardesque delivery which jarred with the costume but was no less pleasing for that.

"We're going in a minute," said Jack. "Are you staying to the end?" He was getting a great kick from the songs and the Sling made him mellow towards everyone.

"I'll just see a couple more turns." Antonia and Steve were behind the drinks table attending to everyone's needs. He wondered what they would do at the party's end. Well he knew what they would do, but where? The Love That Dare Not Speak Its Name. (Except on the *Empire Garvie* where it was daily currency.)

Each time he saw Farley the man was nearer than before, having apparently edged closer under cover of each song. *Mad About The Boy* ended and Penny came off to a rousing cheer.

"Thank you Miss Prentice," said Linda formally. "Leave your name and address. But not with us." Prentice, where had he seen that name before? The next performer was Carol Thomas, who treated them to a poignant rendering of *The Last Rose Of Summer* then came more up to date with an Ella Fitzgerald number. This so captivated Roger it was only at the end he realised with some disquiet that Jack, Batten and Seymour had gone. And that Farley was now standing next to him.

"At last," said he. "I've been hoping to get you alone. I want to ask a favour of you." Before he could hear what this was Penny walked up, now minus hat and wig.

"Roger, Antonia wants you." The peremptory summons was issued quite naturally, as though a refusal would be unheard-of.

"What for?"

"How should I know? Better come and find out." Against his better judgement but anxious to upset no-one, he put down his drink and accompanied Penny over to a corner away from the crowd. Here he found Doreen, in ballet tights and a green shirt, but no Antonia.

"Where's —"

The two men moved so fast he had no chance to escape or call out. Doreen gripped his arms from behind. Penny opened the door of the small office and he was pulled inside. The door slammed shut. He underwent the most abject terror, heightened by the grotesque appearance of his captors. Up close, Penny was nothing like Marie Lloyd. With no hat or wig, the made-up face under the short blonde hair was frightening, the voice cold as iron.

"Roger Wren. Young Roger Wren. Linda's lily-white boy. And now Antonia's."

"But not mine," said Doreen, sounding so masculine it was hard to imagine him sewing a hemline or throwing a public tantrum over a rejected dress. And where the hell was Linda?

"Ooh, I can read your mind," said Penny. "Your pugilist friend's not here to mother you now. She's gone topside for a slash."

"What exactly do you want?" Penny produced a tin of shoe-polish. By a cruel irony, it was the same brand Haji had carried. He felt sick at what was coming.

"We're going to teach you a lesson Roger. You've upset me and you've upset Doreen."

"How?"

"Several ways; your attitude; calling yourself 'normal'; meaning we're all circus freaks."

"I honestly didn't mean that. I'm sorry if I offended you."

"If? There's no 'if' about it; and scoffing about Widow Twankey and the Ugly Sisters. Who do you think you are?"

"And what about me?" said Doreen. "I slaved over that dress for eight days – eight fuggin' days. Then you come along, uninvited, take one look and what does her ladyship do? Dumps it. Runs off and buys a new one. And she couldn't have done *that* if you hadn't been so keen to run messages for her darling rich uncle."

"Listen," said Roger. "Please listen. I didn't mean any of it. I didn't realise the way of things at sea, that's all."

"No?" said Penny. "Well you will in a minute." His voice took on the silky tone of the true sadist. "Ever had your balls blacked, Roger? Takes simply ages to scrub off. They're red raw by the time you're finished. Be a long while before you're fit to go up on B Deck or the bridge again."

The bridge! Now he remembered. Time for a mad gamble.

"Get his pants down," said Doreen, tightening his grip. Penny unfastened Roger's belt-buckle as its owner summoned all his courage.

"Just a minute." It may have been dry-mouthed fear that made his voice harsh. "What about Kropp?"

How attentive people became at any mention of the man!

"Kropp?" said Doreen. "Wha – what of him?"

"Ask Penny. She went to the bridge about him."

"I never did," Penny snapped.

"Oh yes." He drew strength from the lengthening pause. Kropp was becoming a useful bogeyman to wave at his foes. "Oh yes you did, Penny. I saw your name on Quinn's desk the very day I was up there. My thing was first. 1500 hours. Quinn had your complaint down next to deal with; Prentice complaint 2000 hours. And sure enough Kropp goes up at eight o'clock for a bollicking. I saw it down there on the note-pad; your name, no question about it. And you know Kropp's going to kill whoever shopped him. When he finds out who it was. When somebody — tells him."

Penny took his hands away from the belt. "And I suppose you'd do that, wouldn't you?"

"Is he right?" asked Doreen. "Did you report Kropp?"

"No – no! Course I didn't. I'm only glad somebody did. We're all supposed to be girls together on here yet we put up with all that abuse and insults Kropp dishes out. Not to mention the odd black eye or bloody nose. He threw Trixie down the pub stairs in Southampton. Nobody's safe from him, only Linda. And we can't all be sodding prizefighters. I had to stay away from Mike Nelson's cabin 'cos of Kropp. And he's still doing it. Never mind what they said on the bridge, he don't take a blind bit of notice."

During the lengthy lament, Roger had discreetly sized up his position. There was a second door in the room, another exit or a cupboard?

"So what do you want to do?" said Doreen. Penny shrugged.

"Oh, don't know. I suppose he'll drop me in it now if we touch him. Kropp'll get me. There's no escape on here. I'll finish up like poor Henrietta did." Doreen came round to face Roger, gripping him by the shirt as the *Windrush* man had done.

"Roger, take careful heed of what I'm saying. You have no idea what you're getting into here. There's things go on aboard ship you wouldn't dream of. There's some really crazy homies about. So get this. We'll let you go now but you keep to yourself anything you think you know about Penny. If you breathe one word to Kropp you'll have the rest of us after you, 'specially if he lays a finger on Penny. You'll never want to go to sea again. We'll really do you over – clear?"

It was very clear. He did up his belt and took a trial step at departure. Doreen stopped him. God, what now?

"Not this way —" a crafty smile at Penny "— that way." Doreen pointed to the other door. Through this he found another even smaller room. In the middle of it stood Steve. Kneeling down facing him was Antonia, still in the Hadley ensemble and about to perform an act that he'd often heard of but never actually observed.

"What do you want?" bawled Steve. "Get the hell out of here!" Roger obeyed, closing the door on the scene and turning to face his captors.

"Never seen a head job before Roger?" said Penny and doubled up in hysterical laughter.

"Don't tell Kropp," giggled Doreen.

"We live and learn," he said feebly and stumbled back into the main storeroom.

This was no place for him. B Deck was where he belonged, with her. Again everything was the opposite of life on land. Even by consent, sex with a female passenger was forbidden, on pain of dismissal and/or a blotted record. Yet this sort of thing was tacitly allowed. As long as it was only among the crew and down in the bilges where it wouldn't offend decent folk. The hypocrisy of it all took his breath away.

Many of the company were staggering drunk by now but the improvised entertainment went on. A man was reciting a tribute in verse to his (hopefully) fictional mistress.

"Salome. Salome. That's my gal Salome. She's a big fat cow; twice the size of me, with hair on her belly like the branches of a tree. She can run, jump, blow, suck, shoe a horse or drive a truck. That's my gal Salome." It was definitely time to go. He'd seen and heard enough for a lifetime. If he got any more broadminded he would overbalance.

"Hi Roger." Carol breathed whisky fumes in his ear.

"Hello Carol. I liked your songs."

"Thank you. I thought Penny was a bit much though, didn't you?" Finding his drink where he'd left it he took a much-needed swig. He wasn't going to discuss Penny.

"What's the matter? You seem a bit shaken."

"It's nothing." He finished his drink and clawed his way to the exit. Carol watched as he endeavoured to leave. One of the bolts resisted. For a fearful moment he thought they were coming for him again.

"I daresay all this polari has upset you," said Carol. "It must be strange to someone such as you. We're not all the same as Penny you know or Doreen; very temperamental, those two. You'll get used to it. It won't be long before you lose all those silly little inhibitions."

Outside at last, he leaned against the bulkhead. In the past few weeks he'd lost his pallor, his virginity, and a good many preconceptions. So for the time being he would hang on to the inhibitions. Through the closed door he heard a voice announcing something that earned a tumult of applause. There came a scream of horror, delight or amusement; he couldn't tell which as the next act began. A chorus of "oohs" and stamping feet. God only knew what they were up to now.

One o'clock in the morning. Other than her cabin there was only one place to find peace. The voyage had become a kind of two-tier existence. Squalor and fear below decks, beauty and serenity above. The sea was always there, a whispering, enigmatic presence that never failed to soothe him. And tonight when he most needed distracting it had a special trick ready. At first he thought it was moonlight. But there was no moon or stars. The water itself was alight, hissing and sparkling with a strange white fire. As if all the world's searchlights were aimed up from the sea-bed.

He was not to enjoy it for long. Farley was at his side again.

"Fluorescent, Roger. That's all it is, or phosphorescent; something in the salt; chemicals or bugs or some such. Be back to normal tomorrow." Roger had never felt less like talking. "Yes," Farley continued. "Seen it before, regular thing in the tropics." A pause. "What were you up to with those two in that room?" He didn't reply. Farley had wanted a favour. No doubt he would soon hear what it was. "Roger, about the other night. Hope we can forget that."

"OK. It's past history."

"Good — er — I was thinking. You did say you won't be going up there again?"

"That's right. She called it off. Fed up with all the secrecy and creeping about. So was I. Quinn nearly caught me, if it was him."

They watched the whiteness moving like pack-ice all around them. Farley nodded at the empty distance. "What's out there, what's the nearest land?"

"We're passing the Gulf of Siam." To him the very names were romantic, part of the magic of travel, a joy even to pronounce.

"What comes next?"

"French Indo-China. On the other side you've got Borneo, then later on the Philippines. And to port again there's the Gulf of Tonkin." He knew he'd overdone it.

"Clever clogs ain't you? That's how you scored with her. Spun her a line about your travels."

"Mrs Morrell knows more about the Far East than you and I put together. I didn't spin her a line, I just listened to her talk about her life and Hinduism and stuff." He didn't want to discuss her with this man. And he'd guessed what the desired favour was going to be. "I'm off now to turn in." Farley restrained him.

"Wait. What else did you talk about?"

"Oh, the war, her job in Hong Kong."

"And now she's chucked you. I knew she would; quick tumble with a youngster before going home."

"Maybe, maybe not. I'm going to a party in Hong Kong at her house." Pulling free, he tried to go but the man clutched him again.

"Listen, you can still go up there. I'll get some booze. We could both — I mean — I could join you. A threesome for half an hour, say. She likes you. You could get her going about all that other stuff and giving her drinks till she's — you know — then you could leave us and slip quietly away." He couldn't believe his ears. Gina was to be primed into a malleable state and then left to gratify an oaf they both detested. And the picture of a sozzled Gina bore a disturbing and slightly guilty resemblance to his last night with Ruth. There was no way he was going to do it.

"What about it?" said Farley. "We got three days."

"No."

"Why not? What do you care? I'll give you your ten bob back."

"I tell you I won't be going up there again."

"Alright then, get me to this party you mentioned."

Roger decided on caution. At the last count he'd had more friends than enemies. No need to tilt the balance. There might be other girls at the party. Give the man *something.*

"OK. I'll see if she'll agree, though I wouldn't count on it. I'm ringing her up after we dock to fix the day. She'll need time to get home. If we dock in the morning. I'll call her after lunch." In the sea's eerie light Farley's appearance was even more unsavoury.

"Made yourself really at home with her, haven't you? Alright then, I'll expect to hear about it as soon as you fix it up. Properly speaking you still owe me, don't forget that." Ghostlike, Farley faded into the shadows. Roger rested a moment longer at the rail. Far away he thought he saw a number of twinkling bright dots. These, he convinced himself, simply had to be the lights of Saigon.

Over the following three days a sense of anticipation ran through the *Empire Garvie*. After toiling so many long, hot miles, their destination, the Crown Colony of Hong Kong, lay nearly in sight over the brow of the sea. For the soldiers still aboard there was the nagging worry that "Honkers" as they called it might be only a temporary posting. Five years after Japan's surrender the spectre of war had returned. Yet again a clash of ideologies caused simple, homely men of many nations to wearily pick up their weapons and wait to be told who they had to shoot at this time. But the crew had other thoughts.

"We don't want to spend too much there," said Jack. "Now this war's starting we don't know how long we might be in these parts, shuttling about."

Roger heard this with some dismay. What with Kropp, Farley, and now Penny and Doreen having various designs on him, the prospect of staying out here for weeks was not a beguiling one. His life had become a balancing act; hanging on to his friends, placating his enemies and still enjoying the scenery. And during all this finding time to cultivate a brand-new and somewhat random sex-life. He'd told no-one of his alarming experience in the storeroom or the real identity of Kropp's complainant. That he would squirrel away for further use. Roger, it seemed, was learning how to survive.

Although it was still hot below, fewer men slept on deck. The South China Sea was swept by a powerful north-easterly breeze that could be uncomfortable in the small hours. And he'd seen no dolphins yet, or cyclones. Arrival at Hong Kong was at daybreak, but despite this many were on deck to see it. Whatever diversionary trips might come, this was the real turn-around point. The place they all thought about.

Everyone watched the cluster of islands creeping out of the mist.

"Come and see this, Roger," said Batten. "Your first taste of China." The junk was quite large with a patched square sail and high poop worthy of a Spanish galleon. The ancient craft had an angular beauty about her.

"They live on those boats," said Jack. "Spend their whole lives on them. They got a harbour of their own here called Aberdeen, funnily enough." At the stern of the junk an old woman in black walked from side to side holding the upper end of a long sweep-oar. The skill of generations marked her every movement. Back and forth she toiled, twisting the oar at every stroke, fish-tailing the heavy craft along and only raising her face for a second as the ship overtook her.

Roger asked Batten, "Where's Wei Ho Bay?"

"No idea, why?"

"The party."

"Ah, the one Clay's been talking about. Jack might know where it is."

"Yes, like to come?" He owed Batten. The man had saved his bacon more than once.

"Definitely Roger, let me know when."

Soon they were among the islands, a succession of tree-clad humps thrusting from a dark sea. And as they neared the largest one the space between became smothered with craft of every kind. There were junks of all sizes, some boasting an engine. Sampans lively as pond-beetles scuttled among the larger vessels: gaunt, black-bodied steamers from all corners of the world, low-cut warships sulking at anchor, and overladen pleasure-boats darting from island to island.

"Who else is going, Roger?"

"Only you and Clay, and maybe Farley." Few things ever ruffled Batten. This did.

"Farley? After the way he —"

"I know, but he came after me when I left the wedding and kept on and on. I only said I'd try to get him in." Batten shrugged.

"It's your party. Don't forget you can always threaten to tell the bridge he's been taking bribes. Although of course if you did you'd likely drop yourself and Clay in it too." Roger tried to remember the time when his life had been simple. His own colleagues still didn't know it all. Everything needed care. He knew how some could bear a grudge.

"You didn't invite *me*," someone would say. They were all present. Now was the time.

"I'm going to a party in Hong Kong." It took a few minutes to tell the tale. Bill was incredulous. "Do you mean to say you been back up there for more?"

Jack said "He was up there Singapore night, when you were ashore paying for it."

Roger wished he could have kept the thing secret. But he would have to work out something regarding the off-duty rota in port.

"When is the party?" said Bill. "And who's going to it?"

"Tonight, I hope, or more likely tomorrow. She'll need time to settle back home. I've got two from Cabin 21 and maybe a B Deck steward."

"Hold on," said Martin. "Three from outside and none of us?" Trouble already.

"I know, but without Clay and Batten there wouldn't even be a party. They helped bring it about. And the other man had a hand in it too. It was his bloods we called on. He could still drop me in it if I don't keep him sweet, korey-wise." At least he could reel off the slang now.

"Makes sense," said Pat. "Where's it going to be?"

"Some place called Wei Ho Bay."

"I've heard of that," said Jack. "Holiday resort across the island on the south side. Sounds more fun than wandering around Wanchai. I say go for it while you can laddie. Fill your boots."

Toddy spoke for the first time that morning. "Kowloon. Nearly in."

They were easing into their berth right across from Hong Kong. Clay joined him. Once alongside the quay they had an unobstructed view of the island. Dominating everything was the Peak, a high dark mass looming over the bustling beehive that was Victoria, the heart of the Colony.

"Is that where we go for the party?" asked Clay.

"Somewhere beyond that on the far side. I'm going to ring her up after lunch. And I've got to ask if Farley can come. He's making trouble again. I can't keep using Kropp. If I open his kennel door too often someone'll get mauled."

He was tempted to linger there, taking in the ever-shifting scene before them. The water-borne activity was ceaseless; back and forth, an endless parade of sampans, fishing-boats and ferries. And there were junks. Junks piled high with precariously-stacked merchandise. Junks as old as time with blackened timbers and sails like ancient scrolls, trailing stove-smoke and festooned with family members.

"Fragrant Harbour," said Clay. "That's what the name Hong Kong means, according to Batten."

"It is fragrant to me."

Clay sniffed the air. "Do you really think so?"

"Not literally perhaps. Not all the time. But it's ..." How could he explain it? All the different sensations it brought him? It wasn't only Hong Kong. It was the incense of Tommy Wang's, the guttering candlelight and solemn silence in Sri Mariamman Temple. And it was the frangipani blossom reaching out to them along Tanjong Pagar Road, the perfume enfolding them as they strolled away from Chinatown.

"Something about the Far East gets to me. I can't put it into words."

"Don't get carried away," said Clay. "If you fall in love with it you won't want to go home."

The spell was broken, for now. Before they even began work, a man came round collecting laundry.

"Back so soon sir. Very good, you see. Shoe repairs very good also." During breakfast he got his first sight of the Chinese helpers, two young men and an older woman who may have been their mother. This chirpy trio worked willingly, and gleefully scooped up all the spare food that came their way. All instructions were met with the same reply. "OK-you-see." Uttered as one word, this conveyed both acknowledgement and the promise of satisfaction. There was the pleasing novelty of eating their own meal while these keen workers toiled at the strap-up.

Toddy returned from a visit to D Deck square. "Three days. Sail the fourth day. Ten o'clock in the morning."

"Where then, Korea?" said Martin.

"No, Japan then Korea." They worked out the time-off rota. Starting now it would be two men off each of the three days. A coin would decide the order.

"Me and Martin," said Bill. "We'll be one pair." Jack spun and caught the coin.

"Heads," said Bill.

"Heads it is. When do you want it?"

"Today!" cried Martin joyfully. "Let's go!"

"Youth," said Pat as the mess door slammed. "We won't see them again today. Forget the coin. What day would you like, Roger?"

"Tomorrow, if that's alright. I don't think the party'll be till then." The Chinese trooped out with their cardboard boxes of bread and tin cans filled with an unattractive mixture of discarded food.

Jack said, "Right then. Roger and Toddy tomorrow, me and Pat last day. Let's go get our dollars."

Roger changed into his best trousers and a stripy pink shirt he'd been saving for Hong Kong, a sort of special for the main destination.

"When are you going ashore?" asked Clay when they met at the purser's.

"Now, but only to Kowloon, I don't think there's time to see the island and be back by twelve. Tomorrow I've got the whole day off."

"Alright. I'll get the same if I can. Let's go and sample Kowloon before lunch. Oh, and there's no phone on board for crew by the way. You'll have to find one ashore this afternoon to call her."

"I will." On the square they were held up as the last troops disembarked and it was nine o'clock before they got off.

Changing a few pounds had given Roger sixty Hong Kong dollars. Half-a-dozen "tenners", each one such a work of art it seemed too pretty to spend.

"By the way," he said. "If you should happen to see Kropp ashore do let me know."

"I think he's still aboard. In any case he won't get beyond the first bar. I saw Batten and few others going off. Do you know anything about Kowloon?"

"Only what I've read and what Gina told me. I know those hills are called the Nine Dragons and Communist China's somewhere on the other side." Further along the quay another ship was tied up ahead of theirs. Around ten thousand tons, she was painted matt grey overall with a large 107 on her side. The Stars and Stripes hung at her stern and her name was in surprisingly small black letters. Endowed with radar, cranes and life-rafts, and with twin AA guns mounted forward, the *Chester M. Vandemeyer* looked ready for anything. Yet she was but a humble supply ship, an unglamorous maid-of-all-work hauling her loads across the Pacific in all weathers, supplying Uncle Sam's men with everything from ammunition to ice-cream.

At the foot of her steep gangway a gum-chewing American rating stood guard, resplendent in his white bell-bottoms and small white hat. Except for the carbine slung over his shoulder he reminded Roger of his British counterpart in Aden.

"The place'll be full of them," said Clay. "I bet we get called limeys. Here's another one." A young officer in a well-tailored uniform descended the gangway, took a hand from his pocket and put it somewhere near his forehead. Responding, the sentry brought his own arm up in a leisurely forward arc, touched the edge of his

Popeye hat and jerked his hand away in a flat chopping movement as if quartering the air before him.

"The way they salute," said Clay. "Not a patch on ours is it?" Roger became aware the officer was following not far behind them. He'd met a few Americans at home during the war. They had always seemed decent enough; generous, free with their chewing gum and Hershey Bars. No real discipline though; officers and men lounging about, all first names, hands in pockets. Still, no need to be stand-offish.

"Good morning," he called.

"Hi there. Are you fellows from that troop-carrier?" The eternal query.

"Yes," said Clay. "We just got here from England."

"First visit," said Roger.

"Is that so? We've been here two weeks now so I guess I know it pretty well. The *Chester M* is dry of course so our boys go for the taverns when they're on liberty. And the local hookers, there's plenty of them."

"Ah yes," said Clay. "Somebody said the other day if all the hookers in Hong Kong were laid end to end he wouldn't be at all surprised!"

The man laughed. "That's a great gag. I must remember that." He seemed incredibly young for an officer. A cadet maybe or midshipman, or whatever they called them in the Navy. Didn't look as if he would ever dare to order anyone about.

At the dock exit the man said, "If you want souvenirs go to Leung Kee's or the Kowloon Gift Centre. I'm going there myself later. First I've got to say my goodbyes to someone." He hailed a taxi. "Bit of a hurry, got to be back by 11.30. Might see you around." He waved and was gone.

"Off for a last date," said Clay. "With his Chinese girl, then buy presents for his other one back home. At least he never called us limeys."

Kowloon reminded Roger instantly of Singapore; the same wildly fascinating shop names. Yen Tee, Tai Woo, Hung Lee and Yuan Cheong. The reek of joss-sticks and spices. Here again were the dashing rickshaws and taxis clustering around the ferry pier right outside the docks. And there were trishaws, both pedal-powered and motorised. The latter comprised a motorcycle adapted to carry a small cab supported on two rear wheels. All these vehicles jostled together in a noisy stream, mingling with bowed workers in coolie hats hauling overloaded carts or bent under bamboo poles with a load at each end.

"Work and more work," said Roger. "They never seem to stop." There were no idlers here but themselves. No strollers or dreamers to notice (as he did) the last of the morning mist caressing the Nine Dragons, or the olive-green Dakota with throttled-back engines slipping down between the hills towards the Kai Tak airstrip. It was difficult to believe he was actually here, in China. A host of stereotypes ran through his head. Men with pigtails, the Boxer Rebellion, bird's nest soup. And the mind-reeling distance they'd come to be here. Naturally he'd worked it out in the atlas before they sailed.

"Do you know just how far we've travelled?"

"No. But it's a dead cert you do."

"Yes. We've done nine thousand five hundred miles. Or seven thousand eight hundred as the crow flies."

"Some crow. You're making me thirsty." Presently they came to a large hotel, the Peninsula, and turned into Nathan Road. They found Leung Kee's. There was so much to see and admire. Things, hundreds made of ivory. And there were porcelain Buddhas.

"I hear you've got one of these," said Clay. Roger found the Chokai mark.

"The very same. Two dollars I paid." Clay did one of his fast calculations.

"Four and eightpence and these are six dollars Hong Kong money. Seven bob." Batten as usual had been right. His Buddha gained in value the further he took it. Very well, it could squat in the back of his locker gaining interest. Like a bank account.

Nathan Road led directly from the harbour area into a tight welter of interlocking streets full of noodle-stalls, fortune-tellers, tailors and tattoo artists. They saw many of their own crew and several from the *Chester M. Vandemeyer*. The American sailors were usually in groups and conspicuous in their all-white rigs and Popeye hats.

"There's Linda," said Clay. "Gone in that shop ahead of us."

"Walk on then. We don't want to meet any of them now." They hurried past.

"I'll need some change," said Roger. "For the phone this afternoon, that's if I find a call-box. I've yet to see one."

They bought picture-postcards in Heung Chong's, a packed little cavern of a shop sandwiched between a barber's and a steaming noodle-stall. Roger examined a three-dollar wooden fan. Finely made, it was varnished and painted all over with a pattern of swans and water-plants. From behind him came a well-known voice.

"If you turn that down you want your bottom smacked." Linda had caught them up. He noticed the man wore a pink shirt much like his own. "Roger, I heard about Penny and Doreen in the storeroom. Sorry I wasn't there to save you."

"I managed to talk my way out of it."

"I warned you about Penny didn't I? Vicious that one, really horrid. Two of a kind, her and Doreen."

"Morning Linda," said Clay. "All by yourself with these wild Yankee sailor-boys about?" Linda gave a defiant head-toss.

"Don't you fret. I can handle them. Look, you don't want to waste time here. Stick with me. I'll show you a *bona* place, that's got some life to it."

Whenever men of the sea can escape its hold and run free they will find, not so far away, a favoured haunt where all their needs are met. In every major port in the world there is always one. In New York it is the Market Diner. Hot-dogs and Budweiser. In Durban the Criterion will offer you giant steaks and Castle Lager. A thirsty sailor in Hamburg will make for the welcoming lights of the Adler-Bar. Bratwurst, foaming tankards and oompah music. And in 1950, if you were in Kowloon you went to Hanni Lu's.

"Here we are," said Linda.

Hanni Lu's had begun life as a sedate Edwardian chop-house put up by and for the *taipans*, the European bankers and traders who first built up the colony's wealth. Over the decades, ownership and décor had constantly switched.

"This used to be the Sandringham," said Linda. "Not any more. Some old biddy from Shanghai runs it now." The original name had long gone, replaced over the revolving door by a large HANNI LU's in purple neon. Above hung a downward-pointing arrow made up of light-bulbs going on and off in sequence to create a ripple effect. At night it might have had some allure. In daylight it was merely tawdry, and in keeping with the honky-tonk music that greeted them on entry. Three steps down from street level the clamorous clientele sat at circular tables or perched on stools at a long mirrored bar.

"I won't stay long," said Roger. "I'm supposed to be looking for a phone booth. There's a call I must make after lunch today."

"A phone?" said Linda. "Look no further. There's one in here. Come along, I owe you a drink for leaving you to Penny's mercy that night." Décor-wise, Hanni Lu's place had no set style. The floor was an imitation Roman mosaic of very small tiles. Cream and gilt walls were still lined with portraits of bewhiskered and "clubby" gentlemen in frock coats. Windowless, the room was lit by a row of chandeliers under a ceiling heavy with ornate plaster scroll-work. Food and drink were served by a team of Chinese girls in very short black frocks.

"Quite a place," remarked Clay as they took their seats. "Bits of everything." As a final defiant touch, each table had a cloth of homely gingham, a sticky bottle of ketchup and a Bakelite ashtray marked "Players Please".

"I'm meeting Carol here," said Linda. "That's if she hasn't stowed away on the *Chester M*." Hanni Lu catered mainly for European crews. Everything was on offer, from hamburgers through sauerkraut or spaghetti to the dizzy heights of bangers-and-mash. But at this hour of the day few were eating. At every hand he saw beer bottles, tilted glasses and bobbing Adam's apples. Linda called a waitress.

"Roger, what'll you have? Come on, it's my treat. The highballs are on me, as the giraffe said." There was only one drink he'd really taken to.

"Ooh," said Linda. "We're missing Singapore already are we? Right, I'll have the same, and I'll get Carol one."

Clay said, "I'll have one of those Miranda beers."

Linda glanced around the room. "Can you see Carol? Ah!" Putting two fingers in his mouth he gave a very masculine whistle. Last seen in full drag Carol now wore sharply pressed jeans and a kind of blousy scarlet shirt with V-shaped pleats down the front and of course the cat-and-dog brooch. There was a companion, an unusually shy American sailor.

"Hullo all," said Carol. "This is George. He's from — where is it George?" The sailor blushed.

"Hackensack."

"Hack what?" said Linda.

"Hackensack," said Roger helpfully. "It's in New Jersey." George gave him a grateful smile. "Say, you been there?" He didn't want to admit he only knew if from Hollywood films, where it was sometimes mentioned in a whimsical way. Like Chipping Sodbury.

"No, I saw it on a map once."

Clay leaned towards him. "Let's go after we've had our drinks." Linda heard him.

"Not yet. You can't leave yet. It's only ten o'clock in the morning. Don't be unsociable. These boys are our allies." Behind a hand he whispered, "And they've got money." Suddenly there were three more Popeye-hatted sailors at the table. The drinks came and further orders were taken. With bewildering speed everyone learned everyone else's name. "Accidentally-on-purpose" the order round the table was, Carol and George, Linda and Tom, Clay and Douglas, Roger and Irving. *Irving*? Roger twisted in his seat to see where the exit was. What he saw was someone at another table watching him in considerable amusement. It was Batten, smartly turned out for once.

Irving was older than his fellow ratings and the only one not smoking or drinking.

"I don't hold with it Roger. Never did. Unhealthy. Same with broads. Bad for a man, broads are. Sap a man's strength. Broads are the creatures of Satan, an abomination in the sight of the Lord. The other guys chase after them, but not me. I like to keep myself fit. Calisthenics, that's the thing boy. Bends and push-ups every morning before Reveille." Roger began to worry about Irving. The man pointed to a badge on his sleeve.

"See that? I got that for Athletic Merit. I'm 140 pounds. The medic told me I'm the perfect weight for my age and height." Irving looked him up and down. "What do you weigh? When you're stripped naked I mean?"

"Me — er — I never — last time I think it was nine stone."

"What in hell does that mean?"

Someone approached the group. The lady was no more than five feet high, and wearing an orange gown, embroidered slippers and pendant earrings that brushed her shoulders. Red-faced and jovial, she reeled off greetings to all she passed, switching from one language to another as required. Mainly she spoke in Cantonese with a German accent, or English with a touch of both.

"Here she is," said Carol. "The Mother Superior, one of Kowloon's characters."

Hanni Lu had a past. Now seventy, she had gone to Shanghai in 1910 as the bride of a German engineer. Herr Schroeder worked hard, got very rich in ten years and died of exhaustion. Inside a week she'd married Mr Lu, a local merchant who followed his predecessor to the grave, leaving Hanni a doubly rich widow. When the communist revolt came she fled to Hong Kong.

This oriental Rhinemaiden let out a cry of recognition and fell upon Carol and Linda, hugging both at once with a whey-faced George compressed between them trying to balance his drink.

"Again with your comrades you come to Hanni's. Making happy always to see you. Girl-friends and boy-friends come every time to Hanni's." She checked the company.

"One, two, three, four funny-boys. Where is Penny? Where — how you say — Anton? Where other nice funny-boys today?"

"They'll be along," said Linda. "Maybe tonight. We wouldn't miss your dinners. Like a bit of spotted dick we do." The Americans looked startled. Hanni gave a piercing shriek.

"Ow, you funny-boys, so wicked when say such things to Hanni, but she still loves you same." She sailed majestically on.

Tom stood up. "I'm going to the john." Irving was still talking.

"What's that you're drinking Roger?"

"Singapore sling." He listed the ingredients. Irving was unimpressed.

Linda now got up and announced,

"When you gotta go, you gotta go." Smirking at Carol, he also made for the toilet. Irving went on.

"Sounds a real faggot's drink that does. Still I guess your kind have a lot in common. Drinks and clothes and stuff." The truth of his situation came home to Roger then. A truth so hideous he wanted to jump up and shout "You daft bunch of Popeyes. I've been with two women this trip. I'm not one of Hanni Lu's funny-boys even though I've got a faggot's shirt and a faggot's drink and I'm sitting with two of them." Instead he had a little more of his Sling and listened to a ten-minute talk on the benefits of rigorous physical training.

"Kinda young aren't you?" said Irving. "To be doing this. Don't get me wrong, I don't mind ..." He broke off as two other sailors stopped by. Each was accompanied by a giggling local girl of uncertain age but very certain calling.

"Reed, you crazy pervert," said one man. "Why don't you get yourself a woman, same as us?"

"Take off, Curtis. Get lost, or I'll lay you out right here."

The man backed away. "OK, OK. We're leaving."

Linda returned, followed at a decent interval by Tom, who

whispered to Irving and then kept walking right out of the building.

Roger said, "Irving, I've enjoyed meeting you but I have to go now. We're all due back before noon." The next event was so sudden he didn't even cry out. Irving Reed's hand slipped under the gingham cloth and took possession of Roger's genitals in the kind of hold you don't argue with.

"Don't run out on me Roger. We got a little deal to make yet." He couldn't budge, could only sit there; pinned in place by an anchor of pain. The slightest attempt to escape brought just enough pressure to freeze all movement.

To add to his anguish, Clay signalled "Let's go" at him. Roger could only give a watery-eyed shake of the head. "Come on," said Clay. "What's up with you?"

"Roger and me are talking about exercise," said Irving. "Somebody his age shouldn't be smoking and drinking. He oughta be developing his young body. Bends and push-ups, up on deck in God's pure air. Wait for him outside. Roger's not ready to leave yet. Are you Roger?" A squeeze brought a tense

"No, no. I'll stay a while longer."

"Alright," said Clay. "But time's getting on. Don't hang around too long like you did with that boy in Aden. The one you couldn't bear to leave." Roger tried to send a message with his eyes but Clay had gone.

"So," said Irving. "A boy in Aden! Get around don't you? Now Roger, here's what we do. We go out to the yard in back of here where the john is. I give you five bucks, same as Tom paid. That's five bucks American, *real* money. Then you're going to do what all you faggots do. Ten minutes is all it'll take. Afterwards we come back here. Nice and easy. Oh, and Roger, don't try to slip away or I'll have to beat the hell out of you. And I don't want to do that. Finish your drink first." In helpless panic Roger looked around for allies. Linda and Carol were talking to George. Douglas had gone to the bar and Batten had left the restaurant.

He took a sip of his drink and his hand shook so much the glass rattled on his teeth. So he put it down again. As he did so, he lost control of it completely. The tall glass fell over, precisely spanning the distance to Irving's edge of the table. While none went on the cloth, the entire contents emptied on to the man's pristine white uniform. Irving released his grip and sprang up, aghast at the unsightly patch.

"You stupid – you stupid, son-of-a-bitch. I'll ..." He lunged forward, slipped on the mosaic and sat down heavily on the wet and soiled floor. Irving Reed would now have a souvenir of Hanni Lu's displayed both fore and aft.

On winged feet, Roger sprinted for the exit, dimly aware that Linda was approaching. Iriving, as he'd proudly stated, was extremely fit. The man was up and after him in a flash. Roger felt a sinewy arm encircle his neck. At this point Linda reached them and Irving got his second surprise. One minute he was in command; a clear winner. The next he felt as if he'd run his stomach into the sawn-off end of a pine log. He doubled over and sank to his knees.

"Run!" yelled Linda. "Run for it Roger!" Irving recovered and partly raised himself, now doubly incensed. Not only had he been floored, but it had been by a *faggot's* fist.

"Get those two guys!" he roared.

They were at the door. "Left side — together!" said Linda. They pushed and fell into the street. Irving and several companions rushed to follow, in their eagerness pushing both sides at once, with the result that the revolving door couldn't – revolve. At the kerb Batten and Clay were conversing. Batten was about to board a motorised tri-shaw.

"We need this," said Linda, diving into it. "Get in quick, there's a bundle on with the Yanks."

Batten protested. "We can't all go in this."

"Would you rather stay and take them on?" They clambered into the tiny vehicle. This had a low roof and a seat that only took two – Clay and Linda who were first in. The others could only crouch in the floor-well like spaniels.

"Drive Joe!" Linda beseeched the reluctant Chinese astride the motorcycle.

"No can take, too many."

Linda waved a banknote. "Five dollars Yankee?"

"OK-you-see." The wobbling trishaw shot away into the traffic, gathering speed in a series of smoky spurts reminiscent of a V1.

Behind them a number of sailors tumbled out of Hanni Lu's and flagged down a taxi. This happened to be an ordinary car; four-wheeled, stable and fast. Batten peered out of the side.

"The chase, as they say, is on. I believe an appreciable increase in our speed would be in order."

"Step on it Joe," said Linda. "If you want your money."

"OK-you-see."

Chapter 12

The sound of the exposed engine now rose to such a teeth-clenching howl they had to shout to be heard.

"What happened back there?" bawled Clay.

"One of our friends," replied Linda, "came over all physical. Roger tossed his drink over him. It was a Sling, so he slung it!"

"No I didn't. I just lost hold of it. He had me by the balls under the table."

"I thought you had a strange expression," said Clay. "What did he want you to stay for? Bends and push-ups?"

"In a manner of speaking, yes."

They hit a bad bump, causing a brief levitation for everyone. Batten winced as they thudded back. "I'm sure I've got the driver's tool-box under me here."

In addition to having the aerodynamics of a tea-chest, the trishaw was underpowered, overloaded and top-heavy, with a way of tilting on corners. But it was highly manoeuvrable. The single front wheel enabled the driver to turn in the smallest space, and dart like a scalded cat between other vehicles. The Yank-laden car had difficulty following.

"Where are we?" said Clay. Batten seemed unperturbed.

"Still on Nathan, but going the wrong way for the ship. And this road's three miles long." He tapped the driver's shoulder. "Go left here, Nanking Street."

They swung round in a heart-stopping swerve that made the front tyre screech and lifted the inside one a good seven inches. But the other car soon caught up, for this was an emptier road.

Roger said, "I hope you know where we're going." Batten shifted uncomfortably.

"I've been round these streets before. Although to be honest I've never done it while sitting on the point of a file. Driver, turn right here." They plunged into a deserted alley so narrow there was barely room to pass along it. This time the other driver was beaten. No amount of reversing or manoeuvring could get the larger vehicle into the gap.

The trishaw trundled on down the alley, collecting the odd graze from a protruding brick and sending the noise of its engine shrieking up between the high buildings.

"Now what?" said Roger. "Their driver knows his way too. They'll simply go round the block and wait for us at the other end of this."

"They might," said Batten. "Depends how quick they are."

"What exciting times we live in," observed Linda.

Batten said, "I was going to Youmatei in this before it was commandeered. The Jade Market. Maybe I'll try again after lunch, assuming I'm still alive."

"I'm sorry about all this," said Roger. "Trust me to get stuck with Charles Atlas. Thanks for seeing to him Linda."

Clay said, "You seem to attract all kinds. The one I was with, Douglas, he talked about korey. Where to go in Wanchai." The alley took a slight bend.

"What if ..." began Roger. "I mean I don't want to spread alarm and despondency but what if we meet someone coming the other way?"

"Thank you," said Linda. "That's the very thought I need right now."

"This thing doesn't have reverse," said Batten. "We'd have to walk back to where we came in."

"And if they're waiting there?"

"We climb the walls – or it's Goodnight Vienna." They reached the end of the alley, and there was no reception committee.

"To the right again here," instructed Batten. "That'll bring us back to Nathan Road."

Furtively they chugged to where they could rejoin the main street. "Stop just before we get there," said Batten. "Eyes peeled everyone." Glad of the rest, the valiant little trishaw leaned panting against the kerb.

"There's Carol," said Clay. Linda whistled and waved.

"Oh there you are," said Carol. "They're after you and Roger, that Irving homi and a few from another table. They chased you in a taxi."

"We know," said Linda. "Have you seen them since?"

"Yes. They all came back to Hanni Lu's. They had a conflab, got back in the taxi and headed to the docks. I can't stop. I left George over the road. He's lonely, wishes he was in Hackensack. So I'm helping him buy presents. See you later."

Clay said, "Poor George"

"Ouch," said Batten, reached under himself and produced a rusty file. "I knew it."

"Next move?" said Roger.

"Nothing to worry about," said Clay. "They're back on their own ship by now."

"Perhaps," said Batten. "Or they could be lying in wait for us at the gate. They know full well we have to go back that way."

"Yes. But how do they know we're not staying ashore all day?"

Roger began to speak, then stopped. "Tell us Roger," said Batten. "Pray tell us what you have so obviously just remembered."

"I did mention to Irving we had to be back by twelve."

"Clever," said Clay.

Batten stood up, or more accurately crouched up. As best he could in the tight space. "Right, I claim a spell on that seat. First, we'll have a trial run and see. Driver, to the docks." Clay took Batten's place in the floor-well as they rejoined the traffic. At the top of Nathan Road they crept around the corner of the Peninsula Hotel and started down the road to the docks. To their left was the harbour, and beyond that, Hong Kong Island. Roger thought about the other segment of his strange life. Was she home yet? Maybe she was on her verandah. A villa on a bay was bound to have a verandah.

"Stop!" said Batten before anybody expected it. They all lurched forward, briefly smothering the driver. Five faces peered ahead.

"They *are* there," said Linda. A few yards before the dock gate, Irving and six of his friends were stopping and checking the occupants of every likely vehicle. They saw a man dragged out, examined and thrust back in before his taxi was allowed to go on. Their own driver became alarmed.

"Want please no trouble."

"Fear not my son," said Batten. "Go back to Nathan Road and we'll see you alright." Out of sight again, they crawled one by one from the trishaw, unfolding and flexing their cramped limbs like pupating crane-flies.

"Everyone chip in," said Batten. They all gave something. The driver smiled happily at Linda, who handed over a crumpled five-dollar bill.

"Easy come – easy go. Roll on tonight."

The trishaw put-putted away to become part of the scenery once more.

"There goes a contented man," said Clay. "He's earned enough today for a new front tyre and a week's supply of hot noodles." Batten seemed at a loss, which was unusual for him.

"Any suggested plan will be given full consideration."

"Don't look at me," said Linda. "I could handle Irving but with the best will in the world, seven men?"

"What we need," said Batten, "is some American with enough authority to get us past them."

"We met one of their officers," said Clay. But Roger was doubtful.

"For a start we have to find him. Then if we did he's too young to frighten the likes of Irving. You know what they're like, undisciplined. They'd more likely frighten him. He may be an officer, of sorts. I doubt if he's twenty even. Wet behind the ears."

Linda scoffed. "Listen to Long John Silver."

"You're sure he's an officer?" asked Batten. "They all dress so finely it's hard to tell. And you're right about discipline. They don't have much." Clay looked up and down the street.

"Leung Kee's. That's where he was going. Oh, he was an officer, definitely. Peaked cap, one or two shiny bits. We saw him get one salute." At Leung Kee's there were only two uninvolved American sailors, a couple of Chinese and a Polish seaman in black jersey and greasy cap who could have passed for Joseph Conrad himself.

"No sign of him," said Clay. "And it's ten to eleven."

Roger wandered outside. Time, he was plagued by time. And now he'd got three of his friends caught up in his misfortunes. Perhaps they could hire a sampan, get themselves paddled round the outer end of the dock and shin up the *Garvie's* blind side. This crazy notion took a hold and it was a while before he realised what he was absently looking at. Across the street a taxi stood with its boot-lid open. Next he saw a uniformed figure emerge from a shop bearing a brown-paper parcel which he placed in the boot before going inside again. Roger dashed back into Leung Kee's.

"He's over the road. Quick, let's catch him before he goes!"

"Steady on," said Batten. "We don't want to scare the poor kid if he's as raw as you say. Just speak to him, then leave it to me."

"What shall I say?"

"Anything, except possibly – 'hello sailor'."

The Kowloon Gift Centre was similar to Leung Kee's but with the added attraction of a juke-box delivering *Twelfth Street Rag* at ear-breaking volume. By the counter the officer was watching another parcel being wrapped.

"I bet he calls us limeys," said Roger. "When he hears our story." Clay and Roger were recognised immediately.

"Hullo again. How do you like Kowloon? Buy anything?"

"Only some postcards," said Roger. "We've been to Leung Kee's. Their Chokai Buddhas are dear compared with Singapore."

"I know. They've all hiked up their prices since the Korean face-off began. More ships calling. This store's better." He shook hands with the others.

"Glad to know you."

"The pleasure's all mine Captain," said Batten warmly. "Meeting one of you chaps always is. I have many happy memories of you people during the war."

"Nice of you to say so."

"Oh yes." Batten got into his stride. "The greatest nation on earth, America. Although I know some would rather cut out their tongues than admit it. And I'm not just saying that to be polite. It's my honest opinion. I say that as an Englishman. We like to think we're in the tops – empire and so on. But the simple fact is America has come to our rescue twice this century. There's no getting away from that. And now —" he smiled ruefully "— we need help again. We're lost."

During this, the shopkeeper had put a number of parcels on the counter. The officer was given a bill which he carefully checked.

"Thanks for the promotion, but I'm not a captain. Only a second lieutenant, j.g. That's Junior Grade. Lowest of the low some say. Lost? What, all of you?"

"Yes." When he wished to, Batten could actually *look* lost. "We know roughly where we are but not for certain. Took a wrong turn somewhere and there's not a taxi to be had." The lieutenant studied them as he counted out his payment. Two were no older then he was, but thinner. Must be their lousy rations. The older one put him in mind of a podgy bank teller, and the other – he had a strong suspicion what the other one was. He paid his bill.

"How about that? I got something here for every member of the family, not forgetting Grandpop."

"That's sweet," said Linda. "What a pity there aren't more like you in the world today, kind and generous. That's Americans all over. I've often found that. Nothing's too much trouble." The officer put the bill in his pocket and turned to face them. And he didn't seem quite so young any more.

"Right. Now let's cut the crap shall we? You're not lost, you're broke. You've spent all your pay getting stoned in Hanni Lu's and now you're after a free cab ride." They had an unusual treat. The sight of Batten embarrassed.

"Lieutenant, it's not as you think. We are neither drunk nor broke. I can assure you any financial obligations will be fully met. The fact is we had a rather distasteful *contretemps* with some elements of your crew and we wish to avoid further friction with these persons who are now lingering at the dock gate. We believe the presence of a commissioned member of the USN might help us through."

The Lieutenant stared at him and then at the others. "Is this guy for real? *Contretemps*?" They told him the story. He didn't seem surprised.

"We took on some guys at Manila, replacements. They've been troublesome at every port. I don't even know all their names yet. OK, help me stow these in the trunk of the cab and we'll be on our way." There were nine parcels in all. These they put in the boot of the taxi and the journey began. In front sat the driver, Roger and the American, with the latter next to the nearside window. In the rear it was Linda who was sandwiched in the middle. Thus, the two who might be deemed prime targets were rendered harder to get at.

"Been many places Lieutenant?" asked Batten.

"Sure have. Pearl, Midway, Manila, all over. It's a good outfit, the *Vandemeyer*. Most of the crew are OK. You get used to a ship. Kind of ...atmosphere ... you know?"

"Soul," said Linda. "All ships have a soul. A famous person once said the *Mauretania* had one you could talk to."

The officer chuckled. "Oh, come on now. No offence, but that's a very English idea."

"Yes, I agree. But it was Franklin D Roosevelt who said it."

"Ouch, I sure walked into that one."

During the drive, Roger had time to reflect. A mere four hours ago he'd been at sea. Now he was hurtling along squeezed between a Chinese and an American with a new gang up ahead who wished him harm. Just a normal run ashore, really, for him. And another thought. Sometime today he had to go back to Hanni Lu's to call Gina. Back to Irving Reed's hunting-ground. How about a disguise? Irving avoided girls. He could see Carol and get himself done up in drag. Yes, and walk straight into Kropp. These ramblings! What was he thinking of?

The dock gate came in view.

"Here we go," said Clay. "This makes you think of Checkpoint Charlie in Berlin." The seven sailors formed a line across their route.

"I thought so," said the lieutenant. "They're the Manila bunch." Even from here Irving could be identified by his stained clothing. The fitness fanatic darted around to the nearside.

"That's one of them!" he barked. "That's him in the middle. And there's the other son-of-a-bitch in the back, the one who slugged me. Get 'em out!" Doors no-one had thought to lock were snatched open. Hands clawed at Roger and Linda.

"Hold it right there!" Unsure who had spoken, the sailors slowed and stopped, forming a tableau round the car. The lieutenant got out. "What do you think you're doing mister?" Irving grinned at his friends and put a hand on the young man's shoulder.

"Aw, look lieutenant. There's no call for you to concern yourself with this. We got no beef with you. Why not carry on aboard and leave things to us?"

"No. I'd like to know what all this is about."

"Lieutenant, it's kind of personal. Best keep out of it." They could see the effort required of the man. Having to pay some respect to this youngster because he had a modicum of rank.

"Tell me what actually occurred."

"One of them —" Irving hesitated.

"Yes?"

"One of them slugged me." The lieutenant glanced into the car and back at Irving in disbelief.

"You're telling me one of *these* guys hit you?" Two of the sailors sniggered.

"Which one was it?" Irving pointed to Linda who leaned out and gave a royal wave to everyone, using a very exaggerated wrist movement.

"I had to. He was being perfectly beastly to my friend." By now all the other sailors were stifling laughter.

The lieutenant asked Irving, "And what did you do that was

beastly?" Irving longed to pick up this two-bit squirt and toss him into the Fragrant Harbour.

"I don't really know. I couldn't say. I mean I was not ..." Before joining the navy the young officer had never met people like Irving Reed. When the boy had expressed a wish to "be a sailor" this had been fondly granted. And somewhat like Roger, the lessons had come thick and very fast. Annapolis Naval Academy combined the rigours of boot camp with the pressure-cooker confinement of a public school. Here he learned a very great deal about the things that never appeared in Navy Manuals. Yes, he got the picture.

"What's your name mister?"

"Reed."

"I'll ask you again, and this time I'll hear the correct response."

Irving fumed. "Seaman First Class Irving J. Reed – Sir."

"Well now Irving J. Reed, I believe your behaviour today has been pretty bad. It will not do. Not in this man's navy. On top of that you're running around in a soiled rig. You're supposed to drink it, not pour it over yourself." Irving's face turned scarlet at this.

"But I don't drink – never touch it!"

"Don't give me that. There's even some on your butt. Bad example, are you hearing me?"

"Yes Sir!"

"Remember, each time you go ashore on liberty you represent the United States Navy. Your appearance and deportment should reflect pride in that. Do you agree with me mister?"

"Yes SIR!"

"Good. Consider yourself fortunate not to be on Captain's Report." The lieutenant checked his watch. "I have a quarter after eleven here. So if you and your buddies aren't aboard in fifteen minutes you'll be posted AWOL. And so will I." The young man re-entered the taxi and nodded to the driver. They passed through the gate and sped down the dock road.

"Thank you lieutenant," said Batten. "That was the true voice of authority. You'll do well in your career."

"Would you believe it?" said Clay. "Not one of them said they were due back. All that chasing around, we only had to wait until 11.30 and they'd have been back on their own ship."

The *Chester M. Vandemeyer* had come to life. There were men on her decks and a clatter of gear.

"Now hear this," began a message over her Tannoy. The sentry had been joined by a quartermaster ticking names off a list. There was a triple outbreak of air-chopping salutes.

"Put away your wallet lieutenant," said Batten. "We're paying this one, and we'll take your shopping up for you."

"No need." But Batten insisted, somewhat to the dismay of the others who were looking back along the quay. So they all took the things from the boot and carried it in one journey up the sharply canted gangplank. At the top they stacked the parcels on the deck while the lieutenant did another air-chop towards the flag at the stern.

"Thanks. I'm afraid I can't allow you beyond this point —" an ironic smile "— I don't have the authority." A round of hand shakes.

"Lieutenant," said Batten. "It's been an honour and a privilege to meet you." From this high point they could see Irving's party approaching.

"Shall we get going?" said Roger.

"Not only an honour," continued Batten in his best after-dinner style. "But a genuine eye-opening experience, I must confess we'd always thought you people were a trifle too easy-going when it came to discipline. Well, we've learned differently today."

"Batten, come on!" said Clay. With Batten to the fore, they started back down. Halfway, he stopped, which meant they all did. Batten faced the *Chester M.* and gave a snappy Royal Navy salute.

"Give my regards to Broadway!" The officer waved.

"What a nice boy," said Linda "And we never did know his name."

"They're not all like him," said Roger. "What about those others? I have to return to Hanni Lu's this afternoon."

It was a relief to reach the *Garvie* and look back. Led by Irving, the sailors were pounding at AWOL velocity along the quay and up into their own ship. A thought occurred to Roger.

"Go on without me. I want to check on something." Of course it should have been obvious; the frenzy of souvenir collecting, the 11.30 deadline. But none of them had thought to ask. At the *Chester M.* only the ever-chewing sentry remained.

"Excuse me. When are you sailing?"

"What's it to you bud?"

"I'd really like to know, personal reasons."

The sentry shifted his wad of Wrigley's finest from one side of his jaw to the other.

"Real soon. Thirteen hundred today." Roger made his way back. He felt a lot easier now.

For a number of reasons his midday work was an unaccustomed pleasure. All the more irksome chores could be left to the helpers who relished the chance of gainful work. And for the first time Bill and Martin were absent from the mess. He was able to relax in the company of the others, with whom he'd always been at ease.

"And where did the Lodger go today?" asked Pat.

"Only to Hanni Lu's."

"No excitement? No narrow escapes?"

"Give him a chance," said Jack. "He was only gone a couple of hours." They had a right to know, and the other two weren't there. No rolling in the aisles. As expected, they received the story calmly, with the head-wagging amusement of those who'd seen too much of humanity's ways.

Pat said, "That'll learn you not to consort with queers too often. Not in certain places."

"Yanks?" drawled Toddy. "I've shit 'em."

Before going ashore again there was one thing he had to see. On the stroke of one o'clock the *Chester M. Vandemeyer* departed Hong Kong. Even with binoculars he was unable to recognise anyone on her decks. But he watched as her radar scanner began to rotate and the Stars and Stripes flared out from her stern. And even from here he could pick up the start of another squawking Tannoy message, "Now hear this!" before it was snatched away on the scented wind. Irving J. Reed and the baby-faced officer were gone. And during the whole episode no-one had called anyone a limey. For some unfathomable reason he felt vaguely let down by that. But it would not in fact be his last brush with Americans.

Farley was waiting in the cabin. Another complication.

"No need for you to come." But Farley was adamant.

"Yes. I'll give you a hand with the phoning, tell you what to say. Come on, we can swing it. Share and share alike." Clearly, he considered Gina their joint property. Passing Leung Kee's window display, Farley said, "Still got that cheap Buddha thing?"

"Yes, as a kind of investment. Worth more in the UK."

"That's what you think. It's not worth anything. I'll tell you what I'm doing. Waiting for Japan and get hold of one of those samurai swords. What their officers used to wear. A soldier was telling me. His brother brought one back home and sold it for fifty quid."

Hanni Lu's was emptier than before, only a smattering of *Garvie* people and crews of other vessels and of course, no Americans. The same music kept up its steady beat. Barely inside, he was confronted by Hanni Lu.

"You funny-boy here in morning make trouble."

"No Hanni." He found himself parroting her mode of speech. "American do that. Me not make trouble."

"OK. You make to Hanni promise no more trouble."

"Yes. We'll be alright. Americans all gone now." Farley followed this exchange with interest.

"That's your middle name ain't it? – trouble. I never knew you were a funny-boy as well. The old girl's got you sized up; AC-DC, chasing women *and* sailors."

"It was only a silly misunderstanding."

Approaching the phone-booth in the corner, Roger said, "Did Mrs Morrell get away alright?"

"Yes, make that call." As he'd feared, Farley squeezed into the booth with him.

"I can't phone with you here. Wait outside."

"No, I want to be sure you ask about me." Roger lost his temper. Today he'd had a bellyful.

"Get out of this box or I won't call her!" He tried to push the man out, they tussled and the booth swayed. In the background he saw the Rhine maiden snap her fingers at a big Chinese bartender and point in their direction.

A shambling giant in a cream suit and a red bow-tie, this minion plucked Farley out of the booth and held him at arm's length, looking at his mistress like a dog with a slipper. Roger wondered where he'd been that morning when he might have dealt with Irving.

"No more fighting!" barked Hanni Lu. "Make call then go. Both go. You banned. No more come to Hanni Lu's!" He closed the folding door of the booth and scraped his wits together. First he had to figure how a Hong Kong phone worked, then marshal his unfamiliar coins together with the slip he had with her address and number on it. And he was closely watched all the while by the most ill-assorted trio that ever hung around a phone-booth.

In ascending order, Hanni Lu stood with each hand tucked inside the opposite sleeve of her robe and a look on her face that would have scared Kropp. Next was Farley, helplessly fuming. And the towering bartender stood impassive, holding Farley's arm with both hands as if awaiting the order to break it. Roger finally reached the dialling stage and got through right away.

"Gina, it's me. Roger Wren."

"Roger, you didn't waste much time. I'm still unpacking."

"I've got tomorrow off."

"Ah, about that, tomorrow's impossible. I've got to go into Central first thing. I'll be working late tomorrow. This Korean business. I've got some new trooping schedules to learn about."

Was this the brush-off? With Farley waiting to crow about it?

"But it's alright Roger. I'm having friends round for dinner tonight, homecoming party. Come tonight, whatever time you can. Who will you bring with you?" He thought fast.

"Clay and Batten, you've met Clay. And actually, there's Farley. He wants to come too." She didn't answer at first. There was no need. He could sense the outrage coming through the wire.

"Farley?" she said slowly. "Are you making a particularly bad joke?"

"I know. I told him it was out of the question but he kept insisting and making threats. You know how he is. And he got your cabin changed. I promised him I'd ask you." Again for a while she was silent.

"I know you Roger. I do believe you're actually sorry for him. Farley got a tip from me this morning. The room-change was all he did for me, and that had a very ulterior motive. The rest of the time I was fending off his loathsome advances and telling myself I was too soft-hearted to get anyone the sack. As for threats, well I'm sorry but I don't care if he's holding a knife to your throat, he's not coming here." The bartender banged loudly on the glass and jerked his head at Roger.

"What on earth was that noise?" said Gina.

"Another cheetah. This one wants to use the phone."

The sound of her laughing was a tonic. Nothing could spoil it. Not the distortion of distance, the overloud music or the implacable faces outside.

"Roger, you are impossible!" When at last they had to finish he left the booth with a brutal sense of coming down to earth again. Hanni had gone. The bartender was waiting to see them both off the premises.

"What did she say?" grumbled Farley.

He didn't want another scene. "I'll tell you outside." A few paces along the street as they were passing a warehouse Farley stopped and faced him.

"Right. Now you've got us both banned from that place I want some good news."

"She won't have you there. I'm sorry. I tried —" Roger was seized and thrust back violently against a high stack of cloth-covered bales before the warehouse wall.

"Tried?" said Farley angrily. "You tried alright. I've a mind to belt you." Again he was pushed against the bales. "I know what you did, told her a string of lies. Made damn sure I wouldn't be going there." Roger struggled free and edged away.

"No I didn't. I mentioned how you changed her cabin for her but it made no difference. She won't hear of it."

Slightly mollified but still peeved, Farley folded his arms and leaned back against the bales. "Let me tell you something Roger bloody Wren. For a youngster you're getting way out of your depth. I heard you in the after storeroom. Holed up cosy with Penny and that other one." Farley's special talent, he remembered, was eavesdropping. "Talking about Kropp you were. Having a good laugh over him. What if he knew about that? What if somebody set Kropp onto you for a change?"

At times such as this, with all his senses heightened, Roger tended to notice things. Behind Farley, the square bales of silk or cotton were stacked about twelve feet high. Disturbed once too often, they had begun to wobble. He offered his hand.

"Oh for God's sake man, let's go for a drink."

Farley knocked his hand away, then disappeared beneath a tumbling Niagara of what resembled large soft dice, each one stenciled "South China Textile Company". A man ran out of the warehouse and began to yell in Chinese, then English.

"What you do? What happen?" The pile heaved. Farley's head appeared at the top.

"Ask him," said Roger and walked away.

When he got far enough he glanced back. The warehouseman was making quite sure Farley knew the extent of his annoyance. Other men restacked the bales. Farley now had even more reasons for feeling vengeful. He wandered on, undecided whether to return aboard or take a long trishaw ride to somewhere. Communist China, he thought wildly. Over the Nine Dragons to where they'd never find him, away from the *Garvie*-choked dockland, away from them all. Penny, Kropp, Farley *et al.*

No, back to the ship. He'd made his call and the party was on. If he stayed ashore now he'd sooner or later foul up again. It was that kind of day. Nearing the dock gate he ran into more of the ship's personnel. Soon he was meeting someone he knew every few yards. And for the first time on dry land he met the remaining three occupants of his own cabin.

"Everyone's going ashore," said Jack. "Except you. You're coming back. The Lodger – always the odd one out."

Pat said, "Did you make your call?"

"I did. After a bit more trouble. I'm now banned from Hanni Lu's."

"Banned?" gasped Jack, astonished.

"Five minutes," said Toddy. "Five minutes in Hong Kong and he's banned. I don't know."

Trailing cigar-smoke, Batten appeared next. "Roger my boy, sweetheart of the USN. Fully recovered I trust?"

"Now yes, but I'm banned from Hanni Lu's."

"Don't worry, I'll speak to her. I'm off now off to Youmatei. That's where I was going earlier before I got shanghaied. I'm determined to see the Jade Market. Party all fixed up?"

"Yes, tonight. Minus Farley. Just Clay, you and me. She's giving a dinner. Shall we meet by the ferry at six?"

"Fine. Oh Roger, I have to tell you. Kropp's getting ready to go ashore. Be warned. He's sober at the moment."

"I'm obliged to you." The next group included Antonia and Penny. The latter saw him first.

"Ooh, clock the Lodger. Back again after a hard day's being normal! I don't think." Antonia was more friendly.

"What a perfectly dreadful morning you all had. Linda's full of it. Never made and then lost five bucks in so short a time, poor cow."

"Well what did she expect?" said Penny coldly. "That slut's always throwing her weight about. She's got no standards, that one. Like you in that she is." Penny minced off along the road.

Roger said, "I'm only thankful it was Linda."

"Yes, you were fortunate," said Antonia. "And it's not true you know, what Penny said. I have standards. They're low, but I do have them."

Roger said, "Take care of yourself ashore." And he meant it. Antonia was one of the better ones. He liked him/her, and Carol. The numbers thinned out as he passed the scene of Irving's defeat and he was almost at the dock gate when he saw a chin approaching. A jowly, pugnacious chin, followed by the familiar face it belonged to.

He told himself for the last time he was through running from Kropp. There was no way to avoid the man. Other than scaling the nearest crane or leaping into the water. Like the destroyer he resembled, Kropp sharply altered course to intercept him. The man was moving straight and sure, and he remembered there was no known instance of him going on the offensive while sober. But they were off the ship and more or less alone.

"Where you been?" Kropped growled.

"Hanni Lu's."

"So they're saying. Chasing Yankee matelots." Roger stepped to his right, Kropp to his left. Bringing no change. Tired of this ridiculous minuet, he spoke up as boldly as he dared.

"Mr Kropp. Everything you believe about me is wrong, right back to that time in the shower."

"Lies. You're all lying; you and all your dirty, queer friends. I'll get even with you, Jimmy, sooner or later. Don't have any doubts on that." To his surprise and relief, Kropp shoved him aside and marched on his way. He tried to remember how many encounters he'd had with this clearly deranged person. And he thought of the possible outcome if Kropp and Farley should meet in Kowloon and discuss him. Penny was on the loose too. His three worst enemies could join up, pool their common loathing of him and come back tonight fully primed with liquor and hate.

On board again he went to No 21, the Kropp-check for once not required.

"Forget all of them," said Clay. "You're always lucky. Today proves it yet again." Roger told him about the party. "Damn," said Clay. "I can't make it tonight, too busy up top. See what you can fix for some other day. We're back here after Japan." They were alone in the cabin. Roger noticed the small attaché case left on Seymour's bunk.

"Where's Frank? He left his secret box out."

"Gone for a shower, and if you're considering a look in his box – don't. It'll be locked, always is." They tried and it was.

"A grown man," said Clay. "Keeping a hoard of skin books."

"Maybe you'll go that way when you're alone in the world."

"Seymour's not alone in the world. He got a letter today, wouldn't say who it was from."

Seymour returned and silently got dressed. "Frank," said Clay. "How about sharing out your skin-books?"

"What skin-books?"

"The ones you got in that case."

Suspiciously, Seymour examined the catches on the lid. "What I got in here is my own property, no-one else's. If I want to keep skin books in it I can. There's no rule says I can't."

Clay went on. "I'm surprised, that's all, a man at your age. Wouldn't you rather have the real thing?"

"I've — I've got someone at home."

"Leave it be," said Roger under his breath. But Clay wouldn't.

"That's not what they say Frank. They say your people left you over your drinking."

"Oh they left me alright. And they won't be coming back. Now I got somebody else." Seymour fished under his pillow for the letter. "See? Here's the proof. What have you got to say about that? Crazy old Seymour's got a woman in England. Do you want me to read it out or will you take my word for it?"

"Alright," said Clay. "We believe you."

"Good. Now leave me alone and mind your own fuggin' business." Seymour stuffed the letter in his pocket and left the cabin.

"So they did walk out on him," said Clay. "Finally he admits it." Seymour had left his locker open. So he couldn't have left the ship. Probably on deck brooding. Clay put on his white jacket. "I've got to work. They got some special function on, Army brass hats. God knows what time I'll finish tonight." Roger was on his own again. In a couple of hours he'd be at work himself. After he'd done what he knew he had to do.

Seymour was at the stern rail, perched on a bollard reading his letter.

"Frank, I must apologise for Clay. The way he tried to stir things up."

"Doesn't bother me, I'm used to it. Ignorance, that's all it is. Ignorance you could cut into blocks and build a wall with. Did he send you up here to find out more?"

"No honestly. I only wanted to say that." Roger began to leave.

"Hold on, don't go. You're not like them. I don't mind telling you about this woman if you keep it to yourself." He didn't really want this. Secrets, promises and betrayals; as if there weren't enough already, but of course he didn't walk away.

"As I said before Roger, I've had a lot of heartache in my life and I've been on my own a long time. The trouble is you can't trust people. Yes, I more or less trust you, but I've been done so often. That's why I had a go at you that day about Hiroshima. I don't want to see no bombsites. Not when I was in the Blitz."

"No of course not." His conscience eased, he tried to think of a tactful exit line.

"Well Frank, we're all got work to do so I'd better —"

"Listen Roger, I said I've been alone for years. So I have but not anymore. I want to tell you this because I know you won't blab and because you're the only one among this riff-raff who's ever shown me any consideration." Now he couldn't leave without contradicting this. So once again he patiently heard out Seymour's saga of misfortune. Some people get paid for this, he thought.

"That's how it was Roger, for years. Sometimes I felt there was some evil thing, you know, some kind of haunting thing bringing it all on me. I came close to ending it more than once I can tell you. One time I actually climbed the rail and hung by one hand, but I chickened out. This is all between you and me, mind."

"Certainly."

"That's the way it's been till now. I met this woman a couple of months back. In a club I sometimes go to. I live alone see, don't go out much. Her old man ran off and left her so she joined this club, where we met. On a tennis court if you can believe it, never played in my life, till she showed me. We've been out a few times now; here and there. Now she writes and says she's looking forward to seeing me. I never thought anything would come of it." Seymour looked at his letter again, his hand shaking slightly. "I don't know whether I should get tangled up with anyone again. Not after – I mean she seems alright and she knows I've got no money. What do you think I should do?"

A man about thirty years his senior was asking his advice. With all the debauched sexual champions aboard it was him he preferred. It wasn't fair. He didn't need this burden. Playing for time he asked, "How old is she?"

"Forty-five."

"And have you —?"

"No. But it's on the cards."

"Then I can't see anything against it, if you're happy together, then why not?" If anybody deserved a break it was Seymour. "Write to her. Send her something. Women love that. Get her some cute little thing ashore."

Seymour slid down off the bollard. "I will, I'll do it now. Thanks Roger. I'll go for broke on this, come what may. Older women are the best anyway, don't you reckon? I mean you've got one like that yourself haven't you. Over on the Island, Clay said."

Seymour now took on the expression Roger knew so well, and he guessed the coming question even as the man strove to frame it. "What's she — I mean your woman — of course if you'd rather not say — I mean I'm only asking, what's she like — you know — in *that* department?" What on earth could he say to that?

A sampan laboured into view, bobbing cork-like in the wake of a powered junk with a painted dragon on its prow. Dragons and serpents he thought. They were everywhere in the Far East. Fire-belching faces carved high on cornerstones. Painted cobras twisting up temple pillars. The one on her dressing-gown. Reptiles everywhere. He had his answer.

"She shags like a rattlesnake."

The impossible happened. Seymour laughed. Out loud. Laughed in the spluttering, wet-eyed way of a soul too long in darkness. Recovering, he put the letter away.

"I feel a lot easier about it now. They're better out than in, these things. Once you've found someone who'll listen that is. I'll nip off now and pick up something to send her." He headed for the companion steps.

"Try the Kowloon Gift Centre," Roger called. "Or Heung Chong's off Nathan Road."

"Thanks again, I will." Seymour, happy? It was payment enough. Roger, it seemed, could get some things right.

They let him go early from the mess. By six he was at the Star Pier, still sporting his "Hong Kong" shirt. Batten had managed to reach the Jade Market.

"No bargains though, Roger. What I liked I couldn't afford and what I could afford was awful. One thing though. I saw Hanni Lu and explained everything. You can go back there anytime."

"Much obliged. That's another one I owe you."

Named *Evening Star*, the ferry was double-decked and double-ended, like the tramcars they would shortly see. For a few cents this took them across to the island. Batten read Gina's paper slip aloud.

"Penang Lodge, Macau Drive, Wei Ho Bay. Not so much an address, more a geography lesson." Stepping ashore at the Star Ferry's other pier, Roger found a city more noisy, more feverishly alive than anywhere he'd yet been. A human and mechanised tide flowed back and forth in endless bands of colour and clatter. Tramcars, green and top-heavy-looking, trundled along their pre-ordained iron paths, indifferent to the rickshaws, bicycles and cars cutting and weaving a suicidal way among them.

Batten was wearing a dark blazer with tan slacks, a silk cravat and 'co-respondent' shoes. A smooth-tongued charmer dressed to kill. For an appalling second Roger saw Gina in his arms.

"Are you expecting to make a conquest?"

"Hope, dear boy, springs eternal. If Wei Ho Bay is what I think it is we could be moving in exalted circles this evening."

A few enquiries and they were on their way. The single-decker bus was driven by a young Chinese.

"Will you tell us when we get there?" asked Batten.

"Sure. OK-you-see." Before they'd gone three hundred yards the bus slowed and stopped. The driver pressed the starter a few times to no avail.

"I knew it," said Roger. "Things were going too well."

The driver jumped out, gave another "OK-you-see" and lifted the bonnet.

Batten said, "I suppose we could take a cab, although I've no idea how far it is or what it would cost." After some tinkering the driver slammed down the bonnet and resumed his seat. The engine came to life and they were off again.

The bus took them through Central, skirted notorious Wanchai on the left and began to climb through leafy suburbs into the hills that separate the north and south halves of the island. They glimpsed luxury bungalows behind screens of cypress and pine. Velvety lawns and a white mansion half-drowned in wisteria. Now they were passing Happy Valley, where the famed racetrack lay basking in the late haze.

"I'd like to live here," said Roger. "If I had the money."

"So would I. Home from home; a bamboo Bournemouth." Still climbing, the bus rumbled on. The air turned cooler. Wei Ho Bay appeared quite suddenly, when the road took a bend and began an abrupt descent.

This part of the island was clearly given over to the good life, an expatriate haven shielded by its hills from the vulgar commercialism that paid for it all. An indolent sprawl of pink or white villas spilled down the hillside all the way to the shore. Every one had its wide roof of green tiles and most were tethered to the road by a driveway flanked with manicured bushes or slim trees stood to attention. Here and there could be seen the blue rectangle of a swimming pool. The bay itself formed a perfect semi-circle, a giant C taking a bite from the ocean.

"Macau Drive," came the call. They alighted from the bus. From all around came a loud buzzing.

"What's that noise?" said Roger.

"Might be cicadas. That's if they have them here. I've never heard them in Hong Kong before, but then I've never been in this part."

Macau Drive dropped down to the sea in a succession of tree-wrapped minor palaces, no two exactly alike and each set slightly lower than the preceding one. Trees and distance gave privacy to all. The place exuded a kind of exotic domesticity that both seduced and reassured.

"Money," said Batten. "Can't you smell it?"

"Wealth isn't everything. It doesn't bring happiness."

Batten surveyed the sumptuous dwellings all around them. "No, but it sure as hell makes the misery easier to bear."

Penang Lodge scored a point over the others by having an exterior colour-washed in a pleasing *eau-de-nil*. As they turned into the gravel drive a car followed them in, also headed for the single-storey villa. At the wheel was a burly man in RAF uniform with a slim brunette next to him. Standing aside to let it pass they noticed she was an oriental and very much younger than the driver.

"There's your companion for the evening," said Batten. "Someone your own age. I'll take care of Gina."

"Get six," said Roger. A crude rejoinder to hide his nagging worry that Batten might not have been entirely joking.

"One other point Roger. This evening I'm Henry again, OK?"

At the villa they noticed the car had been parked facing back down the drive, as if for a quick departure.

"I wonder who the Raff type is?" said Roger. "And more to the point, who's the girl?" Gina answered the door-bell.

"Roger! Here you are then. I must say I do like your shirt, very up to date. I hope you've not been wearing it in the wrong company though. Some sailors could get the wrong idea about you."

"I have and they did."

She laughed. "You're cheering me up already."

"I'm sorry I couldn't get you to Antonia's wedding."

"Yes, I heard about it from one of the other stewards, quite an evening. Where's Clay?"

"Unavoidably detained."

"Never mind, so this must be ...?" Batten took her hand.

"Henry Batten, charmed to make your acquaintance." For a moment it seemed there might be a hand-kiss or a heel-click but she was spared this. Too continental perhaps. They were led through a hall into a tastefully furnished room bathed in evening sunlight. This opened onto the expected full-length verandah. The place had everything. Carefully spaced antique pots erupting with flowers, a low table with drinks. More blooms in a giant *cloisonné* vase, and several bamboo chairs under a large candy-striped parasol with "Dubonnet" round the fringe.

"Got that cheap at an auction," said Gina. "Years ago on a trip to Saigon; very French that city is." Best of all was what lay beyond the verandah; a breath-catching prospect of the bay in all its curving perfection. And closer to hand a line of steps leading to the beach.

There were more new faces. Wing-Commander Shay was a soft-spoken individual with no "side" whatsoever.

"Evening Mr Wren or Roger is it? Hmm, that's a jazzy shirt you're wearing. Where'd you get it? The UK?" Before Roger could answer he pressed on. "Gina tells me you were Raff yourself." Among these older people he was acutely aware of his youth.

"Only National Service, doing mods on radar."

"Hmm, important work all the same. Every country's got radar now of course, now we've shown 'em how it works. What stuff did you work on?"

"Oh, there was Gee and IFF and H2S."

Shay nodded. "Know why they called it that? H2S?"

"I assumed it was a codename."

"No. It was because the whole device could be a stinker to operate. H2S is hydrogen sulphide – rotten eggs."

Next they met a tall attractive woman of about forty who was introduced as Elaine Halley.

"That's right, Halley. But no comet jokes please. I'm a lot younger and I come around more often. Although I've always believed the stars have a great influence on all our lives. The Chinese are very keen on it." Batten took to her instantly. Smooth as silk, he informed her that curiously, he too believed passionately in astrology and was delighted their "orbits had crossed". The term "fast worker" might have been coined for Batten.

Gina having momentarily vanished to other parts, Roger found himself in a bamboo chair sipping a sherry and hearing about Sam Shay's duties at Kai Tak.

"This business in Korea has really caught them out. God knows why, they should have seen it coming. But that's the Raff for you. You know yourself. Panic stations. Snafu as the Americans say."

"Will you be sent to Korea?"

"Bound to be I suppose. Transport Command, I'm in Dakotas. This couldn't have come at a worse time for me. We should have been leaving for UK next week; going home for good, retiring. My wife's already there, staying in Reigate with my sister, and finding somewhere for us all to live. We were due to go next on the *Empire Fowey*, my daughter and me that is. Now it's all up in the air. Don't know if I'm going or not. I may send her on the *Fowey* without me." Batten and Elaine were at the verandah rail engaged in astrological debate. Gina reappeared and called Roger over. So far there'd been nothing in her face to remind him of that astonishing night. No look or sly smile. Maybe when they were alone …

"I see you've met Sam Shay. He's the one I told you about; another man with a Chinese wife same as Neville and Yingsu."

"And his wife's in England. So that girl I saw him with …?"

"Yes, the daughter. Nineteen she is. Her name's Anna. And you'll be intrigued to know she's very keen on English poetry. Here she is now."

He'd heard of "Eurasians". The word explained itself and in Anna Shay, east met west in happy defiance of Kipling's old assertion. In a strictly western sense she was not conventionally beautiful. Her cheekbones were a touch over-prominent, her body almost too slim.

But attraction takes many forms. Her skin was flawless, her figure perfect for the white *cheongsam* that hugged it. Cut in a page-boy style, her midnight-black hair caught highlights from the dying sun, and in her almond eyes he saw again the goddesses of Sri Mariamman temple. Giving a quick bird-like nod she spoke first.

"Good evening. You are one of Gina's friends from the ship." Her voice was light as air, with a faint upward inflexion at the end.

"Good evening. Yes, Roger Wren. And my associate over there is —" he remembered in time "— Henry Batten." His associate was still engrossed in Elaine and gave them a wave.

"I hope everyone is hungry," called Gina. "It's all ready in here." A small procession moved into a dining-room off the verandah. Roger felt a little out of it, as he had in the Jade Palace. They seemed to be all of a kind here, even Batten. It was difficult to equate this polished gent with the ragamuffin philosopher of Cabin 21. And impossible to see the Gina of tonight as he once had. Naked in her cramped B Deck cell with the monsoon lashing down.

They were left to choose their own places at the table. He opted to sit between her and Anna. At each place was half a grapefruit in a silver dish. "Don't stand on ceremony," said Gina, adding with startling bluntness, "Everyone just get stuck in." In Roger's former life of good but homely food, wartime rations and post-war austerity, things like grapefruit had played little part. The first taste nearly made him pucker up till he saw the others adding caster sugar to theirs. The conversation rippled round the table, with a tendency to slow down when it reached him or Anna. As the youngest by many years they could not help deferring to the others. And despite the free-and-easy humour there was an underlay of good manners that made him speak carefully.

"Wei Ho Bay seems a really fine location. Do you live far away Anna?"

"No. Only just down the Drive. Two houses along." Strange, he thought. Why come by car?

Food was served by the hostess with the assistance of a small silent woman who scurried back to the kitchen between courses. "Maria, my Portuguese cook," said Gina. "I should have let her go after John died but I hadn't the heart." The meal progressed. They had fish, of a kind he'd never heard of. This was accompanied by white wine, ready for the next course. Chicken to him was a treat you had at Christmas. Having it now, in a splendid concoction of spices and bamboo shoots was a novel experience. His father was wrong. You could be only a crew messman and still learn about high-class fare. As long as you got the invites.

Batten said, "Did anyone see a paper today? I hear the North Koreans have crossed the 38th Parallel."

"It's true," said Sam. "I hope to God it doesn't come to anything. I had my fill in the last lot."

"Father." Anna sounded timid after the gruff talk of war. "Father, tell Gina your news."

"Tell me what?"

"I've got to cancel my leave and return to Kai Tak tonight, because of this latest threat. Only got the phone call today but I didn't want to miss your homecoming. I've got all my stuff in the car." A shadow had descended on the company. This was how all wars began. Rumours and reports. Leave cancelled, marching feet in a distant land of which they knew little and cared less.

"When will you be back?" asked Gina.

"No telling. Next week – next month. It might be only a briefing."

Batten said, "There's no doubt the UN are preparing to go in. It's why we were sent. We'll take on troops for Japan."

"That's right," Sam agreed. "Seasoned soldiers. Could be you'll take the Argylls and some of the Wiltshire Regiment. They'll go to Kure for re-equipping then to Pusan in South Korea. The men you brought today will replace them here." Roger stole a glance at Anna. Her eyes were half-closed as if to hide her feelings. He remembered it was her father who might be flying his lumbering, unarmed Dakota through a hostile sky.

"Oh come on," said Elaine briskly. "Chin up everyone." She raised her glass. "Here's to a quick campaign and back to the old days. We beat the Japs and we'll beat the North Koreans." The crude jingoism jarred badly. He saw Anna close her eyes and turn her head away. When the meal was over they all retired to the open air again.

"Anyone want to play mahjong?" pleaded Gina. Nobody did, for which he was grateful. He didn't want to play games. At least not that kind. What occupied his mind now was how this evening might end. There was Gina, whom he still craved. But tonight was surely too soon. And she had to make that special trip in to her office in the morning. There was Batten and Elaine, who they'd since learned was a divorcee with a house nearby. Obviously Batten had plans in that direction.

And there was the mysterious Anna. With Sam called away she would be walking home alone to her empty house. He checked his train of thought. Play it by ear. See how it goes. The satisfying meal and the visual delight of the view were very conducive to talking. Gina mentioned his photograph. "I've not had time yet to get anything done. But I will. That shot's going in the gallery. I'm set on that." It wasn't the kind of party he'd expected. No excessive drinking, no carousing. Not that he minded. He couldn't imagine what Bill would have made of it.

During the meal he'd addressed a few tentative remarks to Anna and got polite if distant replies. Now as they took their ease under the Saigon parasol he tried again. "This is my first visit to Hong Kong."

She stared absently at the bay. "I'm afraid it's changed since the war, although it is still beautiful." He wanted to draw her out – hear those crisp sentences with the little upcurl of sound on the tail of each one.

"Yes it is. There's much I want to see while I'm here. The view from the peak for instance, and the Tiger Balm Gardens." The smooth oval face turned to him.

"Gina told me you admire oriental things. You don't care for the usual interest of seafarers."

"No." Except one, he nearly added. "No. Especially as I've never been overseas before. I want to take this opportunity to see places."

"What of your comrades? Surely they too have such desires."

"Some do. But I fear most are not interested."

She shook her head. "Their eyes are open but their minds are shut. It is so sad." Such solemnity in a nineteen-year-old. As if mixed parentage bestowed wisdom beyond her years.

The time passed too quickly. Sam held forth on the Korean situation. Batten had them chortling over some Cunard escapades. Even Roger contributed. Tales of his Aden and Colombo visits went down well, as did a sterilised version of today's events. The question of how, when or even if he would return aboard tonight was pushed to the back of his mind. At 10.30 Sam left and this signalled the end of the evening. Roger wondered how he got to Kai Tak. "Special arrangement with the navy," said Gina. "Leaves his car at HMS *Tamar* and goes over by launch. He knows the commander." They stood at the entrance as Sam kissed his daughter, made his farewells to everyone and drove away.

Anna said, "Thank you for the dinner Gina. I'd like to leave now. Would you mind?"

"No, not at all. Roger, why don't you see Anna home?"

He'd thought about how to suggest this. Now Gina had done it for him. They took the verandah steps to a path along the rear of adjacent properties. The girl was silent, and he had little idea what to say. Her deadly serious manner didn't help. But when he did think of something and opened his mouth to say it, she spoke first.

"Would you really like to see the Tiger Balm Gardens?"

"I would, yes. And I've got tomorrow free." She made no reply as they walked on. The cicadas whispered busily in the dusk. What now? He thought of a joke and it died in his head.

"I have often cycled there," she said gravely. "But always on my own. The Gardens are not to everybody's taste." At a small gate she stopped. "I have a spare bicycle. If it would please you we could go there tomorrow afternoon." In the velvet-soft twilight the *cheongsam* seemed luminous against the dense shrubbery. He wanted to reach out and touch her.

"I would be delighted. Where shall we meet?"

"At the top of the Drive. Would two o'clock be convenient?"

"Yes, perfect."

Putting out a hand she said, "Goodnight then Mr Wren. Thank you for escorting me."

A genteel hand-clasp. "Goodnight Anna." Her footsteps echoed along a paved path to her house. He retraced his steps, feeling he'd just emerged from the last century. *If it would please you. Thank you for escorting me!*

Back on the verandah Gina sat smoking. It was only the second cigarette he'd seen her with.

"Welcome back. Did you get her home alright?"

"Yes. A very agreeable person, I thought. Good manners."

"That's her mother's doing. Comes from a very well-to-do Peking family, her mother. I think she only married Sam Shay because he was an officer with prospects. I'm afraid young Anna's led a very dull life since the war. Her dad's alright but Mother keeps her on a very tight rein. The poor thing's only ever had one boyfriend and her mother disliked him so he had to go. But I do happen to know Anna spent one night with him. That's strictly confidential Roger."

"But now her mother's in England and her father's at Kai Tak."

She treated him to the cascading laugh that so stirred him. "That's right. A free agent at last. I wonder what she'll get up to." They seemed to be alone.

"Where are the others?" As if he didn't know.

"Gone. Henry took Elaine home too. And he won't be back – if I know Elaine."

He was aware that she derived amusement from watching him. "Roger, I'm afraid the final bus left for Central ten minutes ago. There is now no chance of catching the 11.30 ferry back to the mainland."

"Yes, I rather thought that would happen. Imagine I could have caught it if I hadn't taken Anna back at your suggestion."

"What are you implying?" Almost certainly she was playing with him again. Two could do that.

"Mrs Morrell, it seems I must ask to stay the night. I will cause as little inconvenience as possible."

"No trouble at all. Come this way." It was a small bedroom, not far from a larger one he assumed was hers.

"I'm sure you'll sleep soundly here," she said. "You won't even hear the cicadas – and Maria's gone home. In the morning when I go to work I can drop you off in Connaught Road by the ferry pier, alright?"

Alone, he undressed and lay studying the ceiling. The bed seemed enormous after the succession of bunks. So they were cicadas. One small puzzle solved. Leaving the big one. Her abrupt manner. Was she play-acting or really angry? How easy it was to seem cocky even when he tried not to.

Yes, he'd surely blown it this time. It was a wonder he hadn't bragged of his coming assignation with the Eurasian girl. And yet Gina had sent him off along that path knowing about the damn bus. After five minutes of this he pulled himself together and went to her.

The room was in that sultry semi-darkness that seemed a prerequisite of all his amorous adventures. "Oh there you are Roger. I was beginning to think you'd died."

Tonight she had on a nightdress, a garment that was shed with such alacrity he was reminded of the rhyme. It wasn't the Almighty who – he stifled a chuckle and she rapidly cooled. "You're very sure of yourself. I believe I warned you of that in Singapore."

The nature of their friendship was clear. Mutual pleasure and amusement. As with Ruth but on a more rarified level. And she made the rules.

"I was only laughing at myself. Since joining the ship I've had a nickname – the Lodger. Now I am one."

"Why Lodger?" There were hazards here. Gina appreciated most humour, but finding herself the subject of a bawdy verse might be too much.

"I suppose it rhymes with Roger. Why did you put me in that room if …?"

"Because you've now met Anna. She's prettier, she's your age and possessed of an oriental serenity and charm I can only achieve in shrines and temples. And you both love poetry. You might well have had a change of heart where I was concerned."

"Of course not and we never even mentioned poetry."

On the ship there had always been the fear of discovery. Initially an incentive; a "to-hell-with-them" kind of wickedness, but in the end an annoying distraction. Tonight was special, now the silence held no menace. His ears were not tuned for footsteps or a knock at the door.

The spacious, even opulent room was a perfect setting for what became his most stimulating night to date. Ripened and hardened in a ship that was little more than a sea-going hothouse of carnality, his boy's body and artless demeanour had begun to seem not altogether a bad thing. It was true, they did like them young.

"Come here Roger," she murmured very quietly, and they rolled together like kids on a beach. Blissfully alone at last, they gave way to the animal instincts that lie in all of us. He forgot about Kropp. He forgot about Prentice and Farley, and all the people and things that had plagued him on the long global trek to this spot. But the joys of life are fleeting. By now he really should have known better. Perhaps deep down he did. But he could never have guessed quite how this incredible run of luck was going to end. Or that it would be very soon. In twelve hours' time. In a nightmare of blood and pain.

Chapter 13

Gina drove well. Her car was an old Austin, rather nondescript for such a select area but she handled it with skill. "Maria's husband maintains it for me and in return I let them use it. He charged the battery for me yesterday." They'd shared a light breakfast at seven. After a night to remember. A series of conversational interludes linked by bouts of energetic sex that left him, if not drained certainly depleted.

"I forgot to say how much we enjoyed that dinner. Clay will be sorry he missed it."

Clay – another debt to repay. Without him none of this would be happening. There would have been no Ruth or Gina. No temples or idyllic resorts far away from the jostling docklands where an assailant might lurk round any corner. "Come again tomorrow, same time as before. Clay too if he can make it, and Henry. Well, he may have other plans if he and Elaine are still sharing an orbit."

"I'll look forward to that."

"Tonight's no good. The situation in Korea means we're all busy at the department this evening. They're starting a whole new section to deal with troop movements to Japan. They'll be boarding the *Garvie* today, the first contingent. When I finish tonight I'll be fit to drop. I shouldn't even be going back yet. What a way to end a vacation."

There were no recriminations when he confessed to his afternoon date with Anna. "I don't mind in the least Roger. Do you think I own you? Anna's a splendid person; she deserves someone to go cycling with. Be sure you treat her right though. She's a deep one, Anna. Under all that goody-two-shoes stuff I think she may be quite a girl. I think she just needs someone to bring her out. Now Mummy's not here maybe someone will." He had the distinct feeling he was being pushed towards Anna.

They crested the hill and began the long downward run into the city. In Connaught Road they pulled over to the kerb. She did not even switch off the engine. Leaning across, she kissed him lightly on the cheek. "Bye. See you tomorrow." As he closed the door she said, "Remember what I told you about Anna. Talk about poetry. Tell her you like Robert Browning and then watch her face!"

At the Star Pier he was swept along in the crush of humanity boarding the ferry. Chinese in black tunics and women lugging bundles of goods to Kowloon markets. Harassed men in business suits, cheek-by-jowl with hung-over sailors returning from the fleshpots of Wanchai. Eventually he got a seat next to one of the "commercials", a distinguished gent clutching his newly purchased copy of the *South China Morning Post*. As expected, he saw many known faces, and his name was soon called.

"Hey, it's the Lodger. Where you been all night? As if we couldn't guess!" They were an odd couple, Smith and Nelson. Elastic-bodied and restless, Nelson crossed and re-crossed his legs on the wooden seat, twisting about to study the scene around them. Smith, with his chubby face and fringe of hair resembled Friar Tuck at his most rascally. "Don't tell us," said he. "Been with that widow, right?"

"Correct. And you?"

"Wanchai. Only for the shows though – nothing else. Don't need it. Happily married, me."

In the *Garvie* moral wasteland such a degree of fidelity was a rare gem to come across. So where had they been till 7.30 in the morning? Nelson's face still shone from some recent visual feast. "Round all the joints. Taking in the all-night shows." The businessman next to them shifted uncomfortably and stared pointedly off at a passing junk. "Strip shows and all that stuff. All kinds, right up on the stage. There was this woman, this fan-dancer came on, and I tell you straight Roger, not a word of a lie, she had nothing on behind the fans. Nothing except black shoes and black gloves. That's all – honest. Then at the end of her act she flung her arms and legs out like — like a starfish."

"It's true," said Smith. "Put me in mind of the five of spades."

The businessman snorted and opened his newspaper with a disapproving rustle. Stark headlines leapt off the front page. KOREAN CRISIS DEEPENS. REDS TAKE WONJU. It didn't seem important. Not on this ancient ferry-boat crossing the harbour in the pale sunlight. Here all was in order, at peace. Everyone intent on their own lives; from the amiable fishermen in their sampans, to the families on the lumbering junks.

Roger had been on the go since daybreak yesterday. Sleep must be the priority, otherwise by three o'clock he'd be falling off his borrowed bike. At midday he'd have a bite to eat in the mess before setting off to meet his Eurasian date.

"Wake up Roger," said Nelson. "We're there." Coming off the ramp he stumbled.

Smith said, "He's still half-cut."

"No really I'm ..." But they were gone, lost in the crowd pouring off the ferry. Yes, he must get to his bunk, his "pit". If the others left him alone that is. Bill and Martin would be back now, working breakfast. In the event, when they all gathered in the cabin they did leave him alone, because they needed a recovery period themselves, but first there was a lip-smacking exchange of news, mercifully short, that even included hearing where Jack and Pat had spent the previous evening. Wanchai of course. "I'll have to sample that part sometime," said Roger drowsily.

Jack said, "Roger likes to have more than one iron in the fire. Now he's got some Chinese piece in mind. Only he'll get it for nothing – you see."

"That's because he's young and innocent," said Pat.

"So am I," complained Martin unconvincingly.

"Yes – but he looks it."

"Terrible thing – greed," muttered Toddy. By eight o'clock, an unaccustomed calm descended on the glory hole as all who had a few hours free "got their heads down". When Roger awoke it was lunchtime and the cabin was empty. It was his day off. He could lie there while others worked. Recalling Singapore he thought of Gina's beloved legion of gods. A deity for every human aspiration. Yes, he must be doing something right. Or maybe he believed too much in gods and providence. Maybe he was just a "jammy swine" as they said. Toddy came in with several parcels.

"Laundry's up. Yours is two dollars." Roger leapt down from the bunk, showered and began dressing for his afternoon date. Toddy watched him. "Good time?"

"Last night – yes. Off again now. Bit of lunch first."

"Heard about where you went," said Toddy morosely. "Funny place, the Far East. Strange things happen here if you tempt fate. It's why they got so many fortune-tellers here. Lucky charms and stuff."

Roger paid his laundry money. "I've been OK so far. The gods like me." Closing his locker, he caught sight of the Buddha. Despite himself, he had a second look. The faint, all-knowing smile was still there. And yet, was it quite the same? Not a trifle – sardonic? Of course it was the poor light in the cabin. Move the thing around and it was the same as before. He'd started seeing things. Too much excitement, too little sleep. Not to mention rich food, Camel cigarettes and joss-stick fumes. A spell of cycling up in the hills would set him right. At the mess he joined the queue, getting the expected ribbing from the servers.

"Here comes the Lodger," said Bill. "Feed the bugger up good or he'll never last the voyage out the way he's going."

It was here and now that the overlong winning streak came to a terrible halt. Somebody grasped his arm from behind and swung him round. His face then seemed to explode, the whole front of it becoming an instant mask of searing pain. His mouth and nose burned like fire. Staggering, he fell to his knees. His entire face seemed to be shedding itself, falling in successive layers of agony down to his chin only to start again at the top. There was a buzzing in his ears and his eyes were welded shut with heat and pain. Dimly he heard voices.

"Fuggin' 'ell! Did you see that? Who was it done it?" Somehow he got his eyes open. He was crouched on all fours in a small dark-brown puddle dotted with shards of white. This was all he took in before pain forced his eyelids down again. Someone helped him up.

"OK laddie, hold on to me." Jack's voice.

"Sit him down here." That was Martin. Peering down again through sticky lashes he saw his own feet shuffling forward, making gooey skid-marks as he left his puddle. And he noticed also on the white tiles a spattering of large red spots keeping pace with him, dripping from his chin with ominous regularity.

"Here, put this on it. Hold it in place." A cloth was put to his tormented face and he pressed it there with both hands. Slumped on a chair in anguished darkness, he heard a clamour of voices around him.

"Who done it?" was the main point of interest, followed by speculation as to who the forlorn figure behind the cloth was.

"It's the Lodger. Somebody slammed a plateful of oxtail soup into his dial. Did it so hard they broke the plate."

"Poor bastard. He'll be marked for life." Jack's voice came again. "Let's get him down to the quack's – Bill!" Once more he was hoisted up and led back past the patch of blood and soup, out of the door and down the alleyway.

The journey seemed to take ages. Jack and Bill discussed him as they went along, talking across him as if he was dead or unconscious.

"On his day off too," said Bill.

"No cycling now with his new Chinese bit."

Roger unstuck his lips. "Who did it?"

"Kropp," said Jack. "Lots of people saw him. He must have come to the mess on purpose." No, this was all wrong. This shouldn't have happened here. Not on board, in bright lights among friends. It was supposed to be on shore, where he knew how to be a fugitive. On shore there were murky alleys to run down, a hundred holes to hide in. Where he had a chance. Kropp had misled him. He felt almost as aggrieved by that as the attack itself. At the surgery they sat him down again and he gingerly lowered the sodden cloth.

"What happened?" inquired the doctor. Jack explained as they got his soup-enriched shirt off.

"Oxtail it was," added Bill as if he thought this might have some bearing on treatment. A middle-aged nurse came in with a bowl of water and bathed his face. They found he had five cuts shared among cheekbones, forehead and chin.

"God, what a mess!" said the doctor encouragingly. "Alright, as you say you witnessed it you'd best go and describe it to the Second Steward. We'll be keeping this man here for a few days." After they'd gone the doctor took some iodine and cotton-wool from a cabinet and gave Roger a stern look. "You're the sixth one I've had in here since we arrived. A couple of men fell down steps coming aboard, too stewed to walk. The others had black eyes and assorted abrasions collected in having a so-called good time. So I'll tell you the same as I told them. If you people can't have a drink without getting into a stupid quarrel you ought to lay off it."

Coming at such a moment, the accusation was ill-timed. The cuts were painful and there was the scalding and the heavy initial bleeding. Now came the dabbing of iodine and the sensation of being stung by five bees all at once. He felt entitled to be touchy.

"I was *not* drunk!" he said so vehemently the nurse dropped her swab. "And I'll thank you not to imply that I was. This attack came out of the blue. I have never actually had any kind of fight in my life. With anyone. Neither have I the least love of alcohol. It wouldn't worry me if this ship was dry. Like the – like the *Chester* bloody *Vandemeyer*!" The nurse paused in her work to observe her boss's reaction. The man finished applying the iodine and got some dressings.

"And I'll thank *you* to keep a civil tongue in your head and remember you're talking to a senior ship's officer. But – if I was wrong – I'm – er – I'm sorry. I simply thought – is something amusing you Margaret?"

"No, nothing. Nothing really," said the nurse and hurried off with her bowl of reddened water. Fifteen minutes later Roger was in a bed in the small ward off the surgery, wearing unaccustomed pyjamas courtesy of the Orient Line. The room was all in white with some other beds and a highly-polished porthole. There were four large dressings on his face, the two forehead cuts being close enough to share one.

"There shouldn't be any severe disfigurement," said the doctor and left him alone with the nurse who sat beside him taking down his personal details on a clipboard.

"Sorry I lost my temper," said Roger. "Don't normally swear."

"I think you were right to stick up for yourself. He is rather down on drinkers. We had a busy morning with them. Singapore was the same. We only use this ward for deserving cases. The rest he patches up and sends on their way. He thinks you're all of a kind. I'm always telling him to go easy. Perhaps now he'll be more tactful."

The doctor returned and read the clipboard. "Roger Wren. I thought we'd met before but I couldn't be certain. Nobody could, the state you were in. Had any lunch yet?"

Roger ran a careful tongue over his burning lips. "No, but I can recommend the first course." The doctor threw back his head and roared with laughter.

"Margaret, get him something to eat. He's earned it. Something cold, I would advise." Still chuckling he left the ward.

Margaret said, "That's the first time he's smiled today." Later, finishing his meal on a tray he mentioned his ruined date. "Cycling?" said Margaret. "I must say that's something different. Have you got family here in the Colony?"

"No, some people I met. Expatriates. I was seeing this girl at two o'clock."

"Would you like me to ring them and explain why you can't make it?"

"I thought there were no phones aboard."

"Oh, there are phones, but not for general use; only official matters. And there's a local directory too." The only number he had was Gina's and she was at work.

"Thanks a lot. I don't know her number. It may be under the name of Shay. Wing-Commander."

He spelled it out. "The Wei Ho Bay area." She took the tray.

"I'll see what I can do. Don't tell the doctor."

"Thank you again." He fingered his abused face. The dressings felt huge. Margaret returned.

"Someone to see you." Bill and Martin seemed embarrassed, tongue-tied as they entered his hushed and sterile retreat.

"How's —" Bill began. "How does it — I mean does it hurt much?"

"Quite a lot. Thanks for helping me." Martin was awed by the dressings.

"Got many cuts under there?"

"Five. The broken plate did that. And I've been scalded."

They were at an acute disadvantage here, these men whose cruel tongues he'd once dreaded. You couldn't mock somebody whose red face squinted up at you from a misshapen white mask. They made halting conversation, looking everywhere but at him. "Jack told Candy," said Bill. "And I can guess who he'll tell. Kropp'll be in trouble." Presently they left, taking his soiled clothing and promising to secure his locker and belongings. "Jack'll bring your clean gear and washing stuff – OK?" said Bill from the door.

"Thanks."

Roger tried to estimate the odds on him surviving this voyage. Hardly a tower of strength to begin with, he'd subjected his body to a series of unaccustomed demands. Occasional hard labour and pounding flight. Intense physical gratification and scorching heat. Now this. And soon they would be approaching a war zone. He wondered if the North Koreans had anything in mind for him. Footsteps sounded. First Officer Quinn strode in and sat where the nurse had been.

"Mr Wren, you are clearly intent on making this voyage a memorable one for us both. At least on this occasion you didn't wait till just before sailing time. One must be grateful for that. How do you feel now?" Roger saw no need for restraint.

"Bloody awful, sir."

"Yes, and you look it, quite frankly. Now I've had a full report from Mr Candy and the Chief Steward. This man Kropp has been a trouble-maker from the start. I gave him a severe rocket at Colombo, and to no avail it seems. He's good at his work I'm told but off-duty there's been too much of this malarkey. So as we're now in port a while we're going to straighten him out. What I want to know first is this. Exactly why did he attack you?"

Roger told him. Quinn listened incredulously. "A couple of grievances, weeks ago, and he goes wild now? I think something more recent may be the cause of this. Any ideas?" In his mind's eye, Roger saw two men huddled together in a Kowloon bar. Farley plying Kropp with drink, filling his woozy skull with images of Roger and the queers laughing about him. Or maybe it was Penny, another one terrified of Kropp, pointing the finger at him. And Penny of course, as the true culprit, had an even stronger motive than Farley. Yes, he had ideas. But he wasn't passing them on. He had enough to think about.

"No. I suppose he came back drunk and remembered he hated me. It's been a long time coming. Now it's over and I can forget about him."

Glancing about the ward, Quinn said, "You'll be well cared for here. Fine man the MO. And the nurse is a very kind lady." He looked intently back at Roger. "I can assure you it's not over. We're taking Kropp to court tomorrow. And you're coming with us. As his latest and most heart-rending victim. With any luck they'll bung him in jail while we go up to Korea and back. Then he should behave himself till we discharge him at Southampton."

Roger sank back in bed, appalled. "I can't do that. He'll be after me all over again. Let it end here."

"Nonsense," said Quinn brusquely. "Once he faces a magistrate all the fight'll go out of him. You come to court tomorrow. Think of all the others he's terrorised. In particular some of our — ah — more effeminate employees. You'll be doing it for them and stopping him doing it anymore."

"I don't really feel up to it."

"Not right now you don't of course. But the MO tells me there's no serious damage. Looks a lot worse than it is. Not that I don't sympathise, of course I do. But we want you to do this. You'll be alright after a night's rest." Roger felt too weak to argue further. Quinn stood up. "So that's settled, right? I'll be back later to see you. Can I get you anything?"

"Yes. A plane to England."

"There's no call to take that attitude. You owe it to you colleagues to do as we ask. Now I've got things to arrange. Anything you need, the nurse is right outside."

Alone again, he wanted only to bury his face in the pillow, forget he was twenty and indulge himself in a good long post-adolescent howl. But the dressing prevented this so he lay on his back thinking of Gina, Anna and the Tiger Balm Gardens. And who might arrive next. It was Margaret. "I got through. Here's the number. I wrote it down for you. Your date sounds a nice girl. Sends her regards and hopes you'll be better soon."

"It's very good of you to do this. I appreciate it."

She checked him over. "How's the pain?"

"Still pretty fierce."

"Take it easy. Someone else will be here soon to cheer you up." Half an hour went by. The dressing made it difficult to turn his head and raising it to survey the room brought an aching surge to his cheeks. He was reduced to studying the deckhead girders above him. Cast in the metal of the nearest one was the maker's name, just legible under years of paint. *Stahlwerke Molle*. A reminder of the ship's birthplace, prompting him to muse on the international flavour of his present life. He was in China on a German-built ship. Having been chased by Americans and assaulted by a Scotsman with a Swiss name, when he should be out with a Eurasian.

More visitors – Clay and Batten, the latter looking odd in his steward's clothes. On one so urbane and self-possessed such servile garb seemed wrong. Like an aristocrat disguised as one of his own footmen. "Roger my dear boy. Let me guess. You fell off the verandah. The Wingco caught you with his daughter."

"Nothing of the kind. It was —"

"I know. Heard the story. What an utter *Visigoth* that man is. I never thought he'd go for you on the ship after that last warning. My error, sorry."

"How did it go with the Comet Lady?"

Clay said "Don't get him going. We've heard little else since he drifted back on the morning tide."

"I never knew," said Batten, "how much there is to this astrology caper. By the time we'd gone through the Zodiac twice and decided what Taurus had planned for Pisces it was rather late. I am however pleased to confirm that conjunction duly occurred at two a.m. Earth time." Roger began to laugh then winced as his dressing pulled. Cheering up could be painful. He told them his own story and of tomorrow's party.

"Thank goodness for that," said Clay. "I was starting to feel deprived. Maybe now I'll get to visit this seaside fun-house. Is it true you and Kropp are in court tomorrow?"

"That soon got around. Yes, Quinn twisted my arm."

"Best of luck," said Batten.

Clay said, "Didn't you see him coming with that plate?"

"No of course I didn't. The first I knew of it was when he shoved it at me. I just sort of stood there with this brown stuff oozing down my face. It was bizarre."

Batten said, "I thought it was oxtail."

That evening Quinn returned. "How do you feel now?" The question was academic. Only death would prevent Roger going on show next day. "It's all in hand. At nine they take us to the magistrates' court here in Kowloon. I don't know how we're going. Black Maria or some such. You'll be with me. Kropp, I don't know. Maybe they'll truss him up like that other animal at Singapore, that jaguar."

"Actually sir, it was a cheetah. Who else is going?"

"From the ship? Nobody – me, you and Kropp. That's all. There's no question he did it. The whole mess-room saw him. He didn't deny it. Said he'd been drinking and didn't know what came over him. What we always hear. We shouldn't be there long. One look at you'll settle it." After Quinn left he shut his eyes and awaited the next callers.

They came in strength. Linda, Carol and Antonia. And surprisingly, Penny and Doreen. They entered so quietly he couldn't resist pretending to be asleep. "My God!" whispered Carol. "They got him under sedation. And look at the state of him." Standing round the bed in a reverent arc, their muted voices were in marked contrast to the usual stridency.

"That Kropp," said Penny. "They ought to shoot him. Doing that to the Lodger. Poor innocent kid."

"Ooh, you've changed your tune," said Linda. "He didn't used to be 'poor innocent kid' did he? Not to you. You wanted to black his –"

"Never mind that. I was wrong, I admit it, OK? Anyone who gets this done to them and then takes Kropp to court for it gets my vote.

He's doing what we should have done. We've been moaning over Kropp. Trolling about, weeping and wailing yet none of us wanted to do anything. We couldn't report him. Oh no, that would be sneaky, breaking the unwritten code."

"Somebody did," said Linda. "In Colombo, now I wonder who that was?"

"Not too loud," said Carol. "You'll wake him up."

"What'll Kropp get?" wondered Linda. "That big homi who stabbed Hetty got three years."

There was a pause. He felt compelled to go on with his pretence, just to hear them discussing him. Doreen was still silent.

"I'll tell you what," said Antonia. "This may not be a stabbing but to me it rates a jail sentence all the same. This is really nasty. I mean facial injuries. What if he ends up ugly and unattractive? Can you imagine what that must be like?"

"No," said Linda. "Let's ask Penny."

"Oh, you just had to get one in didn't you?" hissed Penny. "Were you born a bitch, or did you have to work at it?"

"For heaven's sake stop it," said Antonia. "Come on, we've had a look at him. Now let's leave him in peace."

Doreen spoke at last. "Of course I'm sorry for him. But I'm still niggled over that dress." He heard the door close but could sense someone was still there.

"Alright," said Linda. "Open your eyes. You didn't fool me for a second."

"Hullo Linda. Good of you all to come. Antonia's wrong I hope. They said I wouldn't be too marked."

"No but there's no harm letting Penny and Doreen think so. Be a martyr."

Roger hesitated. "Actually I know it was Penny went to the bridge over Kropp."

"Was it? I had my suspicions."

"And I told her I knew."

"Why ever did you do that?"

"To avoid getting the shoe polish treatment."

"Roger you're really learning."

"In that case why am I lying here and who lit Kropp's fuse?"

Linda thought. "Penny perhaps. Thinking you'd only get a black eye. Could be why she's suddenly all contrite. Relief and guilt."

"The thing is," said Roger wearily, "I haven't done anything to anyone. I've not reported anyone or done harm to a living soul on this ship."

"You're definitely a martyr Roger, suffering for us all. I must go. We're all off ashore, Steve and Antonia too. Penny's been complaining we always do the same things. Why don't we go somewhere new she says. Let's have some novelty. So now we're going to the Peking Rose Theatre to see *Iolanthe* performed in Chinese. If that's not a novelty I don't know what is."

Roger had three more callers that restless day. Jack and Toddy brought him some clean gear and Pat his toilet things. "You might manage to clean your teeth," said Pat. "If nothing else." They didn't linger long beyond a short chat and to wish him well for tomorrow. "They detailed a young squaddie to fill in for you. Some lad on fatigues."

Next came the doctor and nurse. This time they put a turban-like bandage round his head to secure the forehead dressing against any hazards of his coming journey. Another bandage was passed down under his chin and back up to his head to protect the other dressings. He suspected it was also to dramatise his appearance even more. "This'll save time in the morning," said the doctor. "And be very careful getting in and out of vehicles." Finally alone, Roger eased out of bed, got his toilet things and moved slowly over to the ward bathroom, hoping there wouldn't be a mirror. There was. He didn't look a martyr. He looked like Sabu – with mumps.

In the morning he had a blinding headache, although the face pain had eased. After a meal they gave him an aspirin, got him dressed and led him up to D Deck Square. Here he found Quinn, carefully adjusting the angle of his cap in the notice-board reflection. "Ah Wren, feeling fit?"

"Well, to be truthful …" But the First Officer had turned away to peer down at the quay.

"They're waiting for us. Follow me." Roger stepped onto the gangway and out into the open, his white ball of a head glowing in the morning light. Word had spread. The instant he appeared a cheer went up. From a line of watchers on board came a string of calls.

"Roger the Lodger goes to town." "The Soup King." "Kropp's best friend." "Give that man a white stick." And mingled with these were more supportive offerings. "Good luck Lodger." "Tell them all about him." "Get the bugger put away if you can." On the quay stood a large grey car with a Chinese constable holding the rear door open. Two more were in the front seat with Kropp between them. No-one said a word. Quinn got in, followed by Roger and the constable. Again he was one of six men in a car whizzing through Kowloon – towards another confrontation.

"Any talking, let me do it," said Quinn. They turned into Nathan Road, hearing a snatch of raucous music as they passed Hanni Lu's. Five minutes later they pulled up before an imposing stone building. The policemen took Kropp off down a corridor and pointed Roger and Quinn towards a room. "Wait in there."

They waited. "The last time I was in here," said Quinn, "it was because someone had been stabbed." Soon they were called out and conducted to a large chamber where they sat in a raised stall facing the magistrates. Under the royal coat-of-arms sat three men, all Europeans. On the bench before the centre man a small name-plate informed everyone that he was Mr F. X. D'Almada. In the well of the court an area of floor was enclosed by shoulder-high railings penning in a mixed bag of defendants, one of who was currently on trial. And here, standing aloof from the rest, was Kropp. The centre official made a short statement and banged down his gavel, whereupon the Chinese defendant was led away, protesting loudly. Mr D'Almada consulted his papers.

"Ian Stewart Kropp and er —" One of the other men leaned over and pointed at a paper. "Thank you. And — er — Roger Wren."

Quinn whispered, "They're doing us first. This'll take about five minutes."

"Mr Kropp," began D'Almada, "from the wealth of written testimony I have before me and your own verbal admission to this assault, an admission made to your own superiors, I can only conclude this was an attack of savagery totally without reason. You yourself can offer no explanation other than an excess of drink. This man was not attacking you; was not even facing you when you approached him. Mr Wren is present in court. I would ask you to look at him."

Many faces swivelled towards Roger and a shocked muttering went round the room. Kropp took a cursory glance. "I never meant to do all that. The plate broke on the deck and he fell on the bits."

"Not true," whispered Roger. The measured tones went on.

"Mr Kropp, I do not believe that to be the case. And even if it were, the injuries are still a direct outcome of your actions, are they not?" Kropp glowered. "You will pay compensation to Mr Wren in the sum of two hundred dollars. In addition you are both bound over for two years." Down came the gavel and they were led from the court.

"Damn," said Quinn. "We're still stuck with him."

"What's 'bound over' mean?"

"It means next time one of you hits the other you'll be punished. Quite how they do that if we're not here I don't know."

"Kropp'll want revenge for this now," said Roger bitterly.

"This way please," said a girl who could have been Anna Shay's twin. In an office she gave Roger two hundred dollars and got him to sign for them.

"That's that," said Quinn. "Orient Line will pay the court and stop it out of Kropp's pay." Back at the police car, the same group got in and they returned to the dock. Kropp maintained a surly silence throughout. As the car left them and they made for the gangway, Quinn stopped. "One moment both of you." The man chose his words with care. "Kropp, I was given to understand this attack was in retaliation for something you wrongly believed Wren had done. To wit – reporting your general behaviour to me, and getting you a well-merited rocket for it."

"Are you trying to tell me he didn't?"

"Yes I am. If you don't believe me you can ask Able Seaman Cardwell, who was there at the time. Wren was ordered to the bridge by me. Over another matter entirely. Namely a complaint by a passenger. A sergeant of the Middlesex Regiment. Wren was involved with his daughter. As a result she became so enamoured of him she somehow ended up in Colombo harbour. Distracted out of her mind by the prospect of parting at Singapore." This was a novel slant on events. And clever too. In one statement Roger had been cleared of the two sins Kropp held against him. There was rather more to the First Officer than a smart pair of shorts.

"In fact," said Quinn, "between the pair of you I've become heartily sick of waiting for the next disturbance. So I don't wish to see either of you before me again. For any reason. What I want at this moment Kropp is for you to apologise to this man now that I've cleared away *all* your misconceptions about him. And to give an undertaking to leave him alone in the future."

Kropp showed only annoyance. "Why does he need an apology?

If he's got two hundred dollars of mine out of it?"

They watched him bound up the gangway. "That's what you'd expect," said Quinn, "from such a man, but you should be OK now. I think it's finally sunk in. Try not to antagonise him anymore. Stay in the sick-bay till you're fully recovered."

At the surgery a man with a black eye sat with his head right back, holding a swab to his copiously-bleeding nose. "Meet casualty number seven," said the doctor. "How did it go Roger?"

"They made him pay me two hundred dollars."

The man clutching his nose addressed the overhead light. "They should hab pud hib idside."

That afternoon while he watched the soldiers boarding Clay came to the ward and heard all. "What will you spend it on? Two hundred Hong Kong dollars is over twelve quid."

"It won't be spent at all till we get back here. I can't go anywhere like this. Tell them all about it at Wei Ho tonight. If Anna's there tell her I still want to see her and Gina too. Tell them separately if you can."

Clay slowly shook his head. "You're insatiable."

"Irons in the fire, that's all. When's the *Empire Fowey* in?"

"Soon I believe. Why?"

Roger sat in the bedside chair and held his head. It felt hot and heavy, about to roll off his shoulders. "Anna might be going on it. With or without her dad. See what you can pick up tonight."

"I hope to do that."

"No, you know what I mean. About her going on the *Fowey*. It's no use asking Batten. He'll be away with the Comet Lady. I'm glad he got fixed up, I owed him. You too. Sorry you missed out."

Clay said, "This Chinese piece sounds promising."

"None of that now. I rely on your loyalty not to be tempted."

Privately, he thought anyone who saw Anna as merely a "Chinese piece" would not get far with one so frighteningly well-bred. But there was also Gina, with her fondness for games. Well, he could hardly claim finder's rights over both of them. As he was learning, no-one really belongs to anyone. Not this far from home. His last caller of the day was Frank Seymour, holding a carrier-bag and edging crabwise into the ward as if expecting to be challenged by a sentry. The man spoke all in a rush.

"Roger, I can't stay long. How are you? I got this stuff where you said at Heung Chong's. I think she'll like it. Fifteen dollars all told.

What do you reckon?" The gifts were laid out on the bed. Here was one of the exquisitely-made fans he'd seen. And a small statuette in ivory. "Have a dekko at this," said Seymour. The necklace was similar to the one Pauline acquired in Aden, but included pieces of polished green jade.

"It's all wonderful," said Roger.

Seymour gathered them up. "I'm not waiting till I see her. I'm sending it all on from here. That way I'll get another letter when we come back here from Korea."

Roger thought three gifts all at once might be overdoing it. "Send one from here and the others from somewhere else. That shows you're thinking of her wherever you go."

But Seymour insisted. "No, it's all going today. I'll get a kimono in Japan too. And more things homeward bound."

Before turning in, Roger looked out of his own personal porthole. Across the harbour the city of Hong Kong made a breathtaking spectacle. A tall building proclaimed in green neon letters that it was the headquarters of Butterfield and Swire. Another defiantly countered this with "Jardine Mathieson" in even more strident colours. The entire side of the island lay under a shimmering swathe of lights blazing from every possible source. Windows, watercraft, neon signs flashing their names in every colour and direction, and the darting glow-worms that were vehicles moving through it. And all of this was reflected in the surface of the Fragrant Harbour. The whole scene hung over an inverted rippling copy of itself wherein each and every bright dot had its dancing twin.

"Quite a sight isn't it?" said a voice. The doctor had joined him.

"It is. It's magical"

"See the Peak? You can go up there. They've got cable-cars."

Behind the dazzling foreground, Victoria Peak could be seen as a soft-edged black triangle, sown with jewels of light that only petered out towards the top.

"Sometimes," the doctor went on, "I think this must be the most glorious harbour in the world. And I've see a few. There's something here for every taste. Take my advice. When we come back here don't be lured into the nearest bar. You said you're not a boozer but I know the way it is below decks. There's better things to do. Take a ride up the Peak as I said or over to Repulse Bay for a swim. Or there's Stanley, lovely place."

"How about Wei Ho Bay?"

"Ah, now, that I think may be a little too posh for merchant seamen."

Next morning it was time to observe the departure, a low-key affair with no big crowd or brass band. This time the soldiers were preoccupied with what may await them twelve hundred miles to the north. So was Roger. Half of him wanted to avoid any more ports. Preserve himself for Penang Lodge or somewhere else along that road. But two new countries. He couldn't pass that up. While he watched the last island and the last junk drop below the skyline the medical duo entered the ward.

"Good morning," said the doctor. "Time for a look at that dial of yours." Removal of the outer bandages was a harrowing process, although the cool air was a blessing. What he dreaded was the final stage, taking off the smaller dressings held by adhesive plasters. But he was spared this ordeal. "Not yet. Do they feel comfortable? What about your skin generally? Still sore?"

"Hot and tingling." The nurse gathered the bandages and left. The doctor waited till she'd gone.

"Been to Japan before? Oh no it's your first trip isn't it? You'll find it's nothing like Hong Kong. I've been there. In the RN in 1945. Kure where we're going. The place was heavily bombed in the war. Believe me it was pretty grim. A grey sort of town, you know what I mean? Grey. All these wretched people struggling to live. Having to get by any way they could. And I mean *any* way."

"Are you about to warn me of something?"

"Japan's still an occupied country. The Americans are in charge. Oh, we've got people there and the Aussies but it's the Yanks who call the shots. Whatever you do, take precautions; that's all I'm telling you."

"I understand."

"So long as you do. They're a strange race, the Japanese. I was there in Kure just after they threw their hand in. What a day that was. Sunken ships right and left. Smoke still rising on shore. We had to meet a local surrender delegation. Like the one in Tokyo Bay on the *Missouri*. And one thing above all sticks in my memory. As we came to anchor we saw these six planes coming. Hellcats or Avengers we thought, doing a victory flypast. Then we saw they were Japanese, heading straight for us as if they meant business. We wondered if they knew the war was over." The doctor pursed his lips and turned away as though reluctant to go on.

Roger waited, then said, "And did they attack?"

"No. They flew right over us and out to just beyond the harbour. Then they formed a circle and flew round and round for a while. Well then, one by one, God I can see it now. One by one they peeled off and dived straight down into the sea. Full throttle, vertically straight down. Instant death it must have been. At that angle and speed the water's like concrete. I guess I'm never going to forget that. I watched six men commit suicide."

Roger was discharged on the third morning. The last plasters were peeled away, revealing five small but fairly prominent scars set in a pinky-brown visage not unlike the one he had after his first "bronzie". His first day back at work was enlivened by inquiries about his condition, the day in court and how he felt about Kropp. "Black eye," said Pat. "That's what he usually gives people. This plate thing is new." Sympathy, as ever, was well-tempered with humour.

"Nobody's going to hit the Lodger in future," said Bill. "Too expensive. Not only that, they'd have the queers to deal with. They all love him now he's had Kropp neutered." Approaching Cabin 21 he felt confident enough to enter without checking the occupants. Kropp was there, on the point of leaving. The man regarded him coldly.

"I suppose you still want an apology?" He was not so scared of Kropp. Wary, yes. But the paralysing fear had gone.

"I never asked you for one. You know the truth now. I leave it up to you."

Kropp shifted his feet and looked away. "Yeah, well. I suppose – och, to hell with all of you." The door crashed shut behind him.

"Almost," said Batten. "Almost, but not quite. Stuck in his throat."

"Forget him," said Roger. "Tell me about Wei Ho Bay."

Clay sighed. "Bit of a washout for me, korey-wise. This time anyway. I did meet someone. Name of Hazel. Only lived a few doors away. I could tell she took a shine to me, but she had her husband with her. The annoying thing is, I had the next day off so I didn't have to come back that night. Next time, well I could strike gold. If there is a next time and if she's on her own."

"Yes and *if* you've got the following day off. What about Gina and Anna?"

"Gina had a fellow called Graham with her. From the office. They knew about your trouble. Anna phoned her at work. And she stayed away. Something about her dad. Still, we had a fantastic meal and played some weird game with all those ivory tiles. Then we went for a walk along the beach. All of us." Clay had caught the last bus back that night. Batten returned with the dawn, after another encounter with the Comet Lady.

"Unfortunately she's got no car," said Batten. "I had to stand at the bus stop again, alone and palely loitering."

"Of course, he *did* have the day off," said Clay.

Roger was still absorbing the item about Gina's new friend. "And what about Graham? Did he get the night bus?"

"No," said Clay. "I think he lives locally. When I left he was still there. And they were arm-in-arm on the beach walk. But I wouldn't read too much into it. They're all like that, these people."

At daybreak on the fourth day they reached Kure and Roger was on deck with the rest of them. To most of those aboard, Japan was a new experience. There was nothing comparable. Japan was as foreign as the moon. This remote, misty land had long stood aloof from the world, then suddenly lashed out to bludgeon its way to short-lived triumph. Beaten now into submission, it lay passive. "Enduring the unendurable" as the Emperor had decreed. Fresh from the D Deck chart, Roger knew they had entered the Inland Sea. And that the dark shapes on either side were the islands of Kyushu and Shikoku. "So where's Kure?" asked Bill.

"Up ahead. We're coming to it. It's on the main island, the big one, Honshu."

"What would we do without you?" said Martin.

He had to curb this love of place-names." I only got it from the chart. It's up there for anybody to read."

First sight of the great naval base bore out the doctor's words. From the scrubby hills, down to the sprawling iron wasteland of broken sheds and skeletal cranes, Kure was unremittingly grey. The colour of ash – or death. And this was echoed in the naval transports and warships in the harbour. Only the ships' flags gave relief. The Stars and Stripes or the White Ensign dancing like flowers on a lake of lead. "What a dump," observed Bill. Recalling the doctor's story, Roger glanced up at the empty sky.

Martin gave vent to his awful braying laugh. "What's the Lodger looking for, a fuggin' *kamikaze*? You won't see none of them, they're all gone."

But Roger was engulfed by his sense of history and he could see them clearly. Emerging from the clouds of time, half-a-dozen planes. Obsolete, patched-up remnants of an air force that once ruled the Western Pacific. Passing over the beloved homeland one final time. He saw the six young men, consumed by the agony of defeat, calling the Emperor's name as they pushed the stick fully forward and closed their eyes ready for the terrible impact to come. Yes they were all gone, long ago.

One of the premier naval ports, Kure had been thoroughly worked over by the USAAF. There were few substantial buildings left, although a number of modest structures had been thrown up to serve the slowly-recovering life of the town. In the docks, gaunt sheds full of holes testified to the bombing. One in particular was of colossal size, a great rusting iron skeleton at the water's edge. As expected, somebody knew what it was. "That's the big dry-dock," said a deckhand. "Where they built the *Yamato*. Biggest battleship in the world. All eighteen-inch her guns were. The main ones that is. And about a hundred others. Bristled with guns that thing did. We had nothing like her. Nor the Yanks either. In the end they sunk her with planes."

Clay called Roger over to where he stood. "Run your eye along there to the right. Tell me when you see one you know."

There were several ships. "What am I looking for?" The words were barely out when he saw it. "No it can't be!"

"Yes," said Clay grimly. "Oh yes my son. Anytime now you'll be doing your bends and push-ups. Up-down-up-down. He'll have you. Irving the wonder man is here. Just in time to take over from Kropp."

Roger focused his binoculars. "It might not be. They turned those things out like they did the Libertys. Peas in a pod. They're identical except for the name and number." But yes, there was the name. And the big 107 on the side. In Hong Kong she'd been all of a bustle prior to departure. Here the *Chester M. Vandemeyer* had a horribly settled look. Her radar scanner was still. No smoke curled from her funnel and her cranes were at rest, cradled fore-and-aft.

"It's no coincidence really," said Clay. "There's a war on. They stopped off at Kowloon on the way here. Same as we did. She's only one of many. See, there's that RFA tanker we saw in Colombo. Look on the bright side Roger. You've only this minute arrived and already there's someone here who's dying to meet you again." Clay laughed.

So did Roger. It covered the moment while he tried to think of a bright side on which to look. According to the doctor, Kure was awash with Americans who considered it their personal territory, won by force of arms. Everyone else would be there on sufferance. The British, the Australians, even the Japanese. Keep your place buddy. And now there would be Irving Reed and his cohorts roaming the streets. Yes, it would be wise to go somewhere out of town. If he got the time. There was to be no shore leave till the afternoon so they spent the morning on deck, observing. As at Hong Kong, the harbour was active. But here the driving force was not trade. This was the assembly point for the forces destined for Korea. They saw their own complement of troops marching off to a transit camp for retraining and re-equipping.

"I hear the town itself is quite lively," said Jack. "Once you get to it." They learned it was to be a two-day stay, followed by the short hop to Pusan and back. There were no local helpers.

"Only two days," said Pat. "So who's the unlucky pair?" A coin was spun, and the odd ones out were Bill and Martin.

"Sod it," said Bill. "But I don't suppose there's much to go for till the evening. We'll have a quick look around after lunch." Jack and Pat had this day off, Toddy and Roger the second. And in Jack's absence, Bill and Martin tended to be work-shy. The other two found they were doing most of the chores.

"Stick with it," said Toddy. "Tonight'll be easier. More people ashore."

That afternoon, for the first time, Roger descended the gangway in company with the two younger men. It wasn't planned, they just happened to leave together. They'd probably soon ditch him. These days there was no longer any talk of dragging him off for korey. "Got your own supply you have. Back in Honkers." Martin still sounded jealous. Roger wondered if he might be the one who incited Kropp and decided he didn't care. It was all behind him now. They were in Japan. There were more strange things to absorb him, a whole new catalogue of sights, sounds and smells. Roger today was a tourist pure and simple, even down to the camera.

"What about your bundle with the Yanks?" said Bill. "You know that same cargo boat's in."

"I'll worry about that when it happens," he replied with a show of confidence he did not feel. They'd changed no money yet.

"I was told you get a better deal on shore," said Bill. "Some services club. This looks like it now." Outwardly a charmless brick barn of a place pock-marked by shrapnel, Osaka House was full of servicemen, mostly American but with some Britons and Australians. All the naval personnel were now in blue rig. Here they changed their money. For three pounds Roger got three one-thousand yen banknotes. Bill made straight for the bar, and Martin hastened to join him.

"Where you from and what d'you want here?" Roger met his first Australian, a man with arms like thighs and skin the colour of Ayer's Rock.

"*Empire Garvie* from England."

"Ah, that's fair enough. Reason I asked is I thought you might be one of them government snoopers sent out by Canberra to check up on us."

"Why would they do that?"

The man replied much too quickly. "No reason. No reason at all! We're not doing anything illegal! Strewth, we fought the war for them didn't we? A man's entitled to make a little extra cash while he's stuck out here. I just thought you might be from Oz. You look too young to be sloping around on your own. Most Poms are stinko by this time of day."

Roger thought he might learn about Kure. "We're not all like that. Buy you a drink?"

"Sure. I'll have a Fuji beer. Make sure they give you cold ones." They sat at a wobbly cane table with their icy beers. On each bottle was a label depicting a snow-capped mountain. "That's Fuji-yama," said the man. "It's miles from here, up near Tokyo. What's your name?"

"Roger Wren."

"Mine's Pete Langham. I been stationed here three years now."

Osaka House was a hybrid of the PX and the NAAFI. He saw no overt signs of disharmony among the various nationalities. "I was warned about Kure being a bit — wild." Pete regarded him over his Fuji-yama bottle.

"The Japs are alright as long as you don't throw your weight about too much. Most of the old people are making the best of it but some of the younger ones are still a bit upset about the surrender. There's a gang called the Yoru-neko – the Night Cats. Tough as nails they are. They love tattooing themselves. The hard way – tap-tapping with a knife-point like the Polynesians. Test of manhood, you know the sort of thing. You don't want to tangle with any of those fellers. As for the Yanks, I don't care much for them either. Think they won the flaming war all by themselves."

"Who *do* you like?"

"I don't mind the English. Poms can't hold their drink but they're OK otherwise. My wife's English. From Nottingham. Is that near your place?"

"About 150 miles."

"You must know her folks then? Name of Roberts?"

"Afraid not."

Across the room a party of Americans linked arms and began to sing *From the Halls of Montezuma to the Shores of Tripoli*. Pete signed. "See what I mean?"

Roger thought the song no more aggressively patriotic than *Roll out the Barrel* or *Waltzing Matida* but he merely said in a "veteran" kind of way, "Yeah. I had a bundle with a whole bunch of 'em back in Honkers. And now the same ones are here in Kure."

"I noticed you had a few scars. Broken bottle?"

"No. This was a soup-plate."

Pete whistled. "That's something different. Big feller, the one who did it?"

"Biggish." Kropp had just become an American. It was too late to backtrack.

"If you're going into town," said Pete, "I'll go with you. Steer you away from where the Yanks are. You don't want them cutting up your dial a second time." Again he had a self-appointed guardian. One inspired by a keen dislike of Americans, and a now unshakeable belief that they had injured Roger. His delicate young Pommie friend who only lived a kangaroo-jump from his in-laws. The man had army friends on every street corner. "Hey Pete, how ya doin'?"

"Meet Roger Wren. The Yanks beat him up in Honkers and cut his face." A mixed set of Aussies and Britons, they examined his scars and stated with blistering candour what they thought of their one-time allies.

"Pete," said one, "I've had another Yank asking about swords again."

"No worries. Send him to the Osaka tonight – ten o'clock." Pete explained to Roger, "The Japs are having to sell off all kinds of gear. Making ends meet. I can shift almost anything. Take swords. Now they're like gold dust. Everybody coming here wants one. The

Yanks'll pay top price. Do you want one? Only fifteen thousand yen to you. Be more if you were a Yank. Worth twice that in UK. You'd make a fortune."

Fifteen pounds! "No, thanks all the same. Can't afford it."

They began to encounter the local inhabitants. Superficially resembling the Chinese, he soon noticed the differences. They were much quieter, shuffling along with closed faces. And they bowed a great deal, speaking in rapid, sibilant bursts totally unlike the melodic sing-song of the Chinese. Coming to the town proper, he was struck by the makeshift aspect of the whole area. "This part's called Hana-michi," said Pete. "That means Road of Blossoms. They tell me before the war it used to be lined down the middle with flower-beds. All gone now of course. The main street's one block over. Sakura-michi. That's where all the action is. Watch out if you go there."

The strung-out rows of unpainted shops and dwellings had a desperate, pitiful air. As if it were all nothing but a hastily applied shroud on the bomb-ravaged carcass of the town. An elderly Japanese approached Pete and showed him something in a bag.

"Mista Rang-um, you buy?"

"You got more?" An eager nodding.

"How much?" The man held up a splayed-out hand.

"No. Too much." The thumb folded inward.

"OK, show me the rest of them." To Roger he said, "Business, sorry. This could take a while. We might meet again. I'll be in the Osaka tonight. Mind how you go."

The two men vanished down a dark alley. Roger continued along Hana-michi. On each side of him an endless succession of stall-holders waited for someone to please buy *something*. A proud nation was still coming to terms with defeat. For the first time in their history they were under the control of a foreign power. And it showed in the extreme politeness, the quick ducking bow before and after every exchange, and the absence of any sales-pitch. He felt intrusive, humbled by their massive dignity.

Then in a gap between buildings he saw a grove of trees and beyond that one of the curiosities he was hoping to find. Leaving the line of shacks behind him he followed a path through the trees to a small, formal square. In the centre stood the *torii*, a thirty-foot high Gate of Heaven. Two slender columns were joined near the top by a straight cross-beam projecting each side. Then came a gap before the heavy crowning piece, a thick stone mass with its ends curved out and up as if cradling the sky. The towering structure glowed honey-yellow in the afternoon light. He touched the nearest column. It was rough and mottled with age. The complexion of centuries. Here was a placid corner of medieval Japan unspoiled by modern war. At this spot time had taken a rest. But again it was time that was pulling him away. He took his photos and went back through the trees to Hanamichi. Back to 1950. And the road that once had flowers.

Chapter 14

Still keeping a wary eye out for both Kropp and Irving, he returned to Osaka House. His mess-mates were still there, fenced in by Fuji bottles and arguing with a bartender. Outside he met a *Garvie* group, noticing too late who was with them. When last observed, Farley had been up to his chin in cotton and curses. Now, surprisingly, he waited for Roger. "I heard about your trouble." The scars got another scrutiny. "Kropp don't like you much, does he?"

"Not a lot, no."

Having made peace with Penny, and won a fragile truce with Kropp, could he now cross another enemy off the list? "Five days I was in that sick-bay. Hurt like hell. I never saw Mrs Morrell again. And I never got ashore again except for the court. Kropp's money is no consolation."

Farley made no attempt to conceal his satisfaction. "Serves you right. Perhaps now you'll keep your hands off other people's korey." A revealing remark. Unlike Farley's, Kropp's grievance had never been over korey-poaching. Yet Farley saw the attack as if it had been.

"Did you put him up to it?"

"Me – no! Could have been Penny Prentice." Maybe he was wrong about Farley.

"Are you still after a Jap sword?"

"If I can get one."

"Come here to this club at ten tonight. See an Australian called Pete Langham and mention my name to him. He'll fix you up."

Roger decided he would stay aboard that evening. The last thing he needed was to run into Irving Reed or the Night Cats. Tomorrow was his day off and he had no wish to spend it as he had his first, on his back in the sick-bay. As Toddy predicted, there were so many men ashore the evening meal was soon over, even though Bill and Martin came back late. None of them was interested in Hiroshima. "Why go there?" said Bill. "There's everything you want here. All the korey'll be out tonight."

"*Pan-pan* girls," said Martin. "That's what they're called here. Thousand yen for all night. That's only a pound and you want to spend money on trains!" He tried Cabin 21. Here he found all the occupants, including Kropp resting quietly on his bunk.

"Good as gold he's been," whispered Batten. "Alright Roger, I'll come with you tomorrow. I fancy a train ride, but I must be back by seven."

Seymour was writing a letter. "And me. I'll go too."

Roger was surprised. "The last time I suggested this —"

"I know," said Seymour with a rare smile and a wave of the letter. "That was then. I might find something special there for her. They say it's a good place for silk kimonos."

Bill and Martin went ashore again and stayed there all night. "What are they like then?" said Roger, mindful of the need to maintain a predatory image.

"Alright," said Bill and seemed unwilling to elaborate.

Later that second morning Roger, Batten and Seymour set off for the railway station. A few inquiries at the Osaka and they learned the first train was not till eleven. While killing time they tried to get an idea of what they would find at the end of their journey, at the "atom city". An American had been reassuring. "OK now. All tidied up. Got to hand it to the Japs, they know how to work, these guys. We helped 'em of course."

"I suppose it's quite safe to go there?"

"Sure, otherwise it would be off-limits to all us fellows. I've been myself. They got a big market there, got my girl a swell kimono." They found the station without difficulty, a huddled collection of concrete and corrugated-iron liberally supplied with multi-lingual signs to aid the assorted races using it. A few yen got them return tickets to "Roshma" as the man at the window pronounced it.

"No camera today Roger?" said Batten.

"No. Not for where we're going. Doesn't seem right." The train was composed of four carriages hauled by an imposing steam locomotive decorated at the front with the crossed flags of Japan and the USA. They climbed aboard and the train started off.

"He's done a good job, MacArthur," said Batten. "In the space of five years. Democracy for all – whether they like it or not."

Outside the window the countryside of Honshu rattled by, a pleasing vista of trees and paddy-fields with scattered farm buildings and small factories. They shared the compartment with a civilian couple holding doll-faced children on their laps. The Japanese maintained an inscrutable silence, even among themselves. Almost unnervingly well-behaved, the little boy and girl gazed wordlessly at the three strangers opposite. Seymour said, "This is worse than being on an English train. Do we know anything of the language? Batten?"

"I only know the words for Hello and Goodbye."

"Try it then. Make contact." An untypical plea from one who had avoided contact for most of the voyage. Receiving mail from his new lover and buying her gifts had worked a miracle. Batten thought, and shook his head.

"Sorry, I've forgotten what Hello is."

"The other word then. Speak to them!"

"That's silly," said Roger. "You can't say goodbye to someone and then not go. They'll think he's mad."

Seymour said, "Let's make them laugh."

He took out a handkerchief, knotted two corners and with some ingenuity made a rabbit. "I used to do this for my own kids." With his fingers inside, this creation performed a Disney walk up and down his leg, wiggled its ears and generally did its maker proud. The children watched, astonished. Then the native reserve gave way. They giggled and gurgled and squealed as only toddlers can. "Contact," said Seymour. In thirty minutes they were pulling into Hiroshima.

"Now's your chance," said Roger.

Batten pronounced his one Japanese word. And it was a word with an exceptionally beautiful sound. "Sayonara." The family bowed, all four of them. The father repeated the word, and added a long sentence in Japanese.

Roger said, "What do you suppose that was?"

"We shall never know," said Batten. "Maybe he was saying, however did you idiots manage to defeat us?"

The station was a shadowed, spooky place, filled with shuffling feet and loudspeaker voices. Emerging into the sunlight, the dusty odour of destruction smote them in the face. Five years had passed since the day death came to call. Yet its presence could be felt still. The rubble had long ago been cleared away. In its place a shanty-town of wooden huts and stalls had sprung up, covering the city-wide bald patch where a man-made sun had fallen from the sky. Like bewildered ants in a disturbed nest, stooped figures moved in and around the blighted landscape. A few surviving buildings glared tombstone-white against the surrounding hills. The very hills that had contained and focused the blast, ensuring that Hiroshima, as the chosen victim of perverted science, would perish as planned.

"We could go all over the world," said Batten, "and we won't see anything quite as awful as this."

Seymour said, "I don't think we should have come here." They wandered among the ramshackle structures, coming across preserved evidence of the power unleashed that day. Iron posts, half-melted and leaning over, recoiling from the hurricane of heat. A graveyard of foundations, rectangular outlines peeping from the dust to mark where entire office-blocks had been vaporised in a trice.

Trailing behind, Seymour said little. "I thought he was opening up earlier," said Roger. "With those kids. It's this place. Let him get his kimono, that'll buck him up." They came to a set of broken walls topped by the rusted ribs of a dome.

"What have we here?" said Batten. A sign-board told them. Cobbled together from a language guide, the skewed construction of the message had a childlike innocence that defied the grim surroundings. "This is remain part of Industrial Promotion Hall. Where was in 1945 Year August True Point of Bomb Explode. After this Time may All Nations of Earth live to Mankind Peace forever And Benefit."

Seymour joined them. "Oh, what a *sweet* thought. And we're taking troops over to another war."

"Never mind all that," said Batten smoothly. "It's lunchtime. Shall we see what's on offer?" Moving on, they discovered a gloomy café with a low roof they had to duck under to enter. A mere half-dozen tables were covered with cloths that reached all the way to the floor.

At one, a drunken British sailor sat singing quietly to himself. The only other patron was a swarthy-faced GI wearing an off-beat mix of uniform jacket and rough civilian trousers. He was eating with his fingers what appeared to be slivers of raw fish on a bed of rice. Next to his plate stood a porcelain cup of cloudy white fluid and a dish of sauce. Roger stopped on the threshold.

"I'm having second thoughts about this, and if you're about to say 'when in Rome' please don't. Where's Frank gone? Looking for a bar?"

"I don't think so. He's been off it since his first letter. That's all it took. Someone to love him."

"Hi," said the man with the fish. "Are you fellas from England?" The sailor now got up and collided heavily with Batten before reeling out into the street.

"Yes," said Batten. "We have that dubious distinction." They became aware of a curious sound. A rhythmic squeaking as something or someone emerged from the dark rear of the café. It was the most harrowing sight yet. An aged Japanese man offering picture postcards for sale. But he was without legs, balanced on a wooden tea-tray fitted with castors and propelling himself along by pushing at the floor with grazed knuckles.

"This is Zero," said the GI. "I call him that on account of he's a great little fighter. Ain't that right Zero?" The man on the tray grinned and held up his fists like a boxer. "He's always hanging around this joint, poor guy. Go ahead, buy a few cards. They're cheaper in the PX but what the hell?" They bought some cards of Hiroshima, the before-and-after kind. There was change due but they hadn't the heart to ask for it.

"What happened to him?" asked Batten.

"He was on fire-watch in the war. During a raid he ran away from his post and hid under a train. The train moved."

"God, can't he have a wheel-chair?" asked Roger.

"He had one," said the GI grimly. "His own people took it away from him and gave it to a wounded soldier. More deserving you see – more honourable. I'm hoping to get him one when I got enough dough."

Producing a few coins he gave them to the legless man. "Get yourself some chow old buddy." Zero smiled broadly and made a sort of bow on his little tray, then squeaked away towards the rear of the establishment. They had hardly watched him out of sight before the next surprise came. The shabby American had abruptly vanished, leaving behind his unfinished meal. Roger had a sinking feeling. A pound (or its equivalent) for a few cards. He sat down wearily next to the raw fish.

"Batten. That GI. Do you believe he was genuine?" Batten's attention was drawn to the entrance which had suddenly darkened. "I don't know but I'm sure this one is."

Roger remembered the military police in wartime England. Red caps for ours, white helmets for the Americans, headgear which soon got them the nickname "snowdrops". In gleaming boots and blancoed gaiters, and topped with a snow-white painted helmet, a six-foot khaki centurion stood before them oozing authority and menace. He was armed with a long, polished truncheon which he held in his right hand while thoughtfully tapping the other end on his left palm. His function in life was made clear by the MP painted on the helmet.

This apparition stared all round the room and spoke. "We're looking ..." He stopped as the ghostly squeaking was heard again. Out of the gloom came Zero, pushing one-handedly and clutching a steaming bowl of rice. In rapid succession, the MP looked startled, curious, repelled and finally deeply suspicious.

"He sort of belongs here," said Batten. Zero began his meal, holding the tilted-up bowl close to his face and scooping up the rice with chopsticks.

The MP reached into a breast pocket. "If he's always here he'll know if this guy's been around." A photograph was thrust at Zero. "You seen him in here?" Zero took one look and went behind his bowl again. The policeman began to shout. "Look at the picture! Have – you – seen – this – man?" Still the wretched one on the tray held the bowl to his face, desperately gulping the rice as if running out of time.

The next event was all the more shocking for being totally unexpected. The MP swung his long truncheon in a vicious side-swipe, knocking the bowl from Zero's hands and sending it rolling across the floor in a flurry of postcards and rice. "Look at the goddam picture!" he bawled and held out the photo again.

"I don't think he understands what you're saying," ventured Batten carefully.

"Yes he does. They all do. I don't trust any of them. They give me the creeps." The man placed a boot against Zero's tray and shoved. Arms flailing and castors squeaking, the hapless victim careered backwards to crash into a table some feet away.

"There's nothing like showing sympathy," murmured Batten.

"For the Japs?" said the MP. "After what they did? I'll tell you where sympathy belongs – in the dictionary, between shit and syphilis." He showed them the photo. "Have you seen him? His name's Private Gatti." They recognised the swarthy GI. But there was no question of what they had to say. Not after that.

"Never seen him before," said Batten. "We only recently arrived by train." The "snowdrop" noticed the plate of fish and the milk-like drink.

"Whose meal is this?"

"Mine," said Roger with mad courage. "I've just got back from the – from the john." He picked up a piece of fish. Batten joined him at the table.

"I'm still waiting for mine, ordered it ages ago. What's it taste like Roger?" With an effort he bit the fish. Yes, it was raw. The MP watched him, then wandered towards the rear.

"What's in back of here?"

"The kitchen," said Batten. "If you're going in there you might ask them to hurry my order along."

"Nobody here. Food cooking – they've all run off."

"I wonder why?" said Batten very softly. The man was on the point of leaving. Batten called him. "Officer, may I see that again?"

"Batten – for God's sake!" whispered Roger. Convinced the MP was still watching him, he was now obliged to eat more of the fish while Batten made a great show of studying the photo again.

"Why are you after him? Is he AWOL?"

"I'll say. His outfit went to Korea last week. Boy – is he AWOL!" Roger tried the white drink. It wasn't milk. He put a third piece of fish in his unwilling mouth. They heard a vehicle pull up outside and another MP entered.

"We're all leaving. We got to check out the railroad station. Let's go." The blancoed leviathans stomped out, allowing the daylight back in. Roger swallowed his current piece of fish and got up.

"Batten, I could kill you for this. Keeping that –" Batten blinked innocently behind his round glasses.

"Mr Gatti must have left by another exit. I was merely giving him time to get clear of the vicinity." He glanced outside. "They've gone tearing off in jeeps. Are you alright Zero?" The Japanese grinned and pointed.

From under one of the tables with its overlong cloth came Gatti. After making sure the police had gone he coolly took his seat and resumed his meal. "I was raised in the Bronx, been ducking cops all my life. I can smell 'em a mile off. Thanks a heap fellas for not snitching. You too Zero."

Batten said, "They've gone to the station."

"Yeah – I heard. I knew that one when we were over at Hamada. Weems his name is. That is one real mean guy – they should send people like him to Korea. Me, I'm through with killing. I was at Okinawa. They'll catch me sooner or later, I know that. Meantime I'm building up a little nest-egg for when I get home. Say, can I tempt you to anything while you're here? I'll pick up the tab."

"I don't think so," said Roger. "I've already –"

"Hey come on. We're all buddies here. Try this. It's called sushi, fish on rice. Dip it in the soy sauce. Zero, you're coming up here and eat with us."

Gently, he lifted the disabled man off his tray and placed him with infinite tenderness in a chair. Batten then eased him up to the table while Roger gathered up his scattered cards and money, putting them all in order on the tray. At long last a waitress appeared. They were all served with more *sushi* and the mysterious white drink. So commenced the most unusual lunch party Roger had ever been at. To his surprise he began to like the raw fish. Flavoured with the sauce, and garnished with pink pickled ginger, it was actually rather tasty. Batten too, after initial misgivings pronounced it "quite good". And the drink? "It's called *doboruku*," said Gatti. "White *sake*. The usual stuff is clear. Funny drink – *sake*. Half spirit, half wine. They always serve it in these little cups."

It was quite palatable. "They put yeast in it," said Gatti, adding brightly, "It can ferment for an hour or more in your stomach."

Zero ate happily but without a word. "Does he ever speak?" asked Batten.

"Sure, when he's got something to say."

Outside in the atom city, life went on. After forty-five minutes of *sushi, sake* and talk, they prepared to take their leave. "We want to get to the market," said Roger. "We've got this fellow with us who wants a kimono for his lady-friend."

"I can help you with that," said Gatti. "So long as you don't tell anyone else. Look for a market stall with a string of paper lanterns.

There's a lot with lanterns but this one has a whole row of them, red and yellow all along the canopy. Ask for Mr Nikuya. Say Nikuya-*san*. You want a kimono – good one. Say *hinshitsu*. Means quality. And say *jiyuna* as well. Got that? *Jiyuna*. Tell them I sent you. But keep all this to yourself. Not a word to anyone, remember that."

"Thanks," said Batten.

"You stuck your necks out for me didn't you?"

As they were going, Zero was spreading his cards ready for new customers. Roger said, "How many does he need to sell to make a living?"

"It's not a living," said the GI quietly. "It's only another way of dying."

Further along the road they found Seymour. "Frank," said Roger. "What about the market? We've had our lunch, didn't you want any?"

"No I didn't fancy lunch. I peeped in and saw you with those two – and I didn't like the look of either of them. And I've been to the market. They're all out of decent kimonos. Not one."

"You could be in luck," said Batten. "One of those unsavoury types you saw told us where to get bargains. Someone in the know. But listen Frank, we're not to tell a soul about this. Top secret."

"If you say so."

There was indeed a preponderance of paper lanterns and it was a while before they found Mr Nikuya's place. Seymour said, "I've been here already. They've got no kimonos."

"Nikuya-*san*," said Roger. The two boys in charge shook their heads.

Batten said, "Gatti-*san*." Instantly the boys became alert. One beckoned, opened a sliding door, showed them in and waited. Mr Nikuya was about sixty, wearing wooden sandals, a loud green suit and a worried face. "We come from Gatti-*san*," said Batten. Nikuya put a finger to his lips, hurried to the door and checked outside. "Friends of Gatti-*san*," Batten went on, pointing to himself and the others. "All his friends. Kimono please. *Hinshitsu*. Oh, and Gatti-*san*, he say *jiyuna*. Must be *jiyuna*."

"I suppose it means cheap," said Roger. Nikuya rapped out an order. The boy said "*Hai*!" dashed into a back room and returned with an armful of silk kimonos in every conceivable colour and pattern.

Seymour whistled. "Twenty minutes ago they claimed they had none."

Roger said, "I've got a bad feeling about all this. Choose one so we can get out of here and out of Hiroshima."

Seymour took his time. "What are you worried about? So you met a soldier who knows where the bargains are. They got his kind in most big towns here I've been told. Since the occupation. In Kure it's more the Aussies." Carefully, he examined the garments. They were all of superior quality. "I'll have this one," he announced at last, holding up a fine creation in lavender shot-silk.

Nikuya wrapped up the robe very thoroughly, using several sheets of paper and a lot of string. When it was done he thrust the parcel at Seymour and ushered them out, again checking before opening the door. He seemed desperately anxious to be rid of them. There was not even time for the customary bowing. "So how much is it?" asked Seymour.

"Shut up and keep walking," said Batten. "Now we know. *Jiyuna* doesn't mean cheap – it means free."

They headed briskly for the station. Seymour fingered his parcel. "I don't get it. I mean, I've heard of bargains …"

"Frank," said Roger despairingly. "You got yourself an expensive gift for nothing. Settle for that. Let's get to the station."

To which Batten added, "Always bearing in mind who we might meet there."

Sure enough, there were no fewer than four military jeeps drawn up outside the station. Roger said, "I think my fermenting has begun." Inside, the entrance hall was dotted with more snowdrops than a forest glade in March. They saw "their" policeman. Weems was nursing the truncheon and frowning at the civilians as he stood under a vast bi-lingual poster that advocated US/Japanese cooperation.

"Don't look at him," warned Batten. At the barrier two more snowdrops barred their way.

"Can we please see your identity cards?" The flinty eyes darted from card to face and back again as though longing to find some discrepancy.

"Where are you going?"

"Kure," Roger replied.

"And what was your business in Hiroshima?"

"Only exploring," said Batten. "I must say you chaps did a terrific job here," he added, leaving them to decide if he meant the destruction or the subsequent repairs.

At any moment, thought Roger, we're going to get the photo. What if Seymour …? He saw a hand going to a top pocket and said quickly, "We've already seen the picture. One of your men questioned us. We've not come across this man Gatti anywhere."

A queue was forming behind them. "So who was it questioned you?"

"That gentleman over there," said Batten, pointing. "A most efficient officer, we were very impressed by his forthright manner and devotion to duty, weren't we Roger?"

The MPs relaxed. Anybody who got past Weems had to be guiltless. "We're real sorry about this inconvenience," said one. "I guess you're wondering why so many of us are after one man."

"What's he done?" asked Seymour.

"Pulled off a robbery, that's what. Two nights ago over at Hamada. There's a big clothing plant there run by us and the Japs. One of MacArthur's cute ideas. Kinda joint enterprise? This Gatti and a few of his buddies got away with a truckload of silk merchandise meant for Tokyo. As soon as the heat's off it'll start turning up on the black markets everywhere. Kimonos and stuff."

Seymour began, "Funny you should say —"

Batten cut him short. "There's our train! Must hurry gentlemen. I do hope you get your man." The MPs waved them through.

"Is it really our train?" said Roger as they climbed aboard. This time they had a compartment to themselves.

Batten leaned out of the window. "At this moment anything leaving town is our train. I see Weems has now joined his compatriots and they're all looking this way."

"Don't tell me we're running from the Yanks again!" said Roger.

Seymour began to look uneasy. "I'm catching on now. That GI you were with, that was him wasn't it? You know I came with you two in good faith. A change from meeting drinkers everywhere. I never thought I'd be assisting wanted criminals and handling hot kimonos. There's never a dull moment when you go ashore with the Lodger. It's true what they say."

Roger took a turn at the window. "What are they doing now?" Batten asked.

"Weems is still staring at this train. I suppose he knows by now we've acquired a parcel. And I was never sure he believed that fish was mine." The train gave a hoot and began to move.

Batten said, "Thank —" and they stopped again. Seymour gave a little moan and huddled in a corner.

Roger said, "I wonder what they'll do?"

Seymour's voice put him in mind of a wound-up spring. "I'll tell you what they'll do. They'll find the kimono, march us back to Nikuya and he'll tell them how we're all close friends of this rogue soldier." He grabbed the parcel. "Out the other window, that's the place for this!"

Batten stopped him. "Calm down Frank. You're sending that home to your good lady."

"He's coming," said Roger. Weems had finished conferring and was marching towards the train. The beloved truncheon was tucked under one arm and his face set in the expression of one on a divine mission. Inching forward again the train hooted, hissed and halted.

Seymour said wildly, "I don't believe I can take any more of this!" Again the hooter sounded.

"No wonder we can't move," said Batten. "All the steam's going on that thing." Finally, when Weems was fifteen or so yards away, the locomotive spun its wheels, got a grip and set off, gathering speed rapidly as if to make up for all the false starts. Weems broke into a run, then shook his head and walked back the way he'd come.

"He's gone," said Roger.

Batten sank back on the seat. "For this relief, much thanks. Well then, gentlemen, that was Hirsohima, what did you think of it?" They were silent. "No comment at all, not one word?"

Seymour stared out at the dreary suburban landscape. "Yes, how about – *sayonara*?"

Roger meditated on the inverted world he was in these days and the actions of those he met in it. A cruelly disabled man brutally bullied by an upright guardian of the law, but treated kindly by a thieving deserter. "I have two points to make," said Seymour. "First are we on the right train?"

"Yes," said Roger. "Same platform, same line, opposite direction. I remember this bridge we're on now. There's that same sunken barge in the river. What's the other point?"

"The MPs. They'll telephone ahead to Kure. We'll be picked up on suspicion."

Batten was confident. "Wait and see. Play it by ear." At Kure the platform was devoid of white helmets. "Told you," said Batten as they alighted. "They saw our identity cards. By now they know who we are and what ship we're on. So they must realise we weren't even in the country when that robbery took place. The unspeakable Mr Weems never saw our cards. It was only that and his zealous nature made him chase the train. Stop worrying, Frank. Tell everyone you got it from a stranger outside the Osaka Club. Some of them may show up here anyway."

Seymour gave a nervous laugh. "I'm not going round Kure with a stolen kimono. The sooner I get on the ship with it the better. I'm off, see you later."

"A changed man," said Roger. "Is he really on the wagon?"

"No doubt about it. And when I last saw him, so was Kropp. He never even left the ship last night although he did this morning. What is this effect you have on people?"

"It's not me. Frank's got a new incentive for living now. And Kropp doesn't want to pay out two hundred dollars every time he hits somebody. A bollicking's one thing, losing money is something else. He's a true Scot."

The hurried departure from Hiroshima meant it was still only 2.30. Batten stopped. "I believe we turn left here. What about Farley?"

"Farley's happy now he's seen me suffer. And Penny's forgiven me. For the moment I'm in the clear. I fear no man. Except Seaman First Class Irving J. Reed of the US Navy whose ship, as you know, is in."

"We'll both keep our eyes open."

Encouraged by an occupying force fearful of communism, the Japanese had embraced Western "culture" in every way. The street they now entered was packed on both sides with clubs and bars plastered with names like the Monte Carlo, the Windsor Bar, Blue Parrot and Rainbow Corner. At each side of the road ran a raised boardwalk thronged with servicemen and *pan-pan* girls. Many of the saloons had bat-wing doors of the kind a man could look over before pushing his way in like Wyatt Earp.

"Welcome to Dodge City," said Batten. Over the roof-tops Roger saw the canted-up ends of the *torii* he'd admired yesterday. So they were only a block away from that street. This must be the notorious Sakura-michi. The town was obviously smaller than it appeared from seaward. The chances of running into someone were high. "How about a walk up in the hills, get a taste of the real Japan?"

"Excellent idea," said Batten.

So they followed the road till the clamorous clubs and jazzy bars thinned out and gave way to pastoral scenes. A lean-to barn with oxen peering out. Neat groves of cherry trees and thatched homesteads that reminded them of England. They walked for an hour. There were wayside shrines, green stone lanterns each having a little roof with upturned corners. Peasants toiled in the fields, backs bent and faces barely seen beneath broad conical hats or white headscarves. No-one looked up as they passed. There was no reason to. Their labours would never change no matter whose flag flew in Tokyo. The road wound up towards the hills where at their highest point they stopped and leaned on a stone wall overlooking the town and dockyard. They heard the distant hum of military vehicles, the tinkling threads of music along the strip of bars and the faint *whoop-whoop* of a destroyer far out on the Inland Sea.

"What we are witnessing," said Batten, "is the western world and the oriental busily bridging years of separation. Tell me, will your avail yourself of the physical attractions on offer down there? You know it's ridiculously cheap?" Roger's life as a seafarer had undergone a startling transformation since his miserable early days. A sea-change in fact. The favours of two women and the possible, if less likely, option of a third. There was surely no need …

"No," he said. "Are you?"

"Roger, I'm not pursuing minor asteroids when I have a blazing comet to call on at Wei Ho. We are very fortunate, you and I. Poor Clay's gone without since before Colombo."

"I know. And we have him to thank for it all. I fear he might not wait for Hong Kong. He may be driven to invest a thousand yen down there. Chancy."

"It's not only chancy. I would call it irresponsible. If he goes back to Macau Drive after being in contact with a *pan-pan*."

"Is it that bad?"

The subject was out of place. A sordid thing to discuss this summer afternoon on a slumbering hill-top. They began the long descent. "I've heard it is," said Batten. "You can take precautions of course." At the base of the hill they avoided the direct return route and followed a quieter road close to a small bay. He was reminded of the Willow Pattern on his family's best china. The water was flat calm and as dark as wine. A slender boat seemed to hover just above the surface, propelled by a standing figure with a wispy beard. The man faced forward, making barely a ripple as he pushed at a long pole. Here also was a curved bridge giving access to a barren rocky island, while closer to hand a line of pines with spiky foliage framed a deserted foreshore. There was even a temple showing above the trees. Supported by burnished gilt pillars, a set of pink and green roofs rose one above the other in a glorious confusion that seemed to mock the laws of gravity and balance.

"Worth the walk?" said Batten.

"Yes. It wouldn't be right, not to see something of the sort after coming all this way. It's a beautiful country, or was. They've ruined Kure, westernised it. The whole country I suppose in time." The man in the boat stopped and cast a net over the side, using a sweeping motion that laid it flat on the water with a hissing sound. In doing so, he noticed them and smiled, making a movement somewhere between a bow and a nod.

"It was bound to happen," said Batten as they watched him. "They're clever and cultured and artistic. All that but they also committed the most appalling atrocities, cruelty beyond belief."

"The atom bombs were cruel."

"Of course they were. All wars are cruel. But don't forget, they did start it. If they'd stayed at home in December '41 they'd still be as they were. As it is they're better off under MacArthur than if the Russians had come here as they tried to in 1945. Right, that's enough potted history. I've got to get back. We don't all have the day off. Why don't you stay here? Continue the walk, see what's round the next bend and tell me later?"

He was on the point of replying when they heard a sound. A shuffling, swishing sound that defied explanation. Along the coastal road came a long crocodile of men marching in files of three. The sight was alarming. They were in ragged, cast-off uniforms and small soft caps of the type he'd seen in war films, where such men were always depicted as fanatical warriors shouting "Banzai!" Festooned with the tools of their trade, hammers and axes hung like weapons from their belts. Workmen – but they looked so much like soldiers. As they passed, each blank face turned robot-like towards the two strangers at the roadside. There was nothing behind such faces. No enmity, no curiosity, nothing. No trace here of even the shallow affability of the Kure traders or the simpering *pan-pan* girls of Sakura-michi.

The whole picture had subtly changed. The fisherman no longer fished, but stood upright in his boat as though these martial figures had evoked thoughts of another time, when the Emperor's men sang songs of victory and the Rising Sun flew proudly throughout the long Far Eastern chain. A sudden unnaturally cold wind rippled the edge of the Inland Sea and above the beach the pines waved like the arms of drowning sailors. He felt he had no right to be here, in this other, different Japan. A trespasser, an invader. "No. Let's go back to Kure now."

Entering the town from a new direction offered fresh points of interest. "All welcome to Kabuki Theater," announced a hastily painted sign.

Batten said, "I saw one of these shows once in Yokohama. Kabuki's really something. Traditional, like the Noh plays. Give it a go."

"What about you?"

"I'll just see a bit of it and try to get a lift back." The "theatre" was a converted schoolhouse brightened up with lanterns and silk drapery.

"They're probably a touring company" said Batten. "Putting on shows where and when they can." Admission was 125 yen. A man with white gloves took their money and gave them a card printed with a description in English of the drama they would see. The performance had already begun. Every one of the cast wore heavy white make-up and long sumptuous robes. There was little dialogue but much gesticulation and face-pulling. From behind highly decorated screens came short bursts of music, a rapid drum-beat, a furious shaking of tambourines and the frequent crash of a high-pitched gong. But when these stopped they heard another sound, the plaintive but sweetly melodious strumming of a stringed instrument.

And this, Roger thought, was the most exquisite music he'd ever heard. Batten knew what it was. "They're playing a *samisen*. When you hear one of those you can't be anywhere but Japan."

"It's gorgeous. I could listen to it for hours. What's the story?"

Batten studied the card. "The English is rather quaint. Let's see now. A girl is promised to a rich warlord but she loves a young musician in another village. So the warlord sends a terrible demon called Minikui to kill him. The boy hides in a cave with his only possession, a *samisen*. Hang on, there's some odd spelling here. Oh yes, the boy plays his *samisen* so beautifully Minikui is charmed into becoming his friend. The warlord then gets very cross and sends a whole army of demons, every one of whom is slain by Minikui. I think we're still in the first act."

A sudden instrumental frenzy startled the whole audience. The drums speeded up and the tambourines competed frantically with the gong. On to the stage stomped a short but fearsome personage in a scarlet cape, a towering headdress and a hideous carved mask with bared teeth and bulging boiled-egg eyes. Batten murmured, "I think we can assume this is Minikui." Brandishing a sword, the new arrival strode about the rickety stage while the other players shrank back in the exaggerated way of silent film actors. "Of course," said Batten, "if we knew what they were saying it would help." He gave Roger the plot-card. "It's six-thirty. Been quite a day hasn't it?"

Quite a day. Alone again, Roger knew from experience it wasn't over yet. Besides, he wanted to see the play out. And as he watched Minikui pause and cock his head towards the unseen *samisen*, he realised he was watching a style of acting quite unlike any other. True, the costumes and faces were highly theatrical, the music (apart from the *samisen*) confused and grating to his ears. But the gliding, balletic movements, the pointed silences and above all the honeyed notes of the *samisen* conspired to hold him there. Somehow the simple story was stretched a further two-and-a-half hours till Minikui finally dispatched the half-dozen actors playing the demon army, put away his sword and knelt before the boy and girl. The melodrama was over. There was no curtain call. A few seconds of respectful clapping and everybody left. He put the plot-card inside his shirt with the Hiroshima cards and groped his way to the exit.

Outside, it was quite dark. This was no town to get lost in. It seemed wise to go the way he knew, even if it might be longer. Perhaps if he walked fast, didn't stop for anything and kept an eye out for Irving Reed he'd be OK. He would run the gauntlet of Sakura-michi. From both sides, a torrent of chattering voices and western popular music poured forth. Every club and saloon had its imported American juke-box filling the night with a din that drove from his head the lingering *samisen* memory.

Near the Blue Parrot a sudden frantic bleeping cut across the general noise. Down the street in its own cloud of dust came an open jeep containing two American sailors wearing SP armbands. One had a gun-holster at his belt. Like characters in a western they slewed to a halt outside the club. He half-expected them to tether the jeep to a rail. In seconds they hurried from the club with a wild-eyed sailor, bundled him into the jeep and sped off. "Shore Patrol," said a bystander. The man had REME on his shoulder. "They're busy tonight. He won't be the last one they pick up."

"I thought it was mainly us were a problem, the English."

"It's everybody. They're all homesick and bored. Wondering if they'll be sent to Korea." Brief though it was, pausing for this exchange had been a mistake.

"Oi you! The Lodger. Come here!" A harsh voice, issuing from the open doors of the Monte Carlo Club. He tried to ignore it, tried to escape the glaring illumination spilling across the boardwalk. "Roger Wren come back here!" Footsteps drummed behind him and he resigned himself to whatever was coming. The man's features were familiar. "You know me. Cardwell. I had the boat when your blonde fell in. And I was on the bridge with you."

"Yes I remember."

"Come inside. Friend of yours wants to speak to you."

The Monte Carlo was a rowdy pit of smoke-wrapped revelry. Animated groups of men sat entwined with moon-faced female companions or jitter-bugged unsteadily before a cheering company. A low ceiling dripped with paper lanterns. In the centre of the room, pumping out music, a huge red juke-box roared and glowed like some chromium-plated log fire. Most startling of all were the *pan-pan* girls, drawn moth-like from the dark streets. Giggling and squealing, with tight-combed hair and lipstick like blood, they resembled over-painted identical dolls. In a corner he saw the "friend" and hung back.

"I don't think —"

"It's OK. He's sober, honest. Saw you pass by and sent me after you. Just wants a word. I wouldn't advise refusing."

Crouched behind several empty glasses, Kropp was not alone. A girl who did not look more than sixteen sat with him, thin as a post and heavily made up. Her mouth was a lurid gash of scarlet and her eyes pencilled out to a taper as if she'd stepped down from a pharaoh's tomb-painting. Behind her milk-white face he saw a weariness, a kind of "oldness".

"I can't believe he's not drunk. All those glasses."

"That's only *sake*. They put it in glasses here. He's been on it for hours, sticking to it. Somebody told him you can have any amount of that. No more trouble." Yet Kropp still had an air of malevolence.

"Look, Mr Kropp, I really don't—"

"Shut up and sit down. Want a drink?"

"Thanks but —" Cardwell kicked him lightly on the shin.

"OK then I'll have *sake.*" There were no introductions. The girl might have been an object, a mere accessory placed on one side while they talked. Cardwell fetched the *sake* and a Fuji beer for himself. Nothing was offered to the girl.

"Right then," said Kropp. "I been talking with Cardwell here. Quinn told the truth. You never did report me."

"That's right. I didn't. And I'm not queer either, I told you that." Kropp's elbow slipped off the table. A classic sign, but as yet the man seemed quite rational.

"So Cardwell said. You had some judy on the ship. But you're still well in with them nancy-boys ain't you? Still like to have a wee giggle with them. About me for instance." The clear *sake* was smooth and mellow. It was liquid *samisen* music. He longed to run away somewhere and hear it again.

"The only time I mentioned your name was when they – molested me. I threatened to set you on to them." Kropp seemed amused by this. "The giggling came later. They made me watch something."

"Alright, alright. Don't tell me what they did. He must have got it wrong, the bloke who told me."

"Who was it?"

Kropp made a contemptuous gesture. "Some bedroom steward. Foley or Finlay – some such name. I saw the same idiot come back last night with a stupid great sword. Paid good money for it. Mad. No wonder he got it wrong about you." So it had been Farley.

"Anyway laddie, here's what I've done. I know you took two hundred dollars off me but, well, after what I've heard some might say I owe you a wee bit more." Like an apology, thought Roger. Kropp took a swig of *sake.* "So here you are. All yours." Benignly, he glanced from Roger to the girl and back. "She's paid for. Only a short time though, you want longer, you got plenty of money, my money."

"No thanks. I've been ashore all day. I'm going back aboard."

Kropp's tiny hint of matiness vanished. "If there's one thing I cannae abide it's ingratitude." A crude jerk of the thumb. "I picked this one out special when I saw you. Now you want to throw it back at me. You claim to be a man, so what are you waiting for? What's up with you?" It was obvious the girl understood. She turned her elongated eyes to Roger and arranged her crimson mouth into a wooden smile

"We go now soldier OK?"

Somehow he had to get out of this. It shouldn't be difficult. Part amicably once they were out of Kropp's sight. Taking her hand he got up from the table, earning satisfied leers from both men. "Fill your boots my son," said Cardwell. "Only mind you don't catch anything." He made a very public exit, seen by most of the company, which inevitably included many *Garvie* people. The next unpleasant surprise came as they reached the boardwalk. Kropp was right behind him, accompanied by another girl plucked from a table *en route*. It wouldn't be easy after all. Led by the girls, they left the boardwalk, whereupon Kropp tripped and sprawled in the dust.

"Fuggin' 'ell. I cannae be pissed, not me."

"How many had you had?" Some way from the club, they turned down a gloomy path between wooden huts. He still hoped some distraction would enable him to slip away without incurring this man's wrath.

"I dunno," replied Kropp. "About a dozen. And I had some in the Osaka and the Blue Parrot. S'alright. You can drink that rice-water all day and it don't 'fect — 'fect you at all." Again he stumbled and lapsed into a short but pungent medley of Caledonian curses. Kropp, like so many before him, was learning how even a mild-seeming foreign product tossed down the throat with contemptuous ease, can work quietly away in a body more accustomed to homely brews.

The unlikely quartet stopped at one of the huts. Roger's girl slid open a door and gestured for him to enter. Kropp said "See you in ten minutes. I won't be far away." Inside the hut sat a wrinkled female of immense age, with few teeth and a skin of antique ivory. This must be one of the fabled mama-sans he'd heard of, women who filled the triple function of doorkeeper/madam/cashier. The girl passed over some money, presumably Kropp's pre-payment, then opened a folding rattan screen. In a tiny space beyond were a mattress and two cushions on the floor beside it. Illumination came from two candles in a flat tin marked K Ration. The girl knelt on the mattress with her skimpy dress rucked up to reveal legs scratched and bruised as though from many a brutal client. Revulsion and pity filled him. How could he tactfully retreat, simply walk out? He imagined her berated by the old crone for failing to satisfy a customer. Feeling a need to speak, he squatted on a cushion.

"What is your name?"

Surprised that he would want to use up any of the "short time" in actual speech, she raised her old-young face, a painted ornament in the candles' feeble glow.

"Name?" she repeated softly.

He pointed to himself, then her. "Ro – Ger. And you?"

"Ah-so. Sumiko, name Sumiko." Slowly she leaned on the hut wall and regarded him with less apprehension. He had a strange face, this one. Sunburnt and pocked with battle-scars, it seemed at odds with his gentle voice. Perhaps there would be no roughness, maybe nothing beyond talk. She could have a rest before dragging herself back to the Monte Carlo.

The halting exchanges made slow headway. The ten minutes went to fifteen. Sumiko had some English, and sign-language filled the gaps. "I came here on ship," he said, conveying this with two "finger-legs" on a rocking palm. Behind her he saw a cockroach sauntering over the floor.

Gravely she nodded. "So. Orways ship come. OK. Many soldier. 'Merican. Osutrarian OK."

"How about the English? You like them Sumiko?" This took more thought.

"Ingrish? Um, Ingrish OK. Much fight. Much ..." she mimed drinking and rolled her head.

They both laughed and some of the sordidness went away. If only there had been a *samisen*! Suddenly, outside the hut a man shouted in Japanese. Sumiko started up and called to the *mama-san*. Someone banged on the hut wall. "Yoru-neku," said Sumiko. "Bad, go quick!" Outside in the darkness he heard many pattering feet all around. An Australian voice called, "What's going on?" There was whispering, shouting and a sense of invisible menace. Instinctively he slipped into the deeper darkness between the huts.

On the other side of the alley a door slid open and a beam of light lit up several figures running past, short muscular young men with tattooed arms. Two of them paused, conferred together and placed themselves either side of the open doorway. One wore an army-pattern soft cap, the other held a knife. Roger's old adversary appeared in the doorframe, squinting blindly into the night.

"Roger!" came that Glaswegian rasp. "Come away out, ye weak-kneed queer lover. Are ye no through yet?" This oafish predator had frightened him for weeks and in the end carried out a vicious attack that hospitalised him for three days. He owed the man nothing. But Roger was – Roger.

"Kropp, look out!" he yelled. The Night Cats pounced. One locked his arm round Kropp's neck, the other held the knife-point to his chest with one hand while groping for a wallet with the other. The assailants' method was well-tried. Terror had always worked. But the split-second warning triggered an instant response. And Kropp knew all there was to know about terror. Kropp had learned what terror was the first time his gin-sodden father took his belt to young Ian. Terror had sent him fleeing from the other tenement kids when they stoned him for having a foreign, un-Scottish surname. Stiffened him as he rose through the ranks of the Glasgow gangs or fought his way back to the Gorbals on a Saturday night. Kropp in his youth had absorbed so much terror he'd spent most of his adult life giving it back.

The knife-man collapsed with a yelp as Kropp's right toe-cap connected sharply with his shin. The cap-man received a head-butt followed by a punch well below the belt that caused him to fold up in sections like a carpenter's rule. Kropp stepped over the writhing bodies and beckoned to Roger.

"Did you get your korey? Come away then, back to the ship." Along the alley they met three dazed Australians retrieving the scattered contents of their wallets. "Strewth," moaned one. "Who was that? They went through here like a dose of salts." The gang's whirlwind descent on the brothel area had served its avowed purpose. To throw a scare into the bumptious foreigners, and the merchants and bar-girls who pandered to them.

"They were the Yoru-neko," said Roger sagely. "The Night Cats. Youngsters with a grievance." They were not molested again as they returned to Sakura-michi. Kropp said little about the encounter, to him a minor street brawl no different from a hundred others. But the man's day-long intake of *sake* was at last having serious effect. There was a tendency to stray off course and collide with things. Outside Osaka House Kropp hesitated, clearly tempted by the offerings within.

Roger said nothing. The strange new relationship was a brittle thing. A wrong word could shatter it. Kropp squared his shoulders. "Nope, I'm not going in there," he announced piously, turned away and sat down in the road, glassy-eyed. Roger coaxed him up and they pressed on.

"Here's the gate," said Kropp.

It didn't look right. There was a broken padlock and no-one around. "I don't think it's the one."

Kropp flared up. "Well I say it is, alright?" He didn't argue.

At night everything was different. The broken sheds took on spectral shapes. There were eerie scuttling sounds among the rusty debris. And they'd come the wrong way. That was obvious, at least to Roger. They were in a disused part of the docks with only a few feeble overhead lights still working. Under one of these his companion slumped down again, this time on a pile of old anchor-chains. Kropp was now at the maudlin stage. "Y'know this place is nothing. Nothing. The Clyde now. John Brown's f'rinstance. That's what you call a shipyard. Never mind Belfast, never mind Newcastle. The Clyde ..."

"Very true," said Roger. "Shall we go on now, back to the ship?"

All around their pool of light he could hear movement, soft voices and tense breathing.

"Kropp," he whispered.

Like forest animals circling a camp fire, a ring of faces appeared. Eight young men in old army fatigues, all with sleeves rolled up to show their tattoos. Egging them on was one with his shirt wide open to reveal a chest populated with dragons. The Night Cats were back, and Kropp could hardly stand.

Fear was a tangible thing, gripping his stomach and running through his body like tropical fever. "*Queen Mary,*" Kropp went on conversationally, "and the *Lizzie*. Clyde-built both of 'em. I worked in Brown's one time." Watching Kropp and ignoring Roger they closed in. But cautiously. Word of this one's prowess had got about. They looked to their leader for encouragement. Kropp at last became aware of them and got to his feet.

"So you're back are you? Come on then. You want a wee bundle, come and get it."

There was a marked reluctance to accept the offer. Until, that is, Kropp lunged forward and fell flat on his face. Someone forced Roger to the ground and pinned him there with a knee in his back. The rest surrounded Kropp and began kicking. Roger noticed one had an army cap and another had a pronounced limp. This was not robbery, this was revenge. First the principal enemy would be punished, then Roger who could be dealt with at leisure. Again Kropp staggered upright, hitting out at his attackers. But the insidious effect of all that *sake* was pitifully clear. Every wild swing and missed target threw him off balance. Like an exhausted Spanish bull he sank to his knees and the end was near.

Poised to administer the *coup de grace* they looked eagerly at their bare-chested leader, waiting for the nod. And it was that chest with its fire-breathing illustrations that gave Roger one last-hope inspiration.

"Kropp!" he yelled from his own cramped and painful position. "Kropp, take off your shirt!"

The weary head slowly lifted and focused somewhere in his general direction. "Go on, take off your shirt!" Kropp got up and fumbled with his buttons.

The Japanese watched curiously. Off came the shirt and the effect was immediate. A sharp intake of breath and a chorus of "Ahhs!" Roger was forgotten as his own guardian joined his friends. Crowding round, they touched the hounds and horses that entwined Kropp's torso. Their own leader stripped to the waist and posed beside him, presenting a bizarre east/west panorama of dragons and foxhounds. Their own tattoos were harshly traditional, a warlike display of ancient symbols, famous warriors and slogans from folklore.

But Kropp's was like nothing they'd ever come across. Kropp's was animated. It told a story. Tracing with their fingers, they followed the hunt. Twice round his navel, over his shoulders and down his back, vaulting a shoulder-blade on the way. "They like tattoos," explained Roger nervously. Unsteadily, Kropp twirled, fiddling with his belt.

"How about if I ...?"

"Yes, show 'em that too."

All was revealed. The fox's lair and the tail that betrayed it. It was too much. As nocturnal creatures do, the Night Cats howled. They fell about with laughter. Even the Cap and the Limp.

"Alright," said Kropp, pulling on his clothes. "So they want to be friends now. I don't. I'll still take 'em all on, nae bother." Suddenly one of the Japanese shouted a warning. Roger saw moving lights beyond the piles of wrecked machinery. The gang scattered, ducking back behind the curtain of the night as though they'd never existed. The lights disappeared, flickered back on and faded again. "They're all mad," said Kropp as they resumed walking.

Roger said, "I think they admired you. As a fighter, and a worthy opponent."

Kropp, not without an effort, drew himself erect. "You reckon that? Then it's a good thing I stuck to *sake* ..." he tripped and swayed, banged his head on a cast-iron post and lurched dizzily on "... otherwise I might have been too pissed to fight them."

They didn't know where they were going. The whole area was a hazardous, ill-lit tangle of jagged scrap metal, derelict buildings and holes in the ground. "Wait," said Roger. "Stop here a minute while I figure out where we are." But Kropp stumbled blindly on and was swallowed up in the gloom. The darkness and the silence were almost tangible, an invisible cavern populated by the ghosts of long-gone shipyard men who lived and toiled here. Forging weapons for a war they could never win.

"Kropp," he called. "Where are you?"

He needed Kropp. Of all the unlikely people, he needed this man's lumbering down-to-earth presence.

Vividly, the Kabuki play came into his mind. A young man befriends his one-time enemy. Together they face a horde of demons. Nothing but coincidence. Life imitating art. But this was the Far East. Home of the weird, the unexplained. The phantom lights showed again, moving, fading, brightening and vanishing. And now somewhere he distinctly heard the twanging of *samisen* strings.

Tired and tense from the hectic day, he didn't feel normal. A *samisen* – here in the docks? At this hour? He was hearing and seeing things. He was hallucinating, he was going mad.

"Kropp!" he screamed at the top of his lungs. "Kropp. Where the hell are you?" His words flew back in a triple echo, mocking his solitude. That echo. The sort you get in a cathedral or an aircraft hangar. Staring upward he could dimly make out an irregular pattern of light and dark squares high above him and he knew where he was. "Listen Kropp. Do you realise where we are? We're in the old *Yamato* shed!"

Chapter 15

He recalled another detail. The *Yamato* had been put together in a dry-dock. So they could be blundering about almost blindly along the lip of a monstrous concrete pit, deep enough to contain the largest battleship ever constructed.

"Kropp, don't move. Call out to me. Tell me where you are." In answer came the sound of a small avalanche of stones followed by a thud and an oath of such decorative and original profanity as might once have shocked him. Tonight it was music to his ears. Inching forward he came to a collapsed railing, a crumbling rounded edge of stonework and beyond that, nothing. "Are you down there?"

"Yes, I bloody am. And I broke something in my foot."

"You didn't answer when I called."

"Why should I? It's not my fault if we're lost." It was, but he let it go. The man didn't sound far away. Certainly not at the bottom of the dock. If that was the case he wouldn't be talking at all. Roger took out his matches, struck one and still saw nothing.

"Hang on and whatever you do, keep still." Groping about, he found a scrap of canvas and rolled it into a tube. Using many matches he got his lit and held it over the edge. Kropp lay on his side about fifteen feet down, glaring up at him like an ill-tempered sea-lion.

Roger knew little about dry-docks, but felt sure a big one would be deeper than fifteen feet. Kropp might be on a narrow ledge, inches from a fatal plunge. There were no steps or access ladders. Only the broken-off studs where they'd been. The only chain he found was too heavy to lift. Neither could he see any ropes. The makeshift torch went out. "I'll go and get help," he called.

He headed vaguely back to where he thought the lights had been earlier. Soon he found a worn track and made better progress. Again the moving lights and faint music came and went behind the shadows. A foreign dockyard at night is no place for blind wanderings. As if to confirm this, he put his foot in a hole and went sprawling. For a moment he lay still, listening to his thumping heart and spitting out dust. He was exhausted and ravenously hungry. But Kropp had to be rescued. How about enlisting the aid of the Night Cats? No – without Kropp they'd beat him up on sight for being a tattoo-less nobody.

A sudden blaze of white light burst upon him, hurting his eyes. He was caught like a rabbit in a jeep's headlights. From the darkness came a sharp command. "You there! Get on your feet and raise your hands, NOW!" This could not be happening. To cast further doubts on his sanity, he was hearing the samisen strings again, now in company with a female singer. Feeling both alarmed and foolish, he stood with arms in the air. A figure appeared on each side of the jeep. He recognised the white webbing, the blue uniforms and those round Popeye hats which had always struck him as faintly comic. The Shore Patrol were indeed busy tonight. "It's alright," he said. "I'm just trying to get out of this place."

The SP on the left was using both hands to grasp an automatic pistol, holding it before him and aiming it straight at Roger. The gun was tethered to its owner by a white lanyard which hung between them like an umbilical cord. It was as though the man had just given birth to the gun and was holding it out for someone to take. This surreal notion made Roger break into a nervous giggle in which relief and fatigue played a part, and caused him to start lowering his arms.

Instantly there was a shattering explosion, a great clap of sound that seemed to burst into his head and bounce to-and-fro against his skull. The SP had fired into the air. "Keep your hands up!" he bawled, and Roger hastily complied. The second man gave his companion a tetchy glance.

"Are you crazy? There's no need for that."

"We can't take any chances in here. This one's got evil written all over him."

"Well don't do it again. And turn off the radio. I don't dig that Jap stuff."

Singer and *samisen* vanished into the ether. "Frisk him Howard," said the gun man. With some distaste, Howard ran his hands up and down Roger's dirt-stained body. "You're a mess," he observed. "Australian? Right? We saw you from way back there, snooping around in a restricted area. Are you the one who's been hooting and hollering, and lighting fires in the middle of the night?"

"Yes – but if I could explain –"

"How'd you get in here? Was it you broke down the gate?"

"No, we just walked in. Me and a friend. It must have been the Yoru-neko broke the gate. They saw you coming and ran away."

"That's the idea. Scare 'em off. So where's your buddy now? Is he Australian too?"

They were big men. Purposely so, he guessed. Specially selected to instill respect in wrongdoers. Roger drew himself up to his full height and looked Howard straight in the chest. "My name is Roger Wren. I'm an English mariner." It sounded better than "crewman". More Drakeish, Nelsonian. "I'm on the *Empire Garvie*." The gun he saw was back in its holster so he carefully lowered his hands. Any minute now he would be called a limey. But no. They checked his identity, his Hiroshima pictures and the Kabuki card.

"He's OK," said Howard. "Get the vehicle. We'll run you to your ship, we have to go that way. Where's the other guy?"

"That's just it. He fell in the *Yamato* dock. And I think he's broken his ankle." There was an awkward silence. "Can you help us?" Howard hesitated, torn between pressure of duty and a natural humanity.

"Alright, we'll check it out. Get in."

His colleague demurred. "Do we have to? Take him back to his own ship and let them send somebody." Roger stood wearily with a foot in the jeep while they argued. Howard's view prevailed.

"Sit in the front." Roger climbed in. Howard took the wheel and the other SP crouched in the back, never taking his eyes off Roger. The jeep shot off down the track.

Why had they been so suspicious, making him raise his hands, searching him? "There's been a couple of bad incidents," said Howard. "Two men stole a gun and went AWOL. This is where we caught them, this area. It's been off limits ever since." Howard was inclined to chat, asking him how he liked Japan and how Kropp came to be where he was. Roger described his day. Howard chuckled. "Hear that Wesley? They mixed it with the Yoru-neko."

"That don't surprise me none," said Wesley. "These English always have a hard-luck story. Always on the liquor and looking for trouble. We shouldn't even be doing this. Waste of time and gas."

Howard spoke out of the side of his mouth. "Wesley don't like Englishmen. His girl ran off to Tokyo with one. It's kind of a sore point with him. Don't worry about it." A man who didn't like him sat behind him with a gun he loved to fire. No of course he wouldn't worry.

"Wesley, get out the flashlight," said Howard a few minutes later. Ahead loomed the huge empty shell that had hatched *Yamato*. Three faces craned over the edge. Wesley switched on the torch, the beam of which was so shockingly powerful it drew a startled "Jesus!" from the still-prone Kropp. Roger saw now that the dock was half-filled with earth and rubble. Kropp was in no danger of a further fall. But he was still trapped.

"You down there!" called Howard. "You got a busted ankle?" Kropp confirmed that he had, supplementing this with a rambling diatribe against Kure dockyard, the Night Cats, *sake* wine and the Japanese nation in general.

"Is he drunk?" asked Howard.

"Of course he is," grumbled Wesley. "These English, I say leave the bum where he is. Let his own people come and get him."

"We can't go now. They need us."

"They don't need us; they need the goddam Texas Rangers." But Howard's persistence again paid off. With the aid of the torch they made a wider search than Roger had managed and a length of rope was found some distance away. One end was lowered to Kropp, who tied it round his chest. They commenced pulling. Now you would think three men could heave a fourth out of a hole. Not so. From the start Wesley was a very unwilling rescuer, dead against the whole business and complaining about the rope which was grimy and difficult to grip. And Kropp himself, at around fourteen stone was not the easiest of victims. Cursing his misfortune, he would first hold his body clear of the side wall then weaken and fall heavily against it, throwing a sudden strain on their arms.

"The hell with this," said Wesley and let go. With a howl of protest Kropp descended swiftly back to his pit. Roger just managed to grab the end of the rope. Wesley jumped furiously into the jeep and reversed up to the edge of the dock. "Right, tie him on!" They did so, shouting a warning to Kropp. Wesley revved the engine.

"Go easy," said Roger. He had a feeling Kropp was about to be towed all the way to the *Empire Garvie*. Wesley let out the clutch. Kropp rocketed up and out, ploughing an eight-foot furrow in the dust before the jeep stopped. Discarding the rope, they examined his foot.

"Looks bad," said Howard. "Let's get him into the vehicle." They helped him into the back, where he half-laid on the seat with the hurt foot over the side. Wesley sulked behind the wheel as his colleague got in. "Let's go!" said Howard.

Before long they left the dark desolation behind and came to the orderly and well-lit section where all the shipping was. Kropp's eyes were closed and his head lolled child-like against Roger's arm. He actually felt a little sorry for Kropp. This man who had doled out so much punishment to others now lay half-dead from too much drink, several falls and an injured foot. Not to mention the Night Cats' activities.

"We got to make a call aboard one of our own ships first," said Howard, always the chattier one. "About a guy we picked up earlier trying to smash up the Blue Parrot. He's off one of our own navy transports. Name of Lomax. Overstayed his shore leave. We took him back to the command post and put him in a cell for the night. So now we have to arrange for him to ship out in the morning. Boy, do I hate night duty!" They were driving along a quayside, past a monotonous grey line of American supply ships. And Roger knew then what was coming. With absolute clarity he saw what would next befall him in this never-ending day of frights. The question was hardly needed.

"What's the name of this man's ship?"

"The *Chester M. Vandemeyer*."

No, he'd had enough. He couldn't face running into Irving Reed. Once they stopped he would walk off and make his own way to the *Garvie*. Abandon Kropp and let the Shore Patrol bring him home. "Here we are," said Howard. She looked exactly the same. The steep gangway up to the open deck, another bored sentry at the foot of it. The identifying 107 on her side. He didn't need to read her name, hidden in shadow high on her prow. This ship he'd have known anywhere.

Wesley parked the jeep next to a large notice in full view of a stream of returning sailors. "Stay here, we'll be right back," said Howard. The two SPs hastened up the gangway. So he stayed, as he'd known he would. The agony began. He was stuck here with a semi-conscious cripple, waiting for Seaman First Class Irving J. Reed to come along and haul him behind the sheds for what? A good beating at least. Irving would see it as a form of exercise. And there were no lieutenants to be seen, young or old.

Singly or in talkative groups the Popeye-hatted ratings trooped past the open jeep. And almost all of them stopped and commented on the Shore Patrol vehicle with its pair of dishevelled villains in the back. He didn't mind the tipsy ones or the banter that broke out. "What are you two suckers waiting for, your lawyers?" "Make a break for it while you can fellas." "Run the jeep into the harbour, make 'em walk back to Sakura-michi."

But some were sober. Upright, deadly, fully in control sober. These were the ones he watched. The ones who walked the way a "supremely fit" man would walk. Kropp stirred himself and took a drowsy interest in the signboard. "What's all that about?" The stark message made its meaning very clear "NOTICE TO ALL RANKS. While on shore in Port of Kure no member of this ship's company, either officer or enlisted man will conduct himself in any manner deemed to reflect adversely upon the honor and integrity of the US Navy. Infringement of this order will be regarded as a serious matter and dealt with accordingly. Elliot C. Adams, Commander."

"They're stupid, the Yanks," said Kropp. "Nearly killed me getting me out of that hole. I heard a shot too, earlier. I bet that was them."

"I wouldn't say anything. They saved you and they're taking us back. Without them you'd still be down there."

"They *are* stupid. Look how they spelt 'honour' on that signs of theirs." Roger held his head in despair.

The SPs returned. "All done," said Howard cheerfully. "Lomax will join them tomorrow. When he catches up with his own ship he'll do time for being AWOL. He accepts that, so long as he gets home."

Roger re-ran what he'd just heard. "I thought that one was his ship."

"Hell no. That's the *Joseph Starbrook*. Only came in today. They all look the same don't they? Like the Liberty ships."

"So where's the *Chester M.*?"

"Gone. They left here at noon yesterday for their home base. There were some bad characters on that one. That's why the *Starbrook* Captain put up that notice. In case his own crew got out of line." God, all that worrying, for nothing.

"What about that 107 on the side?"

"It's a fleet number. The ship's individual number's up on the stack." They drew up alongside the *Garvie*.

"Did you know somebody on the *Chester M.*?" Howard asked.

"Sort of. Yes"

"Well you won't catch them now. Unless you want to swim to San Diego."

Willing hands assisted Kropp up into the ship. The gangway sailor gaped. "What happened to him? No, never mind. You're the Lodger ain't you? If he's been out with you that explains it." He prepared to bid the Americans farewell. "Thank you gentlemen, your efforts are much appreciated." Was this the closing scene of the day? The finale of his own Kabuki drama? Not quite, something was still missing.

"Glad to be of service," said Howard with a wry glance at his companion. "We'll do anyone a favour, right Wesley?"

"Sure." Wesley sounded almost sincere. "Even a stray pair of limeys." Ah yes. That made it complete.

Next day the *Empire Garvie* slipped through the Shimoneseki Straits to begin the overnight crossing to Pusan. Roger's first act on going aboard had been to obtain some food in the galley. His second to take a shower and his third to tumble into bed, promising to tell all in the morning. Which he did, having some trouble convincing them he'd not slept with the prostitute they'd seen on his arm.

"I've said it before and I'll say it again," remarked Pat. "The Lodger packs more into one day ashore than most of us do in a voyage."

His Hiroshima visit interested the older men, but Bill said, "More fool you for going there. Getting mixed up with another set of Yanks." He saw Kropp, aided by crutches, hobbling about the glory hole with his foot in plaster. There was a strange moment when they met and an expression on Kropp's face as if he couldn't remember if he still hated Roger or not.

The short trip was uneventful. When he came on deck again they were entering another Asian harbour. Pusan resembled Kure. The same rounded hills. The smell of war. Distant but insidious. He watched their complement of soldiers disembark, sensing behind the ribald jokes and forced jollity the true thoughts of these young men who would grow up so soon. Jack arrived on deck. "We're away back to Kure tonight. And there's no shore leave here. Roger, that Farley character's below. Wants to show you something."

"I can guess what it is."

Waiting outside the cabin, Farley followed him in carrying something wrapped in cloth. "Roger, you and I have had our differences, I still don't like you much, but I must show you this."

The sword was long and curved and came out of its scabbard with a blood-curdling swish. "Guess what I paid for it? Go on guess."

To please him, Roger upped the figure. "Must have been expensive. Twenty-five quid at least."

"Wrong, fifteen. Yeah, I know it's still a lot but I'll get forty or fifty for this at home. I know I've seen them. This Aussie I got it from —"

"That'll be Pete Langham, who you wouldn't have known about if I hadn't put you on to him."

Briefly put out, Farley muttered, "Yeah, him. Thanks. Anyway, he found it in a ruined Jap headquarters. That's why it's got some rust on it. I'm not cleaning it though. The Aussie said when you're dealing with war souvenirs you want to leave 'em in their true state or the next buyer'll be suspicious. Think you made it yourself!" Roger held the sword. Rather unimpressive, it didn't seem worth fifteen shillings, never mind pounds. It was strangely heavy and rather dull with scant ornamentation. Some of the silk cording on the handle was unravelling.

"You'd expect that," said Farley. "After it's been buried in rubble. I was lucky to get it. He said he couldn't get any more."

"Keep it handy. You may need it before the trip's over."

"What for?"

"Self defence. If Kropp discovers you deliberately lied to him about me and the queers. At present he thinks you were just mistaken. Your little trick cost him two hundred dollars and a lot of humiliation."

"I never did that." Already he was looking nervous.

"Yes you did. Kropp told me. I'm his friend now. He saved my neck in Kure. And I saved his – twice. As he'll come to realise once he regains his senses. So don't let's have any more trouble between us. I'll stay away from your domain, B Deck, you stay away from Kropp. Agreed?"

"Agreed." Farley looked relieved, slid the sword back into its scabbard and gave an anguished "Ow!" when his thumb got caught under the hilt.

The following dawn saw them back at Kure. It was to be a few hours this time, then off to Hong Kong. "No shore leave," said Jack. "And the whole ship's got a big inspection today. The Captain's coming round. You'll find the days go quickly now Roger. Fly by, you see." Homeward bound. What magic lay in those words. From this point on, every mile they moved was closer to England.

It was his first sight of the Captain. Till now, the inspections had been by the Second Steward. Sometimes the Chief Steward himself would come to run a critical finger along the ledges. But that morning he met Captain Baskerville, a tall man with silver sideburns and a seen-it-all expression. They left Japan by the same route they'd come in by, back between the two large islands and then heading south.

"You won't forget this place for a while," said Clay. "After what you got up to. Are you still saying you never actually went with that *pan-pan*?"

"That's right. And you?"

"No. I can't say I really fancied any of them. And I've heard too many warnings."

Their last sight of the country was a low headland at the southernmost tip of Kyushu. He thought about the disabled Zero. And so-young Sumiko waiting in the Monte Carlo with her Cleopatra eyes narrowed against the smoke. And he wondered if the MPs had caught Gatti yet. No, he wouldn't forget Japan – ever.

At Hong Kong was a letter with a surprise at the end. "I met that girl you knew," wrote his father. "Isobel Shepherd. In the High Street with her younger sister. You should have seen her face when I told her where you are. I gave her a copy of the posting dates in case she wants to write. Is that OK?" A letter from Isobel. He couldn't imagine anything less likely. "How long are we in this time Jack?"

"No idea. Pat's gone to ask."

Kowloon again. The Star Ferry. The Nine Dragon Hills – and something else. A ship much like their own, but with only one funnel. *Empire Fowey*," said Jack. "As far as I know we got no problem with her crew."

Pat returned. "Only two days this time." As before in Kure, two people would get no day off.

"Not us this time," said Martin. "It's between you four." The coin spun. Bill and Martin got the first day, Jack and Pat the second. So he and Toddy were out of the running. With no free day he would have no time to go cycling on the island. The double ferry crossing, over the hills, impossible between his hours of duty. In any case, if she was booked on the other troopship …

"When's the *Fowey* sailing?"

"Tomorrow," said Pat. So he'd seen the last of Anna.

Soon after breakfast, with his phone numbers and a handful

of coins, he went to Hanni Lu's. Batten had kept his word. The proprietress greeted him warily but said nothing. He rang Gina, hoping she was at home, she was. There was uncertainty in her voice. "Who? Oh — er — hullo Roger, nice to hear from you again. We were told of your trouble. OK now?"

"Fine thanks."

"Anna was disappointed you couldn't go biking that day."

"So was I. And now she'll be sailing on the *Fowey* tomorrow." A longish pause. He felt sure some surprise was coming.

"I've got a bit of news for you Roger. They told our department first. The *Fowey's* not going home. Not yet. It's been diverted to Japan, same as you were. In the meantime Sam Shay's had a cable from his wife. She wants Anna with her. And you don't argue with Mrs Shay. Especially at long distance. So – Anna's going on the *Garvie*." It took him a while to absorb this.

"Are you still there Roger? Here's something else. Your porthole picture got in the runners-up list. And a couple of mine. So there's 100 dollars there for you to pick up. Go to the Fraser Gallery in De Vouex Road."

"That's wonderful. Thanks for getting it in. When can I see you?"

Again the awkward pause. He wondered if Graham was with her. "Well, not today. We … I've got to attend a function in Central. You could come tomorrow night. Bring Henry and Clay. We're giving a farewell party for Anna. Sam will be here too. And bring your latest photos."

"Right, see you then." Anna, on the *Garvie*, possibly alone. As the daughter of a Wing-Commander she would travel first class. Another deck up and closer to Quinn's territory. He really shouldn't be thinking like this.

On his next call he had to wait. She sounded out of breath. "Mr Wren! Good morning. I do apologise. I was in the garden. Are you fully recovered from your injuries?" Those exquisite manners. If he'd been wearing a tie he'd have instinctively straightened it.

"Good morning Anna. Yes, I'm fine now. And it's me who should apologise for letting you down on our date. I — er — I hear you will be sailing on the *Garvie*."

"Yes. I will be all day tomorrow getting ready. But I could still go cycling with you today. One more look at the island and the places I've known. Before leaving it all behind."

He would have to get there. Someway – somehow. "Then shall we meet this afternoon? Same time and place we said before?"

"Yes, let us do that. I'll have the spare bicycle with me."

Walking back along Nathan Road he remembered he had 100 dollars coming to him. About a fiver. Add this to Kropp's money and he was relatively affluent. By *Garvie* standards. He went straight down to the cabin. Fortunately they were still aboard. "Bill – I need today free. Will you or Martin sell me your day off?"

"How much is it worth to you?"

"Shall we say 30 dollars?"

"Piss off."

"Come on Bill," said Jack. "What do you need all day for? You're a night bird."

"I'll do it," said Martin. "For 50 dollars."

"Done," said Roger and paid him.

Jack said, "Don't forget you got to be back here by six to do breakfast." In fifteen minutes he was on the *Shining Star* watching the approach of that stunning Hong Kong skyline. Today the camera had been left behind as a possible encumbrance. It was still early. He could collect his prize-money and kill some time in town. Then have lunch before traversing the island.

The Fraser Gallery was not especially grand. A narrow porticoed entrance with something about the arts in Latin over the top and a small modernised interior lined with around eighty large photographs. Visitors sauntered about, studying the work and debating its merits. There were six entries by Mrs G Morrell, glossy prints of eastern scenes. Then he saw his own. Now grown to eighteen inches square, it sat alongside the Angkor Wat Temple and a view of Rangoon. A card below it gave the title, a number and his name.

"That's quite interesting don't you think?" The man was elderly and erect, carrying a silver-topped cane with which he indicated Roger's picture. "Does it say where it is? I don't have my glasses."

"No. It's simply called 'Landfall', but I can tell you it's Colombo."

The man shook his head. "That's never Colombo. Singapore maybe." He didn't want to score points this early in the day.

"You could well be right." At the far end of the gallery he approached a sour-faced woman behind an antique desk. "My name is Roger Wren. I was a runner-up in that competition you held. Number fifty-eight."

She sniffed. "The judging took place ages ago." A glance at a list. "And you never collected your prize. Where have you been?"

"Korea," he replied brokenly. Contrition was swift. "Oh I'm so sorry. Do forgive me. If I could just have some identity." As he left with his 100 dollars, he looked back. The old man was consulting the woman. They both stared at him and across at the picture. Back on De Vouex Road, he spent a satisfying two hours wandering through the heart of Central. Here he discovered temples and gardens, museums and bookshops selling every known publication in every known language. There were mahjong parlours where the shouts of players mingled with the rattle of tiles. He felt privileged to be there, so far from home and able to indulge his love affair with travel and strange lands. And for once, free of all perils.

Around 12.30 he went for lunch to Jimmy's Kitchen. "One of the oldest eating-places in Hong Kong this is," said a fellow-diner nearby. About his own age, the man wore one of the bright flowery shirts that were becoming the fashion for travellers abroad. "Same family's run it for years. Good place Hong Kong. Nice and peaceful. Law-abiding people the Chinese. I'm off the *Fowey*. What about you?"

Roger took a risk. "*Garvie*." It seemed alright.

"Thought you might be," said the man. "Have you met the *Windrush* yet?"

"Yes, in Colombo. Had a bundle with them."

The other laughed. "One day they'll get over that stupid boat-race."

As he was still using Kropp's money and the irony was irresistible, he had oxtail soup to start. Then tested his new fondness for foreign food with stir-fried black pepper beef, finishing up with the strongest, blackest coffee he'd ever tasted. A Chinese newsboy entered the restaurant. "Anybody for papers?"

"Yes here." Feeling like a resident, he lit a Camel and settled back with his coffee and a copy of the *South China Morning Post*. The news was not good. In South Korea the military build-up continued and the RAF were fully committed. It seemed unlikely the Wing-Commander would be going home with his daughter and he felt guilty that this pleased him.

"What's the latest?" inquired the *Fowey* man.

"We're getting in deeper and deeper. I hear you're off to Japan tomorrow."

"Yes. And you've just been. What's it like there?"

"Can be rough if you meet the wrong people."

"Is that where you got those marks on your face?"

He'd almost forgotten them. "No, I got them here, in nice peaceful Hong Kong." After paying his bill, he left his paper to the *Fowey* man, walked down Connaught Road and caught a bus to Wei Ho Bay.

This time he recognised the top end of Macau Drive. There was no sign of her at first. Then he saw her a little way down, a very fetching picture in white shorts and dark green top. The two bicycles leaned against a wall under a dazzling canopy of scarlet bougainvillea. "Mr Wren, how good of you to come all this way."

"Please Anna, call me Roger."

She noticed his scars. "You were badly hurt?"

"For a while. I'm OK now really."

"I've been out most days this week. Yesterday I was at Repulse Bay and Stanley. There's only one or two places left to see. Oh and Tiger Balm of course. Shall we visit the Peak first?"

"Fine, I've got the whole day free." Conversation was not always easy. Of necessity she led the way when traffic forced them into single file, and he found himself distracted by her legs as she pedalled along in front. At the Peak Tram Station they left the machines outside, which he thought a risk.

"No-one will touch them," she said. Law-abiding Hong Kong. The "tram" was actually a funicular railway, green cast-iron cars clawing their way at a 45-degree angle towards the Peak a thousand feet above. At the top they alighted with other sightseers and climbed a few steps cut in the rock.

There was a large viewing area, big enough to stroll in all directions and take in the astonishing panorama of the Crown Colony and its sprawling harbour dotted with craft. Again he felt immensely fortunate to be in the place, so far removed from his workaday life aboard. Pausing at the rail, she gazed absently towards the Chinese mainland. "I love this spot so much I had to see it once more. You don't mind?"

"Of course not, I'm enjoying every minute." Not tactful, when it was her farewell visit. "Sorry, I only meant —"

"Please Roger, it's quite alright." His Christian name at last. A break in the formality. Over at Kowloon the two troopships hugged their piers, and the tireless Star ferries shuttled to and fro as they'd done for half a century.

"We thought it would be the *Fowey*," she went on. "Now with an extra day for packing I can finish saying goodbye to Hong Kong. Tomorrow my father's coming to help me and see me off on Friday." So the Wing-Commander would definitely not be with her.

"Have you lived here long?"

"Five years now. Father sent us away to India when we knew war was coming. I finished my schooling there, studying history and English Lit. And poetry, my best subject. I'd like to be a teacher some day." They'd spent worrying years in India, waiting for news and mixing with others fleeing the Japanese advance – while her father flew his missions. "He was involved in those air-drops over Burma. Supplying Slim's men and the Chindits." He noticed the familiar way she said "Slim's men". Years ago, yet still fresh to those who were closer to it. Men like her father. And Pickard, Morrell and so many who had looked into the face of Death and stared him out. Men who might have hurried home to Blighty – yet perversely elected to stay. Some even marrying into a different race, with all the problems that could bring.

"But he did come through it all unscathed?"

"Yes but afterwards —" Something troubled her. Experience told him to wait. "It was difficult even before the war. But my parents were in love and ignored the warnings. Do you know what I mean?"

"Marriage between the races. Not everyone approves."

"They weren't the only ones of course, but sometimes when we showed up in certain circles, you know."

"You and your mum got funny looks." She laughed at his homely words. "Yes but not from everyone, the Morrells took us for trips on their yacht. And they told us of another mixed-race couple they know in Singapore, the Pickards."

"I know them," he said. "They own a restaurant. You and I could go and see them on our way to England."

"I'd like that."

They returned to the upper station, and it was only good manners to take her hand as they negotiated the rough-hewn steps. He knew it was hopelessly optimistic to believe anything would come of this. A girl like her. As a person she was far removed from Ruth and even Gina. And he only had one slight thing in common with her.

"Anna, who's your favourite poet?"

"Tell me yours first." Gina had been talking. He only knew a few.

"Oh, there's so many. Kipling, Masefield." He remembered Gina's advice. "I quite like Robert Browning." Her reaction surprised him.

"Browning, really? Why that's wonderful. Because you see my favourite is – Elizabeth Barrett!" Now he cottoned on. Barrett and Browning had been lovers, drawn together by a passion for verse. Gina was pushing him towards her.

Assisted now by gravity, the carriage rocked merrily on its way down the mountain, pressing them together on the hard wooden seat and making him acutely aware of the warmth of her thigh against his lightweight trousers. Back on the ride again, they headed east along Tai Hong Road to where the celebrated gardens were. On the way they talked of poetry and books, empire and history – a host of literate things. She asked about Japan. So he recounted all he felt suitable for her ears, excising the more sordid episodes. He told her how he'd been captivated by the sweet song of the *samisen*. "You went to the Kabuki? How exciting! I saw that in a movie once." Every passing minute she grew more relaxed. Well, it was difficult to remain formal while riding a bike and wearing shorts.

She had worked at Jardine Mathiesons. "I left the moment I knew I was going to UK."

"Have you been to England before?"

"Once. We flew there. I quite liked it but I'll always love the Colony. It'll be a wrench leaving for good." The Tiger Balm Gardens appeared in all their glory. Eight acres of pavilions and grottoes spread over a hillside. There were Chinese gods, gaudy reliefs and weird statuary, all garishly painted. "It was a millionaire named Aw Boon Haw," she explained, "who put all this here. Tiger Balm is the name of a cure-all he got rich from, selling it all over Asia." There was also a grand mansion to be admired, and the seven-story Tiger Pagoda which they climbed by way of 149 steps to stand at the top with the ocean before them.

As at the Peak, she was taking in these scenes in order to sustain her when they'd gone forever. A Eurasian he thought would be a kind of ex-patriate in reverse. For a long time after settling in England, "home" would still be Hong Kong. As if reading his mind, she asked, "Do you miss the UK yourself?"

"Well it's only been a few weeks but yes, I think I would if I was away too long."

"Oh, to be in England now that April's there." Quotations, he thought with alarm. These colonial wives and daughters. They all had some kind of arcane passion. Mahjong, eastern theology, poetry. Elaine Halley and her whirling planets.

"Yes," he replied. "Browning put it very well."

"Do you know the next line?" What a challenge. He racked his brain. Truth to tell, he didn't read that much verse. Only what really appealed. If it was Kipling now …

"Whoever wakes …" she prompted, smiling.

It came to him. "And whoever wakes in England, see some morning unaware …" He carried on to finish the verse. To her obvious delight. Her hand lightly touched his arm.

"I think it's really wonderful that we both love the same two people. I've read so much of Elizabeth Barrett's life and work. You know she was an invalid for years? When she met Browning they had a secret love affair. I think it was his kindness that drew her to him. And he made her laugh, even when she was ill. Then her father tried to break it up so they got married and ran away to Italy. When you think how prim and stuffy society was then – to do that. They must have been deeply in love."

Events, Roger thought had taken a curious but intriguing turn. Her fixation with Victorian writers, her stilted manners at meeting and now this frequent use of the word "love" – all contained behind that unlined oriental face. "Sometimes," she continued, "I feel very much like her." They started back down the long flight of steps. "I mean — I'm not ill — but I often feel sort of …" her voice petered out. Only when they were cycling into their next port of call, Shek O did the introspection return. "I was ill once in India. Malaria. It took ages to get over. Mother kept all my friends away. Not that I had many. But I got awfully lonely."

Shek O was a sleepy fishing village with an easy-going, unpretentious air about it. There was a sandy beach with a few children romping at the water's edge. "We used to come here," she said as they got off their bikes. "The Morrells would anchor off-shore and we'd all go swimming. Except my mother that is." Wheeling the bikes, they left the road and started up a grassy headland. Everything around him caught the sun. The glittering sea, the chrome on the bikes and the raven-black hair topping her so-smooth features. He had a compulsive need to embrace her. Shading her eyes, she stood perfectly erect looking out to sea and swaying slightly in the breeze like a fragile meadow-flower. To hell with caution. He began to reach out to her when she suddenly turned.

"Do you really like Kipling?" He thought yes, but not right now. If she went on like this his skimpy repertoire would soon be exhausted.

"Well, a lot of his work is good. I lean more towards his military stuff. The Mandalay one for example." His knee gave a twinge. It was some time since he'd ridden so many miles. "Do you mind if we stop here for a while?" They laid the bikes down and sat beside them.

"I'm not entirely happy with all he wrote," she said and stretched out on the grass with her hands behind her head. "It's a very masculine view of the east he puts across." His mind buzzed with possibilities and the old feeling of being in two places at once. Here with her, strolling down sunlit vales of literature with maybe just enough knowledge to scrape by, and back on the ship where she was only "that Chinese bit the Lodger's seeing".

Worlds apart. And soon she would be moving into his world, but like the others be out of reach except by nocturnal forays tight with danger. Three times he'd got away with it. It wouldn't happen again. She'd be another deck up, in the holy sanctum of First Class. And Quinn was wise to him now.

"My main trouble with Kipling," she said, "is the way he tends to ridicule other races. Typical colonial attitude." This seemed an uncomfortable discussion to be having with a Eurasian, and the last thing he wanted was to argue with her. But he couldn't let that go.

"I think you're wrong there. He wrote of them humorously yet with affection. To him the Sudan warrior was 'a first-class fighting man'. And what about Gunga Din? A better man than I am, etc." Making no reply she closed her eyes as if in resignation and he regretted contradicting her. But remembering she tended towards the romantic he saw a way out. Leaning over, he spoke softly.

"Don't forget. Towards the end of 'Mandalay', Kipling's soldier in England is pining to be back east. In the arms of his Burmese sweetheart, who he loves and regrets having to leave." The dark eyes slowly opened and he fancied he saw a mischievous light behind them.

"You're right," she said. "And the temple-bells they say – Come you back you British Soldier. Come you back to Mandalay." There was something in the way she said it. The urge to kiss her got the better of him. Without touching her anywhere else, he leaned a little more and planted his mouth on hers. There was no reaction. In a few seconds she turned away.

"I'm not your Burmese girl-friend." He'd blown it.

"No. Sorry. Must have been the temple-bells."

"A man would not have been so bold in Browning's time."

The difficult moment lengthened, but her apparent indifference at least gave him time to think. Equating herself with Barrett. The reference to "Browning's time". He wasn't the only one who fantasised. Perhaps she learned it from Gina. "Miss Barrett. Forgive my presumption. I would deem it a great kindness on your part if I were permitted to kiss you."

There are many kinds of smile. From a wide white gash that bisects the face to a tiny simper barely enough to move the lips. What he saw was something else. There was much in it. Amusement at his phrasing, a concession to her liking for old courtesies. Curiosity, for it was so long since anything like this had happened. A whole year since her mother sent that other one packing. Her mother's rules, passed down through generations of Chinese forebears, decreed that a daughter be primed and cultivated in isolation until a suitable husband is found. So there was another feeling too, for her mother was half a world away.

"Upon my word Mr. Browning. On our short acquaintance such a request is outrageously impertinent. On the other hand ..."

It was all there in the smile, and this time he read it right. They kissed quickly and then slowly and he sensed in her something of the same hunger he'd felt himself with Ruth and the breathless role-playing with Gina. Presently she broke away and stood up. "Roger – I know what you're thinking but I'm not sure we ought to be doing this. I mean —" she glanced out to sea as if seeking inspiration "... we don't really know each other do we?"

"We know how to take pleasure in one another's company. Isn't that enough? Isn't that how Robert and Elizabeth came together?" The question was no sooner out then he regretted it. The two Victorians had carried out a full-blooded, loyalty-swearing, hand-on-heart romance followed by marriage. Not exactly the comparison he meant. Picking up the bikes, they started back.

She said, "I know what's going on Roger. You believe if you play on this thing about Barrett and Browning or Kipling's girl long enough I might go to bed with you."

To say he was shaken wouldn't come close to it. After Ruth – and especially Gina – with all their unspoken round-the-houses innuendo, to hear this from Anna of all people. Academic Anna, he might have dubbed her. A girl of knowledge, with manners lifted straight from the pages of Jane Austen. The fact that she was right made it doubly disconcerting. He wondered what she really thought of him – what Gina may have told her. "I won't deny it," he said. "I won't deny that I'm very attracted to you. Both as a friend and —"

"A Chinky bit?" Again her bluntness was a jolt.

"I've never used that word," he replied with some heat. "Not even before this voyage. I've learned things in these past weeks. By God, have I learned things!"

"Sorry Roger. But I've been warned by Father to expect it. From some people – some quarters." Laughingly, but with some bitterness she added, "He once told me not to go near Wanchai at night."

"That's somewhere I've never been"

"No, I believe that. You're not the sort. You said it yourself at Gina's. And she told me too."

"What else did she tell you?"

They reached the main road. "That you were amusing – and kind." Her voice trembled slightly as she took a final look at the village. "Farewell Shek O. Maybe one day ..." she stopped and turned away. He put his arm round her. Down at the beach the children splashed in the surf. An elderly junk laboured across the bay, patched sail aflutter like an old quilt out to dry. What occupied him now was what she would do next. As did Ruth, she had an overbearing parent who was now out of the picture. Anything could happen. Or not. So he waited to see which way she pointed her front wheel. Back to Wei Ho or on to somewhere else.

But she stopped as if undecided, so he said, "Where to now?" Her face this time truly defined the word "inscrutable."

"Home," she said simply.

The familiar sight of Macau Drive was both a comfort and a challenge. Past joys – future promise. Anna's villa was a large but homely place in pink wash with blue windows and a paved drive edged with flowering shrubs. Perfect for retirement but the Wing-Commander (or more likely his wife) preferred England. They put the bikes in the garage. She seemed even more assured now that she was at home and in sole charge of it, perhaps for the first time. "Shall we have some tea?"

"That would be very welcome."

"And we'll have some cakes and biscuits as well."

Entering the house he found a preponderance of Chinese furnishing, with many objects and figurines in carved ebony or ivory. There were lacquered black cabinets smothered in swirling gilt patterns. A long bookcase stuffed with volumes. It seemed incredible that anyone would wish to vacate such a home. "Are you having to sell all of this when you go?"

"Some of it. The rest will be shipped to UK over the next few weeks. At least that was the plan. My mother's gone first to find a house meeting our standards. Or rather hers. I've an aunt in Reigate who deals in property. Mother's staying with her now. Father and I should have gone on the *Empire Fowey*. Now it's going to Japan and father has to stay here. Or Korea."

While she prepared the tea he wandered round the room, finally coming to the books. All the expected ones were there. Shelley, Wordsworth, Byron and so many more. A roll-call of talent. Inevitably, Barrett and Browning had a whole shelf of their own. On a wall hung a picture, a reproduction of "The Boyhood of Raleigh." Two young men, squatting down listening to an older one in a straw hat pointing off to the right. On sighting it he was instantly taken back to another time and place, Clay, himself and Batten. All that time ago on the Suez Canal.

Anna returned with a tray and they sat together on an ornate sofa. "I hope you like this tea. It's something different. A very rare blend from Cambodia. Mother always had it specially sent." The tea-tray was rather crowded, the cups made of paper-thin china and the slim, pagoda-shaped teapot tall and rather unstable. And everything stood on a low, spindly table of the kind so easily upset by a misplaced foot. He was almost afraid to move.

"Tell me," she said, passing him some tea and cake. "Have you ever written any poetry yourself?"

"As a matter of fact I've been putting something together during the voyage. Haven't finished it yet. Only two verses."

"What's it about?" His cup was so light and delicate he nearly forgot he was holding it.

"The sea. I've called it "Trade Winds". I would have called it "Sea Fever" but Masefield beat me to it."

"I'd love to hear it."

"OK. If you're quite sure you want to. Here goes – There is a place beyond compare, that some will never know. A magic place upon the sea, where lowly steamers go. There is a breeze upon my face, a sway beneath my feet. My eyes can see astounding things, and every sound is sweet." Very slowly she put down her plate. "Roger – that's wonderful. Really."

"Well as I say I'm still at it. Juggling it about till it sounds right."

"Every poet does it that way. Browning did. And you always know when it's right because of the inner feeling you get. Robert and Elizabeth knew they were meant for each other as soon as they read each other's work. They thought the same way – about life and – everything." Giving a barely audible sigh she stretched out her legs and snuggled up against him. "The other verse please."

"Right – coming up. Sunsets of a dozen hues, and every shade between. The purest air you'll ever breathe, and stars you've never seen. Fluorescent seas at midnight, white horses on parade. Riding by with silver manes in ghostly cavalcade." For a while she lay quiet, then put her arms round his head and pulled their faces together for a burning kiss that took his breath away.

His heart thumped on his ribs and he felt himself responding to the nearness of that incredibly slim body. At the same time he became curiously and intensely aware of everything around him. The shadows forming in the corners of the room, the overpowering jumble of *chinoisserie* that hemmed them in. "Roger," she said shakily. "What are we doing – I felt as if – I was someone else. I can't believe I did that." He couldn't believe it either. "Who did you imagine yourself to be?"

"Her," she whispered.

"Take it easy. You've been reading too much of that lady's writings. Try someone else. Try Edward Lear. There was an old man with a beard …" Recovering, she smiled, dimpling her cheeks. They kissed again, and now they knew precisely what they were doing – and thinking of doing. "This is wrong," she said.

"Not if you really want to."

"I'm afraid if we did, what might happen."

"I have the — nothing can happen, believe me."

Nervously she toyed with the tea-things. He took her hand. "My dear Elizabeth." She looked at him, searching his face, and slowly withdrew her hand. "I must take a shower first." The door closed behind him and he laid his head back on the sofa. Through a French window he could see a long garden with darkness beginning to claim the far end. He would never know what impelled him to utter those last three words. Yes, he'd done a similar thing earlier. But this – this had seemed to spring out of the air. As though, well – as though he'd actually heard the voice of a long-dead Victorian.

He had another cup of the special tea. It had a weird flavour. The whole *evening* had a weird flavour. Another voice in his head. Toddy's this time. "Strange place the Far East. Funny things happen here." Certainly Anna was a deep one. For so long controlled by her mother and unlike Ruth unable to fool a dominant parent with clandestine pleasures. Immersed in the lives of the two poets, her need for romance fed but never satisfied by reading their work, and moping about the house with now only her fond, but rather dull father for company. Perhaps there were moments when her obsessions got the better of her, and she became briefly and only very slightly unhinged.

The minutes passed in thoughtful silence. Outside it got steadily darker. For some reason the term "witching hour" came into his mind. He took out his cigarettes but there wasn't an ashtray in sight so he put them away and ate a couple of oatmeal biscuits. One could never have too much fibre.

"Roger," she called from the door. In that part of the world you were never far from someone in a kimono. This one was pale green with deep sleeves and a sash tied in a bow like a Japanese *obi*.

"I've finished my shower. Would you like one too – after that cycling? I've left towels and stuff there for you. And one of my father's robes."

"Thanks."

"It's along the hall." She paused. "Next to my room."

After the ship's prison-standard amenities, the bathroom was a riot of luxury. A fragrant temple of blue tiles and feet-caressing rugs. Very different. And as he washed he had a powerful conviction that tonight would be different also. In five minutes he stepped out of the cubicle and towelled himself dry. Listening, he heard no movement elsewhere in the house. He put on the Wing-Commander's robe and picked up his own clothes. Her door was ajar, the interior quite dark.

"Are you there?" he called. There was no reply. It was if he was alone in the house. He switched on the light. No, she wasn't there. But many more things were. All around the room was a motley collection of framed photographs and engravings. There must have been twenty or more. They covered the window-sill, the dressing-table and cupboard-tops. Every one depicted the same man or woman in the garb of a bygone age. And he could guess who they were. Her two beloved poets. "Turn out the light," she called from somewhere. He did so, putting his things on a chair. Then he groped his way to the bed, shed the robe and got between the sheets. Here he lay with a feeling somewhere between elation and a vague unease.

Along the hall, footsteps and a spectral yellow glow heralded her approach. Yes, things were different this time. The illumination came from an old brass oil-lamp, with a sickly flame wavering inside an onion-shaped glass shade. The next surprise was the girl herself. Gone was the kimono. In its place she wore a long white night-gown buttoned up to her neck. "Roger, please try to understand why I'm doing this. It's just — me. I know it looks strange – mad even. But it's exactly how she would have gone to bed. In those days — you know — with him." No-one knew better than he did what a part fantasy could play in sex. Some took it a step further that's all. "It's OK," he said quietly. "Really, it doesn't matter." She placed the lamp on a bedside table and slipped in beside him.

"Please don't think me insane. I've got to do it like this — I've got to. Just to begin with. To feel right. I can't do it otherwise."

"It's OK," he said again. "Relax. Have a little rest first." For what seemed an age they lay without speaking. The dead faces round the room bothered him. As did the oil-lamp. "Do we need the light on?" he asked. "No." But something was amiss with the lamp. "I can't turn it off," she said. "It's jammed." Reaching across her he tried to turn the small brass wheel. It wouldn't budge.

So the yellow flame burned on, the shadows leapt about the room and the old poets continued to watch them. Robert, stiff and bewhiskered. Elizabeth with her poke bonnet and long-suffering invalid's face. The cloying Victorian atmosphere pervaded the room. He felt trapped in a fog of sepia-toned rectitude. With no more ado, he took the lamp and blew as hard as he could down the shade. The flame went out, but not before he got a singed nose and a whiff of oily smoke that brought on a terrible fit of sneezing.

Humour, as ever, worked like magic. Putting her face in the pillow, she succumbed to a long bout of uncontrolled giggling. When the sneezing finally ran its course and he reached out to her she was still suppressing laughter. "Roger," she gasped. "I'm — this is —" and now she lost all restraints. For a full half-minute they kissed, squeezing together till arms and lips ached. "Are you alright?" he murmured. "I'm fine," she said, a little breathless. Abruptly, she pulled the Barrett-style garment off over her head, folded and placed it to one side with such cool deliberation she might have been her alter ego checking the linen cupboard. Now, calmly and for a while silently, they made love.

And this too was different. Here he found not the capable, if perfunctory mechanics of Ruth, nor the polished teasing of Gina. What the Lodger experienced now, in that pink and blue house by the sea, was a peculiarly sublime enchantment. The sort that belongs to the (relatively) innocent. He was only slightly more practiced than her. His movements, his remarks could be ill-judged. Yet their very naivety, their alone-in-the-house sense of mischief smoothed the way. When at last there came a pause, she leaned up on one elbow, pale shoulders and pert breasts just visible in the half-light.

"Roger, today has been one of the best days of my life – if not *the* best."

"Mine too."

"Of course I know I'm not your first. You went with Gina didn't you?" He didn't reply. Dealing with post-coital questions was an art he was still learning.

"It's alright," she went on. "I'm not jealous or anything stupid like that. I simply wondered that's all. Curious if you like. Whether — how I might compare. Was it — better with her?" Make them smile. Whatever you do, make them smile. "No," he said firmly.

"Why not?"

"Well for a start there was no poetry. Or Cambodian tea."

Again they laughed and loved together. And it was at this rapturous point that his other life broke in. He remembered things like buses, ferry-boats and his dreary job. "Anna."

She seemed to climb back from some other existence. "What's the matter?"

"It's ten-thirty. I have to get the bus to Central."

"No!" Her dismay was genuine – and flattering. "You don't need to go now. The ferry starts very early in the morning. Six-thirty. And the bus from here at six. Stay here."

If only he could. "I can't honestly, I start work at six."

"Roger – I'm sorry. What am I thinking of? Of course you must leave." Even after such a phenomenal evening, modesty ruled. Before turning on the (electric) lamp, she donned the old-fashioned night-wear once more. And he had more sense than to make a jest of that. After all, it was what Elizabeth would have done. As he dressed, she sat on the bed watching him. He felt like a husband setting off for work. A lightning wash, and he had ten minutes to reach the upper end of Macau Drive. Now also wearing the green kimono, she waited on the porch in the warm darkness. The buzzing cicadas only emphasised the static softness of the night.

She said "Will you be at Penang Lodge tomorrow?"

"I hope so. And I want to see you during the voyage home."

"Yes, that would be marvelous. We'll go ashore together." A final kiss, a whispered farewell and he set off up the Drive, noting as he passed that Penang Lodge was in darkness. It occurred to him that they hardly ever saw any neighbours or passers-by. They've mostly got cars he thought. Then there were the trees and high hedges. Total privacy. At the top of the road the bus approached, and he had to sprint the last two hundred yards to the pick-up point, thereby ensuring he would spend his final minutes here as he had most of the previous eight hours. Panting from one energetic pastime or another.

Shining Star lay at her berth filling up with passengers. He took a seat and watched as latecomers scurried along the pier to catch the last ferry of the day. There were again many well-known faces. "Roger!" This time it was Frank Seymour, carrying a parcel. "Hullo Frank. More gifts?"

"Oh yes. You bet. And I sent that Jap robe off today. By airmail. Right after I got another letter from her." Seymour made himself comfortable, holding the parcel on his lap and beaming at strangers as if he wanted all to share his satisfaction. "What you been doing Roger – seeing that widow again?"

"No, not her. Another one. Chinese girl."

"Yeah?" The man's eyes gleamed in the rainbow light of the neons. "What are they like – any good?" From misery to joy to lust in two weeks. The change in Seymour was startling. The ferry's engine rumbled. The city's illuminations began to recede. "What a really great place this is," said Seymour. "Better than Japan. Oh, I know I got that kimono in Hiroshima but Kure was mostly second-hand stuff. Did you hear that rumour about samurai swords? Some soldiers were making them out of jeep springs and selling 'em to new arrivals. So the story went." Roger heard this with a kind of dull shock. He'd been happy. Now more trouble loomed.

"That can't be true. Jeep springs wouldn't be long enough."

"Well, some kind of scrap metal. Look at that fellow in Hiroshima. There's a lot of smart operators around. And a lot of out-of-work Jap craftsmen. You didn't buy one did you?"

"No, but I encouraged someone else to."

"Well, I wouldn't worry about it Roger. It's only a rumour. Fake swords, stolen kimonos. Who cares now we're on our way home? Anyway it might be a real one he's got. There are some around. I should think the phony ones are easy to spot. Anyone with brains wouldn't be taken in." No, thought Roger. They wouldn't. But we're talking about Farley.

Chapter 16

The following day the real world reclaimed him. Greasy plates and clouds of steam. The Chief Steward's inspection. Before plunging back into it he had a respectful look at the Buddha. Bill caught him at it. "You don't need him to take care of you. Know it all now don't you?" Roger recalled a sign in Tommy Wang's and thought it worth quoting. "A wise man is always ready to learn." Next he sought out Batten. "You, me and Clay. Tonight at 6.30. We're off to Wei Ho again."

"Well done Roger. See you at the gangway." During the afternoon he got his latest photos from Byfield. Again they were perfect. Then for the first time he went ashore with Jack and Pat. "Where are you off to?" asked Jack.

"I'm getting presents. Six to be exact." And was he still barred from Hanni Lu's? "No, it's alright now. I've been back since. I got a friend to fix it."

"Of course you did," said Pat. "Are you quite sure this is your first trip?" As they turned into Nathan Road he was thinking how he might pay for their drinks without appearing too bumptious. These men, and Toddy too, had been amiable and supportive the whole voyage.

Hanni Lu's dominated the street. Thumping with music, the entire building reeked of hot food, beer, smoke and men. "Well," said Pat. "You're the one who's made three hundred dollars since you first hit this town."

"That's right. So I'm buying." They ordered Miranda beers and asked about his "Chinese".

"She's half English. Eurasian. And she's coming back with us."

"So are you thinking of taking up with her at home?" asked Jack. "Only you see, Roger, that can be tricky in England – if you married her. Out here is one thing but at home she'd stand out. Don't get me wrong. I'm sure she's a fine wee lassie but you know how people are."

"I know. Her parents had a spell of it." He hadn't told anyone about last night. Altogether too odd to repeat. After buying two more rounds he made his excuses and left.

At the Kowloon Gift Centre he got his brother Phil a two-tone silk shirt and his father a souvenir leather wallet boasting gold corners and embossed with the Chinese word for Hong Kong. His last buys at this shop were a fluorescent tie for Gordon, his friend in the UK, and a small picture of Repulse Bay to hang on the wall at home. Four down, two to go. Crossing the teeming street, he dived happily into Leung Kee's where the Chokai Buddhas were now six-and-a-half dollars. After a lengthy search he still hadn't found what he wanted. So he tried elsewhere. Yan Chun's, Hung Lee's and many others. Only when he left Nathan Road and explored the side-alleys did he strike lucky, make his final two purchases and hurry back to the docks in time to see the *Empire Fowey* leaving for Japan.

During the bus ride that evening, Clay was pessimistic. "If Hazel's not there I'll find some excuse to come straight back and go to Wanchai. You two have had it all. Me – nothing east of Colombo. And I did all the groundwork. Back in the Red Sea."

"I don't see the point of fretting," said Batten. "There won't be time for anything like that. We've all got to come back tonight. It's just a matter of a few drinks, a meal and say goodbye to — to —?"

"Anna," said Roger. "I've got presents for her and Gina. And photos to show them."

"I was curious about that carrier bag."

"What do these people see in us?" wondered Clay. "I mean – on the ship it's different. Everyone's at it. But why do they invite us into their homes?"

"They're ex-pats," said Batten. "Colonials. They have similar jobs, do the same things, go to the same local spots. Conversationally, they become sort of – inbred. But you get an experienced merchant seaman –"

"Like you?" said Roger.

"Yes if you wish. Like me. A merchant seaman's been around – seen the world. A breath of fresh air. He can tell of things outside their stuffy little society. Places far away and different. Istanbul, Cape Horn, the sidewalks of New York, exciting, gritty places."

Clay said, "You've never been within a hundred miles of Cape Horn."

"Well don't tell 'em that."

At Penang Lodge Gina inspected his scars. "Very impressive. You've really been in the wars." There were two more people for him to meet. Graham Hyde was a pleasant enough man of about forty in a blue suit and a Yacht Club tie. "Hello. So you're Roger. I've been hearing about you from Gina."

"Nothing bad I hope."

"On the contrary, you seem to have done some good. When she went on that vacation she was very low. None of us could pull her out of it."

Talking to Sam was the other stranger, Clay's potential partner, a woman in her late twenties with reddish hair and the face of an angel. But this angel had come down to earth and stayed rather too long. Although still attractive, Hazel Townsend betrayed signs of rather too many parties, that more early nights and fewer gin-and-tonics might be a good idea. On sighting Clay she winked.

"Why – it's Mr Clayton. Are you ready for another late-night stroll along the beach? I'm afraid Harold can't be with us tonight. The poor man had to attend another do over at Repulse. So you're stuck with me and the poetry girl." As she turned away to meet Batten, a crestfallen Clay took Roger aside.

"Can you *believe* it? Last time when I had the whole night and following day off he was with her. Tonight she's unattached – but I've got to catch that bloody night ferry. Of all the ..." He put on a brave face as Gina took him to meet Anna and Sam.

When he could, Roger put his photos in his pocket and stowed the rest of his package in a corner of the hall, ready for a suitable time. With eight people present it was a while before he could talk with Anna. The Eurasian girl was in a plain pink frock with a single row of pearls. It was an awkward moment. "Did you get back in time?" she asked guardedly.

"Yes. I had to run for the bus but the legs were in good shape after all that exercise – I mean the cycling of course."

With a nervous titter quickly checked, she glanced over at the company. "No-one must know about last night Roger. Not ever. Even now I can't think what —"

"It's our secret," he said, wondering how old they had to be before it wasn't a secret.

Gina came over. "Roger, what did you *do* yesterday? Taking her all over the island and then expecting tea and cakes. The poor girl's still getting her breath back. You sailors are so demanding when you want something." The line was so loaded with innuendo they didn't know where to look. Another person was missing. "Sorry Henry," said Gina to a disappointed Batten. "Elaine is over at Repulse with Harold Townsend. Somebody's wedding anniversary. Her horoscope mentioned a journey in the near future. So when the stars command – you obey. If your name's Halley and you believe in all that. Now Roger – Anna and I would like to steal away somewhere and see your photos. We've neither of us been to Japan. Did you collect your prize at the gallery?"

"I did, thanks again."

They entered a room at the rear of the house, where they were surrounded by such a host of religious artifacts he imagined himself back at Tommy Wang's. "My own private collection," she said. "They're all here, every shape and size. Any more and I'll have to start another room. Photography and religion. What a hobby. Cameras and cults you might say."

"I'm the same," said Anna, chuckling. "Poetry mad." Quite a light-hearted comment on her abiding passion. Anna was "emerging". He spaced his pictures out on a table. Gina's were already displayed. Her shots of Singapore were sharp, professional and full of interest. Even the one of himself clutching the Buddha outside the temple. The cheetah pictures had fared less well. "I was wrong about the lighting," she said.

His own shots of the Kure gateway won the approval of both women. "Very good," said Gina. "I've been almost everywhere, but Japan – no. Too soon after the war for me."

Sam looked in. "Anna – can you spare a minute? Graham wants to hear about our new home in Surrey."

He was alone with Gina. And about seventy-five paintings, statuettes and hanging scrolls covered with esoteric writings. Absently she gathered up her photos. "Roger, about Graham. I've known him for donkey's years. I'm confident you won't be silly over it. You and I — it was the ship. The damn ship. Can you really understand what I'm saying?"

"I know all about the ship. The heat and the boredom – all that. There was no harm in it, what happened. And Graham seems OK." He studied her collection. "How do you remember them all – and all these languages? Can you actually read any of it – that, for instance?" Under a set of Hindu miniatures ran a golden line of embroidered Sanskrit.

"Oh, yes. And quite a bit of Chinese too. Well, not Mandarin so much. The local dialect – Cantonese." They heard a burst of voices from the party and she turned to go. "Shall we join the others?"

"I'll never forget you," he said suddenly, knowing they would have no other private time.

"Yes you will. Anna's going back with you tomorrow. You're bound to meet on the voyage. And you're a very young man."

"I don't always feel like one."

She nodded at the Sanskrit text. "Perhaps I'd better translate that for you. It says – Do not fear the coming of old age. Many are denied the privilege."

Dinner was a convivial affair. When he came to look back on that last night in Hong Kong, he would remember most vividly how every person merged seamlessly into the group. However diverse their origins or social level, being there together on that island at that point in history seemed to sweep away all affectation. So Sam Shay, a Wing-Commander no less, talked earnestly to Clay, a seven-pound a week steward. Roger, even lower at the abysmal depth of mess attendant, described his travels to Graham Hyde, a high-salaried government official. "Hiroshima? That must have been an experience for you. And they actually run trains there?"

During this, by ways of smiles and eye-contact, he shared a

wordless conspiracy with Anna across the dinner-table. Batten, even on his third visit had anecdotes for everyone. And Hazel Townsend flirted shamelessly with Clay every time she got the chance. Democratic licence was complete when Maria the cook was invited to join them, although she declined the offer. Towards the meal's end, Gina rose and called for quiet. She began to speak.

"Friends —"

"Romans and countrymen," interrupted Hazel and was quickly hushed by the others.

"Tonight we are gathered to wish *bon voyage* to Anna Shay, the daughter of my long-time neighbours, Wing-Commander and Mrs Shay. Sam was due to go with Anna to join her mother in the UK. But certain people north of the 38th Parallel are being a nuisance so he's been asked – or ordered – to postpone his retirement. Anna will be sailing alone at eleven o'clock tomorrow on the troopship which we've all seen across the harbour. So here's to you Anna – the very best of luck in your new life."

Glasses clinked, the toast was repeated and Anna smiled shyly. "Thank you all very much. I — really don't know what to say."

Hazel gave a rather unpleasant smirk at the others. "You could always recite a poem."

"Alright – I will," said Anna boldly. They watched the slight figure in pink who now seemed so self-assured.

"Here's something appropriate. For me anyway. 'Sea Fever' by John Masefield." Roger knew it well. She took a deep breath. "I must go down to the sea again, to the lonely sea and the sky." The audience sat entranced by the small, clear voice. "And all I ask is a tall ship and a star to steer her by." Nine more lines and she came to the final one. "A quiet sleep and a sweet dream when the long trick's over." She gave Roger a glance that was only for him. And he was the first to applaud, followed by the others when they realised it was finished.

The meal was at an end, the guests free to do as they pleased. "No rules here," said Gina. "Except the ones in mahjong. Or poker if you prefer it. Who wants a game?" Inevitably the younger ones did not. So it was Graham, Gina, Batten and Sam who gathered round the card-table while the others paired off for a walk along the beach.

"I'm not mad about cards myself," said Hazel, taking Clay's arm. "Harold's a keen player. Probably in a game right now over at Repulse. With Elaine I shouldn't wonder. He won't be back till dawn."

"Don't you mind?" asked Roger.

"Good lord no. We discovered the secret of wedded bliss years ago. Both do as you want and no recriminations."

As the two couples drew apart Anna said, "Isn't she awful?"

"Yes – I'm sure the Brownings weren't like that."

She stiffened slightly. "Do you think I'm a — I can't think of the word — yes I can – a bluestocking?"

"No, I certainly do not. If you're the same person I was with yesterday. I saw no stockings, blue or otherwise." Again she gave the guilt-tinged low chuckle that was so beguiling.

Completely deserted, the beach was long and smooth with silky sand that warmed their feet. Startled by their approach, a tiny green crab scuttled away ahead of them, racing for the sea. "He's a bold one," said Roger. "Coming this far up the beach."

"They do that sometimes. I once found one in our garden. They're usually much bigger than that."

"I loved your recitation. That was for me wasn't it?"

"Yes. I thought you'd like it." Poetry, he thought. It would be a long time before he heard any more. But he was quite wrong in that. And there is more than one kind of poetry.

Clay and Hazel were very close. "She's seducing him," said Anna with amazing candour.

He checked his watch. "Then she's wasting her time. We've got to be back aboard tonight. He must have told her. Has she got a car?"

"Yes, but Harold went to Repulse in it." The others had now drawn a long way ahead. "Where are they going?" he asked.

"Well – I think she's going to show him the Glade. That's the wooded area behind the beach. It's a pretty place to walk. Full of beautiful plants."

"And is that what they're going in there for – plants?"

"I'm sure I couldn't say. And as this is my last night in the Colony I'd rather not spend it discussing Hazel Townsend."

"No. We'll stay away from the Glade." They walked on past the wood to where the beach ended in a line of smooth boulders. Here they sat and talked of England till it got late and they started back to the villa. "What time will you come aboard tomorrow?"

The light was fading fast. "About nine I should think. Father's seeing me off."

Passing the Glade again, he said, "I hope they realise it's ten o'clock." Before she could reply, they heard a piercing scream from the wood. Looking shocked, Hazel appeared and hurried away up the beach.

"I'll see what's the matter," said Anna and followed her. Roger waited. Clay emerged from among the trees, his expression that of a dog chained up just short of a prime steak.

"It's all a plot," he croaked. "An evil plot by fate to deprive a man of what he's a perfect right to."

"What happened?"

"I'll tell you what bloody happened. We are getting on like a house on fire weren't we? Kissing and snogging – well away. Having a good old laugh over Gina's speech and the poetry and all that. Then she says I want to show you this lovely place so in we go —"

"Just a minute. You mean she was actually —"

"Yes I'm sure of it. There in the wood. All for it she was. We lay on this grassy part didn't we — looking up at the trees and getting all — you know. Then —" he seemed unable to describe the coming horror "... then this huge great green crab popped out of nowhere and ran over her legs. Monster of a thing." Roger collapsed on the sand, helpless and choking with laughter.

"Well thanks," said Clay. "I'm glad you find it amusing. Me – I've had enough of Wei Ho Bay and its well-bred residents. They're all overpaid layabouts with the morals of alley-cats."

"I thought that's what you were counting on."

At the house they heard no mention of Hazel's crustacean encounter – and it was time now for the many farewells. Anna was leaving first. "I'm still packing even now. Lots of books and things." One by one she received their hugs and kisses. Slipping out to the hall, he retrieved her present and waylaid her and Sam at the head of the verandah steps. "Anna, another book to read on the ship." It was a small leather-bound selection of Shelley's works.

"Oh Roger – that's really sweet of you. Really kind."

"I guessed you'd have everything ever published on Barrett and Browning so I got him instead. Look inside." Her father waited patiently. She took out a folded sheet of paper. "Well I never. 'Trade Winds'. You finished it!"

"I had to rush the last part. Did Hazel tell you what happened in the wood?"

"Only me. No-one else. What a shock."

"I think Clay's suffered most." Heedless now of her father and one or two faces at the window they kissed again – there under the Saigon parasol on the long verandah, the one he'd always known would be there. When he released her she ran down the steps, waved and was gone.

"Roger." Sam seemed almost timid. "I'm glad I've got you for a private word. Didn't seem I ever would." He cleared his throat. "I don't know what your job is and I'm not going to ask. Or what sort of life you have planned in the future." Roger had a distinct "cap-in-hand" feeling. "All I know of you as a person is what Gina's told me and what I've seen of you myself. You – ah – seem straight enough."

The Wing Commander glanced down the beach path. "I know you and Anna spent a long time together yesterday and I won't inquire as to what you may or may not have got up to. She's nineteen years of age, highly intelligent and knows her own mind. Definitely not the foolish dreamer my wife is apt to call her. Whether you continue to see her in the UK is up to her – and almost certainly her mother. So all I'll say is this. I know you can't watch her day and night on the ship but if you take her ashore I expect you to see she comes to no harm. Will you do that?"

"I will."

"Fine, then I'll say goodbye and *bon voyage*." They shook hands and the officer faded into the twilight.

"Roger – we're leaving," called Batten. Again he fetched a gift from the hall, this time for Gina Morrell, the woman who had led him to all this. They went to her artifacts room, where she carefully unwrapped what he'd scoured the streets of Kowloon to find. "Roger — I'm — I don't know what to say. Thank you. It's the most pleasing present I've ever had." It was pleasing. A perfectly sculpted ivory cheetah about seven inches long with twinkling glass eyes and inlaid ebony spots. "He's lovely," she said. "I can see him now on the quayside. Singapore in the rain. He wasn't the only one to slip his leash that night was he? By the way, I've heard from Neville. The old lady's on the mend. And I wrote back saying you might call on them – with a friend."

"Thanks. I will, given the chance. Oh – and here's something else. I'd like you to have all the negatives of the *torii* gate at Kure. And all those I took before. The prints'll do me. You take these and blow them up for the next showing, if you want to."

"Are you sure? Thank you." It was quite an evening for kisses.

"Come back to Hong Kong. Come back and see me and Graham."

"I may not get another voyage. I may get the sack for – being on the wrong deck." Their friendship was such that he could say this and cause only amusement.

"Well if you do it'll be my fault. I should never have introduced you to her."

Batten appeared. "Roger, that bus won't wait for us."

Gina said, "Let me get my car and run you all into town."

But they declined. "We're in plenty of time," said Batten. "If we go now." Hazel had disappeared.

Graham said, "I think she was tired. Or something upset her. The poor thing went home. Alone for once."

And so it ended. The Lodger's last night in Wei Ho Bay. One more round of farewells and Penang Lodge was history. Thoughtfully, they walked up Macau Drive, past the ornamental gates and blossoming hedges of one exclusive property after another. Clay said little, but Batten was in one of his informative moods. "Of course, one day all this may have to go. Hong Kong is only China at one remove. We took a ninety-nine-year lease on it in 1898. When that runs out we have to give it back to them." The place was redolent of the home counties. House-names rang down the decades of imperial rule. Green Gables, Oakdene, Hillview and at least one Mon Repos. They exchanged Good Evenings with a well-groomed lady walking her equally well-groomed cocker-spaniel.

There was no great hurry. They were in plenty of time, but Roger had the old sensation. As usual he could find no reason for it – but it was unmistakable. The evening's events were not over yet. Perhaps the bus wouldn't come. Or there'd be no room on it. Something.

He asked Batten, "Who won the card game?"

"In the end, Graham. I won a couple of hands but I tell you they're experts. We've been very fortunate, the three of us. With these visits. Fine company, wonderful food. Not to mention ..."

"Go on," said Clay. "Don't mind me. Say it. Korey – plenty of korey. For you that is. For me – nothing. Nil. Zero. The big 0. That redhead gave me the old come-on all evening. And the same last time when her old man was there. Now at last she's alone and what am I doing? Going back to the rotten ship!"

"Where does she live?" asked Batten.

"Ocean Heights. We're passing it now."

"Next trip," said Roger. "Wait till then. She'll still be here."

"No!" Clay halted by the entrance. "No," he repeated rebelliously. In the lush undergrowth all about them the cicadas whispered like excited gossips. "You're mad," said Batten. "How will you get over to Kowloon tonight after the ferry's finished?"

"I don't know. I'll bloody swim it. All I know is I'm not passing this up. You go on. I'll see you – when I see you." Brushing past a long bank of white jasmine, Clay started up the driveway of Ocean Heights.

Batten called after him. "You'll be an hour late on sailing day. That's a DR for certain."

Out of the perfumed darkness came a faint "Too bad."

Batten sighed. "That boy will go far. Mostly downhill."

"Why are they so strict about this sailing day?"

"Homeward bound. If you went adrift coming out they could always get you on the way back. Now you'd be left behind."

Dead on time and almost empty, the bus came and they got aboard. There were only five other passengers, three Chinese youths and an elderly couple. In ten minutes they were over the brow of the hill and heading for Central. "Clay's asking for it," Batten went on. "A DR limits you in your choice of ship and hence where you can go in the world. But I understand his frustration. I only hope the Townsends' morals are as flexible as we heard. Time will tell."

As they began the descent towards the northern half of the island Batten's instructional mood continued. "To survive in the Merchant Navy you need to know a few rules. First and foremost, never drink to the point where you don't know what you're doing. Second, treat all women courteously. All women, never mind who they are or what they do for a living. And thirdly, if you're going to disobey orders for your own pleasure, do it in a way you won't be caught. Bribe the right people and have a good alibi."

At this moment, when the city lights already shimmered in the distance, Roger's fears were confirmed. The bus engine faltered. "Rule four," said Batten. "Never get on a worn-out bus. Is this the same one we first had?"

"Now I come to look at it – yes." This time the driver was not the cheery optimist of before but a morose individual with no mechanical knowledge. "Very sorry. No can fix. All must walk. I give money back. Very sorry." Reimbursed, everybody left the bus and started down the road. The driver disappeared. "Gone to phone the depot," said the elderly gent. "It's not the first occasion this has happened. High time they scrapped that bus."

Comrades in misfortune, the seven formed a little company as they trudged along. The Chinese were students returning from a day at Repulse, while the old couple were Colonel and Mrs Foyle. None of them were going to Kowloon. "No good rushing now," said the colonel. "You'll never make the Star Pier by 11.30. Unless you can hitch a lift." But there were almost no passing vehicles, and what few there were ignored their upraised thumbs. "What are you going to do?" asked Mrs Foyle. The students had heard "Star Pier" and clustered around offering advice in their own tongue. The colonel translated. "They suggest you go along the waterfront – try and hire a sampan. And that's easier said than done. I can tell you. I think you'll have to wait till morning." One by one the students left them and then the colonel and his lady reached the point where they too had to turn for home.

"Bit of exercise plus money saved," said the colonel. "Can't be bad. Pity about you two though. Why not try the stone frigate? Royal Navy. Merchant Navy – you're all sailors. They might help you." The couple departed. It was now definitely too late for the ferry, even if there'd been a taxi or another bus. And they hadn't even reached the city yet. "Do you know the way?" asked Roger.

"More or less. I'm not too familiar with this part. And I wouldn't bank too much on the Royal Navy."

"Sam has an arrangement with them for getting across to Kai Tak. What if we rang him up and see if he could help?" Batten stopped to read a sign-post. "It's this way. Yes, we could try." Another tiring twenty minutes brought them to the main gate of the "stone frigate", HMS *Tamar* – a shore establishment.

"On second thoughts," said Roger, "don't let's mention the Wing Commander. This scheme he's got might be strictly on the q.t. I don't want to drop him in it.

"Quite right. And his daughter would hate you for that." Batten approached the young sentry on the gate. "We're merchant seamen and we've missed the ferry."

"So?"

"Through no fault of our own. The bus packed up on our way here. Now we're in trouble if we don't get over the harbour tonight."

"So?"

"I'm an ex-RN man myself."

"So?"

Inside the gate a hut door opened and a Petty Officer came over. "What's going on?"

"Cadgers," said the sentry, proving he could when required manage more than one syllable. "Couple of free-loaders. They think we'll get a launch out and take 'em to Kowloon."

"I realise it's asking a lot," said Batten. "But if you did have anything going that way we'd be extremely grateful. We're sailing tomorrow on the *Garvie* and should have got the night ferry. Only we had a nasty bus accident on the road."

"Oh – it's an accident now is it?" said the sentry treacherously. "You said it only broke down."

"I'm sorry," said the PO with genuine sympathy. "If we laid on transport for every one of you fellows who spent too long in Wanchai we'd be always at it. Can't be done I'm afraid. Try and hire a sampan, or why not go back to Wanchai and make a night of it – then catch the morning ferry?"

"Too late," said Batten. "Thanks anyway."

"You're both well adrift now ain't you?" sneered the sentry. Batten put a hand on the young man's shoulder.

"My dear boy. I suggest you get a little more service in before you become too smart for your own good. We had somebody just like you on the *Illustrious*. In the end we got so fed up with him we tied him up and forced him to drink a cup of vinegar a day. A cup of it – every day." The sentry shifted uneasily.

"How — how long for?"

"Till his balls were pickled." The PO leaned on the gate and wept with laughter. The other man reddened, drew himself up and looked to his front. "That's the beauty of sentries," remarked Batten as they walked away. "They're stuck there. You can say anything and they can't chase you." By now they were near the waterfront. "Sampans," said Batten. "We need to find the sampans." But it was late. Inquiries led nowhere.

"Aberdeen's where they gather," said Roger.

"Yes. Unfortunately Aberdeen's way over on the other side of the island." They passed the ferry pier, now closed and empty, and went on into Central, where the night-life had not yet finished. Batten said, "We'll avoid getting in a state over this and have a quiet drink to think it out." The Lotus Bar was a modest little wedge of a place striving to breathe between an insurance company building and a bank. Reminiscent of a Paris *bistro,* it was narrow but deep, having two long rows of tables and a bar at the far end. Even the Chinese waiter seemed slightly Gallic, with his white apron, slicked-back hair and frequent shrugs. Batten asked for Miranda beers. "For economy Roger. We may need every dollar we possess before the night's out."

It was strange to be sitting there with the problem unsolved. Roger recalled his companion's deft handling of the Irving crisis in Kowloon, the ghastly Weems in Hiroshima and Kropp at his most lethal in Cabin 21. Batten's Micawberish outlook inspired confidence. Something would turn up. And before long something did. A man sidled over and leaned on their table. He wore dungarees and a blue jersey with an anchor motif on the front. Aged about sixty, and an obvious seaman.

"You're English ain't you?" he muttered, and the smell of drink broke over them like a wave. Before they could answer he sat down between them and ordered a whisky.

"Yes we are," said Batten.

"Thought so. Saw you back there going on about sampans. You don't want no sampans. I got a boat. Help me and I'll help you."

"What do you want doing?" said Roger.

"Sweet's the name. Nathan Sweet. I been coming here for years. Sweet by name, sweet by — by —"

"Nature?" prompted Batten.

"Yes, but I don't take no crap from anyone." His voice rose. "Not from anyone. You got that?"

"Yes Mr Sweet," said Batten carefully. The man gulped down his whisky, ordered another, drank it and ordered a third.

"I'll help anyone out, but I won't be imposed on. You want a boat across to Kowloon – alright but don't think I'm one of them sampan boys doing it for money. I'll help anyone out, me." Nathan Sweet was at the stage of inebriation that had him wavering between fear of mockery and the need to be understood.

"What do you want help with?" said Roger again.

Sweet swallowed his third whisky. "I had a woman here," he said wistfully. "Name of Helga. Swedish lady. Every trip I came here I'd be up to her flat. That's till today. Turned me away she did. She's only getting married. Some Yank I bet. More money than me. Turned me away she did. That's Swedes for you. Can't trust them an inch. So what did I do? Went on the booze in Wanchai. Me and old Fritz. He's alright, Fritz. For a Kraut. Used to be a POW. Got back here and Fritz passed out on me. He's never done that before. I had to leave him in an alley someplace."

They exchanged glances over his head. Batten said. "So what can we do for you?" But Sweet was in no hurry, seemingly unconcerned over the fate of Fritz lying somewhere comatose and forgotten. A lover spurned, he would unload his grief on someone.

"Right after the war I got this ship. General cargo. The Coles Line out of Til — Tilbury. And I met this Swedish blonde doing a strip act in Wanchai. Coup — couple of years back." Mr Sweet had begun to hiccup. Not the rudely audible "hic" of the stage comic, but the discreetly silent kind that registered a mere break in speech. "Two years of bliss. Bliss I tell you. I lived only to come here. Then she goes and does this to me. What do you think of that? What kind of wick — wicked person could do that?"

The ever-pliant Helga obviously preferred marriage to a life spent in a Hong Kong flat waiting for a sailor to call once or twice a year. But they had to cross that harbour. So they readily agreed that the heartless hussy had displayed a fiendish cruelty unsurpassed in the history of humankind.

In the course of this tale, Sweet had consumed alcohol at a rate that had the Sino-French waiter almost out of breath. And still he rambled on. "It's gone midnight," said Roger when a break came.

Sweet jumped up. "So what? You're in a hurry? Can't you have the com-common courtesy to listen to a man? I'm off. Go and make your own way to Kowloon. See if I care."

They chased after him "Wait," said Batten. "You said you needed help."

Sweet stopped. "Oh yes. So I do. Fol — follow me." The embarked on what became an after-dark tour of the waterfront. The increasingly wobbly Sweet led them down various dark ways and dead ends.

"Are we looking for Fritz?" asked Roger.

But Sweet had vanished up an alley. Batten said, "Either that or the boat – if it exists."

"Up an alley?"

"Perhaps he's been trying to sell it – raise money to win back Helga."

They found him standing over the insert form of a large man in khaki shorts and a white polo-necked jersey. "I'll lead the way," said Sweet generously. "Pick him up and follow me."

They took one end each and struggled along. Roger said, "Is he dead or alive?" The body's lips moved. *"Fritz liebt – und zehr kranken."*

"There you are," said Batten. "And he's sick too so watch where you walk." Sweet eventually stopped at a wooden jetty where they laid Fritz down. In the gloom they made out a shabby motor-boat. So there was one. But reaching it required descent of an iron ladder fixed to the jetty. It was Kropp all over again – in reverse.

Sweet said, "I'll go down and stead — steady the boat." This he achieved by stumbling down half the rungs and falling the rest. The following minutes were the most nerve-racking Roger had yet experienced. He went carefully down the ladder with the German's feet on his shoulders while Batten followed with one hand on the ladder and the other grasping the man's arm. In this way they shared the weight between them, to finish in a tumbling heap in the bottom of the boat. "Wel — well done," burped Sweet.

Once on their way, clutching the wheel both to steer and to keep from falling down, Sweet seemed to brighten. The cool breeze and the lively note of the engine bucked him up no end. Perhaps thinking of Helga, he broke into song. "If I had the wings of an angel – it's into your arms I would fly." Roger permitted himself to believe their troubles were over. A happy state of mind all too soon dispelled. Batten said, "We're going the wrong way for Kowloon." Stepping over the slumbering German, he attempted to question Sweet which took a while owing to the engine's roar and the man's relentless singing.

Returning, he explained. "Sweet wants to go to his ship first. A little matter of getting Fritz aboard." Abruptly, the singing stopped. Ahead was an anchored ship of about eight thousand tons, with the standard three-island profile of a typical cargo-steamer. Foc'sle, bridge-housing and poop. She had a grim, cheerless aspect. Apart from her feeble riding-lights, there was no sign of life. Roger read the faint lettering on her stern – *Palmirindo. London.* "Sweet," called Batten. "Is this your ship?" But Sweet was now prostrate behind the wheel, trying to raise himself by pulling at the spokes. This caused the boat to describe a wide circle, scraping her whole length against the ship's anchor-chain and taking them back round the stern again.

"Sweet – wake up!" yelled Batten. The man got to his feet and took the wheel again.

"Sorry. Don't know what happened there. Must've tripped."

Someone had seen their erratic progress. "Ahoy!" came a voice over the water. Now there's a word, thought Roger. A word to put salt on your lips and wind in your cheeks. Until now he'd not heard "ahoy" once, anywhere on the voyage. "Ahoy there, the launch," came the call again. "It's only me," was Sweet's rather un-nautical reply. They came alongside to where the boat-falls still hung down.

"Just lash her on," said Sweet. Roger rather inexpertly tied the painter to the forward fall. Hung down the ship's side was a Jacob's ladder which Sweet very slowly climbed to vanish in the darkness. They waited, rolled gently on the black water. Roger said "How exactly do we get Fritz up there?"

"I presume Sweet's gone to get some assistance. That's if he hasn't forgotten about us." Suddenly the big German stirred, leaned over the gunwale and performed a Technicolor yawn of truly Wagnerian splendour. "Fritz – he OK. Now – board ship to sleep." The giant stood and towered over them, swaying so dangerously they only avoided a capsize by rapidly changing their own positions to counter his. The man's remarkable recovery showed in the positive way he mounted the Jacob's ladder. "Auf wiedersehen Fritz," said Batten.

They heard several voices above. "Hey – you there below. Come aboard!"

"I could see this coming," said Roger. "We'd better go or we'll never see Kowloon. But I don't relish it at all. It feels like going on board the *Bounty*."

Among his other talents, Batten was a born mimic. The rasp in his voice was pure Laughton.

"Is this mutiny Mr Christian? Get yourself up that ladder and right smartly or by God sir I'll flay your hide." Up they went. The *Palmirindo* was of a class beloved by readers of sea sagas. Laid down in 1927, she had trudged her way over almost every stretch of salt water known to man. Where there was a cargo, there she would go. A tramp – yes, but a hard-working one. Following the steamer routes of long ago, those unglamorous tracks on faded charts that never saw liner or cruise-ship. There were four men on her weather deck, all similar to Sweet save one who was quite bald.

"We helped him with Fritz," said Batten. "And he promised us a lift to Kowloon."

The bald one said, "Don't worry about that now. Come below and have a drink." They followed the quartet along a dark passage and down an even darker companionway. "Sweet got the old heave-ho from his girl," said the bald man who they heard the others address as Powell.

"Yes we know," said Batten. "It's why he's been boozing."

"Ah – not really. He's the same every time. First he calls on Helga, then it's off to Wanchai with his old friend Fritz. Probably worse this time through her dumping him."

Somewhere in the grimy bowels of the ship everyone entered a room containing a few chairs and tables. Two tables had been shoved together stage-fashion in the centre of the floor. Out came the beer-bottles, grubby glasses and the amber liquid Roger felt he'd been swimming in most of the voyage. Powell put his sea-booted feet on the table and tilted his chair back. There were several other men present but no sign of Sweet. "He's making sure Fritz is alright. Then he'll be along here to do his stuff."

"Stuff?" said Roger.

"His turns. It's always the same when he's had too many. Entertaining his friends he calls it. Loves doing it. Always right as rain next day."

The door burst open and in came Sweet, now wearing nothing but his underpants and a towel safety-pinned round his head as a makeshift turban. None too easily he climbed onto the "stage". The hiccups still plagued him. "Gentlemen of the *Palmirindo.* Once again I am come among you. A selection of mon — monologues for your education and pleasure. First, that immort — immortal work by Mr J Milton Hayes. 'The Green Eye of the Little Yellow God'." Someone said quietly, "Oh no, not again."

"There's a green-eyed yellow idol," announced Sweet in a deafening shout that seemed to startle even him. More moderately he went on, "To the north of Khat-Khatmandu." Roger knew this one. The legend of Mad Carew, the subaltern besotted with his CO's daughter who gets himself killed stealing the jewel she asks for. "Have another beer kid," said Powell. So he did. Because it was that kind of night. His last in this enchanting city. A short while back he'd been at an opulent villa on the shores of a sparkling bay, embracing a slender oriental beauty, mixing with moneyed people, savouring the best of victuals and cultured discourse. Now he was aboard a rusty old freighter in the company of rough-edged working men who were equally as ready to call him friend. And oddly, again listening to verse. "There's a little marb — marble cross below the town. Where a broken-hearted woman tends the grave of Mad Carew, and the yellow god forever gazes down."

The audience fidgeted. "Come on – get to the end of this and let's hear something new." Sweet jerked his head round so sharply the "turban" came loose and fell to his shoulders, becoming in effect a scarf over which he glared at the heckler. "If you can do any bet — better, got your ass up here. If not shut your mouth." Sweet replaced the towel and resumed. "He was known as Mad Carew by the subs at Khatmandu ..." The night crept on. There seemed no end of Nathan Sweet's ability to remember verses, control an audience and remain upright while drunk. All at the same time.

They got "Gunga Din", "Shanghai Lil" and "The Charge of the Light Brigade". Sweet paused for a drink and the offerings got steadily more salacious. Now it was "The Sad Tale of Tommy Brown", "Mary-Sue's Downfall" and "The Bearded Bint of Barcelona". Roger whispered to Powell, "Does he go on all night?"

"Why – don't you like it?"

"Oh yes, it's very good but —" He realised the man was joking. Powell got off his chair.

"Come on. I'll take you to Kowloon." Batten joined them. Sweet stopped in mid-verse.

"And just where do you think you're going?"

"They're leaving now," said Powell.

"No, they're not. I hate bad manners. They'll leave if and when I say so. Maurice ..." A muscle-bound seaman crossed to the door and leaned on it with arms folded. They were prisoners.

"It's alright," said Powell quietly. "Go along with him for a while longer."

Sweet finished his current rendition. "Now – the piece I know you'll all enjoy. The finest piece of lit — littera – chewer ever written. Eskimo Nell!" Roger was aghast. He'd heard this once in the RAF. "Eskimo Nell" was stupifyingly long. There were many, many verses. The men knew it too, scuffing their feet and openly grumbling. He wondered at the hold this man had over them. Another Kropp he supposed. Another King of the Foc'sle.

The lengthy poem was clearly Sweet's favourite. Fragmented by burps, the words and gestures became ever more theatrical till the inevitable happened. Sweet forgot he wasn't on a real stage and simply stepped off it into thin air. Without undue haste a couple of men went to his aid. "Now!" said Powell. The three of them confronted Maurice. "Come on man," said Powell. "He won't remember any of this in the morning. Tell him I threatened to kill you." The man stepped aside and they hurried up the stairs and along the deck.

Batten said, "Do you think he hurt himself?"

They heard an angry shout about bad manners from the stairwell. "He's indestructible," said Powell.

Somebody had pulled up and secured the Jacob's ladder so more time was lost while this was deployed. Next came further panic when it seemed the boat was gone. But it had only drifted out a little. "You didn't lash it up close enough," said Powell. Feet pounded on the deck above. "Find them!" came Sweet's voice. Powell stepped over to the engine. "Oh dear. Sweet took the ignition key." The engine started and Powell chuckled. "Only joking."

"Too late. I've shit myself," said Roger.

Batten said, "I thought you liked poetry."

Only as they slipped away from the *Palmirindo* did Roger feel the end of this momentous shore excursion might actually be in sight. At Kowloon Powell coasted up to the pier and held the boat steady as they scrambled ashore. "Thanks," said Batten. "Will Sweet take this very badly?"

"No – he's alright if you know how to humour him. It's only this Helga business made him worse tonight."

Roger said, "What about the rest of the crew? Don't they get fed up with him? Somebody ought to speak to the Captain."

Powell stared. "Sweet is the Captain." The boat sped away back to the steamer.

"You know," said Batten, "I quite often have a mind to leave the Merchant Navy. Go straight as it were. Live a normal life where you only meet normal people." Their feet echoed eerily in the lifeless streets. Three a.m. is an ungodly hour. Especially if you are far from home. Even Hanni Lu had locked up and gone. Kowloon was gripped by silence and a darkness that contrasted with Victoria over the water, where the long parade of colour was only partially reduced and the tireless neons still blinked at the night. They were so late that everyone, including Bill and Martin were asleep, enabling him to snatch a couple of hours rest before stumbling wearily to Candy's office to "tick on" or report his presence on board. It was 5.45. After reporting he had a few minutes to go on deck and observe the quayside activity.

And as he watched the different groups, soldiers and officials mingling with Chinese workers, he saw a figure at the far end. A young man striding vigorously through the crowd with head held high and a spring in his step. As if all the angels in heaven sang in his ears. Smiling at strangers, he ran up the gangway like a mountain goat. Mr Archie Clayton, in every sense had quite obviously – Made It.

At nine o'clock when Roger, complete with binoculars, was again on deck watching for Anna, Clay told his story. "'What kept you?' Those were her first words. I kid you not. What a woman. Mad for it — like — like —"

"An alley-cat?" said Roger drily.

"The amazing thing is how I got back. You remember what she said on the beach – about doing what they like and no rows? Well, it's true. Harold came back about 4.30. I tell you I had a bad moment when I heard him. He'd had a few, no doubt about it. I thought he'll kill me when he comes in and finds us. But no – it was all pals together. The three of us. And he told her all about his skylarking over at Repulse. Cool as can be. What a weird pair. Likeable, she called me. After going hammer-and-tongs all night – likeable!"

"So how did you get back?"

Clay leaned on the rail with the air of a storyteller at the climax of his tale. "Harold drove me to Central, to some boathouse he's got a share in. Then brought me over in his own private motor-launch." Roger clutched his forehead. "You spend the night with a woman and in the morning her husband gives you a lift home? Nobody's that likeable!"

"Well it happened. I just got aboard in time."

"I know, I saw you. All I can say is – well there's nothing I can say. But I'm glad you didn't lose out after all."

Clay motioned at the crowd below. "I suppose you're looking for Anna. Do you expect to see her on the way home?"

"It'll be impossibly risky on board. But I could maybe take her ashore. Comfort her if she's lonely." He scanned the faces clustering at the gangway. There was no sign of her. Of course he hadn't been watching all morning. There'd been too much to do. The crew mess had received its most rigorous clean-up yet, and been inspected by a veritable phalanx of officers. He'd used the last of his Hong Kong dollars to pay his laundry bill, which in the light of past events was not small. By 10.45 there were no more arrivals. "Changed her mind," said Clay unkindly. "Staying home with Dad after all. Now you can meet her mother at Southampton and comfort her."

So the *Empire Garvie* left Hong Kong. True to form, Roger savoured his memories as they went. He knew that years from now he would want to reach back to this time. Now as they passed that extraordinary island backdrop there was one more reminder. An anchored ship, a nondescript sea-rover he instantly recognised. Smoke at her funnel and men on deck suggested a possible departure that morning. Through his glasses he studied the men on her bridge, one of whom stood apart. Yes, it was him. Miraculously sober in a brass-buttoned uniform, arms folded and legs braced as if for a storm, Nathan Sweet today was the very model of a veteran sea-captain.

In the cabin that night he noticed an atmosphere of quiet contentment. They were only at the mid-point, but the mere change of direction was enough. They were going the other way now. Towards home. Towards – England. The Lodger felt it deeper than anyone. For he was not, in the words of the old song, Saying Goodbye To Them All. He was taking one of them home with him. If she was aboard.

Bill's voice now held no envious undertone. "I suppose you'll be making your white-coated way up to A Deck anytime now."

"That's as maybe. Quinn's made it his life's work to catch me."

Martin said, "You took a risk going to B Deck. But A Deck – that's his personal playground. I wouldn't chance it myself. Not if you hope to come back next trip." The more he thought about it the more insane it seemed. Anyway there was no certainty she was even on board. A last minute change of plan …? And she was not Ruth or Gina. Away from home, beset by strangers and mindful of the proprieties, she would be much less inclined towards secret assignations. But the very next morning on deck it all began again.

"Hullo – you're the Lodger." The man's face was vaguely familiar. "Don't know me out of drag do you? Trixie. Trixie Haynes. At Antonia's wedding, remember?"

"Oh yes. I think you were Marie Antoinette." Trixie gave a girlish giggle, then broke the illusion by hawking coarsely and spitting over the side.

"Penny said I looked more like Old Mother Riley. But listen – I've been talking to Henry Batten. Your friend I believe?"

He wondered what was afoot now. "Yes, I know him."

"And you got a girl-friend on A Deck."

"Have I?"

Trixie glanced around furtively. "I know you have. Batten told me when he spotted her in the saloon. Anna Shay." So she was aboard! "I've met her too," said Trixie. "For the simple reason I'm her BR. She's on my section – A15. Single cabin. So if you've got any ideas ..."

Money, he thought wearily. "You want paying I suppose. B Deck's ten bob but it's more on A Deck, right?"

"No!" said Trixie coldly. "Nothing of the sort. I was offering to be your go-between that's all. As – well as a reward if you like. 'Cos of what Kropp did to you. And then you marching him off to court. All the homi-polones are still talking about it. See this —?" The man pulled up his vest to show a livid scar running from his navel to halfway round his side. "Kropp did that. In a pub in Southampton. Pushed me downstairs and threw a bottle at me 'cos I didn't get out of his way quick enough. Now he's suffered for a change. Forced to pay 200 bucks in Hong Kong – kicked half to death in Japan then dragged behind a jeep after breaking his foot falling down a hole. The swine's gone through hell since meeting you."

"That wasn't me. It just happened that way."

"Well – I don't know. He'll never terrorise me or my friends again, that's for sure. And he's getting the boot at Southampton."

"I'm sorry. I thought you were putting the bite on me."

Trixie pressed his arm. "It's usually a quid on A Deck but not for you Roger. When you want to see her tell me and I'll fix it. Only keep my name out of it won't you?"

"Of course, and thanks."

"I'm a fool to myself I know but there you are. That's me."

The man hurried away. Roger found his thoughts drawn again to the upper decks. For the third time in the voyage there was someone up there to call on. He remembered the light in her eyes as she enthused over the Brownings, and her slim legs on the grass at Shek O. And – First Officer Quinn. When he came to consider it, Quinn was not all bogeyman. There had been a certain amount of rule-bending diplomacy at the Colombo meeting. Quinn had also pushed through the court case to the benefit of all, even Kropp's in a way. The ironic thing was, this had so endeared Roger to certain people they couldn't do enough for him. Hence the offer of access to A Deck. Back on Quinn's patch. Three times lucky. How often can you roll dice before they come out wrong? His life was not really a Kabuki play, despite all the demons he'd got away from.

The South China Sea stretched almost to infinity, stopping only where a long bank of cloud concealed the horizon. And here something caught his eye, an intrusion in the regular mix of sea and sky. A gyrating black column, thick at the top and tapering almost to a point where it met the surface. An inverted witch's hat of unimaginable weirdness, the water-spout was distant yet fearfully fascinating. The thing was a perfect symbol of the oriental world he was leaving behind.

Chapter 17

One thousand, four hundred and forty miles from Wei Ho Bay, the Lodger waited on a Singapore quayside. As expected, there had been no word from Isobel. He'd thought of writing, but adopted his new attitude of "wait and see". Irons in the fire, he thought. What an apt phrase. True to his promise and utterly discreet, the steward Trixie Haynes had arranged a date for him as soon as Anna had settled in. Meeting on shore had been at Anna's request. Trixie offered a reason.

"I reckon she's a bit self-conscious. Worried about being seen going off with a crew member. Once you're away from the ship she'll be alright." Roger considered this. Maybe she also wished to save him from trouble. Gina may have warned her of the ways aboard ship. The perils of trespass.

Again it was to be an overnight stay, departing at noon next day. No-one had the day off, but Jack let him go early from the mess, overriding others' objections. "Let him go Bill. His Chinese is a decent wee lass. Afternoon tea type. And he's got to be back at five." This gave him around four and a half hours. But it was closer to one before she appeared. Anna was immaculately turned out. Hatless, in a simple white long-sleeved blouse, powder-blue skirt and tan shoes. A minute white handbag hung from her shoulder.

"Roger, I'm so glad to see you. Somebody I can talk to at last." He wanted to kiss her but her nervous glance up at the ship told him she wasn't ready for public affection. "Why – aren't you happy where they've put you?"

"I'll tell you about it. Where are we going?"

"I thought we might walk around and I'll show you what I know about the town. That's not a lot. Or we could go and see the Pickards. Gina told them about us. You'll like them."

"Yes alright then."

Walking to town would take a sizeable chunk out of his limited time. They crossed over to where the taxis gathered at the foot of Tanjong Pagar Road. Was he there? Yes, the moustache was visible even from the rear. "Ah – you come back to Singapore. You want temples again sir, yes?"

"No. We're going to the Jade Palace. And I do know the way from here to Sago Street." Taking the hint the man grinned, imparting to the moustache a brief dihedral, like a seagull considering flight.

"OK. For you – quick ride." On the back seat speeding away from the ship they kissed unrestrainedly. As if they were back at the pink villa and it was years instead of days ago. He told her of Nathan Sweet and she described her four days of adjusting to life on A Deck. "What are your fellow-passengers like?"

"I haven't spoken to many. Most of them regard me as an oddity. It's the sort of thing I told you about. They're quite civil but you can see they're not used to a young Chinese travelling all by herself in first class." She smiled wickedly. "Maybe if I offer to do their laundry, or nanny their children? I've a nice friendly steward though. Mr Haynes. All the other women like him too. And he keeps his cabins so clean and tidy. Not a speck of dust. In fact —" her puzzled tone was quite genuine "... he seems almost, well – like a woman himself." He decided not to explain. Repeated too often things got distorted, and he didn't want Trixie upset.

"I hoped for a letter today," she said. "Or a cablegram. From

Father. Maybe there'll be word from him at other ports along the way. I'm terrified he'll be sent to Korea." Reaching the lower end of South Bridge Road they entered the heart of Chinatown. Singapore again. What if they ran into Ruth or Pauline? He assured himself this was unlikely. Anna peered excitedly out of the window. "This is like parts of Hong Kong. See there – that same shop's got a branch in Central."

The Chrysler drew up at the Jade Palace and he noticed she was a little uneasy. "Three dollars," said the moustache. As he paid the man, she was looking doubtfully at the garish façade and seedy surroundings. Appearances of course could deceive and Hong Kong had similar places. But it was unlikely the Wing Commander ever took his family to one. Certainly not Mrs Shay.

The moment they entered Neville Pickard greeted them warmly. "I said to Yingsu when we knew the *Garvie* was in, Roger will be here with his new friend. Have you had lunch?" They said they had, which in Roger's case was untrue. But he could hardly expect her to wait while he had a meal. Besides, he only had a short while to show her round. Anna said, "Roger's got to go back by five, so I will too." He loved her for that. "No need for you to return early."

"Yes, I'll stay with you." It was tacitly understood – they were a couple. Yingsu joined them, introductions were made and they went through the teeming lower restaurant to a private room at the rear.

Here they took their ease while a waiter served drinks. Anna had lemonade. By way of a change, instead of a Sling Roger had a gin-and-lime, the first taste of which brought a rush of memories. Yingsu wore a bright red *cheongsam*, seemingly her favourite style of garment. He remembered to ask after her mother and learned she was now fully recovered. Conversation took a few moments to develop but once begun it was clear they knew of his doings in the two previous ports. Or at least what he'd confided to Gina. "She told us about you being attacked," said Yingsu. "And that business in Kowloon!"

Full details were definitely not for mixed company. Neville however, with his knowing service background, took a fiendish delight in probing for more. "But Roger – why was the American sailor chasing you? What did he want exactly?" Yingsu rescued him before the story got too convoluted. "What have you both got planned for today?"

"I don't mind where we go," said Anna. "I'm content just to wander."

Neville said, "A better idea would be a conducted tour – by car. We'll show you around."

Protests were useless. "What about the restaurant?"

"Reliable Ali. He can handle it. I gave him a rise last week. Best manager you could wish for. It's in the evenings things get lively. I have to be here then. Don't worry, we'll get you on the ship by five."

So they followed the Pickards out to an alley where Neville's car was parked. This was a sedate open tourer of uncertain vintage – the kind once to be seen nudging along native streets in a lofty, imperial way – as if the occupants were forever heading for a meeting with local chieftains. "Better at the back," said Neville. "See more from there." The rear seats were indeed slightly higher, offering an unobstructed view as they drove up past Sri Mariamman and the top end of Hokkien Street. Neville commenced a well-informed description of the area beyond.

"Here's the river now. Over this bridge and we're into the posh end. The cathedral, the cricket club. All your theatres and government offices. Heart of the empire they call it. But for how much longer I wonder?" Yingsu turned round to face them. "Neville will now treat us to his forecast of how the communist insurgents will first take over the Peninsula, then turn all of Singapore into a workers' cooperative. Starting with the Jade Palace."

"Well it might just happen," said Neville. "I know we've only got a few on the mainland at present, but look at Korea. They're not settling for a half a country. We ought to rush as many troops as we can up there. Stop them in their tracks. The North Koreans I mean. Scatter a few bombs even. Here too. Otherwise it'll be 1942 all over again. Caught napping. Too busy making money and playing cricket to see them coming."

Anna spoke then, her first words for some time. "My father's being sent to Korea."

There was an embarrassed silence. "Sorry," said Neville. "I should have remembered. Gina mentioned him in her letter. He's in the RAF I believe."

"Yes. C47s. Dakotas. But I'm afraid they don't carry bombs."

Neville's discomfiture moved Roger to help him out. "Never mind the communists. We're enjoying the ride. What part are we in now?"

"The expensive part. Just coming up to Raffles." They passed St

Andrew's Cathedral, went another block and there was the famous hotel. "I'll admit it's very imposing," said Neville grudgingly. "You can drink an over-priced gin-and-tonic at Somerset Maugham's favourite table and have a bath in a marble tub. Or come to the Jade and get real value for money."

The next thing they saw was a large open space, green and orderly with a few stylish houses along the edge. "Fort Canning Park," said Neville. "Still recovering from the war but they've restored it quite well. The art gallery's been re-opened if anyone wants to see it." There were no takers.

"I'm very partial to museums," said Anna. "If you should have one handy."

"We have," said Neville. "But it's shut today – sorry."

"We'll see one somewhere else," said Roger. "Colombo or Port Said. That's a promise."

"Is there a zoo?" she asked next. There was. Some way into the park they left the car and entered an arched gateway.

"They've only just begun it," said Neville. "It's touch and go whether it gets enough visitors to survive." The animals had the bemused look of new tenants getting the feel of their surroundings. Anna was delighted, moving happily from cage to cage and dutifully reading the printed details below each one. He wondered if Hong Kong had a zoo. Perhaps her mother had never allowed her in such places. From what he'd learned, the absent Mrs Shay had assumed the guise of a female Sergeant Newbury. She would be mindful of the unspeakable practices some animals, particularly monkeys, could get up to when innocents were watching. And then as they moved away from the chimpanzees (who behaved impeccably), the snakes, antelopes and many others, they came to a cage with but one occupant. The cheetah was almost motionless. Only the head moved, very slowly as if assessing the protein content of the visitors. This lack of animation, the animal's very tranquility soon bored the others and they moved on. Roger stayed.

More people arrived, but now the cheetah took not a scrap of interest in them. For it was watching Roger. Intent, unblinking, showing no movement beyond a twitching tail-tip. A young keeper paused on his way to another cage and noticed the odd staring contest. "He seems to know you."

"How long have you had him?"

"This one? He came to us about two weeks ago from Mozambique. We haven't even decided on a name for him yet. Any suggestions?" It was the same animal, of that he was certain. This feline face had stared up at him before. In those smouldering eyes he saw every element of that extraordinary night. When the rain was a solid curtain, lightning split the sky and a woman poured out her heart to him. When they'd talked of thunder, life and death. And gods. Oh – those gods!

"Yes. Why not call him – Thor?" The keeper nodded uncertainly, and looked at him as he left.

Outside the zoo, they went further into the Fort Canning enclave, along neat paths between sparkling fountains and vivid floral carpets. "Marvellous isn't it?" said Neville with a wide gesture. "You wouldn't believe how this part looked when the Japs left." More darkly he added, "Or what they got up to here." The others had become a little restive. Neville veered between the roles of amusing guide and grim historian to such a degree they approached each new sight with mixed feelings. Yingsu drew Anna aside. "There's something here I'd like you to see. You men go on. We'll catch you up."

The women passed through an elaborately carved and painted moon-gate, a huge circular stone ring set on edge between rampant lions of green marble. "It's another temple," said Neville. "I'm sure you've seen enough of those in your travels." His demeanour had changed. As they walked he no longer pointed left and right at things of interest. "How well do you know Anna?" he asked suddenly.

"Since Hong Kong outward bound. We have slept together. Is that what you were wondering?"

Clearly surprised by this, Neville was silent for a spell, then began again. "Roger, you're a friend of Gina's. So is Anna. It's a case of any friend of hers – you know what I mean. Otherwise I wouldn't be saying this. You and this girl are decent enough people, I can see that. But I wonder if you're aware of the other side of the picture. If you should get serious." More warnings.

"I know all about that," said Roger. "And I don't care. Anyway there's no suggestion of marriage. Not yet anyway."

He didn't really want this discussion, however well-meaning the man was. Neville continued. "It's none of my business I know. Of course oriental women make simply wonderful partners, that I can tell you. Well – look at me and Yingsu. And Anna's parents, although I've never met them. It can work – out here. But —"

"England's different?"

"Yes. We've got friends there and we've heard some tales."

"The Shays seem willing to try."

"They're used to it. And they move in different circles. According to Gina they're quite well-off. His wife won't be standing in a bus queue. Sorry, no offence intended."

When the women rejoined them he could tell from Anna's face she had received similar advice. Back on the road, the somewhat condensed tour of Singapore continued on its humid, sun-bright way. They saw Little India, Mount Faber and the Nagore Durga Shrine, followed by a visit to the former home of Sun Yat Sen. At 4.30 Neville drew up at a roadside tea-garden. "Back at five you said Roger?"

"Afraid so, yes."

"Right then. As it's time for afternoon tea why don't we drop the ladies off here while I run you to the ship. Then we'll all come together again tonight around seven for dinner." It wasn't what they wanted. They wanted to be together, stroll among the crumbling old streets of Chinatown – savour the last of Far East before sailing away from it. Maybe forever. But they didn't refuse. She gave him a wistful smile and entered the tea-garden with Yingsu.

In South Bridge Road, Neville said, "About Anna. Do you get any chance to meet her on the ship, or are there rules about that?"

"There are rules, and I've broken them too often to risk it again."

"In that case why not stay ashore with her? You're here overnight. I'll fix it for you. Little hotel tucked away on Taiping Street. I know the owner. Quick phone call." A startling suggestion. He couldn't see her agreeing to it.

"Thanks. I'll see how things turn out." They were nearing the dock area and journey's end. He felt a need to change the subject. "What make of car it this?"

"It's a pre-war Fiat. Belonged to a major stationed here. When the Japs came they commandeered everything with wheels but they didn't get their paws on this. The major hid it away so well they never spotted it. He ended up in Changi camp with me and John Morrell. Told us all about it. Said if we survived we could have it. Can you imagine that? Three half-dead skeletons racked with dysentery talking about a car! But that's how it was then. Anything to keep your sanity. When we finally got liberated Morrell was too ill to walk, never mind drive. So – after six months in hospital, I got possession."

"The major never made it?"

"No. He's — still there. At Changi. No 20. Row 15. Plot 12. Sometimes I go there – to where he is. Just to talk. Stupid I know. But I like to think he's listening." At the gangway, Roger thanked his host for the afternoon's hospitality. "Don't mention it." Neville was back to his jocular self. "We'll look after Anna and take her back to the Jade. You come there tonight and we'll treat you both to a real Singapore dinner. About seven. Afraid I can't come and pick you up though. Always on call in the evenings – busy time." As usual, the gangway sailor was taking a keen interest.

"What do you make of us Roger?" said Neville unexpectedly. "How do you see us ex-pats out here in our tropical paradise? I suppose to you we're living the life of Riley."

"No. I may have thought that when I first came. But since then I've got to know enough of the Far East and the war to see something else. There's another side to all this. A black side. Memories. Everyone's got them. Whatever they make of their lives here they've earned it. I wish them well."

Neville laughed. "Roger, you may be young but you're a shrewd bugger." The Fiat purred smoothly away.

"So," said the gangway sailor. "The Lodger returns. I must say that thing's a big improvement on the jeep." Down in the cabin he sensed in the men around him an urge to get the tiresome chores over and done with, climb into decent clothes and escape the ship. Outward bound, Singapore had been their first overnight stay. Going home it would be their last.

"Oh yes. We're all ashore tonight," said Bill, nearly salivating at the prospect. "Except the Lodger of course. He don't even need to go ashore for it do you? I don't know why you went off with her today, your Chinese. Spending money on her if she's coming back aboard anyway."

Jack said, "I rather think this one's different."

"Phooey! They're all the same out here." Bill's attitude to other races was the standard one. An unyielding xenophobia strangely allied to an urge for intimate contact.

"I am going ashore," said Roger. "For an oriental-style dinner."

"Another posh blow-out?" said Martin weakly.

"Personally," said Pat, "I don't care for food that grabs hold of the plate when you go to eat it."

By six-fifteen he was off the ship with time enough to make the town on foot, conserving his remaining supply of dollars for whatever the night might bring. Her and there he saw crew-members, but it was soldiers who filled the streets – riding rickshaws, thronging the bars and shops, chatting with every girl in sight. The Far East, seldom truly stable, was again stirring. In the north, the Koreans marched to war, red banners flying. And here in Malaya the same ideology drove other men to attack the perceived enemy. So the troopships ploughed the seas, and the pale young men again trudged the alien ways – seeking what tawdry pleasures there were before the horrors that may come in a week, a month.

Turning into Sago Street, he passed a cluster of six soldiers outside a bar. This particular hostelry called itself the Wee Hame, an attempt to bring a homely touch to a structure that looked as Scottish as a Shinto temple. As he went by, a corporal with red hair strode away and was recalled by the others. "Hey – Jamie! Where ye going?" The Glasgow accent he now knew so well, sawing the sticky air like a rusty knife. "Come away man. This place'll do us fine." He noticed that every shoulder-patch bore the name of a Scottish regiment and each man wore the Glengarry cap with its chequered band and short black ribbons.

At the Jade, a man in a cream jacket with a green sash introduced himself as Ali, the restaurant manager. "Please to follow me sir." Heading for the marble steps, Ali led him through the lower restaurant where more *Garvie* people were partaking of the Jade's offerings. A real Singapore dinner Neville had said. With some trepidation he recalled the items he'd seen on the upstairs menu that first day – and his stomach wanted to run back to the street. But surely, if he could eat bamboo shoots in Hong Kong and raw fish in Japan …? At this hour the upper room was livelier than before, but still had an air of genteel restraint noisily absent downstairs.

Yingsu and Anna were at a four table. "Hello Roger," they said at exactly the same time, looked at each other and laughed. He greeted them and took his seat, feeling unexpectedly *gauche*. They were so coolly elegant, these oriental women. They never seemed to slump, or put on weight – or even *sweat*. "Where's Neville?"

"Downstairs," said Yingsu. "It's our busiest time of the day." He glanced at the menu. The grisly list was still there. Everything, it seemed, that crawled, swam or flew was fit to eat.

Presently Neville joined them; greeting Roger with such rascally, secret-sharing good humour he regretted confiding in the man. If he'd told his wife, and she'd told Anna …! But all seemed well. Anna was quite at ease, telling of the place they'd had tea. "We had muffins Roger. And cucumber sandwiches. Getting in practice you see, for England."

"I hope the tea was Cambodian." At the reminder she was briefly alarmed and warned him with her eyes.

"Now," said Neville. "What are we having? There's an old Chinese proverb – anything that moves with its back to the sun is edible. And no – I don't quite understand that either. How about baby squid? Now they really are delicious. Or the old staple, sharks-fin soup? We've also got eel curry, although that's more of a Saigon speciality." Already reeling at the thought of baby squid, Roger underwent further panic when Anna, reading the menu, said, "How about steamed pigeon hearts?" He realised they were watching, and his face betrayed him. "Whatever you say." They broke into peals of laughter.

"I think we've scared him enough," said Neville. "Don't worry Roger, we're only having you on. To anybody fresh out from England these dishes are very much an acquired taste. Besides, we promised you an authentic Singapore dinner. There are differences. And we won't make you use chopsticks." Guests of the owner, they rated the very best of service with two waiters in attendance. The food dazzled in variety and taste. Portions were not large but very numerous, each following the other in a colourful parade. One in particular he liked so much it must have showed.

"You like that?" asked Yingsu. "It's called *mee siam*. Can you guess what it is?"

"Not exactly but it's very good."

"Vermicelli," said Neville. "With soya beans, eggs and grated nuts. In a sweet and sour sauce."

The exotic dishes came and went, his wine-glass was never empty, and as the evening wore on the three figures before him acquired the unreal aspect of creatures in a dream. The lean, bearded man talking with all the assurance of the long-serving ex-pat, and the two achingly beautiful women, Yingsu in the inevitable *cheongsam*, this time of pale lemon – and Anna in her more homely, but no less stylish attire. A waiter whispered to Neville and he stood up. "Excuse me, I've got to attend to something. Back in a minute. Carry on."

"Evenings are when we get these disturbances," said Yingsu. "Somebody argues over the bill or they just can't behave. Ali or Neville can usually deal with them. We only need to call the police about once a fortnight. If it's outside in the street someone generally calls the redcaps."

Neville returned. "Who's for dessert?" Another taste-bud adventure.

"This is called *chendol,*" said Yingsu. "It's jelly and palm sugar with iced coconut milk." They had their *chendol,* and very strong coffee in tiny cups.

"We'll be gone from this country one day," said Neville. "We all realise that. I just hope the communists don't get their way. Somehow I don't think they will."

Roger said, "You weren't so confident earlier."

"I know. But the more I think about it the less likely it seems. They're good people, the Malays. They all are, all the different races here. Good, honest and hard-working. They enjoy life, especially the Singaporeans. And you can't be a communist and still enjoy life."

The banquet was finally over. While the women went off on a mission of their own, Neville took Roger aside. "Well, you'll be pleased to know I rang my friend and he's quite happy to accommodate you both for the night. The Niagara Hotel on Taiping Street. You pass it on the way to the docks. I couldn't get him to waive the bill but it'll be small. Around nine or ten dollars."

"Thank you. I remember seeing it." He wasn't sure how he felt about this. Would she need an oil-lamp again? So much could go wrong. It was an alluring thought though. There were hurrying footsteps on the stairs. Ali appeared.

"Mr Pickard sir. I'm sorry. Please come. A man's gone mad, holding another man by the throat. I didn't want to call the police till I told you. He's – on crutches with his foot in plaster."

"Good Lord – why would anyone attack a cripple?"

"No sir. He's the attacker – the one on crutches." Yet again, thought Roger. Yet again that Neanderthal enters his life.

"I may know him," he said. "Is he a Scotsman?"

"Yes sir I believe so."

"Drunk?"

"No. He's got one drink in front of him but he's had it a while." Well, the man was said to have moderated his ways. They descended the stairs and his fears were confirmed. In the middle of a small crowd was Kropp, his fingers clasped around the neck of a purple-faced young soldier who was on his knees. This time the shoulder insignia was of an English regiment. Oblivious to his own injury, Kropp was balanced on both feet and his two crutches. With his arms stretched out and his head sunk between hunched-up shoulders, he had a six-legged appearance, as of some monstrous insect. Hampered as he was, he must have pounced like one to seize his prey.

"Let him go please," said Neville.

"No I won't. Not till he takes back what he said."

Carefully, Roger allowed himself to be seen and received a grunt of recognition.

"Kropp – if you go on with this it'll be the police again. Let the man go."

But the new Kropp had retained all the sweet tolerance of the old. "I'll kill the bastard."

Roger had a thought. "If the police come they'll arrest you. They have night courts here. You could be fined again. Another two hundred dollars – or three!"

Kropp frowned at this awful possibility. "OK. But first he takes back what he said. Come on, let's hear you."

The luckless victim blinked and licked his dry lips. "Scot – Scotland is not where all the queers in the world first came from."

"Right – now say about the kilt. Go on!"

"And the — er — the kilt is not just a girl's skirt by another name." A titter ran round the bystanders and was quickly stilled by a glance from Kropp.

Released at last, the soldier made a hurried exit, massaging his neck and muttering. "Crazy. Ought to be locked up. Bloody lunatic."

Kropp hobbled to his chair and flopped down, let his crutches fall with a clatter and almost delicately took a sip of his drink. "Anyone else?" he growled. "Anyone else want to make remarks about Scotland or the Scots?"

The invitation was not taken up. The buzz of conversation restarted and Neville gave a sigh of relief. "Another crisis over."

The women came down the stairs. "What was all that about?" said Anna.

"What one might call a border clash," said Neville. "Roger, I didn't hear what you said to him but it worked. Is he a close acquaintance?"

"Too close. He's the one who gave me these scars."

"Ah, so that's the gentleman is it? The original 'ugly customer'. Now you're quite sure you can find your way back?"

"Yes we'll be OK. Thanks for the dinner and everything." The Pickards accompanied them to the door where the final farewells were said. Coming from the bright interior they paused for a second adjusting to the change, for it was now dark – that steamy, sensual dark that falls so swiftly in the tropics.

"Which way?" said Anna.

"To the right. Make our way back. It's late. We can see the shops as we go. Would you like that?"

"Yes. I'll get some cards." As they left the Jade, a figure was lurking behind a square pillar near the entrance. He recognised the recent recipient of Kropp's displeasure. The man came over.

"Is that mad Jock a pal of yours?" Anna had walked on a little way.

"No," said Roger and at once felt strangely disloyal. "No, not really – why?"

"The bugger nearly did for me," said the soldier. "I don't care if he has got a bad foot, he had no call to do that. Thinks he's hard. Well – he's got to come out sometime. Then we'll see who's hard. If you don't want to get involved take your Chinese tart and scram."

Roger caught up with Anna, thankful she'd not heard the last statement. They passed the Wee Hame. Across the street was a small souvenir shop. "Let's go in there," he said with a backward glance.

Kropp was a foul-tempered loner who brought all his woes on himself. Why should he care about him? But he did. He just did and there was no explaining it. While she wandered among the offerings he stayed in the doorway observing events. The soldier still loitered by his pillar watching the Jade Palace. Presently the man put two fingers in his mouth and whistled. Another man crossed the street and joined him. With his upright stance, cropped hair and neatly pressed shirt he might have been a soldier in "civvies". The first man fingered his throat and spoke rapidly, pointing at the Jade. The accomplice peered in the door and nodded back at the other. Again, it seemed Kropp was to be ambushed and set upon. But there could be no warning this time. And even if there were, Kropp would insist on doing battle. He would be felled and beaten senseless with his own crutches.

Once there had been a time when he couldn't have visualised

these things. But that was long ago. Before Weems and the hapless Zero. Before this voyage and the constant reminders of what men did when driven by rage or contempt – or drink. Engrossed in the goods on display, Anna went further into the shop, and he took another look along the street. The two men had been joined by a third. And he knew there was only one solution to this – a bundle. It took but an instant to dash over the street and into the Wee Hame. Would they still be there after all this time – and not too drunk?

The place was a conglomeration of eastern and pseudo-Scottish décor. Phony-looking stag heads drooped miserably over Shanghai silks and tartan drapes. Crossed claymores gleamed in the light of flickering paper lanterns. The half-dozen Scottish soldiers sat in a corner alcove. They were chillingly – and amazingly – sober. He recognised the red-haired Jamie. Boldly, he plunged.

"Excuse me." One by one the Glengarries turned his way and his nerve nearly went. Whichever way he put it the words would be a challenge. A gauntlet tossed at the feet of a troupe of glowering medieval knights. "Are there any Glasgow men here?"

"Who wants to know?" said one.

"And why?" said Jamie.

"I'm from Glasgow," said the first man.

"And me," said another.

"Why?" repeated Jamie.

"There's three people waiting to beat up a Glasgow man when he leaves the Jade Palace. A merchant seaman on crutches. He fell into an empty dry-dock."

"Why three of them, if he's a cripple?"

"He's strong, this one. Really hard. I've seen him fight."

There was no discussion. Wordlessly the pint glasses were drained, cigarettes stubbed out and the proud chequered caps carefully folded and tucked into shoulder-straps. "One thing," said Roger. "The owner of the Jade is a personal friend. I mean I wouldn't want ..."

"Dinna fash yersel' over that," said Jamie. "We'll get 'em outside." He studied his team. "Henderson – Macleod, stay here and get another round in. Four of us'll do for these jokers." The quartet marched out. Henderson (or Macleod) said, "They shouldn't be long. Stay and have a drink."

"No, thanks all the same. I've got someone with me."

Hastening back, he found her still at the rear of the shop. "I've bought some cards," she said. "I didn't change much money with the other ports to come."

"Let me get you something." But she wouldn't hear of it.

"I shall treasure that Shelley you gave me. And 'Trade Winds', your own piece." On the street again he glanced back at the Jade Palace. Jamie's group had confronted the waiting attackers and commenced a nose-to-nose argument. Then came the pushing and shoving – and the first blow. More men arrived and quickly polarised into opposing sides. "Something happened down there," she remarked.

"Yes. Let's steer clear of it. I promised your dad I'd take care of you."

"I know. He told me."

It was still depressingly hot, but turning the corner into South Bridge Road they faced a welcome if feeble breeze. As she took his arm he experienced the peculiar thrill he always felt when the atmosphere got to him. All over Chinatown a mantle of light had sprung up. Yellow lanterns and guttering naphtha flares, a clutter of neons all striving to banish the gloom. The ebb and flow of exotic odours and sounds, the changing pattern of colourful signs along the street and the jewel-hung sky overhead. The sheer other-worldliness of it.

And above all the presence of the girl. Like him a stranger here, yet with features identical to those around him. In a complex way, she was a part of the very thing they were sharing. Sighing, she glanced about her. "It's sad seeing this. I know it's not Hong Kong but it's so much like it I feel I'm leaving home all over again."

"We don't really have to return yet. I don't need to be back on the ship tonight." He paused. "So — if you'd — rather stay ashore somewhere ...?" He left the words in the air, not entirely sure she'd heard him. They came to a part where the merchandise spilled out over the sidewalk, obliging them to cross the monsoon gully and run the hazard of hell-bent taxis and rickshaws. "No place to be riding your bike," he joked.

"I notice you like to remind me of that day."

"Does it trouble you?"

"No. It was a wonderful time."

Carefully he said, "I know of a hotel. We could go back late. As late as we wish."

"Oh I don't think I could. Not a hotel." They said nothing more, and he wasn't going in for any persuasion. Let things take their course.

If he had to venture up to A Deck – so be it.

It was the sixth time he'd travelled this road. He knew they would soon be at Taiping Street.

"Tell me," she said. "What exactly is your job on the ship? Gina only said you were in catering." The question they all asked sooner or later.

"It's not very grand." He told her what he did, and there was no way of making it sound important, or even interesting.

"But you won't always be doing that?"

"No, I may try in the future to become a waiter – a steward. I'm in no hurry. Plenty of time to see the world. Hop around on different ships for a few years."

"You don't sound very ambitious."

Before he could reply, a small open-top truck shot out of Taiping Street and squealed to a halt before them. There were two men in the front and in the back four more sat facing each other. All six wore peaked caps with red tops. MPs again, British this time. The driver beckoned.

"Do you know this town?"

"Some of it."

"We're new here. Replacements. Where's Sago Street?"

"Up here, third on the left. Opposite Erskine Street. What's up – trouble?"

"Yeah. Street bundle. Bunch of jocks outside some night-club." All this mayhem. And he'd started it. But no, he told himself. Kropp began it. And his victim had sought revenge. It would have occurred anyway.

"These things can get out of hand," said the redcap. "I've seen it in other places. They can spread. If I were you I'd get off the street. Both of you, before they come down this way." The truck roared off in a sharp curve, and the red-topped heads swayed in unison like flowers in a window-box.

She gripped his hand, and her amazing almond eyes reflected the lights of the street. Her voice was scarcely audible. "Where exactly is it – this hotel of yours?"

"Along this side-street."

"You've done this sort of thing before haven't you?"

"No never. Not here or anywhere else."

The two-storey Niagara Hotel had seen better days, but still retained an aura of crumbly pretension. He sensed her nervousness as they neared the reception desk. It was in fact new ground for them both. At home was one thing. This was a hotel – akin to promiscuity, wantonness. And how would she react if someone said "Ah – Mr Wren. We were told to expect you"?

The Malay clerk watched their approach. Here was another one with some girl picked up in a bar. He'd pay whatever he was asked. When he spoke there was just the trace of a leer.

"Yes – can I help you?"

"We'd like a room. One night." To his relief, she crossed over to a couch and sat pretending to study her postcards. The clerk picked up his pen.

"It'll be sixteen dollars and fifty-five cents. What name is it?"

Sixteen dollars! "Wren. Roger Wren." The clerk looked up sharply, said "One moment" and darted into an office. He heard his name repeated and the man returned. His attitude had undergone a remarkable change. "I'm really most sorry sir. My mistake. It's only eight dollars." Roger paid up and was given a key. "First floor. No 42. And you get your own bathroom with it," he added proudly. As they ascended the stairs he saw a second man watching him from the office. Neville's friend, if it was he, was a thickset Chinese wearing an old-fashioned smoking jacket.

The room was plain, but clean. Dark wood furniture and ochre walls. A medium-sized bed and an open window looking out on the street. From the ceiling hung a single bulb inside a glass cone adorned with blue and green triangles and a fringe of two-inch tassels. There was a door marked Bathroom in three languages. On a wall was a framed magazine photo of Edward, Prince of Wales on a pre-war visit to the colony. "Very cosy," said Roger to break the silence.

"I can't go through with it," she whispered. "Not here. It's not the same." From the street outside came a shouted oath and a gale of raucous laughter. He closed the window and drew the threadbare curtains. The sounds were reduced but with no breeze the heat soon became oppressive. When he turned back she was sitting on the bed fingering the white handbag. He couldn't believe the sudden barrier between them, as if their former intimacy had never taken place. It was the setting of course. The strange room, someone else's bed. A distinctly sordid feel to it all.

He sat beside her. "You're right. If you'd rather not it's OK. We can go back now if you like."

"But you've paid them."

"We had Wei Ho Bay. I'll never forget that fantastic day. Or the evening! That oil-lamp!"

"I can't imagine what you thought. A madwoman."

"Not at all. I've often felt quite strange myself. Ever since I got to South-east Asia. What with all these gods and dragons and joss-sticks." For a moment he thought he may have blundered. She herself was half-Asian. But she gave a wan smile so he continued. "We're both of us a long way from our homes. In an unfamiliar place. Like the Brownings." His friends from another century. The two lover-poets reaching across the decades to cast their spell. His arm stole round her shoulders. "This is how they must have felt after they'd escaped to Italy. Remembering the home country and trying to recapture what they'd known there."

With a cool deliberation she put her lips to his ear. "You're doing it again aren't you?" The bathroom door closed softly behind her, leaving him to his own thoughts. Quite clearly she was of like mind, only hampered by some rediscovered inhibitions, the seedy surroundings and the lack of any decorous way of preparing for this. And the deadening, tenacious heat. A brief rattling came from the bathroom and she gave a little cry of annoyance. Look after Anna her father had said, and so far he he'd done so. Desperately wanting her, he was equally resolved to do this right. God knows, he thought, I've been lucky. Leave it up to her. There was also the small matter of getting aboard the ship by six.

He lay back on the bed, staring up at the hideous lampshade and wishing it was one of Neville Pickard's ceiling fans. This time the only other face in the room belonged to the Prince of Wales, and he was busy taking the salute. After an age, she reappeared. Her sleeves were undone, her blouse hung outside her skirt and her hair was damp at the edges.

"Your turn. Mind the cold tap. The handle's loose." In the bathroom he stripped to his pants and ran the cold water, forgetting her warning. The handle clattered off into the sink, and he heard her laugh. When he emerged again, her clothes were on a chair and she was on the bed with only a sheet as cover. Her dark hair lay on the pillow and a bare shoulder peeped over the sheet.

After the short-lived relief of the cold wash the room heat seemed even worse, so he opened the window wide. The narrow street was peaceful now except for a subdued jazz beat issuing from a rather shabby drinking-club opposite the hotel. Above this, on the same level as the window hung a giant vertical sign made up of bright Chinese characters in alternating pink and lavender neons.

Room 42, despite royal pictures and private amenities, did not run to a bedside lamp. But by now dark rooms gave him no trouble. He switched off the light and right away noticed a startling effect. The street-sign outside cast an eerie two-tone glow over the entire room. Everything was bathed in a soft-edged pattern of pink and lavender.

Turning slowly onto her back she murmured, "Roger – this is so wicked." But in her voice was a tiny note of devilry she failed to hide.

"I know," he said, getting under the sheet. "But it would be even more wicked to pass it by."

"How very true," she said solemnly, and broke into giggles. After a few minutes of mutual caresses she slowly sat up and looked down at him, seemingly unaware of the extraordinary twin colours now rippling across her naked body.

"Who needs poetry?" she said teasingly. He could hardly speak.

"Not us," he gasped. Throwing off the sheet he reached up and pulled her down to him. And as they lived and loved, there in their third-rate hotel at the fag-end of town, he knew there would never be a time quite like this. When so many sensations came together at once. The lurid hues dancing over them, the distant keening of jazz filtering in the window and the ever-present humidity moistening their limbs as they writhed. Time passed unnoticed, a trifling thing with no place in their world.

For him, the thought that they would part at Southampton was unbearable. Surely they could go on with this. Get married? No – from habit he shied away from that. For the moment. Maybe later. See how they got on away from the ship and surrounded by relatives.

"I don't want this to end," he said tensely. "When we reach UK will you – will you …?"

She put a finger to his lips. "Roger, is this a proposal?"

"Well, it's more of a *proposition*." The chuckle this caused was definitely one of relief. As if like him she wanted to ride the wave a while longer before enormous decisions were made. Leaning over he kissed her long and lightly as he'd done the first time at Shek O. "I was going to suggest we carry on seeing each other in England. You can tell me where you'll be living. Surrey wasn't it?"

"Yes. Reigate. But it could never be the same as now, you must see that." Why not, he thought, but decided against pressing the subject. Lying back again he turned towards the window and the strident neon shapes over the way. Those glowing glass tubes – they were a part of it. The magic of this night. Everything was. A dingy retreat in Chinatown and this sweet-faced half-oriental who brought such bright joy into his life. Even the brawling in the streets. He felt he was living in a film. One of those Hollywood B-movies with a moody soundtrack, sultry heroines and a villain who always had a rumpled white suit and a name ending in a vowel.

For a while longer they talked, and there was much to say. For all their new expertise, they were still relatively innocent. They discussed life with a kind of quasi-maturity which vanished when they remembered where they were and precisely what they were doing. Eventually Roger held his watch up to one of the pink beams. "It's one-thirty. We needn't leave till around five to make it by six."

Horrified, she said, "No – we can't return in broad daylight. They would all know – or guess. I can just hear them, those officers' wives. That Chinese girl spent the night ashore with a man! No, I'd rather go now while it's still dark. That way as far as they're concerned we've been out dancing or to a late party. Like a lot of them." Before turning on the light he had a last look at the sign.

"What *is* that thing telling us? Can you …?"

"Read Chinese? Well I should hope so. It says – May Lee's Junior Dance Academy."

"Over a bar?"

"Perhaps one pays for the other. Or they share the rental." The humour served to bridge the cheerless minutes of dressing and taking their leave of the rainbow-lit room.

"Don't forget your bag," he said. In the foyer the clerk dozed at his desk. Roger hung the key on its numbered hook. Out on the street they turned their backs on the Niagara Hotel and May Lee's Academy. "We could have a taxi," he suggested.

"No, let's go on foot and slip aboard quietly." Not for the first time Roger was walking in an Asian city at dead of night. They didn't speak much now. The wild excursion to freedom was nearing its end. The ship beckoned — and the ship was reality. She said, "There's three more places we might go ashore."

"Two," he corrected her. "I daren't show my face in Aden."

"Yes, you mentioned that story at Gina's." A taxi whizzed past heading for the docks, and a ribald cheer told him they'd been spotted. To his dismay, it stopped.

"Well – well! Look who it is. Roger Wren's got himself all fixed up for the night. Bit late I'd have thought. Where you taking it Roger?" He recognised the men crowding the taxi. Two seamen, a steward and a barman. Faces flushed and perspiring with the evening's indulgence, they ogled Anna like starving jackals. He didn't reply. Together they merely stared back at the men. The guffaws petered out and the spokesman gave a parting cackle. "Don't do anything I wouldn't do."

The taxi went on its way. He said, "I'm sorry about that," and couldn't have meant it more. There was no response other than a weary sigh. At the ship they waited out of sight till the taxi had emptied and departed. "Have you got your pass ready?" he asked her.

"Pass? Nobody gave me a pass. Have you got one?"

"I don't need it. I've got my crew card. They should have given you a re-boarding pass when you left the ship today. What about your passport?"

"It's in my cabin. Surely you can vouch for me, tell them I'm a passenger." More trouble. He hated the thought of a scene at the gangway. There was another route. The gash-bin access, the short work entry astern. At this hour the galley would be deserted. "I know – this way." They retreated behind the sheds and emerged again near the stern. "No!" he groaned. The short cat-walk was gone, the shell-door closed. It would have to be the main entry.

The entire dock area was devoid of humanity, the ship itself dark except for a few up-lights at the base of each funnel. Yet as they walked along the quay it seemed a hundred eyes followed them, that every porthole watched their lonely progress. The Lodger and his Chinese bit. Crawling back at two o'clock in the morning. No matter that they were quite sober. At that hour everyone was said to "crawl back". As they commenced the gangway climb he said, "Better let me go first."

The friendly sailor of the other watch was long gone, replaced by a doleful individual who clearly detested his job. This man checked Roger's card and then studied Anna who was still at the top step. "Who's she?"

"A passenger. They never gave her a boarding pass when she got off."

"Oh really? She don't look like no passenger of ours. Why were you trying to smuggle her aboard by the galley down aft? I saw you." Anna took a pace forward and the sailor put out his arm.

"No you don't. Wait there."

"I tell you she's a passenger. Her name is Anna Shay."

"Well I'm sorry sunshine, but I got my orders from Mr Quinn himself. If you don't like it, see him. He'll be coming back aboard too – anytime now. They've tightened up security tonight. Somebody actually got one of these girls on board earlier and took her down the glory hole. Can this one talk English?" Anna stood silent, icily dignified under the rain of clumsy insults. Roger exploded.

"Oh for God's sake man. Does she look like a ...?" Too late, he stopped.

"Has she got anything what shows who she is?" asked the sailor. Anna searched in her bag and produced a snapshot and a slip of paper. The picture was of her parents. Her mother was a grim-visaged woman wearing a traditional tunic-style garment, standing apart from Sam who was in uniform. "That's her mum and dad," said Roger, showing it to the sailor. "He's a Wing Commander." The man glanced at Anna with a grudging respect. "They're going to UK to live," Roger added, implying they were all aboard now. The thought that tomorrow he could be on the receiving end of a Wing Commander's wrath convinced the sailor, who barely glanced at the other item, a dining-saloon ticket with her name and table-number on it. "OK," he said with a wave of his hand. There was no apology. She turned to Roger.

"Thank you Mr Wren for a most enjoyable day." The brittle formality served to mask her anger and embarrassment. "Thank you. We must do it again." He tried to soften the little act with a squeeze of her hand but her face remained cold and he sought in vain the warmth that had been there throughout the day. With a belated attempt at courtesy the sailor said, "Will you be alright Miss – you know the way to your cabin?"

"Yes I do," she replied tightly, and mounted the staircase. The sailor stared pointedly at Roger. "And you know the way to yours – *don't you?*"

Back on the crew well-deck and utterly exhausted, he leaned on the rail. What a day. And what a way to end it. God only knew what she'd be like after such humiliation. One of these girls! But it might have been even worse he thought, trying to find some way of dealing with what would surely be a setback to everything. At least they hadn't had to go to her cabin for her passport. Or send for the purser. He heard car-doors slamming. A number of ship's officers were climbing out of a taxi and marching up the gangway. One of them remained, paying off the driver. It was First Officer Quinn. Oh yes. It might have been much worse.

Chapter 18

Turning north-west, the travel-stained ship set a lively pace towards the top end of Sumatra, passing once more through the Malacca Straits, where they'd endured such appalling weather. Now it seemed a welcoming place of bright seas, candy-floss clouds and – at last, dolphins. From the after deck, Roger watched them frolicking around the ship. Gleaming wet, they leapt and plunged up and down continually. Like his own fortunes had been doing these many weeks. And all the time they kept that unique half-human smile at the end of their snouts. As if saying "Look Roger. That's life – up and down all the time."

Earlier that day he'd sought out Trixie, hoping for news. "Ah now Roger. There's a girl who's not at all happy."

"You heard about it?"

"Yes, she told me. I'm the only soul up there she can really talk to. What an idiot that gangway man. Still it's what you expect seeing it was Singapore and somebody'd already sneaked a girl on board. That one was only on ten minutes before she was sent packing. I tell you this sort of thing upsets a person like Anna Shay. That and some of these stuck-up officers' wives. Never mind. I'll keep you posted. I'll see you again nearer Colombo."

There was another aspect to consider. Being frank about his job and lack of high ambition had been an error. And she'd ducked the chance to tell him her UK address. England could never be the same as now, she'd stated. Along with the voyage, the affair could be already ending. Now there was this complication. He recalled her light-hearted dismissal of mixed-race problems in Hong Kong. But that was then. Last night's unpleasantness had been different. Coming as it did after Yingsu Pickard's well-meant warnings and four days of sub-zero politeness from the ladies of A Deck, being twice mistaken for a prostitute must have been the last straw.

All of this of course he kept from his colleagues, giving a toned-down version with just enough detail to satisfy. "I can't keep up with him," said Bill. "Fornicating his way round the world. And how about that big bundle ashore?"

"I saw that happening," said Jack. "And I saw Kropp there too. He came out of the Jade when it was all over. Seemed sorry he missed it. Not that he could have done much. Did you see it Roger?"

"No, nothing to do with me. I was otherwise occupied."

"I bet you were," said Martin. "Will you be seeing her in England?"

"Maybe. I don't know." And he wouldn't know till he saw her again.

But a new blow came three days later when he saw Trixie. "Bad news Roger. Anna's not going ashore in Colombo. It's 'cos it's a launch port."

"I don't see —"

"Those two Singapore incidents. Some of the ghastly women on A Deck have put two and two together."

"And made five?"

"Yes – all their suspicions confirmed. She can't face the thought of being stuck in a boat with them. I don't know yet about Aden. That's another boat trip."

"Alright Trixie. Thanks for trying. Forget Colombo. And I can't risk going ashore at Aden anyway. Tell her there's still Port Said." So it came about that he stayed aboard at the next port, the first time he'd done so anywhere except Pusan. But he had no regrets. Colombo held bad memories for him, and missing it seemed to speed the homeward leg even more. He wrote home, enclosing postcards and recounting some of his activities. Needless to say there was no word from Isobel.

The *Empire Garvie* slipped into Aden harbour at five in the morning. Again there was no mail for him. After breakfast the others lost no time getting off the ship. Roger lay on his bunk thinking about Sergeant Fouad. When the cabin was empty he slid off the bunk and studied the view from the porthole. Aden still had that air of parched indolence. From here there was no hint of the bustling town beyond the waterfront. About to turn away, he caught sight of a ship's launch heading for the shore. Idly he watched it, then noticed another craft approaching the ship. Only another boat in the harbour yet he knew it was coming for him. Because that was his life now. Things happened to him. Wonderful things, awful things – every few days.

Chugging closer, the craft now revealed itself in all its frightening officialdom. A foreign flag at the stern, an Arab at the helm and another one in police uniform sitting amidships. On impulse he took a quick look at the Buddha, trying to take heart from that tranquil, "fear not, all will be well" expression. Someone entered the cabin and he jumped a little.

"What's up Roger?" said Batten. "Not still worried about Kropp? I'm off ashore with Clay and Mike Smith. I suppose you're staying below in case that sergeant's looking for you with a telescope." He told what he'd seen. "Oh dear. This is goodbye then. We'll come and see you next time. If you're allowed visitors."

"For God's sake – this is serious."

Clay came in. "Batten, are we going or not?" Hearing the news, he was dismissive. "That's all over and done with. They're not here for you." There was a shout in the alleyway outside. "Roger Wren – you're wanted!"

"Then again," said Clay, "I could be wrong."

A deckhand glanced in. "Somebody called Wren live here?"

"That's me," said Roger brokenly.

"D Deck square. Policeman's asking for you."

Batten said, "We'll stay below in case they spot Clay and grab him too."

On the square stood the policeman, a younger man than Fouad in a slightly different uniform. The deckhand said, "This man's come to take you ashore. Know anything about it?"

"Yes. It's a long story."

"Ro — ger – Wren," said the policeman laboriously.

"That's all he can say," said the deckhand. "No English, no papers or anything. I've sent for Mr Candy." The Second Steward arrived and Roger told him the story of Haji. "Well, I've heard some yarns in my time. If you were involved in a road accident I suppose ..." He thought for a second. "I'll send for the purser." The purser was a tetchy, officious little man who bustled onto the scene with the air of being the one everybody was waiting for.

"Now then – now then. What's all this about?" Apprised in turn, he attempted to question the Arab, who could only indicate that he'd come for Roger and wasn't leaving without him. "How about phoning ashore?" someone suggested. "Can't," snapped the purser. "No ship to shore line here. Don't stay long enough. One of you will have to go up to the bridge and get someone with – with more authority than me." It seemed to pain him that such a person might exist.

"Ro — ger Wren," said the policeman.

"Alright my friend," said Candy. "We're just waiting for someone. Here he is now." For anyone else it would be coincidence. Not him. It was ruled by fate that he should forever collide with this man. Tall, handsome, and resplendent as ever in snow-white shorts and open-necked shirt, First Officer Quinn strode onto the square and stopped dead at sight of Roger.

"You again! What the hell is it this time?" Quinn listened without interrupting. "Sounds to me like you asked for it. Very well, I'd advise you to go with him now. Sort it out and get back here as soon as you can. We sail at four. There's no way we'll allow this ship to be delayed. Not for you or anybody. And see me when you return."

Once again Roger was speeding across Aden harbour, remembering the first time when they'd all been together in new-found friendship. At the police station his escort pointed to the same long bench under the same antique clock, entered the inner office and shut the door. The same clerk stared at him then resumed typing. It was all horribly familiar. Voices murmured. He sat on the bench and told himself not to even look at the time till he'd judged an hour had passed. Presently his young escort reappeared, accompanied by – Sergeant Fouad, whose cap was still seemingly welded to his head. The man gave no sign of recognition. Roger could contain himself no longer. "Sergeant, what is all this about?"

He got the expected reply. "You will know soon enough. Somone will explain to you."

"The commander?"

"No. He is again not present." The mystery deepened.

Footsteps announced a new arrival, a young Englishman in a honey-coloured suit, white shoes and a red tie. This man had an urgent debate in Arabic with the policemen. The man who had delivered

Roger seemed to have incurred the displeasure of both Fouad and the new man. The latter approached Roger. "Mr Wren? My name is Boyle. I'm with the British Legation here. Nobody very important I hasten to add. Junior Second Under-Secretary. One up from the chauffeur. You must be wondering about all this."

"I am."

"Well, first of all I must apologise for the way you were brought here. Total shambles I'm afraid. Entirely my fault really. I've got a letter here explaining everything. The man should have taken it with him but I got delayed and he went without it. Rather jumped the gun. Anyway it's over this business with the street boy. The accident."

"I'm in trouble for running off."

"Good Lord no. Quite the reverse. His father's here. Come with me."

They all entered the office. Including himself there were no less than seven people in the room. Predictably, Fouad sat in the big chair. Standing around the room were the young policeman, a tall middle-aged Arab, and another one holding a black leather bag. And in the cane chair, the one he'd occupied himself, was Haji. The boy smiled at Roger then looked at the grown-up faces all around and assumed a more solemn expression. The man with the bag opened it and took out a rather weighty Speed Graphic camera. The tall man came forward.

"Mr Wren," said Boyle. "This gentleman is Mr Hassan. Actually his name is rather longer but anyway the point is Mr Hassan wishes to express his profound gratitude to you for saving his youngest son."

"I don't know that I actually ..."

"Yes you did," said Boyle firmly. Mr Hassan shook Roger's hand and spoke at length in Arabic. A flash-bulb went off. Boyle said, "He will be eternally in your debt. He offers thanks and deepest respect for your kindness and hopes that all your own sons will one day bring wealth and honour to you and your esteemed family. Haji is now almost fully recovered and only at times needs to rest." Everyone beamed – except Fouad. Mr Hassan posed with a hand on his son's shoulder, the flash-bulb popped again and the touching little ceremony was over. Roger shook everybody's hand and left with Boyle.

Walking back along the oven-hot streets, Roger said, "I hope the young cop won't be in trouble."

"Unlikely," said Boyle. "He's Fouad's nephew." The youthful official seemed relieved his task was done. "They gave me this assignment my first day back from leave. Hassan is a respected figure locally. Man of some standing."

"Yet his son is only a shoeshine boy."

"Ah yes. But this is not England. You don't get snobbery as such here. Hassan believes a menial occupation is good for a youngster. You learn humility, respect for your elders. Then you're more prepared for better things later. Difficult to disagree with that. Haji was well-known and liked in the area he worked. It's why feelings ran high that day."

"Did they find the driver?"

"Yes. Fouad tracked him down personally. He's doing time for it now. As for the accident itself it's not absolutely certain Haji would have been paralyzed but what you did was definitely the correct drill in a case like that. Rough handling could have caused further damage. So you *did* save him. That's the general belief and we see no reason to deny it." Around them the town went about its business. There was no tension in the air – no feeling of "us" and "them". The purpose of life was living. No war clouds old or new gathered here.

"Of course," Boyle went on, "the legation knew a public relations coup when they saw one. Hence a little project for yours truly. Organise it Boyle. A picture and story in the local news-sheet. Arab boy in a lowly job saved by an English one also in – er – who's also got …" The diplomatic skills faltered.

"A lowly job?" said Roger.

"Um – yes. No offence. I read Fouad's report. Two of you, brothers under the skin. You know what I mean."

Roger laughed. "For all I know he may make more money than me."

At the quay, the troopship was a comforting sight. Boyle's gaze fastened on her thoughtfully, as if he wouldn't mind joining her that minute. Roger asked, "Do you mind being stationed out here?"

"Yes, it's alright. They're nice enough, the people of Yemen." The same sentiments he'd heard more than once in this travels. "Of course there's been some friction, but it's early days yet."

"I suppose – like India and Malaya, in time …"

"We'll pack up and leave? Oh yes. Who knows when though? Ten years – fifteen? Of course we'll have to go. Same as everywhere. But don't quote me on that!" They came to where the police launch and its patient helmsman waited. This time he would leave with nought on his mind but Haji's happy face, his father's rolling phrases and Sergeant Fouad reigning all-powerful at his boss's desk. He asked Boyle, "Why do we never see the commander?"

"Too busy. Lots of meetings these days. Changes on the way. The sergeant can handle things very well, as I'm sure you must have noticed. I know he's rather cold in his manner but Fouad is an exceptionally fine police officer. It was him who told everyone how you helped the boy."

As Roger returned across the water, the junior diplomat stood with one hand shading his eyes and the other raised in farewell. A solitary figure, following the routine of empire until the day of that last sunset.

"They let you go then," said Martin, concealing his disappointment.

"Yes. Now I have to go up and report to Quinn." On the way he checked the mail office again. Still nothing from Isobel.

The First Officer listened warily. "So it was not simply paperwork."

"No sir."

"And this time it didn't involve the Orient Line, the passengers, Kropp or me. For which I am profoundly grateful. Especially as this is my last voyage on the *Empire Garvie*. I shall be joining the company's new ship *Orcades*. An appointment which I am sure will be both less strenuous and more rewarding." Quinn gazed longingly out of his square window, as if already on a luxury liner. Holding a dry Martini and charming the women back to their cabins. "Very well Wren. That would seem to be that. But I trust that you and I will spend the remainder of this trip in a state of blissful separation."

Crossing the Sun Deck, Roger paused for a parting look at Aden. Like so many other locations, the seaward aspect of it would be forever etched on his mind. Now there was the Red Sea to come, and the canal. And then the last place of all, Port Said. God willing, he would take Anna ashore there. But the prospects were not good. "I wouldn't count on it," said Trixie when they were three days into the Red Sea. "There was still no mail from her dad at Colombo or Aden. It's all she thinks about. Whether he's gone to Korea yet or still safe at Kai Tak. Maybe if she gets good news at Port Said it'll buck her up."

"It's very good of you to carry messages like this."

"Not at all. Every time I see Kropp on his sticks I'm grateful. Actually I did suggest she might pen a note to you, or you send one to her but she declined. No notes either way. Probably afraid they'll be seen by the wrong people. That's the state she's in at present. It's how some females are Roger. The least thing spooks them." It was sadly obvious his affair with Anna, once ablaze was now at best – smouldering. His galloping imagination sketched in a vivid simile. She was a delicate Asian orchid wilting steadily with every westward degree of longitude they crossed.

Isobel too he must put from his mind, albeit reluctantly. She wouldn't write. They had their good times back in Southampton. But he wasn't doing any more chasing. If he heard from her at Port Said they could maybe start again. So the Lodger and the troopship, both equally battered but unbowed, made the crawling transit of the canal and the three placid lakes to fetch up once more in that crowded harbour at the corner of the Mediterranean. Returning to the cabin after breakfast he found a letter from his father on the bunk. The envelope also contained a picture-postcard of Brighton. "Phil sent this," his father wrote. "His firm treated him and some others to a week at the seaside. Reward for boosting company profits." He stowed the letter and card behind the Buddha and went on deck to watch the bumboats, the traders' craft clustering round the ship.

Port Said again. The voyage, everything seemed to be winding down. Anna clearly would be unapproachable for the remainder of the trip. Equally, Isobel had finished with him. Otherwise she'd have written. If only to make him suffer long-distance guilt pangs, which he was determined not to do.

"Roger!" It was Clay. "Did you get your mail?"

"I did – thanks. A letter and a card. Is that all there was?"

"Yes. You weren't there so I chucked 'em on your bunk. Listen – I think your luck's changed. Trixie's got news of Anna."

He hurried to No 25 where Trixie lived. All six occupants were present, including the Captain's "tiger", a tall, dark man who liked to be called Hortense. As usual he found these men a little overpowering *en masse*. "Roger!" cried Antonia, sprawled on a bunk in Hong Kong silk pyjamas of scarlet and yellow. "Come in lovey – what can we do for you?" He caught a glance from Trixie and they went outside. "Roger, young Anna's heard from her pop at last. He's staying at Kai Tak, not going to Korea. She overjoyed."

"That's good to hear."

"If you can get away she'd like to go somewhere after lunch. We don't sail till seven so you should be alright. I'm just going on duty.

What do I tell her?"

"Trixie, you're a real pal. Let's see, there's nowhere easy to meet here is there? With that snake thing. Oh – tell her D Deck square. I don't think she'll care if we're seen now her dad's safe. Tell her 1.30. Thanks a lot." He had to work again at five so he had three hours or so. "Take her to the Simon Artz shop," said Bill. "Big department store. Turn right coming off the snake."

So he went to the purser's bureau and had all his assortment of currencies changed into sterling, did his lunch-time work and arrived on the square dead on time. Right away he noticed the change in her. She was much bolder, viewing her surroundings with the same vivacious interest she'd shown at Singapore, in those priceless hours before it all went sour. And as if to emphasise a new pride she wore the white *cheongsam* again, flauntering her "eastern-ness" in the face of all.

"I've had simply marvellous news Roger. Father's staying at Kai Tak for a few weeks. Then they're letting him come home at last – on the *Empire Halladale*."

"That's wonderful. I heard how miserable you've been, with those women and all." They went carefully down the steps to the snake, well aware of the sidelong darts of curiosity. He felt possessively proud to be the one escorting this raven-haired girl whose oriental features and figure-tight white costume made her stunningly unique in that crowd. "Have you got your pass this time?"

"Oh yes." She patted her handbag.

At the quayside along with everyone else they were plied with offers by the tireless army of vendors. But he wasn't so churlish as to hurry her. Anna had missed two ports and souvenirs were a part of travel. She bought him a tie with a yellow sphinx embroidered on it and he got her a small circular brooch. This depicted a tiny red disc with a number of thin hands reaching down from it. "The Sun God," he said, drawing on his book-read knowledge. "The hands symbolise the protection he gave the people of Egypt."

"Another god," she said. "I wonder if Gina knows this one."

"Wear it now."

"I will – if you'll put the tie on." So they did that, using a shop-window as a mirror. Apart from a small wristwatch, the Aten brooch was her sole item of adornment, and set off to perfection the plain white *cheongsam*.

"Anna, you look really good in that."

"Thank you. By the way, where are we going?"

"Nowhere in particular. There's a big shop we might see. Or just walk – cup of tea later."

"Sounds fine. Oh – what happened at Aden?"

Telling the story, he belittled his role in it. "Haji would have got better anyway, but it's good to think I helped."

The town seemed quieter than he remembered it, or maybe it was because they were heading for a different part. There was a sign – Postes Francaises – and one or two other Gallic reminders. "De Lesseps and his canal," he said, resolving this would be his last piece of unsought information. "France has been involved with Port Said ever since he dug it."

Her mind was elsewhere. "I'm sorry about Colombo," she said. "I've been an absolute weakling since leaving home."

"What about Singapore? That was a bright spot."

With a giggle she said, "What a day that was."

"And those women on A Deck – all over now?"

"No, not really. I don't care. Now I know Father's coming home and not going to Korea. His letter today makes up for all the looks and whisperings. Even that misunderstanding at Singapore. I was twice outlawed then. Racially and morally. Only by the wives though, never the husbands."

He tut-tutted gravely, saying with mock solemnity, "Isn't that always the way?" Again she gave that knowing chuckle, and the attendant dimples made her seem both mature and doll-like at the same time.

Passengers or crew, nobody strayed far from the ship. This was the final call. The cravings were all satisfied, the gifts all bought, the snaps all snapped. After seventeen and a half thousand miles the novelty of "abroad" had worn thin. Up ahead he spied Batten, Clay and Nelson. Clay was pointing in another direction and urging the others to follow him. Then they split up and Batten continued alone. Passing the pavement cafes and bars, he noticed many more known faces and received one or two wolf-whistles and jocular remarks.

There was no doubt she attracted attention. Slim and cool, she strolled the scorching street with the assurance of a princess. A rush of affection ran through him. With a shock he realised he was falling for her. He almost said it there and then – "Anna, will you marry me?"

But then the vision abruptly changed. With savage clarity he saw her in another place far away from this sun-dappled fairyland. Hanging out washing on a grey Hampshire day, the bright eyes dulled by care, the smooth complexion long banished to memory. Tight-lipped housewives nudging each other and muttering about that foreign woman – "you know, the one who talks posh and makes out she's as English as we are". Oh God – would it really be like that? Would either of them care? If they loved each other – but they'd never mentioned love. Only that of the Brownings. And you couldn't sustain a mixed marriage on memories and poetic dreams – not in 1950s Britain.

"I saw a notice earlier," he said. "There's a museum up ahead. I promised you one didn't I?"

"You did, and there's nothing I'd like more."

The museum was hushed and cool. Admission was free and they seemed to be the only visitors. The moment they entered he thought of the Sri Mariamman temple. Another refuge from the heat, the abode once more of mystic writings, effigies and masks.

"Awe-inspiring," she whispered. "Gina should see this."

"She probably has." There were unblinking faces everywhere. Carved, moulded, painted or bejewelled. Even the aged curator in his alcove by the door watched them closely. The whole place had a musty, funereal stillness. He couldn't resist a quote.

"The silence 'ung that 'eavy you was 'arf afraid to speak."

"That's from Mandalay isn't it?"

"Correct." Already muffled, the street noise receded as they ventured further, as though they were slipping away from the modern world and through the curtains of history. Back to an age when all these artefacts were the currency of daily life, and the host of painted figures with their sensuous lips and kohl-ed eyes lived and breathed here in this very land. For a while neither spoke again. They passed down between the long glass cabinets filled with relics and photographs of long-ago expeditions. Here was Howard Carter, posing like a prize angler in the tomb of the boy-king. Tutankhamen's golden countenance, after thirty centuries in darkness, gleaming in the candlelight and presenting a majestic calm far removed from Carter's schoolboy grin of triumph.

"I'm glad we found this place," he said. Glancing about, he found he was alone. He went to the end of the display. Nothing. It was as if she'd been spirited away. And the hushed atmosphere of the place was such that he couldn't bring himself to call her name. But she couldn't be far away. Left or right, up one of the aisles. "Anna," he whispered. The artificial faces glared back at him. He had a sudden ghastly fantasy. They'd captured her, these phantom figures. Taken her behind the glass, turned to stone like them.

Only now did the obvious thing occur to him. Stooping down, he looked under the cabinets and between the supports. Three rows away were two pairs of legs, hers and a man's. Relieved, he went to them. Batten was in his man-about-town rig first seen at Penang Lodge, when he'd got the Comet Lady to share her celestial pursuits in more earthly ways. "Roger dear boy, where have you been? I see my two favourite people come in and then one of them promptly vanishes."

"My fault for wandering off," said Anna. "Sorry Roger."

"No harm done." He addressed Batten. "We saw you with the others."

"Yes, I told them I was coming here. You can guess the reaction. Me – I'm not averse to bit of culture." They continued the tour of the museum, while Roger considered the implications of having a third person along. Shrewd as ever, Batten divined his thoughts. "Fear not my friends. I shall not impose my presence on you for long. After I've seen this I shall wend my weary way to the Casino Palace Hotel, where I intend to enjoy a cigar, a read of last week's *Times* and an expertly-made Manhattan. Thus refreshed, I must then alas return to His Majesty's rust-bucket and resume my role of underpaid lackey to a pair of colonels, one lieutenant and their more than usually repellent wives."

"Before you do that," said Anna, "why not have a cup of tea with us somewhere?" Batten glanced at Roger, who nodded. The man was delightful company, she clearly liked him and he wouldn't stay long. "OK by me."

"Thank you – and I insist on treating you both."

They found a pavement café a short distance from the museum. Here they relaxed in wicker chairs under a scarlet awning. A waiter in a red fez drew near, sizing them up in seconds as all waiters are wont to do. An odd group he thought. The female was unusual. An oriental. You didn't get many of those in the café. The two men with her looked hot. He hoped they weren't Americans. They were always impatient, never said please and wanted ice-water with everything. Good with tips but you had to work for it. By instinct the waiter approached Batten, whose clothing, age and demeanour seemed to mark him out as the leader.

"Yes sir?"

"Tea please. Earl Grey if you have it. And some of those excellent wheatcakes of the kind they serve in the Casino Palace." English, thought the waiter. Courteous, easy to serve but tighter with money. The tea *was* Earl Grey, the wheatcakes *were* excellent, and the small group of travellers sat under the awning talking as if they were lifelong companions – three of a kind. Which in a way they were, for surely they had all been affected by past events. The Lodger had been to paradise and back, with side-excursions to terror. The girl, bound for a new life and a new home, had found *en route* the illicit joys long denied her.

And the older man, who thought he'd seen it all, on this particular voyage he too had trodden new by-ways. The hills of Kure, Hiroshima's haunted streets and the perfumed paths of Wei Ho Bay. Roger leaned back in the wicker chair, watching the passers-by and surreptitiously eyeing Anna, erect with her legs primly folded and the Sun God glinting on the high-collared white outfit.

Batten gave a doomed sigh. "Someone's coming over. Passengers. Not mine I'm glad to say but of similar mould. Major Hart and his lady-wife. Joined us at Colombo. He's alright but I heard from their steward she can be a tartar. I'd better do my company servant act. A steward ashore is still a steward to them."

"I've met them too," said Anna. "She's scared me ever since we met but not anymore. Just watch me."

Major Hart was a short figure in a well-cut tropical uniform. "Good afternoon," he smiled. "Mr Batten isn't it – one of our stewards? And you're Miss Shay. How do you do?"

"Good afternoon sir," said Batten. "And you madam."

"Oh – er – how do you do – Mr – Batten."

Her words were an obvious effort, the "Mr" only a temporary title till they were back aboard and he would be merely "Steward" again. Mrs Hart was by no means unattractive. Clear-skinned and slim, well-dressed and sporting a smart sun-hat, she had "presence". But her face was cold, her mouth ever-ready to pull into a frown. Roger was introduced, and remembered to stand up for the handshakes. The next thing to be heard surprised everyone.

"Mrs Hart," said Anna, "would you and your husband care to join us for afternoon tea?"

"That is most kind of you," replied the major. "We'd love to." The man sounded sincere. Mrs Hart, on the other hand, was not especially eager to hob-nob with any old trio met casually on the street. Particularly one comprising a ship's steward, that Chinese girl and some person with scars and a perfectly dreadful tie. But the major had pulled out a chair for her so she sank reluctantly into it and the hallowed English ritual began.

The major downed his tea and munched his cake as to the manner born, "harrumphing" at intervals and speaking in the peculiar clipped style of the professional soldier. He reminded Roger of Toddy. "Actually we aren't Ceylon people at all. Only went down to Colombo to get the ship. Home leave. Visiting relatives in UK. Been stationed in India since '45. Little place outside Mysore. Very nice. Get on well with the locals. To be honest we can't wait to get back there can we dear?"

"No," his wife murmured with rather less conviction. "*Most* of the time the house is no trouble *at all* to run." Mrs Hart did not so much hold a conversation as dissect it, speaking with surgical precision and stressing key words with a marked change in tone. "Although staff can be a *little* tiresome at times I find a certain amount of *firmness* can usually persuade them to see one's point of view." The tinkle of cups, the faultness manners and the ebb-and-flow of small-talk followed an almost religious conformity. As at Wei Ho the social rampants began to fall, although Mrs Hart defended them courageously. "Tell me Miss – er – Shay. What precisely *do you do?"* I mean, are you *with* anyone? Or are you – how shall I put this? – *self-employed?"*

The male members of the group waited, uneasy spectators at a kind of female David and Goliath match. The major's wife continued. "Of course I don't wish to *pry*. I'm only curious because most of the other ladies on A Deck regard you as something of a *mystery* passenger. Some sort of *incident* at Singapore I believe. Some difficulty about being allowed on board?"

The major fidgeted. "Steady on Melanie. None of our business, her occupation. We only got on ourselves at Colombo remember. This young lady's been here what? – fortnight or more. Got on at Hong Kong." Melanie stirred her tea slowly – very slowly. "Yes. Of course. Those women. Someone should tell them. Since the war times have changed. One must expect to – run up against *all kinds* of people when travelling nowadays."

During this, Anna had remained unperturbed – listening to the feather-soft drip of innuendo. Now she took a sip of tea, dabbed her mouth with a paper napkin and spoke. "Mrs Hart, I am travelling alone because my parents at this time are each at opposite ends of the earth – Hong Kong and UK. With regard to my occupation, until two weeks ago I was secretary and shorthand typist to the Senior Accounts Manager at Jardine Mathieson's, 214 De Veoux Road, Central District, Crown Colony of Hong Kong. I am now going to Reigate, Surrey, England where we are buying a house." She paused for another sip of tea and continued.

"My mother's family founded the largest textile corporation in South-east Asia. My father is a twice-decorated RAF Wing Commander awaiting retirement, who is now at Kai Tak supervising the transport of men and equipment to a war zone. He is doing this to help preserve democracy for those of all races throughout the Far East. There are communist regimes in China and Russia. Now people of similar persuasion are in armed revolt in Korea and Malaya. Unless they are stopped the whole of Asia could be at risk. You won't be safe anywhere." She smiled disarmingly. "Even Mysore. May I pour you another cup of tea?"

The lady in the sun-hat slowly changed. The corners of her mouth took an upward turn for the first time since her arrival. Her eyebrows, hitherto arched in disdain, relaxed. Melanie Hart was climbing down to where the rest of humanity dwelled. "Ye – es. I – will have some more tea thank you. Miss Shay, please forgive me. I've been *unbelievably rude*. That's the whole trouble with being on a ship isn't it? One hears such ridiculous stories. Women with little else to do, gossiping away. I – do hope now we know one another better we might meet again during the voyage. Perhaps we could play a little *bridge* one afternoon?"

Anna tried not to look at the others in case she faltered. "That would be most agreeable. We often played bridge at Hong Kong. Sometimes the Chairman of Jardine's and his wife would pay a visit. My parents have known them for years." It was the final telling shot. By now Melanie was beaming. A person's background was so *desperately* important these days. Here was someone whose pedigree positively *shone*. And they were friends! The major was equally taken with Anna. Why, even her father outranked him. They sat watching as two totally different women talked like sisters. Roger had his mind on the possible layout on A Deck while Batten ate the last wheatcake with an amused detachment. Soon the major began to fidget again, a sure sign he was about to address his wife.

"Melanie, I don't want to rush you but you did mention something about Simon Artz."

Still talking, she rose. "Don't forget now Anna. I shall look forward to seeing you in the lounge, or maybe we could have a turn at deck quoits."

"My favourite game," said Anna, straight-faced. Mrs Hart bestowed a grudging nod on the others and the couple melted into the passing crowd.

"Well," said Roger, "that beats all. Anna, I'm proud of you."

Batten said, "That woman had it coming. Trouble is, she now wants to adopt you."

Anna laughed. "Better than getting the cold shoulder."

Batten paid the waiter, surprising him with a generous tip. "I've got to go. Casino Palace. Like to come along?" But it was 4.30. They had to return. So they waved him goodbye and commenced the walk back. It was so hot even their shadows seemed to be withered, struggling to exist. Yet she was quite at ease in the clinging dress with the high tunic collar. He loosened his tie. "Simon Artz. I was going to take you there. Along the dockside. We might just squeeze it in."

"No. Let's give it a miss. I'm not ready to face Melanie again quite so soon."

How he ached to embrace her, there before everyone on the baking street with the sight-seers and Arabs, hustlers and young soldiers jostling about them. By the time the ship was in sight he'd made up his mind. "Anna – I've got to see you again – like before. I've got to come up to A Deck. I know your cabin number."

"I don't believe it's allowed."

"Pretend we're in the Niagara Hotel. Or perhaps – Italy?"

She smiled guiltily. He saw the thoughts running through her mind and couldn't believe what he was suggesting. By all the odds they must be caught. He was risking not only his job but her reputation, only today restored. But as they reached the snake and saw that old ship waiting they faced each other and forgot everyone. Very quietly she said, "In seven days it'll be goodbye."

The words were bullets tearing him apart. "Does it have to be?"

They were on the pontoons now and talk was difficult on the shifting surface. At the lower platform she stopped. "I'm afraid it does."

Sick at heart he wanted to clutch her tight before the ship devoured her. Anguish coarsened his words. "Why – just because you've got a Chinese mother?"

Her eyes moistened. "No. That is *not* the reason." A noisy group came along the snake and they had to wait for them to pass.

Suddenly she gripped his arm the way she did at decisive moments. "Roger – don't say goodbye now. Say it tonight."

"You're sure?"

"Yes. I'm sure. Nine o'clock?" Before he could reply she was up the steps and into the ship without a backward glance.

Despite everything he had to make one more mail-check, half-hoping there would be nothing from Isobel. There wasn't. Next he visited Trixie again. "Hullo Roger, I knew you'd be along. You want to go up there now don't you? Unfortunately there's a snag. All the way from Hong Kong any time might have been OK. Tonight however will call for extra care. It's Mr Quinn, the First Officer."

"No! That man again! He haunts me – he—"

Trixie put a finger to his lips. "Hush now duckie. Let's go on deck." On the hatch they lit a couple of Roger's Camel cigarettes. "Quinn thinks he's clever," said Trixie. "Laying down the rules while he goes cabin-hopping. We're all wise to him, all us bedroom stewards. Now he's got this party he's been cultivating since she came aboard at Colombo. She's a WAAF would you believe. Section Officer Wakefield. They were ashore together today. Came back looking very pally. Port Said seems to affect women that way."

"You're right, it does. That's why —"

"I know. I saw you too. I suppose you couldn't make it some other night?"

He recalled Anna's last entreaty, the telling spark in her eyes. The moment was now. The next seven days, even tomorrow night were too far away. They would lose the momentum generated this day. "No. I believe it's now or never."

"Alright. I said I'd help you and I will. What time – nine o'clock?"

"Fine."

"OK. I'm going on duty now till 9.30. This WAAF's cabin is on someone else's section. Aft of A15 on the same side. Couldn't be worse really. You can only hope it's not next door. I don't know the actual number and I can't find out 'cos the stewardess and me don't get on. She'd shop me if she could. So I'll keep a watch. If and when I see Quinn go in anywhere I'll give him time to get his pants off then nip down and tell you. Meet me here around nine and if he's out of the way we'll go up. After that you're on your own. And wear a white jacket."

They got off the hatch. Roger said, "I know about that, I wore one a few times on B Deck."

"Yes, it does allay suspicion if you're seen going into a cabin. Or coming out. It's how long you're in there gets the tongues wagging. You should be alright. Once Quinn gets settled in nothing short of a boiler-room explosion will shift him. Another thing – avoid stewardesses. You never know where you are with them. Some are good, some aren't." Very much like everyone aboard he thought.

"Thanks Trixie. I really appreciate all this." At seven o'clock he watched the departure, vividly recalling the morning long ago when he'd first set eyes on Port Said. Now they slipped out of the harbour, past the Simon Artz store they'd never got around to, and De Lesseps on his high column pointing back at his canal as though imploring them to stay. Then it was the blue Mediterranean once more – heading west into the sunset and the final stretch.

Freshly laundered and now on permanent loan, Clay's coat came out of Roger's locker. "Here we go again," said Martin. "Where to now?"

"A Deck."

"Fuggin' 'ell," said Bill. "Nowhere's safe from him."

Pat asked, "What tanker will you go on at Southampton?"

"Tanker?"

"After they hit you with a DR and you can't get a job on anything else."

It was 8.45 when he arrived at the foot of the steps leading to the upper regions. Trixie sounded edgy. "I was right about Quinn. He sneaked into a cabin ten minutes ago. Are you sure you want to go through with this?"

"Yes." He had to see her before the voyage ended. To settle things one way or the other. As for Quinn – well he had Trixie to help him. Someone who knew Quinn and his ways, and all the room-hopping.

French-farce manoeuvres of life on a troopship. They went up to B Deck, then inboard and up a carpeted stairway to the exclusive enclave of A Deck, that sanctified ground where only the great and the good set foot. On the starboard side the cabins followed the custom in having only odd numbers. Unlike on B Deck, they were not in groups of four accessed by small side-alleys. Here each one opened directly onto the main corridor. Nowhere to hide, he thought.

"Quinn's in one of these," whispered Trixie. "I saw him from the forward pantry then when I looked again he'd gone. So which one he's in is anybody's guess." They walked almost to the forward end. Trixie suddenly halted. "Here's your one. A15. Now when you leave, do a quick check then get off this deck – fast. And remember, you did all this on your tod." Trixie hurried away. Roger knocked and was instantly admitted. Darting in, he shut and locked the door.

"Roger, are you on duty?"

"Eh? Oh – the white jacket. No it's so people will think I am."

After so many days of deprivation they embraced and kissed with the fervour of wartime sweethearts at Waterloo Station. "Roger ..." she began, when appallingly there came a knock at the door. "Who is it?" she stammered.

"Melanie." They exchanged stunned glances. He checked the room. Furniture too small, bed on a solid base. All he could do was flatten himself against the wall on the hinge side of the door.

"Anna?" came that polite, but commanding voice.

"Better just see her," he mouthed. "Or she'll wait till you do." The door was half-opened. "Anna my dear girl – are you alright? You look a trifle – *wan*."

"I've got a headache. All the excitement today. What was it you – I mean why have you —?"

"Oh, I won't come in if you're not well. I merely wondered if you'd care to make a fourth at bridge in the forward lounge. But never mind if you're not up to it. I thought you and I could be partnered against my husband and Colonel James. At the moment they're having a drink with the Sibleys. We met the Sibleys in Simon Artz you know. Alright in their way I suppose but I can't say I really care for them. By all accounts they had a reputation in Singapore for throwing somewhat *scandalous* parties. They held one in their cabin only last night. Them and their friends. Their own kind. And the sort of *songs* they sing! They've got two sons in the navy and another one's a film actor which they seem to think makes them special – lets them do as they like and never mind offending *decently-behaved* people." She paused for breath and ploughed on.

"I mean to say, it's all very well being patriotic but there are *limits*. Only the other day I was saying to Mrs Goddard and her husband ..." Anna stood in the doorway, visibly wilting under the tide of trivia. But finally even Melanie Hart ran out of people to dissect, condemn and categorise. "Well, I do hope you feel better soon. Have you got any aspirins?"

"No – I mean yes. Yes I've got plenty of aspirins thank you. I'll take one now and get to bed."

At last she was gone. Anna closed the door. "I was with her all afternoon and evening. With a short break for dinner. And I had to explain all about my pass at Singapore."

He smiled. "You ought to cultivate the Sibleys. They sound like more fun."

"I hardly think so." It was not the answer he expected. Something bothered her – again. Maybe it was the series of encounters with Mrs Hart. A sledge-hammer of respectability whose very manner drove home the fact that she wasn't really this sort of young woman at all – indulging in clandestine meetings away from home. "Roger, we're still not very accomplished at this are we?"

"I thought we were." They were using the hushed and furtive tones he'd got to know so well on these upper decks. There was no drink to ease things along, and in any case he'd known from the outset she didn't care for alcohol and cigarettes. And the proximity of Quinn bothered him. But with the door safely locked and the distant sounds of footsteps and voices eventually dying out, a single ship's cabin becomes one of the most intimate places on earth.

She was in the green kimono, a garment that gave a faint seductive swish as she moved, and brought a welcome oriental touch to the functional, western-style room. "I'd like to chat for a while," she said. They embarked on a wonderful, nostalgic journey through all the events they'd both experienced. The cycling tour of Hong Kong and the pantomime of the oil-lamp. The Singapore episode. They laughed (quietly) at Clay and Hazel's misfortune in the Glade. And Melanie Hart's cut-glass pretensions got a little well-merited ridicule.

The breeze drew them to the porthole. Silver-tipped and restless, the dark sea rushed and tumbled past like life itself, ever speeding –

ever warning that now was the time. Now – when things might never be right again. "Moonlight," she said. "Each night I've stood here and this is the first clear moonlight night."

"Well – there you are then. It must be telling us something." Wordlessly they shed their clothes and climbed onto the bunk.

Days ago, in one of his analytical moods he'd drawn in his mind a graph on which his varied sexual exploits appeared. A straight line rising steadily from his short initial coupling with Ruth to the heady perfection of the Niagara Hotel. But he couldn't have guessed with what sadistic symmetry it would plunge back to the base line. In the beginning little was said. They both knew some kind of end was near. Soon the friendship would lose the worldly, faraway quality that fuelled it. He wondered if there was the smallest hope of carrying on with this in England. During a pause he just had to broach the subject.

"What would you say if I said – I was falling in love with you?"

"Well, I might say the feeling could become mutual." A qualified reply, but his heart leapt.

"Then why can't we —?"

"Get married?" The word was out, and she'd said it first.

Emboldened, he said, "Yes. Why not?"

"There is a reason."

"Then tell me what it is."

She made no answer, but sat up and glanced first at the door, then the porthole. "Roger – something's wrong." Now, coming down from his own personal cloud he could feel it too. Throughout the voyage there had always been that sense of the ship around him. Far below, the engines' thundering voice ascending through the body of the ship, muffled and softened as it passed successive layers of steel to end as a gentle, silent tremor. Now it was gone. He felt an awful dread and tried to keep it from his voice.

"The engines have stopped."

"Why?"

"They've broken down – or been stopped on purpose. And you don't suddenly do that unless ..."

The ship developed a quick and violent list to port. Somewhere a man was shouting. They heard running feet. "Roger, you must go. There's some kind of emergency. Go now before someone comes knocking at the door." The words had a depressingly familiar ring. But he couldn't leave her. "If it's a real emergency I'll stay with you."

"No Roger. You must go – you might be needed."

There was genuine panic in her voice. He could see she was totally "spooked". As if outside the cabin all the forces of conventional behaviour were massing. Led by Mrs Hart, they waited to swarm in and catch Wing Commander Shay's oh-so-very-well-bred daughter doing what they'd all suspected her of from the start. "Roger – please!"

"Alright." Throwing on his clothes, and only just remembering the white jacket, he kissed her for what he knew could well be the last time. "I'll see you again before you get off – that's a promise."

He peeped out, saw nobody and hurried down the corridor, heading aft. The list to port was still there. A steward turned a corner and grabbed him. "What's going on – why are we listing?"

"I've no idea." Behind him, a door opened and a man in pyjamas stepped out. "I say – is anything wrong? Why is the ship leaning over to the left?"

"I don't bloody know!" barked the steward and rushed on, pursued by the man bleating "I say!" Roger set off again, and another door was wrenched open. This time it was a woman in a blue nightdress. He noticed her lipstick was smudged, possibly as a result of the sudden list. "What the hell are you *doing*?" came a man's voice behind her. "Shut the damn door!"

At that instant the ship swiftly righted itself, and caused the door to swing wide open revealing First Officer Quinn sitting on a bunk, still wearing his immaculate shorts. Unfortunately he wore nothing else, other than an obscenely thick crop of chest hair. For three appalling seconds, he and Roger stared at each other, then the woman slammed the door shut. Head reeling, he hurried on down to C Deck and the open crew space. Here he found several men leaning on the starboard rail and pointing aft.

"What's up?" he asked the nearest person.

"Somebody's gone over the side."

"My God – who?"

"Don't know yet. They've lowered the starboard launch. That's why they did a sharp turn to starboard after stopping the engines. Kills some of the speed and creates a patch of still water for the boat. Bit drastic. Somebody's bright idea I suppose." The unscheduled halt had brought most off-duty men up from below. His own cabin was fully represented, like everyone speculating on who had fallen overboard. "We thought it might be you," said Bill. "Thought maybe you had a fight with Quinn and he chucked you over."

"It's no laughing matter," said Jack. Roger spotted Batten standing alone and joined him. The man had a grim expression on his moonlit face. "I know who it was," he said softly. "Don't blab it around. They'll know soon enough. It was – Seymour. And he never fell, he jumped."

"Oh God – no! I thought he was alright now."

"Apparently not." They stared across to where the remains of the wake were still dispersing, and at the countless wave-crests, any one of which could have been a man struggling. The other launch had been lowered, and the two boats could be seen circling desperately – and it was becoming obvious, in vain. "We were with him," said Batten. "Right here on deck. Him, me and Smith – talking. Out of the blue he says, 'Well, I'm going now. Goodbye.' Then he climbed the rail and jumped. I threw a lifebelt and Smith ran to raise the alarm."

Batten's face betrayed his emotion. Normally so blasé, the man was shaken to the core. "I've seen men drown. But never like that. Like he was just leaving a room." Smith returned, told the crowd all about it and came over. "Have they got him?"

It was brutally clear they had not. Even in so short a time as two or three minutes, a ship travelling at seventeen knots covers a lot of sea. And with a man in the water moving aft, reversing screws is out of the question. So the search went on while the *Empire Garvie* wallowed dead in the water, and the chattering line of watchers remained at the rail.

But Frank Seymour had made his final exit, his last defiant walk-away. Much later came the sad decision to recall the boats, get back on course and resume the voyage. Everyone talked of Seymour. "Always a bit strange, him," said Martin. "Snappy sort of nut-case. You couldn't talk to him. Same as Kropp."

"Hard luck for the Lodger," said Bill. "Short and sweet tonight wasn't it?"

Roger's thoughts were such that he didn't know what to consider first. Seymour's tragic end affected him deeply. The man had been happy. He'd helped make him so. And his relationship with Anna was back in turmoil. It seemed she sort of loved him, but they must part at Southampton. For reasons not yet given. On top of all this had been the shocking confrontation with Quinn. His DR was now assured. If only because he'd caught the man himself in the act, a detail he purposely omitted from the general story. "Don't worry," said Pat.

"You're inseparable, you two. He'll take you on the *Orcades* with him."

Next day the suicide was on everyone's lips. A shadow had been cast that would take days to shake off. Trixie was not encouraging. "You've had it Roger. It's not good, the feeling on A Deck. Anna's got the willies. And I don't know what's got into Quinn. I guess he never got his oats either. I've never seen him in such a foul mood. Roll on Southampton." The troopship sped on over the Mediterranean. Back to UK. Back to Blighty. That tiny, rainswept island that once marched civilisation across the globe. Now the imperial sun was long past its zenith. But it would still take over a decade to set.

Chapter 19

Over the next four days from Port Said to Gibraltar, Roger was unable to think of anyone but Anna, Quinn and Seymour. His erratic love-life, his future employment, and the awful demise of a man he'd advised and befriended. Expecting any moment a call to the bridge, he worked like an automaton, ignoring the heartless banter around him. Even Bill's best efforts.

"You know what I think Roger? She's been seeing Quinn after you go. It's been Goodbye Roger – Hullo Mr Quinn every time. What a man – six feet and good-looking with it. You got no chance. You'll end up like Seymour, too frustrated to go on."

Smith came to the cabin on the third day. "Roger, we're on the bridge. Me, you and Batten. Captain's cabin – right now. It's about Seymour." They dashed off before the others could comment and began the long ascent to the Sun Deck.

"They're making some kind of report," said Batten. "For when we get to UK. Candy's been round already. They searched Frank's locker."

Roger was puzzled. "I know you saw him go, but why am I wanted?"

"We told them you knew him."

Short of climbing the foremast, the bridge was as high as anyone could go. Close by were the Captain's day-cabin and sleeping quarters, comfortable rooms in easy reach of the wheelhouse and chartroom. "Come in," said a voice when they knocked. Three white-uniformed men were in easy chairs round a coffee-table. He was relieved to see that Quinn was not present. To the right was Mr Pryor the Chief Steward, a pale, paunchy man rarely seen except for inspections. Captain Baskerville sat regally in the centre, finger-tips together and silver sideburns combed back like tiny wings. On the left was Mr Candy the Second Steward, from his expression clearly wishing he was somewhere else.

"These are the men in question sir," said Pryor. "Batten, Smith and Wren."

"Good," said the captain. "Well, they're not on trial. They don't need to stand." A settee was pulled up and they sat facing the men in white. "You'll have guessed why you're here," said the captain. "We need to ascertain what facts we can regarding Mr Seymour's death and lay them before the authorities at Southampton. First I'd like you to describe precisely what happened that night."

Batten and Smith told their sad story, while Pryor wrote everything down. The captain then addressed Roger. "Mr Wren, you are here because I've been told you were rather closer to him than most. The man confided in you, is that correct?"

"We talked sir, yes." He couldn't think where to start. "He told me of his troubles. About his drinking habit and difficulties getting a job. At one time he did think of suicide. He told me that."

"Anything about family?"

"No. He always shied away from that. Refused to discuss it." They heard about the favourite fantasies. The lake rescue, the skirmish with a gang of Germans. "These things were quite real to him?" asked Pryor. "In his mind they really happened?"

"Oh yes," said Batten. "He'd get quite angry if he thought we didn't believe him. So we humoured him. The details would change almost every time but we never pointed this out. It all became rather pathetic."

Roger said, "Then he began getting letters." He told them of Seymour's affair with the woman at the tennis club. "After his first letter he was a reformed character. Off the drink. Going ashore buying her presents. Writing from every port and getting mail back. Cock-a-hoop he was."

"In that case," said the captain, "why did he take his own life?"

There was a knock at the door. It was a deckhand. "The cases sir. One of them's still locked and we found no keys anywhere. They probably – went with him."

"Very well." Seymour's two cases, a large one and the "secret box" were dumped on the floor and the man left. "I had these brought up here for a reason," said the captain. "I want to find out why this man did what he did. An official search by me in the presence of witnesses."

He opened the larger case. "Mr Pryor will make a note of anything significant." The contents were laid out on the floor. There was nothing but the normal things found in a suitcase. "Now this one," said the captain, picking up the attaché case and examining the catches.

The three subordinates exchanged glances. Batten said, "Sir, I really don't think anything will be gained by opening that."

"Why – do you already know what's in it?"

"Well – yes. A strong suspicion. Judging by the way he guarded it and always kept it locked. We guessed what he had there – books. Special ones. He never denied it."

"Skin-books," blurted Smith boldly.

Candy coughed nervously. "Sir, I think they mean – a certain *type* of magazine. Indecent illustrations — and — and pictures of —"

"Thank you Mr Candy," said the captain gently. "I am not unacquainted with such things, having as it were risen from the ranks myself. Nevertheless, I believe the circumstances justify a search." Reaching into a nearby drawer, he took out a letter-opener and in a few seconds forced open the catches. The lid was carefully raised.

There were no books. Lying on top were two folded newspapers, the first of which was a *Daily Mirror* dated August 1940. It more or less fell open at the centre pages. The captain said "I think you owe Seymour an apology. A posthumous one at any rate." He laid the paper out for all to read. And there it was before their eyes.

"TOY GUN HERO NABS NAZIS," crowed the headlines. Below it the piece went on in the old wartime blend of humour and jingoism. "Four members of Herr Hitler's much-vaunted 'master race' had a big surprise yesterday when they crawled from their damaged Heinkel. Mr Francis Seymour of Canfield Close, Weymouth was waiting for them holding his young son's toy revolver. Convincingly realistic, it was of course quite harmless. But he courageously held them at bay until reinforcements arrived. Inspector Leigh of Dorset Constabulary said it was the bravest thing he'd ever seen. Readers may recall Mr Seymour's other valiant feat last December. On that occasion he was on hand to save six-year-old Emily Perry when she fell through the ice at Pickett's Lake near Weymouth."

The main picture showed Seymour demonstrating to Home Guardsmen how he'd pointed the gun. Behind them could be seen an elliptical tail-fin, tall and black and with a stark swastika that still carried menace. Depicted in a smaller photo were four dejected young men in flying-suits, one nursing a bandaged arm.

"So it's all true," said Smith weakly. "He could have proved it anytime. Why didn't he?"

"We shall never know," said Batten. "Seymour was odd in every possible way. Small wonder his family left him."

Captain Baskerville spread out the other paper – a *Daily Express* of late 1944. A front page picture now, but this time no humour, no camera-smiles. Fire-hoses, ambulances, ARP men and a mountain of rubble. "MASSACRE AT CHISWICK. V2 Hits Packed Suburb," ran the headlines, adding in a shocked aside: "See Centre Pages." They were silent, for each knew there was worse to come. "Shall we – see the rest of it?" asked the captain.

One by one they nodded. Batten said, "Let's find out why he kept this one." There were more graphic photographs, lists of the dead, the injured, the missing. And over to one side was a single half-column headed "Dorset Man's Tragedy".

Pryor shifted uncomfortably. "This is all years ago. I don't quite see the point ..."

"I do," said the captain. "Something sent him over that rail and we're here to discover what."

He began to read aloud. "One man most cruelly bereaved by yesterday's rocket attack is Mr Francis Seymour from Dorset, whose wife and two children died ..."

"Do we really have to go on with this?" said Candy. The captain paused, and continued.

"... along with Mr Seymour's own parents. Mr Seymour stated that he held himself entirely to blame for the deaths. Talking to the *Express* he said his wife had been unwilling to make the long rail journey but he had insisted that she take the children to visit his parents. At this point Mr Seymour became so acutely distressed our reporter discontinued the interview. Mr Seymour is at present under psychiatric care at Chiswick Royal Infirmary." Captain Baskerville laid the paper down and rubbed his eyes. Nobody quite knew what to say.

"We all thought they'd walked out on him," said Smith. "Why didn't he show us this?"

"Grief is a strange thing," said the captain. "A private thing. Some can never bring themselves to share it with anybody. Bottling this up for five years is enough to tip anyone over the edge. But you say he was getting better – receiving love-letters?"

"He was full of it," said Batten. "His lady-friend at the club. Sending her gifts, getting mail at every port from — oh — Hong Kong outward bound to Port Said coming back."

"So – discounting Japan which wasn't on the itinerary we're talking about six letters. Probably stowed away in this very case." He searched. "Lots of snapshots and keepsakes – wife and kids mostly. Yes, here we are. Now I realise this is a distasteful thing for all of us but it must be done if we're to solve this puzzle. I think the answer lies in one of these letters. We'll read one each till we find it."

Of all the situations Roger had been in, this had to be the one to cap them all. And it was the wrong place for such an unhappy task. Six men reading a dead man's love-letters while sailing over a sparkling blue sea in a bright room shot through with sunbeams. Batten spoke first. "This is the one he got in Aden. All I can say is – I wish a woman would write me a letter like this."

Pryor said, "If she still loved him at Aden maybe there's some clue in the last one."

The captain nodded. "You could be right. So who's got the Port Said letter? I believe it's you Mr Wren."

Roger could scarcely believe what he was reading. "It's not a letter, it's a death-warrant."

"Never mind. Read it out please. Exactly as written."

With an effort, he began. "Dear Frank. Well this is hard to write but here goes. Last week someone came in the front gate and you could have knocked me down with a feather it was Larry come back all lovy dovy and wanting to start again so what could I say but yes I mean he is my husband and he says he will be different and better from now on so we are going to try again I won't be seeing you any more he don't know about us it's better if you don't come round any more all the best Joan Walker. PS Thanks for the presents."

They all watched dumbly as the captain took the letter and placed it with everything else in the case. "Now we know," said Baskerville, seeming to avoid their eyes. "A broken love affair. That'll be a matter for the inquest. Thank you gentlemen." His brusque manner was obviously to hide his true feelings. He was clearly moved, as indeed they all were. The meeting ended and they all went their separate ways.

Roger said, "That must be the most brutal rejection letter ever sent."

"I've seen a few," said Batten. "In the navy. Dear John letters we called them. But he was only just getting himself together. That makes it worse."

Each sought in his own way to erase the savage headlines that wrecked a man's life and the curt note that ended it. Smith muttered, "I can't get over her ditching him like that. After all that leading him on. Poor devil."

Perhaps by way of relief, Batten managed a small touch of humour. "We might derive some wicked comfort from one thing. The thought of her having to explain to Larry where all the gifts came from." Roger was disinclined to tell the others what they'd discovered but soon all was known, and the glory hole had even more to talk about.

One person not remotely interested was Farley. Roger met him on deck as they were passing Gibraltar. Farley was basking in thoughts of home – and profit. "Roger, it's all fixed up about my *samurai* sword. I been in touch with a fellow in Southampton."

"Is he a proper dealer?"

"No, but he's mad about oriental weapons. You may care to know he's offering fifty quid for it – if he's happy with it. And I know he will be. I don't even have to take it to him. He's meeting the ship."

"How will he get it out of the docks?"

"That's his worry. What about your Buddha?" Yes, that was another thing to think about.

And so, three days later the great moment came. No more blistering heat, only the fresh breath of England coming down the Channel to meet them, a whisper of rain in it to remind them of home, and the comforting four-engined roar of a Coastal Command Sunderland greeting them with a low pass across the bow. At seven in the morning they crept up the Solent to the Western Docks, there to moor at 103 Berth. Everyone with a spare moment was on deck to savour the inestimable joy of arrival. It was the last act in the drama, and the Lodger was there with the long cast of players who had filled twelve weeks of his life. "What will you do?" said Clay, taking back his white jacket. "You won't be returning on this one will you? Myself I'm thinking of going on a Cape boat – *Union-Castle.*"

"What about Hazel Townsend?"

"No. Too nerve-racking. Too weird that crowd. And it's too damn far to go. So it's pastures new I think."

Roger pointed. "How about that one then?" A ship's length behind them the *Winchester Castle* waited at her berth like an impatient greyhound, the very epitome of seagoing style with her lavender hull, white upperworks and handsome funnel.

"No. That's 101 Berth and it's Thursday so she'll be going at four o'clock today. But there's one every Thursday. They're regular as trains the Cape boats."

Right after breakfast Roger went up to A Deck. He didn't seek out Trixie and he didn't have a white jacket. All the decks were alive with personnel of both ship and shore. He was merely one of many strangers milling about the corridors. Several cabins had luggage stacked outside, including A15. After a long delay his knock was answered.

There was a nervous look on her face. "Oh – come in Roger. My – mother's here." The word, he thought, was "formidable." Nothing else would serve. The woman standing in the centre of the room was short yet possessed the look of absolute authority. Poker-faced and passionless, her Chinese features bore no trace of her daughter's eastern charm. Yet Sam Shay had fallen for her. Once she must have been as attractive as Anna was now. Maybe Anna too, in the course of time – it wasn't a theory he cared to pursue.

"So you are Mr Wren." When she spoke her mouth hardly moved at all. "I understand you have on occasion been my daughter's companion."

Her manner impelled him to reply in the same stilted fashion. "Yes. Wing Commander Shay asked me to be her escort if she wished to visit anywhere *en route.*"

"I see. Well we are here now and I have a car waiting. So if there is nothing else – oh one other thing. If you incurred any expenses I shall of course ..."

His face gave him away. "Mother!" said Anna in a small voice.

"Mrs Shay ..." Not quite sure how to put it, he plunged. "Mrs Shay, I have become very fond of Anna and I wish very much to continue our friendship here in England." Anna sank into a chair and gave him a despairing glance. Her mother's face twitched and registered an infinitesimal change which he realised was the beginning of an actual Expression.

"I do not believe for one moment such a thing would be in my daughter's interests. When I heard of you I prevailed on her to tell me all she knew of you and your future plans. It appears that aside from some literary interest you have nothing whatever in common. Also your present occupation and your stated desire to – as it were – coast along at it indefinitely do not inspire confidence. Anna in due course will marry and it will be better then if there are no previous – entanglements." To his dismay, Anna got up and stood close at her mother's side. His cheeks burned.

"Mrs Shay. When I first met Anna —"

Her mother held up a hand. "If you please, there is no more to say."

"Anna?" he said incredulously. Anna shut her eyes tightly and opened them again.

"Please Roger. Mother's right. I tried to tell you."

"But what about —" The hot memories flooded his mind, clamouring to be heard and lived again. And the dark panic on her face told them they never could be.

"Mr Wren, you must realise this trip had not been altogether a pleasant one for Anna. The other night's tragic event will not be easily forgotten. The sooner she is off this ship the better I think. So thank you again. We must not keep you from your other duties."

Almost in a trance he found himself back in the corridor, only to hear his name called. "Wren!" A well-known voice, issuing all the way from the forward staircase. Quinn stood there, staring over the heads of everyone else. "Wren – my office – now!" So here it was then. The DR. The push. Goodbye to it all.

"Come in Wren and shut the door." The First Officer sounded just a little ill-at-ease. He was no longer in tropical whites, but the dark-blue long-trousered rig of temperate zones. It made a change not to see his legs. "Now I want you to clearly understand that everything I said to you on previous occasions still applies. That night of the suicide you were wandering A Deck for what I'm quite sure was another rule-breaking expedition – and what you may or may not have *imagined* you saw makes no difference. So if you think for one moment you can make trouble for me I strongly advise you not to try it."

"I can assure you sir I've never had any such intention."

"Good. Because the fact is I've had a bellyful of you Wren. You – unsettle me. You may not be intentionally bad but you have an unfailing knack of – attracting trouble. I could have you put off the ship along with Kropp and one or two others but as I'm sailing on another company vessel I'd feel better knowing you were still on this one. But I'll tell you this. If in the future you should think of joining some other ship, first make sure I'm not on it. Because if I am I'll see your name crossed off the crew list before the bloody ink's dry. That's all."

After the two harrowing interviews his head was awhirl, making it something of an effort to go to the forward lounge where the crew were receiving their discharge books and accumulated wages. His pay was a pleasant surprise, being rather more than expected. "Danger money," explained Pat. "We all got it for going to Korea. And you didn't draw so much out did you? You got money other ways – and you got free treats ashore. Now let's see your DR." Another surprise. There was no DR. Only the usual conduct stamp they all got.

Back in the cabin everyone was packing, but they all paused for a disbelieving study of his book. "Jammy to the last," groaned Martin. "I don't know how he does it. Have you got some kind of secret hold over Quinn?"

"Hold?" said Roger innocently. "Now what could I possibly know about Quinn?" He asked Jack, "When are we free to go?"

"After lunch. Ship's staying three weeks. A fortnight's leave, then work on board the third week. That's if you *are* coming back."

Jack glanced out of the porthole. "Your Chinese girl's ashore. Come and see." She was threading her way through the cluster of soldiers, dockers and onlookers towards a car. A smart, black limousine parked well away from the crowd and clearly no taxi. The chauffeur got out and opened the boot. Behind Anna trailed Trixie and another steward with four cases. They stowed these in the car and received a tip from her. Obviously waiting for her mother, she stood shading her eyes as she looked up at the ship. There would be no other chance for a private goodbye.

He tore through the ship, down the gangway and across to where she was, not caring a damn about anyone or anything, or realising it was three months since he'd stepped on home soil. "What on earth —?" He closed her mouth with his and they kissed for a long and lip-crushing half-minute. Fascinated, the chauffeur watched them. "Anna — I can't believe — after all we did —."

"She doesn't know about that! If she ever found out she'd – she'd disown me. It's got to be like this I'm afraid. I thought you understood that." Over her shoulder she saw her mother descending the gangway. "Our ways are different Roger. In things like this they are. It's how it's done. I can't go against her wishes, I just can't. You must see that. I mean how could we possibly ...?"

"Mr Wren!" Her mother's voice sliced them apart. "Mr Wren, will you please go away now. Otherwise I shall ask someone to remove you. Anna – get in the car." Meekly, she obeyed. Her mother joined her and the engine started. "Thank you for being of some assistance to my daughter on her long voyage. Now we must make some further calls before starting another tiresome journey to – to where we are going to live. Driver!" Swiftly the car departed. The girl didn't look back. As he turned away there was a sudden screech of brakes. The car had almost hit two men running across the road towards the ship.

Ashen-faced, Farley was being hotly pursued by a burly figure wearing a leather jacket and brandishing the *samurai* sword. With a quick spurt the man caught Farley, they struggled and the sword was dropped. A small circle of onlookers formed. Someone asked "Who started it?" and was no wiser when Roger said, "An Australian – in Japan." Breaking free, Farley reached into his pocket, flung down a bundle of banknotes and fled – in the wrong direction, towards 104 Berth. The man gathered up the money, glaring at the watchers who soon dispersed. Roger stayed, for he had to hear the end of this. Now the man grabbed the sword, whirled it round his head and flung it as far as he could past the *Garvie*. The blade flashed twice before falling Excalibur-like to the water, where alas no ghostly hand reached up to catch it.

"Con artist," said the man. "Nearly got away with it he did. Sword was a fake. Rubbish. And I had a bloke in London ready to pay a hundred quid for it if it was genuine." Roger again felt a sneaking sympathy for Farley, for whom nothing had panned out right the whole voyage. "There's nothing some people won't try on," he said consolingly. The man counted his money.

"Fifty. All there. Lucky I caught him. I was just hiding the thing in my van when some of the fancy work on the hand-grip came undone and I saw some faint words on the metal. What somebody had tried really hard to grind away then painted over. Well I rubbed off the paint and made out a couple of words and I knew what I had there. I mean – I dunno where the Japanese Army got their swords made but I'm bloody sure it wasn't General Motors."

The final meal on board was an unusually subdued affair and soon over. After they'd done all the chores, paid Linda for the cabin-care and cleaned everything in the mess, it was time for each of them to go his own way. Roger was still packing when the moment of parting came. The farewells varied from a sober handshake to poke-in-the-ribs mockery. It was all vastly better than on that first terrible day when he met them all. "So it's goodbye to the Lucky Lodger," said Bill.

"Not so lucky as regards Anna," he replied ruefully.

"Why – because you're not Chinese too?"

"No. Nothing to do with that. Her mother won't allow her to go out with a plate-washer."

For the final time Cabin 17 shook with mirth, Martin's hee-hawing drowning the rest. Eventually they left him, sitting on Pat's bunk as he had twelve weeks ago. Alone, except for the Buddha, the small porcelain figure squatting in the dim recesses of his locker waiting to be packed. He took it out, wondering what to do about it. Declare it and pay the duty – or smuggle it. The Customs were aboard, prowling the ship.

While he thought about it, he heard once more the evocative notes of *The Old Master Painter*. And again, as on that distant sailing day he wandered along the alleyway towards Cabin 21.

"He put the purple in the twilight haze – then did a rainbow for the rainy days.

Dreamed up the murals on blue summer skies, painted the devil in my darling's eyes."

And he loved the lyrics and the pictures they formed, for had he not seen all that and more over these amazing weeks? Batten and Clay were alone as he entered, still holding the Buddha. "Come in Roger," said Batten. "And your little friend too." The man had suitcases with labels marked "Henry Batten Esquire", and a number of scratched and wellworn hotel stickers, one of which read "Carlton Hotel Cannes".

"Is that where you're going?"

"No, but one can dream. You never know – one day. I collected these things when I was with Cunard. The bloods had spare ones lying around. They looked good on luggage."

Clay stopped the record and picked up his gramophone. "I hear you never got a DR. That Buddha's been your guardian angel."

"I lost Anna."

"Yes, but now you can join me on *Union-Castle*. Two weeks off and then back here for a Cape boat. There's eight to choose from."

"I may join you," said Batten. "If they don't call me for the inquest on Seymour."

"Alright," said Roger. "I'll see you then – two weeks." Turning to go, he forgot the door was open and knocked against it. The Buddha fell to the floor and smashed into a dozen pieces.

Clay said, "Whoops! Now he can't bring you any more luck."

"I wouldn't be too sure of that," said Batten, with a strange certainty in his voice. Roger gathered up the bits. "Porthole?" suggested Clay.

"Yes. That seems fitting. Back to the good earth he was made of. I wouldn't like to see him in a dustbin. But not here, too near the quay." He found an empty portside cabin and dropped the remains of his two-dollar investment into the River Test to join Farley's sword. Back in his own cabin he sat on Pat's bunk undergoing the most extraordinary feelings. What was the matter with him? His cases were packed. He had only to take a taxi home and the whole huge experience would be over.

And yet – Isobel. He should have swallowed his pride and written to her. There might have been someone special to come home to. Well – there wouldn't be now. And it was entirely his own fault. Chasing after unsuitable females all the way to the Far East and back. His father's letter and a card. There'd quite definitely been nothing else. He'd checked and double-checked at the mail office.

And Clay had said quite clearly, "I chucked 'em on your bunk."

Something clicked in his mind. "Them" is plural. But the two items had been in one envelope. Clay should have said "it". Perhaps there was something else. He stood and rummaged under his mattress where it pressed against the bulkhead. Nothing. Sitting back on the bunk he spoke aloud to himself. "You are being extremely stupid, selfish and over-imaginative. She never wrote. Pull yourself together and go home." And then he slowly knelt and peered under Pat's bunk. Far back in the murky corner, a pale-blue spot. Yanking up the mattress, he reached down between bunk and bulkhead. Torn and wet, wrinkled by seven days of Linda's wet mopping, the airmail letter just readable.

Clay looked in. "Still here? Everyone's gone. Batten too. Can't you tear yourself away?"

"I'm just coming. Don't wait for me. I'll see you at *Union-Castle* in a fortnight."

"OK. Try and get on as a steward."

Alone again he read the letter. It was hard to believe she wrote it. Isobel had never been overly romantic. Even now her words conveyed surprised approval of his trip rather than excitement. Yet there was no doubt she was impressed, showing a keenness to hear about it and even apologizing for calling him unadventurous. He would ring her. This minute, before even going home. Then maybe, this evening ...?

Picking up his cases, he walked off the *Empire Garvie* and asked where the nearest phone was. "Down at the end of 101. On the far corner of the shed." As he rang her number, the *Winchester Castle* moved into mid-river and got under way. He thought how great it would be to sail due south all the way to South Africa. To Cape Town, where they had a strange, flat-topped mountain and the Delmonico Club where the cabaret was *bona* and the prices cheaper than Bernie's in New York. A voice came on the line.

"Yes – who is it?" He recognised her younger sister.

"Hi Jean. It's Roger Wren. Could I speak to Isobel?"